CW00515451

BOTH ENDS BURNING

PETER DARLING

Peter Dar—
25/11/2023

BOTH ENDS BURNING

Published by
Useful Publishing
web: www.usefulpublishing.com.au
eMail: usefulpublishing11@gmail.com

This edition published 2022 Copyright © Useful Publishing 2022

The content contained within this book may not be reproduced, duplicated, or transmitted without direct written permission from the author or the publisher.

Under no circumstances will any blame or legal responsibility be held against the publisher, or author, for any damages, reparation, or monetary loss due to the information contained within this book, either directly or indirectly.

Legal Notice:
This book is copyright protected. It is only for personal use. You cannot amend, distribute, sell, use, quote, or paraphrase any part, or the content within this book, without the consent of the author or publisher.

Disclaimer Notice:
Please note the information contained within this document is for educational and entertainment purposes only. All effort has been executed to present accurate, up to date, reliable, complete information. No warranties of any kind are declared or implied. Readers acknowledge that the author is not engaged in the rendering of legal, financial, medical, or professional advice. The content within this book has been derived from various sources. Please consult a licensed professional before attempting any techniques outlined in this book.

By reading this document, the reader agrees that under no circumstances is the author responsible for any losses, direct or indirect, that are incurred as a result of the use of the information contained within this document, including, but not limited to, errors, omissions, or inaccuracies.

ABOUT THE AUTHOR

Peter lives in Aylesbury, England which sits about 30 miles to the north west of London. He is married to Caroline and they have two kids, Thomas and Lily.

Peter thrives on popular culture – music, tv, books, sport and cinema and for his sins has been an ardent follower of Chelsea FC for over 50 years through the thin and thick and, hopefully not, thin again.

'I always felt I had a novel in me, whether good or bad, and a few years ago in a burst of creativeness I produced Both Ends Burning. The manuscript has sat on a shelf gathering dust for a while now. The guys at the publishing company, Useful Publishing, have taken it on and, thanks to them, I will be a published author. It's all a bit emotional really!'

I may not have another chance to do this so there are a few names here.

To my wife of twenty-five years, Caroline, and our offspring, Tom and Lily, who despite my trying to, and thinking that I do, influence them, actually influence me much more than I care to acknowledge.

To my old man, who we lost some years back, 'thanks for the creativity' and Mum, who we lost last year, 'thanks for everything else.'

To the guys at Useful 'thanks for the opportunity'

And finally to all of those affected by the hideous pandemic 'God bless and stay well'

Peter Darling

CONTENTS

CHAPTER ONE

'Do we know who he is at all?' asked Jamieson to no one in particular.

Evason answered, 'he had a wallet in his inside coat pocket. It's over there with SOCO. Some papers in it appear to show that his name is Brian Wilkins. Lives in Penfold Street, which is just... 'she looked up to get her bearings '... over there.' She pointed vaguely off into the distance. 'Just around that corner. Five minutes or so, walk away.'

Jamieson nodded and looked down at the body on the pavement before him.

An old man, seventy, maybe even older, lying on his back, arms open wide, palms up, head thrown back, mouth slightly open, eyes shut. 'Neighbours see or hear anything?'

Evason looked at him. 'It's a bit early yet. Paperboy found him at six o'clock this morning. Luckily, he had a mobile on him. Called 999 and reported it.'

Jamieson looked at his wristwatch. It was just before seven-thirty. 'Yes, I suppose it is still a bit early. Pathologist?'

'Already been. Doctor...' Evason flicked through pages in her notebook 'Jenner. Here by six forty and gone by seven.'

'He didn't hang around then,' said Jamieson.

'She, Sir, the pathologist was female.' Corrected Evason.

'Oh,' said Jamieson, feeling slightly chastened. Evason was a champion of women's rights, and Jamieson always felt that despite his best intentions, he constantly managed to trample over them. 'Did the doctor have anything to say?'

Once again, Evason referred to her notebook. 'Time of death is estimated to be between four and eight hours ago. So between ten o'clock last night and two o'clock this morning. Cause of death was likely to be a series of blows to the head with a blunt object.'

Evason knelt beside the body. 'The first blow was here...' she indicated the back of the head with her pencil. 'Fractured his skull. Doctor Jenner believes from her preliminary investigation that there was enough force in that initial blow to knock the old man out cold. Any further blows and the doctor believes that there were at least another four or five to here.' Evason used the pencil to indicate the man's right cheek. 'Here...' The right temple. 'And here.' The right jaw. 'Were unnecessary. He was already down and probably dead.'

Jamieson looked around. Injuries to the right-hand side of a victim's face usually meant a left-handed attacker. There were two large wheeled waste bins outside one of the houses, presumably awaiting collection by the waste disposal lorry at some point. Jamieson turned to Evason.'Have the Scene of Crime Officers had a chance to have a good look around yet?'

'No,' she replied, hiding the exasperation in her voice, 'too early.'

'Ah yes, so you said before', Jamieson, deep in thought, 'Make sure they do a thorough job around these bins, won't you? It's highly conceivable that's where our attacker was lying in wait. You know the old man comes along, and the attacker leaps out and...' Jamieson mimed a left-handed assailant wielding an inanimate object above his head 'first blow to the back of the head as the old man passed by. He staggers, and the assailant comes round the front and delivers an uppercut to the right side of the jaw bone. Jamieson mimes the uppercut that puts the old man on his back. He's out cold, so he can't defend himself and then whack, whack, two more strikes for good measure, and our attacker's away and gone.'

'Motive?' asked Evason.

Jamieson pulled a face. 'Not robbery,' he said, shaking his head. 'Pretty sure of that.' He pointed to the dead man's wrist. 'That watch must be worth a few bob, and whoever it was didn't even try to look for a wallet.' Again Jamieson was thinking aloud. 'We'll know more about motive when we know exactly who Brian Wilkins is, or I should say, was.' Jamieson looked back down the road and picked out the figure of a man in deep, apparently jovial, conversation with the police officer manning the police tape which closed off the road. Eventually, the man tore himself away from the conversation and ducked under the tape, clapping the police officer on the shoulder as he passed.

Jamieson walked back down the slight incline to meet him. 'Sandy. Good morning,' said Jamieson.

'Morning, Sir, and a lovely one at that.' Detective Sergeant Pete 'Sandy' Stone, forty-nine, five feet six, twenty-three years, a Detective Sergeant and no genuine desire to progress to a higher rank. The absolute opposite to DS Claire Evason, standing some fifteen yards away, twenty-nine, five feet eleven and although only nine months in the rank, already pressing for the next promotion. Jamieson turned and joined Stone in walking towards where the body lay.

'What have we got then?' asked Stone, in his usual manner, which implied he was leading the case rather than the other way round. Jamieson didn't mind; Stone was good at his job.

'Interesting one', said Jamieson, 'Man in his mid-seventies in an apparently motiveless attack, fairly brutal too, judging by his injuries.'

They reached DC Evason and the body. Stone looked down and then tilted his head to his right as if studying a piece of fine art. There was sudden recognition, followed by anger, in his eyes.

'You've just got your motive.' He pointed at the dead man. 'I'd know that bastard's face anywhere. That's Lesley Wallace'

CHAPTER TWO

The door burst open, and through it came Sandy Stone. He struggled to carry two cardboard storage boxes and used his chin to hold the top box in place. Evason followed, carrying two more. She looked far more comfortable and was, it seemed, stronger than she looked. Just as it seemed Stone was about to run out of steam entirely, he made it to his desk where he clumsily half placed, half threw the boxes down. The top box slid off and crashed to the floor. The lid came off, and half the contents spilled out.

Evason glided smoothly across the floor and neatly placed the boxes she was carrying on her desk.

Stone, red-faced and out of breath, stooped to pick up the stray papers. Jamieson could see that the top box was marked 'Case Files - Lesley Wallace -Box 1' and assumed the other boxes were numbers two, three and four.

Jamieson was somewhat annoyed with Stone. Back at the crime scene, Stone had refused to shed any real light on what he knew about the deceased, other than to comment that he was 'a real piece of shit' and that his demise 'could be down to any number of people'. Stone's argument against saying any more was that he wanted to fully reacquaint himself with the facts before making his views public. Jamieson felt that given Stone's reaction, his and Wallace's paths had crossed professionally, and the outcome had not gone Stone's way.

Back at the crime scene, Jamieson had briefed the local sergeant. Door-to-door enquiries of the local area, including Wallace's neighbours. Find out what you can about Wallace and what he was doing out so late at night. One of the constables pointed out that there was a pub in the direction that Wallace had come from and that it was a fair bet that he had had a few pints and was making his way home for the night. 'Good point,' said Jamieson and made that particular constable responsible for interviewing the landlord of the pub to see if anyone could recall seeing Wallace last night and therefore putting some timings around his movements.

Then Jamieson and Evason returned to the station in Evason's car, leaving the silent Stone to drive himself back. Jamieson left his car at the scene as he knew that both he and one of his Detective Sergeants would be returning later- the department was facing cutbacks, and Jamieson was keen that petrol consumption was kept to a minimum. During the ten-minute drive back, Jamieson and Evason said very little. Both were wondering what this Lesley Wallace had been responsible for that had put the usually upbeat, optimistic Stone into such a foul mood.

When they all arrived at the station, Stone was already there. He had stopped off at the control room, left his jacket on the back of his chair, and then gone downstairs into the bowels of the building where they kept the old case files. After half an hour, he called on the internal telephone and told them he'd found what he was looking for but would need some help bringing everything he needed back upstairs. Evason volunteered, and Jamieson, mindful of his earlier faux pas when automatically referring to the pathologist as 'he', gestured with his arm in a 'be my guest' kind of way. 'I'll make us some coffees, shall I?' was all he said. Evason didn't reply. She was already out of the door.

Stone collected the stray papers, put them back in the box, and replaced the lid. He sat down behind his desk and picked up his mug of coffee. Jamieson and Evason waited. Evason agitated, thinking, 'God, he's in his element here - the centre of bloody attention!'

Stone sipped the coffee and put the mug back on the desk. 'It's exactly as I remembered it,' he said, 'even though it was over twenty-five years ago -you don't forget dealing with people like Lesley Wallace.'

Jamieson was in a spot. Technically, both he and Evason should do this by the book. They should pick their way through the files and put together their own picture of Lesley Wallace rather than rely on Stone's version of events. He was very emotional about this individual and what happened twenty-five years ago. Perhaps he could not be relied upon to give a clear, concise version of events without letting his feelings interfere. Jamieson took a view:

'Claire, why don't you work your way through these boxes? Get a feel for what we're up against here. Make some notes, get some names, see what you think.' Evason glared at him. This was donkey work and should be shared amongst all the Detective Sergeants, not just one.

Jamieson turned to Stone. 'Get your jacket on, Sandy; I'll buy you a pint.' Evason simmered quietly.

CHAPTER THREE

In the bar of The Duke across the road from the station, Jamieson placed a pint of best bitter in front of Sandy Stone. He had opted for a half of lager himself. They had settled into a booth away from prying ears, not that there were many customers to be seen at noon on a Wednesday afternoon.

Stone took a good slug from the top of his drink and placed the glass on the table in front of him. Jamieson waited until he appeared to have settled fully. 'Okay, Sandy, tell me about it but in a controlled, level-headed way. I see you're upset, but I want a policeman's view of this man.'

Stone looked him squarely in the eye. 'Fucking kiddie fiddler, wasn't he? Our victim Wallace.' Jamieson winced. So much for a controlled recount.

Stone sniffed and looked down at his beer. 'Sorry,' he said and paused. 'It was one of the worst cases I ever worked. I'd just made a DS...' He smiled, albeit without any humour. 'My career progression has stalled somewhat since then.' He puffed his cheeks out. 'Anyway, I was working with Scott back then; Detective Inspector Jack Scott came with a big reputation. It was a good first placement for a young Detective Sergeant keen to get on, and I loved it for the first couple of months or so.' He rubbed his chin with his hand. 'Then one of Scott's snouts came up with some info about a pedophile ring working in the Luton area. Talk about naïve, I had to look the word up in the dictionary to begin to understand what we were dealing with, and even then, it came nowhere near the true horror of what was being done to these kids — it was something that was just totally incomprehensible to people in those days — if you'd told my old Dad what these bastards were doing to these kids he'd have just looked at you and asked you 'why?' Jamieson said nothing and let Stone continue.

'Of course, back then, the Internet didn't exist, so most of the material was magazines, photos and videos shipped in from the Far East and available from mainland Europe, places like Holland, where they claim to be more liberal, more perverted, more like. That was the inn; that's what the snout gave us. A group of pervs buying this filth and then watching it on their VCRs behind their closed curtains.

Only it wasn't that. It was much worse than we ever expected. We'd got names and addresses, one of them was Wallace, and we put them all under surveillance — staked them out for the best part of three weeks every now and again; they'd all gather in one place and have a sort of party, I suppose you'd call it — Scott made a decision that we'd raid the next party, gather up the magazines, photos and videos and expose these bastards to the world, lock them away for five years and when they got out make sure that everyone knew what they'd done; get them shunned by society, I suppose.' Stone picked up his beer and took a long draught. He wiped his mouth with the back of his hand. 'Anyway', he continued, 'We got wind of the next party and set up the raid for eleven o'clock that evening. We hit them hard and fast. Fifteen of us through the front door before they'd even had a chance to wonder what the hell was going on. It was a smooth operation right up until Scott went into the living room. 'Stone paused whilst he relived the moment. Almost involuntarily, he put his hand to his mouth, unable to continue. Jamieson waited patiently. 'They'd got two kids in there, two boys, six and seven, who'd they'd snatched off the street in Birmingham that afternoon. 'He paused again. Sniffed, tightened his jaw, and stared straight ahead, not wanting eye contact with Jamieson. 'You should read the file. I don't; I can't even bring myself to say it.'

Jamieson put his hand on the older man's shoulder: 'Wallace?' he said. Stone raised his eyebrows: 'That's just it. He wasn't there.

He would've been there, no doubt about that, but he had 'flu. He was at home in bed.'

Stone continued, having regained some composure. 'Scott sent a team round to Wallace's place, and they pulled him out of his bed and dragged him down to the station. Searched the house from top to bottom. He had some mags and a couple of videos, but nothing that would get him more than a fine and a suspended sentence.

Got himself a clever brief and gave a 'no comment' to everything he was asked. So Scott made a decision. He didn't ask anyone else what they thought because I think he knew that nobody else would have agreed — as far as we were all concerned, Wallace was as much a part of this group as any of the others — he was just fortunate not to be there that night; he'd been at previous meets, no doubt, and he'd have been at future ones if we hadn't had burst in on them when we did. Anyway, Scott offered Wallace total immunity from prosecution if he'd testify against the other four. Wallace snatched his hand off. He agreed so quickly that we knew there and then that there was more to come, and we'd just guaranteed that he could talk and walk. Scott was crushed. He had no idea how deep it ran.'

'Wallace's solicitor got Scott to sign a warranty to say that his client would not face prosecution for any offence that predated the night of the raid, and Wallace began talking and talking. And the more he talked, the more obvious it became that the other four were almost bit part players. They were worthless individuals, puppets, all being worked by Wallace. Wallace was their ringleader. What he said went, they were his contacts in the Far East; they were his ideas. Then suddenly someone thought to ask what Wallace did for a living and when we found out, it was like a cold shiver running the length of my body.' He paused. Jamieson gently prompted him: 'What was it that he did, Sandy?' Stone gave a resigned look. 'He was the night warden at a foster home in Dunstable.' Jamieson closed his eyes. The implication was plain to see.

Stone continued. 'Scott was in the middle of an interview with Wallace and his brief when this piece of information came to light. We got a message from Scott in the meeting. Through the two ways, you could almost visibly see him turn white. He immediately suspended the interview and had Wallace taken back down to the cells.

Wallace was cool as a cucumber. Knew that he was untouchable. His brief was muttering about civil rights and the like, but it was all half-hearted.'

'There were nearly a hundred officers working out of Luton nick at that time, but only four were female. Scott rounded the four of them up, no uniforms, all in civvies, and went straight to the foster home. He felt that the kids were more likely to open up to a woman — a kind of softly, softly approach — quite forward thinking for the time.' Stone drained what remained of his drink and pre-empted Jamieson's offer of another. 'Early, I know, but I needed just the one; I had a shock this morning.'

Jamieson prompted further: 'What did Scott do when he got to the foster home?' 'Well, I'd phoned ahead and told the Manager of the home that the boss was on his way. I didn't tell her why, just that he was coming. When Scott and his team arrived, I gather they were taken straight to a room away from the kids. The Manager joined them, and Scott dropped his bombshell on her. She'd had a pervert working unsupervised on her night shift. Not her fault. There was no such thing as the sex offenders' register or CRB checks in those days, and besides, Wallace had no previous anyway, so it wouldn't have been picked up. She'd taken references from his last employer, and everything had stacked up. She'd done all she reasonably could be expected to do in the circumstances, and Scott assured her that this was the case. She was still distraught, though. Scott got her calmed down and asked her if any of the kids were showing any unusual signs of stress, you know, problems with behaviour either way. So kids who were normally well behaved starting to act up or kids who were normally more outgoing going into their shell, things like that.'

'The problem was that there were over a hundred and twenty kids in that home at the time, all of them damaged in some way or another. The manager couldn't pick out any boys specifically. So Scott asked her to divide the current residents of the home into four groups whilst he made a call to the Institute of Psychiatrists. Told them it was important and got put through to the top man. He explained the situation and asked what questions he should be asking and what responses or behaviour he should be looking for. Then he briefed his team. Each of them was to interview thirty boys over the next three days. They were to follow his script and look for responses. The script consisted of ten questions, eight of which were general, you know, what's the food like? Who's your favourite member of staff? That sort of thing. The other two questions pitched in at number seven and nine on the list were the ones to watch out for; Does anything strange happen during the night? And, Is there any member of staff that you really don't like? The top man at the Institute explained that no child was likely to open up and come out that he hated Mr So-and so because he made him do things during the night, but most kids would give funny answers like such-and-such a kid sleeps walks or another farts in his sleep, and they didn't like a warder because he smelled or had a big nose, that sort of thing. The kids that didn't, the kids that were evasive, took a long time to answer and then didn't really say anything; they were the ones to watch.' 'So off they went, and for the next three days between them, they interviewed one hundred and twenty boys aged between six and eleven. It was hard work. If you ask an adult ten questions, they'll finish answering them in ten minutes maximum. You ask a lad of six ten questions, and you'll be lucky if you're through after three-quarters of an hour, and all the time, you're listening and watching them to see how they are reacting. Finally, after every child was interviewed, Scott collated all the information and came up with five boys who appeared to show signs of stress when they were asked Scott's killer questions.

One, in particular, a boy of nine called Darren Hughes, had clammed up completely after question seven and refused to answer any more questions. He was on the verge of tears, and it seemed the only fear was preventing him from spilling them. Scott pulled the lad's file. He'd been in the home since he was seven. His Mother had had a breakdown, and his dad couldn't cope with holding down a full-time job and caring for a sick wife and young child. Something had to give, and that something was Darren. So he was moved to a foster home, initially on a short-term basis, whilst Mum got better, but it soon became more evident that his Mum was in a much worse state than anyone first thought. So Darren stayed. Two months previously, he had been formally put up for adoption, but he didn't know that, and there had been no takers. So for the next round of interviews, Scott called in professional help but stressed that it needed to be a female who carried out the interviews. The Institute recommended one of its most highly rated female members who came to the home. After speaking to them, she sat with all five boys and was satisfied that four of them, although they had their own troubles to contend with, had not been physically abused. Scott and his team breathed a collective sigh of relief. However, continued the female psychiatrist, the last boy had been systematically groomed from seven. The physical abuse had started as soon as he turned eight and had continued ever since. Scott asked what she meant by 'groomed'. Singled out, chosen for a specific purpose, she replied, in this particular case, sexual abuse.'

Stone stopped talking and considered what he had just said. It had clearly had a profound effect on him twenty-five years ago and still does to this day. 'Who was the boy singled out, Sandy?' asked Jamieson. 'It was the Hughes lad.'

CHAPTER FOUR

Constable Roger Johnson pressed the doorbell for a further five seconds and looked up to the window on the first floor, where the occupants were most likely to be. There was still no sign of life. He checked his watch — nine forty-five. Was he being reasonable to expect a pub landlord who probably doesn't get to bed on any night earlier than, what, one, two o'clock, to respond to early morning callers?

When it was the police dealing with a case of suspected murder, Johnson felt it wasn't unreasonable and pressed the doorbell again. This time, there was a movement from upstairs, and eventually, one of the windows opened. A big bleary-faced man looked out and blinked as the bright morning light hit him in the face. Surprisingly he wasn't angry. He finally got his blinking under control and, through slitted eyes, looked down at Johnson. 'Hello,' he said. 'Police,' said Johnson, holding up his identity card, wholly unnecessary as he was in full uniform. 'Are you the landlord?' The man grunted in the affirmative. Johnson continued, 'can you spare me some time to answer a couple of questions, please, sir?'

The big man sniffed and ran his hand over his face. 'Give me five minutes, and I'll be down,' he said and disappeared back inside, closing the window behind him, which promptly reopened. His head came back out: 'I'll put the kettle on. Do you want a coffee?'

Having declined the offer of a hot drink, Johnson sat on one of the benches outside the pub that he supposed were used by the smokers — outcasts since the smoking ban came into force a couple of years ago, banished to the cold outdoors to continue with their disgusting habit — Johnson was glad, he was a bit of a health freak. He toed a pile of dog ends that sat on the ground between his feet. He looked at the pub sign — The Happy Farmer — and thought back. As a kid, he lived around the corner from here, and his dad used this pub on Friday and Saturday evenings. So that was how he knew it was here.

When he mentioned to Jamieson that there was a possibility that the deceased was returning from The Happy Farmer, Jamieson seemed impressed by his local knowledge and specifically asked him to follow it up. That made Johnson feel good. He'd heard about Jamieson, that he's not afraid to delegate tasks to more junior officers. This may be his chance to impress. The initial door-to-door enquiries hadn't really brought anything to the table. A few of the neighbourhood knew of the deceased, but only next-door neighbours knew his name. Those that knew of him had seen him out and about, and it seemed that he had a routine of going up to the pub — Tuesdays, Thursdays and Saturdays — evidently, he left home at just before eight on those evenings and returned home just after eleven on Tuesdays and Thursdays and nearer half-past eleven on Saturdays. Although he hadn't actually interviewed the next-door neighbours, Johnson had heard from other officers that he was a man known locally as Brian Wilkins and had lived at 15 Penfold Road for the last twenty or so years. Originally with his mother, but she had died about fifteen years ago, and ever since, Wilkins had lived on his own. People saw him as a harmless old man who always said hello but rarely passed the time of day away with anyone. He never had visitors. He didn't drive a car and was now retired. Before that, he was a document processor working from home.

One of the local Detective Sergeants had used the deceased's key to access the house — a small two-bedroomed property — and the forensics team had been the first to enter. There was nothing untoward with the house, certainly no signs of a break-in. Forensics had spent an hour inside the property dusting for prints and anything else that showed signs of activity not involving the deceased. Eventually, they left and moved on to another job south of Luton. The DS locked the door and left an officer on guard at the front garden gate — no more than a precaution really, and given the shortage of available man-hours, it seemed an unnecessary waste — but DI Jamieson had told him that he himself would be returning later in the day to have a look around the property — and as Jamieson didn't have a key, the only means of access was to leave a key with the officer standing guard.

The DS knew that he would probably get it in the neck from the Duty Sergeant at the station for unnecessary waste of police man hours, but what was his alternative? Leave the door key under the doormat with a note on the front door? He was damned if he did and damned if he didn't. Better to risk the instant wrath of a lowly Duty Sergeant than the ongoing irritation of a Detective Inspector.

Johnson closed his eyes, turned his face towards the sun and took in the warm May morning. He quite fancied working as a detective and was pleased that he'd impressed a Detective Inspector. He'd put his name down to take his Sergeant's exams and was confident he would pass them without too much trouble. The sun warmed his face, and he'd almost drifted off when he heard the bolts inside the door being unlocked. He quickly opened his eyes and took his notebook from his pocket in anticipation.

The door opened, and the man appeared — he looked even bigger at ground level — he carried a massive mug of steaming tea or coffee. He looked over at Johnson, who had stood up. 'Inside or out?' he asked. Johnson saw that he had a packet of cigarettes in his hand. 'In', he replied. Although he had the feeling that the man would light up as soon as they got inside, he wanted to see what the place looked like.

The man ambled back to the main pub doors, took out a bunch of keys, unlocked the door, and pushed his way into the bar area. He indicated that Johnson should sit in one of the booths, which he did. The big man then sat opposite. Johnson felt his side of the booth lift under the man's weight. 'Sorry to have woken you,' began Johnson and waited for an acknowledgement that never came. He continued: 'There's been a murder about half a mile from here, and we think the victim may have been coming home from a night out at your pub. We wondered whether you could help us at all?'

The big man took a slurp of his drink, plucked a cigarette from the packet, pushed it between his fat lips, and lit it with a match. He inhaled deeply, then turned his head and blew a raft of smoke into the air, away from Johnson. Johnson felt a debt of gratitude toward the man. The man nodded. 'Go on,' he said.

'No photos yet, I'm afraid, but I've got a name and a full description. We understand that he may have been a regular visitor here on Tuesdays, Thursdays and Saturdays.' Before he could continue, the big man cut in; 'That'll be Brian then. Don't know his second name.' His voice was deadpan, emotionless, almost as if Johnson had told him that the local football team had lost rather than a man had died.

'Could you describe your 'Brian' please?' said Johnson. It was the same man, of course, it was, but there was the need to be thorough, to be sure beyond any doubt. The big man thought for a few seconds and sniffed again. He pursed his fat lips: 'Seventies, wore those big glasses, thick white hair, always wore a shirt and tie probably about five, six, seven and thin. He couldn't have weighed more than eight stone tops. Came in every Tuesday, Thursday and Saturday and drank three pints of bitter. Kept himself to himself.' Johnson nodded. 'He was in last night?' It was the big man's turn to nod this time; 'Yep. Arrived at around quarter past eight, drank three pints of bitter and left at just after eleven. The whole time he was here, he spoke no more than ten words, and that was to me behind the bar — 'Evening', 'the usual, please', 'same again please', 'one more please' and 'Goodnight'' he counted up the words using the fingers of his hands 'make that eleven. Sat in that booth over there' He pointed to a grimy cushioned booth in the far corner; he always sat there. Well, when it was free, he did.'

Johnson was impressed. 'How'd you remember all that?' he asked.

'Tuesday evening,' said the man, 'the place is all but empty. I had no more than ten people in last night. I could tell you, everyone who was here and exactly what they drank. Cost me more to run the bloody one-armed bandit than I made in profit last night.'

'Trade poor?' asked Johnson, genuinely interested.

'Tell me about it,' said the man. 'I'm not sure how much longer I can keep the place going. It's losing money hand over fist. I blame the supermarkets — cheap booze, too easy for people to stay at home and drink — it'll kill the pub trade altogether in the end.' 'That's a shame,' said Johnson.'My old man used to drink here a long time ago.'

A short silence fell between the two men, both contemplating better times. Then Johnson spoke again: 'Did you notice any strange faces in here last night?' The man thought: 'No,' he said, shaking his head, 'All regulars.' 'Monday night?' asked Johnson. This time the man thought longer and harder: 'yeah, now you mention it. A guy came in just after nine and ordered a bottle of Bud. Never seen him before. He sat there... This time the man pointed to a booth in the opposite corner to the one where the older man had sat. '...read a paper, drank his beer, stayed, about twenty minutes or so. I guess then just upped and left.'

'What did he look like?' Johnson asked.

'Mid-twenties, I suppose, blonde hair, pretty average all round, I'd say. Although he did have an accent, I'm sure of that.' The man threw his cigarette end onto the floor and crushed it with his foot. 'What sort of accent?' Johnson was intrigued by this development 'difficult to say. He was another one who didn't say much. It wasn't a foreign accent though, you know, French or German, anything like that. It was American or Canadian, something like that.' Finally, the man stood, and Johnson felt his side of the booth return to its usual position. 'Is there anything else? I've got the pumps to clean before I open.'

'If you saw this man again, would you recognise him?' asked Johnson. 'Yes,' replied the big man, nodding.'Pretty sure about that.'

Johnson nodded. 'I just need to take a note of your name and contact number, and I'll be going. You've been a great help, though. Thanks for your time.' Having gathered the required information from the pub landlord, Johnson left the pub and walked the route he assumed Brian Wilkins would have taken. It was a reasonable assumption, as there was only really one direct route between the pub and where Wilkins lived. He slowed his pace to what he thought a man in his seventies who had drunk three pints of beer might walk at. From the pub, there was an initial gentle incline of around three hundred yards or so which then levelled out as you turned right into Peverall Road. A further five hundred yards along Peverall, he took a left turn into Montague Avenue. He walked a further five or six hundred yards down Montague, then right and an immediate left onto Penfold Street, where Brian Wilkins lived.

The entire journey took Johnson just under twenty minutes and made its way through residential housing estates the whole way. Any potential attacker was taking a risk anywhere along the route. The attack happened at around eleven thirty, which is not particularly late. People were constantly walking dogs or making their way home from a night down the pub. Johnson retraced his steps to where the body had been found. Johnson didn't believe the body had been moved to where it was found. However, he was almost certain that was where the attack took place. If you planned to attack someone in public anywhere along the route between the pub and where the victim lived, this was probably the safest place along the whole route to do it. It was a proper avenue — tree-lined — and the leaves on the trees would have blocked much of the brightness from the street lighting. Johnson tried to imagine what it would be like at eleven o'clock in the evening — dark and shadowy, no doubt — the houses were terraced with no garages, so at that time of night, a lot of cars would be parked up on the pavement giving it all a strange and eerie close-ness. Johnson could see how someone who knew the route that the old man took could very easily hide and then, as the slightly drunk seventy-year-old walked past, leap from the darkness and attack him. Five whacks with a weapon, and then you could be on your way; if the whole attack took more than ten seconds, it would have surprised Johnson.

He stood and considered the scene for a further two minutes or so before setting off back to the station where he would write up his first ever report to a Detective Inspector.

CHAPTER FIVE

After leaving the pub, Jamieson and Stone took Stone's car back to Wallace's house on Penfold Street. The officer on duty outside the property recognised them as they approached and opened the front door, ready for their entry.

The inside of the property reflected the outside; Tired and in need of redecoration. A long, thin, rectangular kitchen was equipped with equally ancient 'white' goods. The small fridge/freezer could no longer be termed a 'white' good. It had turned a shade of yellow a long time ago. The cooker was at least twenty years old. There was no electric kettle — an old-style kettle sat beside the hob, its surface thickened by years of grease. Jamieson opened a cupboard. The inside reflected a single person. There was an eclectic collection of cups, mugs, dinner plates and side plates, few of which matched, and Jamieson was certain that there was nothing like a complete dinner service in there.

With the front door closed, the hallway was dark, save for the rectangle of light being thrown in through the small window set high in the door. At the bottom of the stairs over the bannister sat an old overcoat, which Jamieson assumed was too hot to wear except during winter. The coat smelled stuffy and reminded Jamieson of the kind of smell that he always associated with death — ironic, really. Under the stairs, there was a collection of shoes and a pair of Wellington boots, but not much more of note.

In the front room, there was an old armchair pulled round to face the television and make the most of the heat thrown out by the electric fire; Jamieson assumed that this had been done during winter, and now that the milder weather had kicked in Wallace hadn't bothered to return the chair to its usual place, further back in the corner away from the fireplace. There was a coffee table by the side of the armchair with a pair of glasses and a packet of mints resting on it. The television wasn't huge but looked reasonably new, maybe four or five years old, certainly the newest item on view in the whole room, if not the house. A bookcase was in the corner of the room, housing a few classics. Jamieson noticed Treasure Island nestling next to Great Expectations, but in the main, it was dominated by paperback versions of detective novels set in Britain and America. Jamieson eased one from its position in the bookcase. The inside cover indicated that it had been bought secondhand for 30p. He pushed the book back into its space.

The rest of the house followed a similar pattern. There had not been much investment in the property for a long time. Jamieson remembered one of the officers mentioning a neighbour had said that Wallace had lived there with his Mother until she died almost twenty years ago. Possibly that was the last occasion when the house was redecorated or indeed anything new, apart from the television, had been bought.

The second bedroom, Jamieson presumed it was the one used by Wallace's Mother while she was alive, had been turned into a makeshift office. In the corner, a desk showed a clear patch on the surface, otherwise surrounded by a film of dust. Again, Jamieson recalled an officer saying that Wallace had been a data inputter working from home when he worked. The computer had been removed by the forensics team and taken back to the station. They would access the hard drive to see what Wallace had been downloading recently. Jamieson mused: the film of dust would indicate that the computer had not been used for some time now. He tried a drawer in the desk, which came open easily. Inside there was a folder containing bank statements. Jamieson flicked through to the last few statements, which he assumed would be the most recent.

He was surprised that Wallace had substantial balances on his current and deposit bank accounts. A monthly entry into the current account indicated that Wallace had invested wisely.

Money clearly wasn't an issue, particularly as judging from the state of the property, it appeared that Wallace didn't spend much, anyway.

He put the folder back in the drawer and had a cursory look around the rest of the room. The scene of crimes team had already given the place the once over, and a smaller team would return sometime over the next two days to go over the place with a fine-tooth comb.

Whilst Jamieson had been looking through the rooms in the bungalow; Stone had taken on the task of checking the small shed in the back garden and the loft space.

Again SOCO had already done a preliminary search, but Jamieson felt the experienced eye of a Detective Sergeant would give the search an extra dimension. So Jamieson went looking for Stone: it wasn't immediately evident where he could be found.

'Sandy?' called Jamieson, coming out of the kitchen, looking about him.

'Up here', came the reply. Jamieson looked up; the hatchway leading to the loft was open. Stone's head peered out.

Jamieson looked round and frowned. There was no noticeable sign of how Stone had gotten up into the loft. 'How the hell did you get up there?' He asked. Stone smiled for only the second time that day and the first time since he had seen Lesley Wallace's body lying on the pavement: 'I might be pushing fifty, but I'm still pretty fit. Lateral pull-downs,' he explained when he noticed the puzzled expression on Jamieson's face. I jumped up, grabbed the edge of the open hatchway and pulled myself up using my arms,' he explained. Jamieson nodded.' Impressive' He pointed to a stepladder in the corner. 'I'd have used that. Anything up there?'

Stone sat down on the edge of the hatch with his legs dangling down. Jamieson stepped back. The agile Stone pushed himself off and dropped the eight feet from ceiling level. He landed almost gently and bent his knees on impact, much as a parachutist would. He straightened up and dusted his hands off.

'Nothing of interest,' he replied, reaching for the pull string to shut the hatchway. He couldn't reach it and made a leap for it, knocking it away with his open hand as he did so. The taller Jamieson reached up, casually caught the swinging pull string, and gave a gentle tug, easing the hatchway closed. Stone grunted and flicked the light switch on the wall 'off.

'Anything in the shed worth knowing about?' asked Jamieson. 'No,' replied Stone,' an old hand-pushed lawn mower and some rusty tools, a few old paint pots, but nothing unusual.' Jamieson nodded, apparently deep in thought. 'Where did we find the house key?' he asked suddenly. 'Wallace's coat pocket,' answered Stone.

Jamieson pursed his lips and looked at his wristwatch — it was nearly two thirty.

'Okay, let's go," he said. 'Leave the key with the uniform on the door. He may as well lock up and go back to the station. I think he'll be of more use there. I don't think that anyone'll come knocking here. There doesn't seem to be any reason for anyone to come.'

CHAPTER SIX

Back in the car, Jamieson outlined his thinking aloud to Stone. 'Okay, here's what we need to be looking at. When we get back, we concentrate on the old case files that you brought up from storage this morning. That'll give me a clearer picture and will refresh your memories. Then we'll need an official identification, so we'll have to search out next of kin, if there are any, or dental and medical records if there aren't. Once we've established that it is indeed Brian Wilkins in the morgue, we need to track down when the change of name took place. If I was a betting man, I'd say it was very soon after all Wallace's misdemeanours came to light, probably twenty-five years ago. Then I'll need to see the pathologist get his take on the matter, although I'm not sure he'll.' He stopped himself as a vision of Evason appeared in his head 'she'll be able to add much; it's fairly evident that someone bashed Wallace on the head a few times, smashing his skull. Then we start considering who and why.'

The remainder of the journey back to the police station went relatively quickly. The two men didn't speak — Jamieson sat considering what he knew of the case up to now, and Stone sat reliving the horrors of the case from over twenty-five years ago, wondering whether he would be able to approach the pending murder case with full conviction knowing what he did of the victim. He eventually decided that he would act in the professional manner expected of him in every aspect of the case. By the time they'd returned to the incident room, Evason was halfway through the third of the boxes she and Stone had brought up from the storage facility in the basement. By her side, she had a pad of lined paper and was making notes as she scoured each and every individual document. She seemed distant and thoughtful to Jamieson. He'd worked with her now for six months and had found her to be an excellent detective, a little opinionated and stubborn at times, but on the whole, he enjoyed working with her and listening to the ideas that she put forward, always well considered and always well presented. She had a promising future ahead of her. Nevertheless, the overall mood in the room was sombre.

'Coffee?' said Stone, breaking the silence. Jamieson and Evason nodded, and Stone went down the corridor to the hot drinks vending machine.

When he had left, Evason stood and shut the door behind him. 'Pretty harrowing stuff,' she said to Jamieson, indicating the boxes. A leading comment inviting an open reply. 'Yes, I imagine it is', replied Jamieson 'Sandy told me all about the case earlier.' 'Did he mention that the DCI made a deal with Wallace and his brief without getting clearance from a higher authority? Or that the whole thing backfired, and they caught four sprats but failed to land the mackerel? Or Sandy and at least two other officers had to have prolonged counselling after the event: Sandy tried to resign from the force, but they wouldn't let him.' Jamieson nodded, although the last two points that Evason had made came as a complete surprise to him.

Evason continued: 'Do you think it's wise to let Sandy work on this one? He was traumatised when it all happened before. He may not be able to treat the victim compassionately, you know, having lived through it all the first time round.' Jamieson considered her point: 'He's a good cop, a professional. He won't let anything get in the way of that.'

'Read the file, please,' said Evason, and catching sight of Stone through the window in the door as he approached, she lowered her voice and urgently added, 'Sandy went through an awful lot.'

Using his elbow to push the door handle down and applying his hip to ease it open, Stone came back into the room, balancing two plastic cups of coffee on a file and carrying a third. 'Shit, that's hot,' he said, grimacing and placing the cup in his hand on the desk in front of Evason.

'Thanks,' she said, flicking over a sheet of paper and moving on to the next in the file. Jamieson plucked his coffee from the top of the file and peered at it. A brown slurry, he sipped it. The overriding taste was one of sweetness. The team's method of removing the acrid taste of the instant coffee that the machine provided was to add two or three times the recommended sweetener — it improved the taste, but only slightly.

Stone took the remaining cup and moved to his desk. He put the coffee down, took off his jacket, and slipped it over the back of the chair. He reached over and hauled the box marked 'one' from beside Evason's desk and up onto his own. He took a deep breath, sat down, lifted the lid off the box, and prepared to return to a time and place he secretly wished he would never have revisited. Jamieson moved to his own desk and sat down. He picked up a typed sheet of paper that someone had placed in the centre of the desk and began to read. It was the report by Constable Johnson outlining the meeting with the landlord of the Happy Farmer. Jamieson speed read through the report and then, as was his habit, reread it, this time more thoroughly.

When he'd finished, he spoke to Evason: 'When did this come in?' he asked. Evason looked up: 'Erm... about twelve or thereabouts, I'd say.' 'Did you read it?' continued Jamieson.

'Briefly,' said Evason. 'Why? Shouldn't I have done?'

Jamieson held his hand up as if to say no problem. He had an open desk policy in this office. If people wished to communicate with him only, then it was up to them to put stuff in envelopes and mark them private and confidential. Otherwise, whatever was on anyone's desk was open to all the other members of the team to read. That was how it worked, and everyone understood that.

'What did you think?' he asked.

'Of the report?' Evason wrinkled her nose. 'Okay. Fairly thorough seems to cover all the salient points. The prose was probably a bit flowery for me, but that's being picky.'

The team had been running one man short for the last three months, and there had been little headway in returning the numbers to the full complement. The report had been written by Constable Johnson, who had impressed Jamieson that morning with his local knowledge and his natural thought process in thinking that the victim may have spent the evening drinking at the local pub. The findings in Johnson's report proved that he had been right. Maybe he should try to get Constable Johnson seconded to the team for the foreseeable future or at least until they had got more idea of how the case was going to progress; it seemed likely that there would be a lot of legwork necessary, far too much for the two Detective Sergeants in situ to take on. He made a mental note to speak to the Chief Constable's office.

CHAPTER SEVEN

Jamieson checked his watch — five fifteen — incredibly early to go home on the first clay of a murder case. The police training manual stated that the Key to solving most murder cases was often found in the first forty-eight hours after death, and Jamieson agreed that in most cases, that was probably right. However, most of these cases involved either lots of witnesses, overwhelming circumstantial evidence and, sometimes, a suspect standing over a body holding a smoking gun. This case didn't fit into any of those moulds. Jamieson was convinced that this was a revenge killing for an act or acts that took place a long time ago and, as such, didn't feel that the forty-eight-hour rule applied.

He had suggested to Evason, who had been pouring over boxes and files for a straight six hours, that she would be better prepared for the morning if she were to head off home, relax and rest her eyes ready for the next day. That was at around four-thirty. Surprisingly Evason didn't argue but merely gathered the files she was working on and placed them back into the relevant box. Next, she tidied five plastic coffee cups around her desk and dropped them into the wastepaper bin. Finally, she slipped her overcoat on and picked up her shoulder bag. She looked at Jamieson and mimed that he should keep an eye on Stone by pointing at her eyes, then at Jamieson and finally at Stone. He nodded and said, 'goodnight Claire. See you in the morning.' As the door closed behind Evason, Jamieson spoke to Stone: 'What are your initial thoughts?'

'Someone got him, no doubt about that, and there'll be no shortage of suspects. He was a bad man, evil to the core.' Stone sniffed and indicated the four boxes lying in various places around the floor. 'In my opinion, the killer's name is in one of these files, and it's our job to find out who it is.' Jamieson studied Stone's features closely; 'You had a bad time with this case before. Do you think you're up to facing it all over again?'

Stone kept his eyes on the desk in front of him. 'I'm older now, more experienced,

I've seen more — not that it makes the likes of Wallace any more palatable — but I'm a Detective Sergeant on a murder squad, that's my choice, and I'm paid to help solve murders. It's not a prerequisite that I like the victims. Most of the time, I don't even know the victims. I need to do what I am good at doing and act professionally and when I go home in the evening, I need to leave all this behind until the next day when it all starts again. It's my life, it's my choice, and I can handle it.' Jamieson nodded slowly; 'Okay'.

That was almost an hour ago, and since then, nothing had passed between the two men as they sat at their desks and systematically went through files and other papers documenting the deceased's life from more than a quarter of a century ago. Finally, Jamieson flipped the file he was reading closed and puffed out his cheeks.

'Sandy,' he announced. 'I'm calling it a day. Why don't you as well? Get yourself off home and spend some quality time with Margaret.' Stone sat back in his chair: 'It's her yoga night this evening. She won't be home until gone seven.'

Jamieson ran his fingers through his hair, interlocking them at the base of his neck, and sighed. 'Okay, so much for the subtle approach. Now, as your direct line manager, I'm ordering you to go home and forget about this case for the evening. We'll all start again in the morning refreshed after a good night's sleep.' The smile of resignation that gradually crept across his face betrayed his authoritative tone of voice. 'Com'on, I mean it. Go home.'

Stone considered his options: 'Another half an hour, I promise, no more.'

Jamieson took his jacket from the hanger on the coat rack, slipped his arms in and shrugged his shoulders until the fit felt right. Then, he picked up his briefcase that was sitting next to his desk and made for the door. 'Okay, but no more. I mean it. And I will check with the Duty Sergeant downstairs in the morning. See you bright and early.'

On his way downstairs to the station's front entrance, Jamieson took out his mobile phone, scrolled down until he found 'home' and pressed the dial button. The phone rang seven times before it was answered.

'Hi, it's me,' he said.

'Hi, Dad. What's occurring?' He hated that phrase. 'Is Mum there?'

'Hold on', and then in the background, 'It's Dad for you', and some indistinguishable noises whilst the phone was handed over.

'Hi, how's it all going?' Lucy, this time, on the other end of the line.

'Fine. I'm on my way home.' Jamieson pictured Lucy looking at her watch and getting into an almost immediate panic. 'It's only twenty past five. I haven't even begun dinner yet. I thought you'd started a new murder case. I wasn't expecting you until around eight at the earliest.' Jamieson interjected, 'It's okay, don't worry about it. I'm just phoning to say I'm on my way, and can I pick anything up at the supermarket for dinner or do we push the boat out and get a takeaway tonight?' The thought of an Indian takeaway made Jamieson's mouth water in anticipation.

'No, we're okay,' said Lucy. Jamieson could hear that she was opening and closing the kitchen cupboards as she spoke.'We've got some pasta and a sauce here. That'll be nice and quick and a much healthier option than a takeaway. It'll be on the table for six thirty.' 'Good. That's great,' said Jamieson, trying to keep the disappointment out of his voice. He wasn't a pasta lover. 'I'll see you in about an hour.'

He pressed the button to disconnect the call just as he reached the front desk, gave a wave of his hand to the duty sergeant on his way past and was out through the double doors and into the station car park. He unlocked his car using the remote, opened the door, threw his briefcase into the back seat, climbed in, put his mobile into the blue tooth holder, fastened his seat belt, and started the car. The journey home was uneventful. Traffic was slightly heavier than Jamieson was used to, but then again, it was rush hour when he wasn't usually on the road. He used the time during the journey home to think about the Wallace murder. He had no doubt that Stone was right — it was a revenge killing, and in all probability, the name of the murderer was in one of the boxes that currently sat in the office back at the station. But whose revenge? One of his victims or one of the four who had been locked up based on Wallace's evidence against them whilst he, Wallace, the main perpetrator, had walked away scot-free.

He reached home at twenty past six and let himself in with his front door key, calling out 'Only me' as he crossed the threshold. He put his briefcase down at the foot of the stairs and went into the kitchen to find Lucy standing over the hob, stirring a pan of tomato sauce. He moved over to where she stood and kissed her on the cheek. 'Hi, good day off?' he asked.

She screwed up her nose while considering the day's events: 'So-so, I'd say. Went over to Mum and Dad's and took Mum out for her weekly shop. Then had a late lunch with Samantha in the new coffee shop in town. Got home about half three, and I've been catching up on some work I brought home with me since then.'

This time it was Jamieson's turn to screw up his nose: 'You brought work home with you? Some day off!' Lucy had recently started a new job as a marketing manager for a local gym. The role was part-time, covering three days a week, but it was her first job for a considerable time. She was a fiercely determined woman and wanted to make a good impression, and if that meant her putting in some hours on her day off, then that's what she would do. Jamieson knew this and knew that his little jibe would have no effect whatsoever.

'Updating membership details, with particular interest in those which have lapsed since the beginning of the year,' explained

Lucy. 'Speaking of the gym, I was thinking of going for an hour or so this evening. Do you fancy joining me?' 'Normally, yes, but I was thinking of going to band practice tonight. Especially as I haven't been in ages.' Aged fourteen, over thirty years ago, Jamieson and his best friend, Billy Watson, formed a band at school, The Wailing Bunnies, and in various guises, the band had continued into their adulthood. Billy was the main driving force behind it all, primarily because it provided a decent living for him. As Jamieson initially went through university and then onto police school, his input had fallen away to the extent that he occasionally 'guested' whenever he could make it. The band didn't need him as both Billy, and Jamieson's direct replacement, Tony Standish, were accomplished guitarists in their own right, but Billy was adamant that there would always be a place in the band for his founding member and best friend. The band did cover versions of popular songs, careful to continually refresh their repertoire to include up-to-date favourites. They played at weddings, birthday parties, pubs and other events. During the summer months, they often found themselves booked from Thursday through to Sunday and at a fee of fifteen hundred pounds a go, they made good money. Additionally, Billy hired himself as a session musician and tutored young and old in the basics of guitar playing.

One drunken evening Billy lavished praise upon an embarrassed Jamieson, telling anyone who cared to listen that 'he owed everything he had to Alex Jamieson' explaining that 'the day a tall skinny kid with messy black hair approached him at school with his guitar case slung over his shoulder, and his beat-up amp in his hand saying 'let's play some rock'n'roll' was the day that his life changed forever'. Jamieson supposed there was merit in what Billy said. Up to that point, Billy had no idea where his future lay. With the birth of the Wailing Bunnies, they had, without appreciating it at the time, taken the first steps to build a serious business — a business whose longevity and sustainability had surprised everyone. Here they were, now in their mid-forties, still going strong. And there was Billy, never having settled down and married, still living the life of a sort of rock star. Okay, Bono and the rest of them could rest easy, but there was rarely an appearance when Billy wasn't approached during the break in the set with an offer of some kind from a female aged anywhere between nineteen and sixty-five!

Conversely, Jamieson knew from age ten that he wanted to be a policeman, specifically a detective. His doggedness and determination matched Lucy's, and his career path after university took him to a fast-tracked officer scheme which he passed with flying colours. He quickly rose through the ranks and made Detective Inspector before he was very far into his thirties. Since then, he had stalled somewhat. Perhaps he'd reached his level of expertise. Perhaps subconsciously he didn't want to continue with his initial upward trajectory and felt safe where he was, doing what he did.

'That sounds like a great idea,' said Lucy enthusiastically. 'You haven't seen Billy in ages.' She stopped talking and gave the matter some further thought. 'I'll tell you what; I can drop you off on my way to the gym, then I'll swing by when I've finished and give you a lift home. That way, you can have a drink, and I can listen to any new stuff the band is working on.'

'Great', replied Jamieson. 'I'll get my stuff together". He was pleased that his idea had gone down so well. He didn't feel that he was imposing on Lucy. I was, after all, her suggestion, and he knew that she adored Billy and loved listening to the music the band played.

She loved live music, particularly rock'n'roll. Jamieson had first met her in the students' bar at university, listening to a local band knocking out standard stuff. Their recollection of the band's quality on that evening differed, to say the least. Lucy, who at that time didn't drink and as a consequence was stone-cold sober, thought they were awful — bad drumming, tuneless playing and flat vocals — whilst Jamieson, who had been playing for the University rugby team that afternoon and had been in the bar since the match had finished at five, thought the band was 'one of the best he'd ever seen'. At the end of their set, he'd staggered onto the stage and insisted that he sing the encore with them. The singer seemed completely unconcerned or uninterested and stepped back from the microphone, spreading his hands as if to say 'it's all yours' before disappearing towards the back of the stage and a couple of waiting female students. Jamieson turned to the rest of the band and asked them if they knew 'Bad Moon Rising' — a rock standard in anyone's book — they did, and the drummer counted them in. They began badly. Jamieson didn't know the words or, at least in his drunkenness, had temporarily forgotten them and got worse. By the time they had reached the chorus the second time around, the original singer had reassured control of the microphone, and some semblance of order had resumed.

Jamieson's exit from the stage had been undignified. His claims that the guitarist deliberately lifted his guitar, causing the lead to his amplifier to rise up just as Jamieson stumbled past, causing him to trip and pitch head first from the front of the stage/were greeted with hoots of derision when he returned to where his rugby playing mates were gathered. Lucy and some of her friends were with them, and despite herself, she found his goonish antics somewhat endearing. That was nearly a quarter of a century ago.

Jamieson went upstairs to change into his band outfit, jeans and a t-shirt and to get his guitar and amplifier ready. He paused at Justin's door and knocked. On hearing a muffled 'come in', he pushed the door open and poked his head in. His youngest son was sitting in darkness with just the glow from the computer screen in front of him, illuminating his facial features. Justin quickly turned his face from the screen, saw it was his Father and just as quickly looked back at the screen again. 'Hi Dad,' he said. 'Hi Jus,' replied Jamieson. 'What are you doing?' He narrowed his eyes to see what was on the screen and made a mental note to visit the opticians in the near future. 'Killing aliens' came the reply as if it were the most natural thing in the world for a four-teen-year-old boy to be doing.

Jamieson stepped into the room and looked around. He realised he hadn't been in Justin's room for a while now and, consequently, wasn't entirely up to date with the boy's tastes. He was pleased to see that the Manchester United poster previously on the wall above the bed had been replaced by one of the local rugby teams. The poster of Britainy Spears had suffered a similar fate. In its place was a dark, gloomy drawing of a young woman dressed entirely in black and looking out of the picture into the eyes of the person standing directly before her. Her right hand was extended out from the picture. In it, she held a gun with the handle facing outwards and the muzzle facing her as if she were offering it to the person looking at the picture — Jamieson wondered whether it was the sort of picture that you should be wearing 3D glasses to fully appreciate — across the top of the picture in clear block capitals it said 'Revenge is everything'. Jamieson widened his eyes and thought to himself. 'Not sure about that one,' but decided against saying anything to his son. It probably wasn't worth the grief.

Jamieson was pleased to see a pile of books on the bedside table, which indicated that at least his son still had time for reading. The iPod they gave Justin on his last birthday was sitting in the charging dock alongside the books. And in the corner of the room, the last vestiges of Justin's absolute youth, an action man, sat forlornly, looking on as his friend and master grew up, leaving him behind. 'Done your homework?' Jamieson enquired over Justin's shoulder. 'Didn't get any today,' replied Justin, his eyes not leaving the screen. 'How is school?' 'Um...er... yeah... well, it's good.' The boy's fingers skipped across the keyboard, and another green alien on the screen disintegrated into dust.

Jamieson watched for a further ten seconds, then gave up trying to engage in a conversation. Instead, he walked across the room to the door, turned and said: 'Dinner's ready in about five minutes.' As he reached the top of the staircase and just before formulating an internal comment about 'the trouble with kids these days', an image of his Father appeared in his head.

'Christ,' he said aloud. 'I'm turning into my Old Man!'

CHAPTER EIGHT

Lucy dropped him outside the Jennings Arms pub and told him she'd be back in around two hours. Jamieson checked his watch — seven-fifteen. He felt much as he did when he and Billy first set up the band. He had his guitar slung across his back and his old amplifier in his right hand. He made his way round to the back of the pub. There was an old entertainment room used for parties and weddings, but it was empty for most evenings during the week. The pub landlord let the bank rehearse there free of charge, providing they played a set at the annual fundraiser run by the pub every September. It was an equitable agreement that suited both parties.

Jamieson shouldered the door open. It was a reasonably sized space with a bar at one end and a stage at the other. In between, there was a dance floor with tables and chairs set out, ready for a forthcoming event, probably at the weekend. Jamieson could see how easy it was to serve people a sit-down dinner and then move the tables and chairs to the edges of the room to allow the real partying to start later in the evening as drink freed people from their usual inhibitions.

The stage was about three feet off the ground. There was a drum kit already set up. Jamieson recalled that Jim Dunne, the longstanding drummer with the Wailing Bunnies, always arrived at rehearsal and gigs early because he had so much to set up. Consequently, he was always ready significantly earlier than the rest of the band and usually disappeared off to find a bar where he could have a drink. Jim always maintained that he kept time better with at least one alcoholic drink inside him. There were three other people on the stage — Liz Willis, the backing singer and Johnny Williams, the bass player — the third person was instantly recognisable to Jamieson even though he had his back to him.

Jamieson walked down the middle of the hall, slaloming through tables and chairs. Johnny Williams looked up when he was about ten feet from the stage. As he recognised Jamieson, a huge grin spread across his lace: 'Look what the bloody cat dragged in.'

Liz Willis, in her mid-forties but looking as goddess-like as ever in a sleeveless blouse, tight jeans and knee-high leather boots lifted her head, spotted Jamieson, grinned and took a running leap from the edge of the stage towards him. Jamieson managed to get his amplifier safely to the ground just as she reached him, almost knocking him backwards and planting a huge kiss on his right cheek.

'Oh, Alex,' she said. 'As gorgeous as ever. I haven't seen you in almost a year and a half, and you haven't aged a bit.' She used her thumb to wipe away the lipstick mark that she'd left on his cheek.

Alex smiled. 'Hello Liz,' he said. 'Looking good.'

He looked up at Johnny Williams and winked. 'Johnny. How's tricks?'

Finally, the third figure on the stage turned from what he was doing and faced Jamieson. Jamieson would never admit to being an emotional sort, but it had been a long time since he'd since Billy and a nice warm feeling welled up inside him and his eyes glistened. He grinned sheepishly.

Billy beamed down at him from the stage: 'Wella, wella, wella, look who's shown up for band practice almost two years late — the prodigal guitarist returns' He jumped down from the stage with a little more decorum and significantly less energy than Liz had and approached Jamieson with his right hand outstretched, fingers facing upwards. Jamieson responded, and the two joined hands in one of those new style handshakes - less formal, more matey — with his free left hand, Billy planted a friendly but firm slap on Jamieson's right shoulder.

The remaining band members turned up for the next fifteen minutes, and Jim Dunne, the drummer, was recalled from the bar next door. Everyone was delighted to see Alex, and they could have spent all evening catching up. However, just after seven thirty, Billy announced that they were here for rehearsal, and rehearsal is what they would do. However, he conceded that they might finish a little early tonight to enjoy a celebratory drink with the returning hero.

Although Jamieson hadn't played with the band in a while, he had occasionally practised at home in the spare bedroom just to keep his hand in, as it were. He considered himself a reasonable musician for someone who, in the main, was self-taught. He had had some initial lessons at school but found the basics boring and preferred to go off and create his own music. As a result, he had an excellent ear and knew how to play the basic chords.

Billy was kind enough to start rehearsals with two songs that the band had been playing for years. They probably could have played these songs in their sleep and didn't really need to practice them, but it gave Jamieson an easy re-introduction to playing with other musicians. Initially, Jamieson found that he was slightly off tempo, but quickly the fingers of his left hand loosened up and started to skip their way across the fretboard of his guitar whilst the fingers of his right hand grasped the plectrum and struck the right strings pretty much at the right time.

After the first two numbers, Billy used the old internal telephone system to call a drinks order through to the bar and called for 'tenners in the kitty, please'. Everyone coughed up except Jamieson, who stood with a horrified look on his face, patting his empty jeans' pockets. He had come out without his wallet.

'Nothing ever changes, does it?' Mocked Tony Standish gently. They played some new songs, which Jamieson picked up as they went and strummed the appropriate chords. Then, finally, the drinks arrived, and they took a ten-minute break. Billy cornered Jamieson and told him that the band were finding themselves getting more and more bookings. For some, at bigger venues or functions, they could up their prices. It seemed that mobile discos were finding times tough, and more and more people wanted live music at their weddings or parties, and the good reputation that the Wailing Bunnies had built up had stood them in good stead. They were known on the circuit for their reliability, their flexibility to change their set to reflect the tastes of their audience and their good quality musicianship. Jamieson was pleased with his old friend. He knew Billy worked hard and put his heart and soul into the band.

Billy looked older, thought Jamieson, but then he suspected so did he. It had been almost two years, and they were both at that age when things began to change and change quickly. Hair greyed or thinned or even disappeared altogether, waistlines expanded, faces creased, and joints started to ache. He cursed himself for leaving it so long between catching up with an important part of his life and vowed not to leave it so long next time.

Billy asked how things were going at work and then in general. Jamieson responded that work was work. Home life was great. Xander was away at university, and Justin was heading towards his GCSEs with the usual lack of commitment that he showed towards anything educational, but they weren't overly worried. The kid always pulled it out of the hat in the end. Lucy was well. Jamieson knew Billy had a soft spot for Lucy and hadn't mentioned that she would show up later to pick him up. That would be a far nicer surprise for him after the shock of seeing Jamieson himself. They played on for another couple of hours, occasionally stopping for refreshment. Most of the stuff they played was new to Jamieson. There were some ballads when Liz would step up to the microphone and deliver a killer performance. It amazed Jamieson that she hadn't ever been approached to go professional. The comparison between Liz and some of today's so-called female singers was non-existent — Liz simply blew them out of the water.

Then there was some stuff by the newer bands, mainly from the States. Jamieson had probably heard stuff on the radio in his car, and whilst it was good enough to get you home at the end of the day, it wasn't exceptional enough for Jamieson to go out and buy the CD. Jus probably had most of the stuff downloaded onto his MP3 player. Jamieson kept up with most of the new stuff, kept it simple, played his chords, strummed along, and stayed in his comfort zone. Finally, Billy announced: 'Just two more songs, people, and we'll go straight through with both of them. It's a couple of old numbers that I thought we may resurrect and get back on the playlist.' He grinned and looked across at Jamieson. 'The first one is Johnny B Goode.'

Now it was the turn of the rest of the band to grin. Jamieson had always, in the past, taken a back seat whenever the band played on stage. He played the rhythm guitar and provided occasional backing vocals. Except for the one song — Johnny B Goode — that was his song. For that one song, he took over on lead vocals and lead guitar. That was his time in the spotlight. That was when Billy stood back and left centre stage to him.

He smiled: 'I haven't played it in ages,' he protested. Nevertheless, he moved centre stage and adjusted the microphone stand to accommodate his slightly taller frame. He turned his amplifier up to a level that befits a lead guitarist. Finally, he settled and looked at the rest of the band. Fingers of his left hand pressed firmly against the fretboard. The fingers of his right hand clutching the plectrum posed over the bridge of the guitar.

He was telling the truth. He hadn't played the song for some years, but it was one of his favourites, and the whole lead guitar part and vocals were burnt indelibly into his memory banks.

It was a short, frantic, breathless song. Blink, and you'd miss it. From an initial burst of machine gun notes from the lead guitar, drums and bass joining in and driving the whole thing forward, a voice telling of an illiterate young boy living in Louisiana who 'played the guitar like nobody could' and the plinky plink of the piano coming into the chorus.

The band was a little rusty, and the song was not as tight as some of the earlier songs they'd played tonight, but by the time

Jamieson brought his raised fist down, jamming the plectrum across the strings for the closing note, he had reached a high that he had not enjoyed in a long time. Everyone had beaming smiles across their faces. Liz Willis clapped her hands together above her head and whooped and hollered. Jim Dunne and Tony Standish exchanged mile-wide grins and high fives. Billy raised his pint high above his head and shouted to Jamieson above the noise, 'You haven't lost it' Then, in unison, they said to each other: 'I never had it!' and burst out laughing.

Eventually, the high dimmed down.

'How the hell am I going to follow that?' said Billy, moving front and centre stage again, using his hip to nudge Jamieson back to his customary place on the stage. Jamieson knew the whole band knew what was coming. 'Okay', said Billy, 'Summer Breeze.' In the old days, this was the song that closed the set, and it always came straight after Jamieson's moment of glory. Jamieson was never sure whether it was Billy's way of reasserting himself as leader of the band or whether it was the good old-fashioned way of lifting the audience, whipping them up into a frenzy and then hitting them with a piece of real quality and the way Billy played this particular song it was, without doubt, authentic quality.

Whereas Johnny B Goode was fast and furious with sharp edges and crashing cymbals, Summer Breeze took itself seriously; it was a modern-day classic with a haunting guitar piece as smooth as melted chocolate and vocals to match. And Billy played both parts to perfection. This was the song that sealed it with the ladies.

Billy's hands caressed the guitar, his face portrayed agony, and his voice oozed pain — and the ladies in the audience loved it. Then, two minutes into the song, Jamieson noticed the door at the back of the hall open. In walked Lucy, hair wet from the shower and face reddened by her exertions. She pulled a chair out from behind one of the tables and watched in awe, as she usually did when Billy held centre stage.

Finally, when the song finished, Billy looked at the other band members.

'Bloody Hell, that felt good. I wonder how it sounded out there,' he said, indicating the audience area with the neck of his guitar. Not sure," said Jamieson with a big smile. 'Why don't you ask your biggest fan?' Billy spun around to catch sight of Lucy making her way towards the stage.

'Woo-hoo', he shouted, scrambling to get his guitar strap over his head. He propped the guitar against the amplifier and turned and leapt from the small stage to meet Lucy, who ran into his arms.

'Hey baby, long time no see,' he said, sweeping her into his arms and spinning her round. Lucy laughed with delight. 'You've not lost any of your magic,' she said. 'That was brilliant.' Not as good as your old man earlier. We got a fantastic version of Johnny B Goode out of him' Jamieson smiled modestly and held up his hand in acknowledgment, but the conversation had already moved on.

As he packed away his equipment, he looked around him. People were talking and laughing animatedly. These were good people. This was a strong support network. He could not believe he had neglected it for the past couple of years. Billy approached him and clapped him on the shoulder. 'So if Lucy is a designated driver, you can have a couple of pints then.' He beamed, 'Fantastic, we've got some catching up to do.'

CHAPTER NINE

'Okay. What have we got then?' asked Jamieson. 'Hopefully, most, if not all, of the names should match up.' He looked down at his notepad. 'I'll start.'

He cleared his throat.'Andrew Soper, David Sargeant, Thomas Winslow and Malcolm Lewis.' He looked up at both Evason and Stone, who nodded their agreement back at him. These were the easy ones. These four men were put away for lengthy prison sentences on the back of evidence given by Lesley Wallace almost twenty-five years ago. Each of these men unquestionably had a motive to harm or even kill Wallace.

'Okay,' said Jamieson, 'we continue. Known victims next. Darren Hughes, James and Charlie Marshall Hughes were the boy that Wallace had groomed at the foster home, and the Marshall brothers were the two boys in the house the night the raid took place. Again Evason and Stone nodded. 'That's not an exhaustive list by any means. It's currently made up of actual known victims of Wallace. It's more than possible that there are many more that can be added to this list.'

'Moving on, it gets more difficult. Next are victims who were not directly affected by the events but bore a degree of suffering by association, shall we say?' Jamieson checked his list. 'Mr and Mrs Marshall and Mr and Mrs Hughes, as parents of the victimised children, Mrs Worthington, the manager of the foster home, Stone cut in. 'She'd be in her eighties now, so it's unlikely.'

Jamieson acknowledged Stone's comment with a nod of his own. Nevertheless, we need to speak to her, even if it's just to eliminate her. Plus, she may remember something we haven't got documented in our files that might prove of significance.' 'Fair point', said Stone. 'Finally,' continued Jamieson, 'and I'm sure you understand it is imperative that we accept the need for thoroughness in this investigation...' he paused 'We need to consider the effect of Wallace's actions on the team of police directly; involved in the investigation.' He looked directly at Stone. 'That would include you as an investigating officer and Detective Inspector Scott as the head of the investigation.' Stone nodded slowly but said nothing.

'Does anyone have any other names that stood out from the initial trawl of the files?' asked Jamieson. Evason spoke. 'Not in the files, but a possibility would be wives or children of the four men jailed. They may hold a grudge against Wallace for his part in that.' Jamieson replied. 'Whilst that's worth consideration, we need to be crystal clear that these four men were still dangerous individuals. We need to take care not to classify them as victims of Wallace. Without Wallace's intervention, we may never have put them away.'

Silence descended whilst each of them thought about the situation some more. Then, finally, Stone spoke: 'Well, I can clear some names from the list straightaway' he counted on the fingers of his left hand as he spoke. 'Thomas Winslow died not long after going inside over twenty years ago. He wasn't afforded segregation like the sexual offenders these days. He was found in the shower block with a stab wound through his heart, and his dick hacked off and shoved in his mouth. They found the weapon, a crudely made knife, but despite having strong suspicions, they could never pin the offence on anyone. I don't think they tried very hard — many people in that prison, including the warders, thought that it was just desserts.'

Jamieson winced at his colleague's chosen terminology: 'Wife or any other relatives?'

Stone pulled a face: 'Single man. His father had died long before, and his Mother had disowned him. No siblings."

'Okay,' said Jamieson. 'Move his name and the likelihood of anyone connected with him to the bottom of the list. Who else can you clear?'

Stone pushed the ring finger on his left hand back to indicate number two: 'Scott died a few years ago. He was in his eighties by then, living in a nursing home. I used to visit him every so often. Funny thing was that he never mentioned retribution of any kind against Wallace. He always thought that twenty-five years ago, Wallace was there for the taking, but he blamed himself for panicking and acting too quickly in striking a deal with him to bag the others. I'd say he was full of remorse and, perhaps, guilt for what happened, but retribution? No, I don't think so. He left the force not long after it all broke.' Stone paused for thought. 'Well, he was pensioned off. Never had the chance to make amends, put things right. He went from a legend to a nobody in no time at all. Every time I saw him after he'd retired, that case was all he'd talk about. It consumed him. He'd re-examine events over and over. Where he went wrong, what he should have done. It was his own failings that concerned him. Not any kind of revenge on Wallace.' Stone finished up. Evason was leaning forward in her seat — her eyes intently on Stone.

Jamieson waited for Stone's words to sink in before asking, 'he had a son on the force, didn't he?'

'That's right,' said Stone 'Jim. He'd be about my age — last I knew was that he was a DI up in Merseyside somewhere.'

'Anything there?' said Jamieson.

'What?' said Stone. 'Would Jim have picked up the baton for his old man and sought revenge on Wallace?' He sucked air in through his lower front teeth while he considered his answer, then shook his head. 'No, I don't think so. It doesn't feel right. Jim was a policeman in his old man's mould. You catch and convict them fair and square. If you do your job right, then that's what happens. If you don't, then they go free until they re-offend again — then you get another chance. That's what happened with Wallace — only as far as we can tell, he's never re-offended. He's never given us another chance.'

Jamieson nodded. Whilst he trusted Stone and knew that he had an excellent instinct in these matters, he made a mental note to make some follow-up enquiries that might or might not involve speaking directly to Jim Scott. He looked at Stone. 'Any more names that we can cross off?'

Stone paused then started talking, seemingly picking his words carefully: 'Twenty-five years ago, when I found out about Lesley Wallace's crimes and the fact that he would be walking away without facing any kind of justice, it sickened me, absolutely. If you'd have put me in an empty cell for five minutes with just Lesley Wallace for company, I'd have murdered him, no question. I felt like that for a few years after. I had a lot of anger, and as a result, I wasn't a good policeman or husband. Initially, the counselling that I was given just made me more annoyed, some poncy over-educated university type telling me it's okay for me to be angry...' he gave a resigned snort of laughter 'but the more sessions I attended, the more I could see that he was right. You can't take responsibility for life's anomalies like Lesley Wallace. You do your best to catch them and put them away where they can't hurt anyone anymore, but sometimes, despite your best efforts, it doesn't always work out like that. Gradually I stopped hating Wallace with quite so much vengeance. If I saw him in the street now, if I'd even recognised him in the street now, I'd viewed him as a pathetic individual and nothing more.' Stone looked Jamieson directly in the eye...besides Margaret, and I had friends round for dinner on the night Wallace was killed. They didn't leave until a quarter to two in the morning, so I've got a cast-iron alibi.' He smiled. It broke the tension that had been building up all morning.

Evason also smiled: 'The doctor says that death occurred between 10 pm and 2 am — that still leaves fifteen minutes unaccounted for.' Then, she widened her eyes and gave him a knowing look.

Stone joined in with their gentle mocking of him. 'If you want to phone Margaret and ask her what we were doing between one forty-five and two o'clock in the morning, then be my guest, but don't be shocked by her response.'

Jamieson and Evason looked at each other. Jamieson raised his eyebrows: 'Washing up?' he said. They both laughed. 'Eh! There's life in the old dog yet!' said Stone, laughing with them.

There was a knock on the door. 'Come in', shouted Jamieson, trying to suppress his laughter. The door opened, and Constable Johnson walked in. For a moment, Jamieson didn't recognise him and was about to ask him what he wanted. Johnson beat him to it. 'Constable Johnson, Sir, I was told to report to you immediately.' Jamieson remembered. 'Ah, Johnson,' he said.

He recalled his telephone conversations on the way home in the car last night. The first was with the Chief Constable's Office bemoaning that the team were still light, and they had a murder investigation underway, which would take up a lot of man hours. Having secured agreement from the Resources Officer that he could approach the station sergeant for one extra body, Jamieson then phoned the station and requested the secondment of two officers, as agreed with the Chief Constable's Office, to assist in the enquiries of the ongoing murder investigation. 'Impossible,' came the reply. 'We can't spare two officers. You can have one.' 'Okay,' replied Jamieson, 'but it needs to be someone good, someone, like Johnson' 'Hold on', Jamieson could hear pages being flicked at the other end of the line. 'Okay, you can have Johnson — he's due on duty at ten in the morning. I'll have him report straight to you.'

'Thank you,' said Jamieson before hanging up. He had learnt long ago that you had to pitch high and be prepared to negotiate down to get what you initially wanted.

'It's Roger, isn't it?' Jamieson asked Johnson. 'Er, Rog, Sir,' answered Johnson.

'Um, right.' Jamieson introduced the others in the room in case Johnson didn't know who they were. 'That's DS Claire Evason, and this here is DS Pete Stone, Sandy. We're reasonably informal on this team, so it's Claire and Sandy. I'm Alex but if you find that difficult just 'Sir' but not 'Guv' please, we're not on a television show. So you'll be Roger unless you're getting a bollocking, then you'll be Constable Johnson, and I'll be Detective Inspector Jamieson. We share a lot of ideas in this office, so don't be shy even if they might sound a bit limp or even downright far-fetched — if they are ridiculous, Sandy here will let you know pretty swiftly. One of his strengths is the savage putdown.'

Johnson awkwardly thrust his hand towards Evason, who briefly shook it. Stone stood and leaned over, extending his right hand, smiling at Johnson as he took the younger man's hand and briefly squeezed.

Jamieson pointed to a nearby desk; 'Take this desk for now. I'll give you a full briefing later, but for now, you'll be working with Sandy.' 'Thank you, Al... Sir.' Said Johnson correcting himself, his face visibly reddening as he sat at the desk.

Jamieson divided up the tasks. Stone and Johnson would be looking into the current whereabouts of and, if necessary, interviewing the remaining three men who were locked up based on Wallace's evidence and the foster home manager.

They would also be responsible for finding any witnesses, which would mean further to all the houses; Wallace took the route on his way home from the pub. Additionally, and as Johnson had already done the groundwork, they would be responsible for anything that may be of interest involving the Happy Farmer Public House.

Jamieson and Evason would be responsible for tracking down the victims, as Jamieson had badged them earlier, and their parents. They, or rather Evason, would also be responsible for tracking the movements of Wallace after he had given his evidence — when he changed his name, where he had been living, who he had been working for — up until when he had been found battered to death yesterday morning. Although Jamieson didn't mention it out loud, he would be responsible for dealing with the police involved — the two officers who, along with Stone, had been through counselling and Jack Scott's son, Jim, the Detective Inspector based somewhere in Merseyside.

There would be a briefing meeting every morning at eight-thirty sharp — everyone to attend unless an exceptional reason was provided beforehand — and Johnson, as the newest recruit to the team, was responsible for providing coffee and croissants — not the instant muck provided at the station — proper stuff for the local café three doors down. Evason would start a coffee fund; it wasn't fair to expect Johnson, on a constable's wages, to pay for everyone's morning pick me up. All mobiles to be kept fully charged and switched on, please.

Johnson put his hand up: 'I don't have a police issue mobile, sir,' Evason said: 'There's one in the top left drawer along with a charger. I'd get it put on charge now.' So Johnson rooted in the drawer found the mobile, charged the nearest electrical socket, and put the mobile on charge.

While this was happening, Jamieson took Stone to one side: 'Don't let Johnson read the files. I don't want him getting any preconceived ideas. He's an intelligent lad and might come up with some angles we haven't considered. Take him for a coffee down to Giorgio's and give him a detailed outline of what we've got so far, but only limited information about the events of twenty-five years ago. Bring Claire and me a decent cup of coffee back.'

Stone and Johnson disappeared down to Giorgio's. As they passed through the door, Evason called after them: 'Cappuccino, please' and smiled. She continues to tap away on a computer keyboard, finding out what she can about how Lesley Wallace became Brian Wilkins. The 'why' and 'when' were more obvious.

Jamieson picked up two box files, took them into the glassed-off office area A at the back of the room, and then returned for the other two. He meant what he said about it being a team that worked together and shared ideas, and to demonstrate this for the majority of the time; he would sit out in the open plan office with the rest of his colleagues. But there were times when privacy was needed, such as now, when the small office came in handy for more private work, including telephone calls of a sensitive nature.

Jamieson sat down behind the desk and delved back into one of the box files. He soon found the file he was looking for and from it wrote down the names of the officers who had counselling alongside Stone — Detective Sergeant William Mitchell and Constable Simon Atherton — he added the name Detective Inspector James Scott to the bottom of the list. Next, he fired up the computer on the desk and clicked on the icon for the police index. He entered the name 'William Mitchell' but left the section for rank blank, as he didn't want to limit the results based on information from twenty-five years ago. Unfortunately, the police index database had only been computerised since the early 1990s, and, whilst there had been a population of much of the data prior to that date, nothing was available to help him. Thankfully, he was wrong.

The computer whirred for a while before coming up with three 'William Mitchells' currently working or having previously worked for the police force. The first, William Alan Mitchell, was born on 14th April 1976, which would have made him nine or ten at the time of the initial investigation, so it was easy to discount him.

The third name on the list was William Keith Mitchell, who was listed as a Community Officer working in Manchester. He had only joined in 2000, and again, eliminating him was a simple task.

The middle William Mitchell, William James Mitchell, seemed the most likely candidate. He was born on 13th March 1962, making him around the same age as Stone. He was currently a Hostage Negotiator working in the Metropolitan Region. His home address was listed as somewhere in Bedford, around twenty miles from where Jamieson now sat. Jamieson jotted down the contact number listed with the Met and other relevant details.

Jamieson deleted the details for Mitchell and inserted 'Simon Atherton'. This time only one result was returned, and the record was marked 'resigned 25/9/1985' — three months after the case first broke. Apparently, Simon Atherton had been more badly affected than either Stone, who had remained with the police force, even though his promising career had initially stalled and subsequently stagnated, or Mitchell, who had reached a reasonably senior level. There was a home number listed on Atherton's record, which Jamieson noted along with the date of his resignation.

Finally, Jamieson typed the name James Scott into the search engine of the index. This time there were eight different 'James Scotts' listed, but Jamieson quickly found that James Scott, son of Jack, was indeed still a Detective Inspector working in the Liverpool Region. Again, Jamieson noted down all the relevant details, including contact numbers.

He decided that he would meet both Mitchell and Scott face to face and would call the given contact numbers to set up meetings. Atherton was slightly different in that the details he had were from twenty-five years ago. He would call the number listed and find out more about Atherton's whereabouts.

He picked up the phone and dialled the contact number for Atherton. Five minutes later, he was confident that Atherton could be crossed off the list of possible suspects. An elderly lady had answered the phone. Jamieson had explained who he was and that he was looking for Simon Atherton. Unlike the majority of people who treat the police with suspicion, the elderly lady opened up completely. Simon was her son, and although he had never told her completely what had happened, she knew it wasn't good. Having dreamed of being a policeman for many years, that case, the first which Atherton had any serious involvement with, had made him decide that he wasn't cut out for police work after all. He had tendered his resignation not long after, and the police had been good enough to make a severance payment to him for the mental and physical anguish that he had suffered. Simon had taken that money and decided to start a fresh life in Australia. He had been there for almost twenty-five years and had an Australian wife and three children. He'd taken citizenship up five years after going out there. He'd never been back to England since. Every two years, he would send money back to his Mother so she could fly out and visit. She was seventy-five now and was worried whether she could still manage such a long journey.

Jamieson felt that Mrs Atherton could have continued their chat for hours, but time would not allow him to do so. He poked his head out of the office door. Evason looked up from what she was doing and said, 'you wouldn't believe how simple it is to change your name these days — you can do it all online.' She indicated the screen of her computer. 'However when Wallace did it on' She shuffled through the papers on her desk "the 24th October 1985. It was slightly more difficult. He had to go through a firm of solicitors.' More shuffling of papers "...Jeffries Hawkesworth & Co based in Dunstable. I've phoned and made an appointment to speak to Mr Hawkesworth in about half an hour's time.' She locked the computer screen, stood up and put her jacket on. 'I won't be long,' she said. Then as she reached the door, she stopped and looked back. 'Oh, by the way, the autopsy's been done. I've made an appointment for you to meet with the doctor at the Luton General Pathology Department at around one o'clock.' And she was out of the door and heading down the corridor. Jamieson skipped to the door, stuck his head out and called after her: 'Remind me, what's the doctor's name?'

Evason didn't look back. Instead, she just called out: 'Jenner' and under her breath to herself, 'and she's a lady.'

CHAPTER TEN

Jamieson parked in the main hospital car park, eschewing the invitation to pay and display. He was on official police business and, as such, was entitled to such privileges as free parking. He found the main entrance and asked the receptionist where the pathology lab was. The receptionist frostily used her pen to indicate a sign above her head that told anyone who cared to read it that pathology could be found along the long corridor leading off to the right. The sign also told Jamieson that if he followed the yellow route marked out on the floor, that would also take him to where he wanted to go. He noted that the haematology department was indicated by a red line on the floor and wondered whether that was some kind of a staple joke in the world of hospital administration.

After ten minutes of walking, Jamieson finally found Pathology, which appeared deserted. Eventually, a nurse appeared wearing green with a mask tied behind her head and hanging just off her face. She was reading a chart attached to a clipboard in her hand. 'Excuse me', Jamieson attracted her attention. 'I'm looking for Doctor Jenner.' The nurse looked up: 'Congratulations,' she said.' You've found her.' She thrust her hand out.'You must be Detective Inspector Jamieson.'

Jamieson took the proffered hand but looked somewhat confused. *'I'm* Doctor Jenner,' explained the figure in green.

'Ah,' said Jamieson with a pained look on his face.'Sorry, I was very slow on the uptake there. You must think I'm a bit dense.' Idiot thought Jamieson, Evason told you it was a female pathologist.

'Not at all," said the Doctor kindly. She indicated a door to her right. 'Shall we talk in the office?'

Jamieson passed through into the office, which was little more than four walls, two chairs and a desk — no windows, no personalisation of any kind, hospital white walls and grey lino on the floors — Doctor Jenner followed him in and had to squeeze round behind him to get to the other side of the desk.

Earlier the Doctor had followed the now accepted protocol of telephoning the incident room on the number shown on the business card that Evason had given her yesterday morning to invite the principal investigating officer to attend the autopsy. However, Evason had declined on Jamieson's behalf and instead had made an appointment for after the procedure for Jamieson and the Doctor to discuss the findings in what Jamieson always referred to as a more respectable environment.

Jamieson wasn't put off by attending autopsies; if he felt the situation warranted it, he would do so. But he also felt that violent death was an incredibly undignified process for anyone to go through. A body was invariably found by someone who didn't know the deceased, and then the police were called in, and at least another twenty people, including police officers, police photographers, police doctors, et al., would traipse past without a by your leave. Then the humiliation of being wrapped in a body bag and heaved onto a stretcher in front of a crowd of onlookers before being manoeuvred into the back of an ambulance or hearse. Then the autopsy, the final ignominy. No, if Jamieson could possibly avoid it, he let the Pathologist have his or her time alone with the deceased to do his or her job, and Jamieson would wait patiently and collect the results when they were ready.

In a case like this, where Jamieson thought he already knew the cause of death, there was less reason for him to be present at the autopsy. In truth, he didn't expect anything important to come out of this meeting that he wasn't already aware of.

Doctor Jenner tapped at her computer keyboard. The autopsy report filled the page on the screen in front of her. 'Right', she said, 'the autopsy report for who is believed to be Brian Wilkins, age currently indeterminable, thought to be mid-seventies

Jamieson cut in: 'Actually we're pretty sure it's a man called Lesley Wallace, although we are still awaiting a formal identification.' The Doctor nodded. 'I see,' she said. 'What about the papers in the wallet? Your officers were pretty sure about the name found on them.'

'Um,' said Jamieson. 'He definitely *was* Lesley Wallace. He may now *be* Brian Wilkins. We're looking into whether he changed his name by deed poll.' 'Well, whoever he was, he was killed by a powerful blow to the back of the head by a blunt object, possibly a rounded bat of some sort. The angle of the injury to the right side of the back of the head would indicate a left-handed assailant. The second blow was delivered from the front. Again, this was done with some venom, and the last three whilst he was on his back. The last three wouldn't have had any effect on him because he was already all but dead after numbers one and two.'

'Not a lot of blood?' Jamieson thought out loud. 'Old man, chilly night,' explained the doctor. 'if he'd been a twenty-five-year-old on a hot August afternoon, you'd have had blood. Plenty of it.'

Jamieson nodded: 'Anything more I should be aware of?' The Doctor scrolled down the screen.

'Previously broken arm, appendix removed. The general wear and tear you'd associate with a man in his mid-seventies, really.'

Jamieson rubbed his hand across his lower face whilst he took this information in. 'Oh, and did you know that he was on *cyproterone?*'

Jamieson didn't have a clue what *cyproterone* was. Why should he? He wasn't a chemist? So instead, he said: 'Wow, a toxicology report already, you people don't hang around.' A half smile played across the lips of Doctor Jermer.

'No,' she said. 'We are efficient, but not that efficient. One piece of paper in the deceased's wallet was a prescription for *cyproterone,* made out in the name of Brian Wilkins. One of your Scene of Crime Officers referred it to me this morning.'

'I see', said Jamieson 'What exactly is *cyproto?*' *Cyproterone*' finished the Doctor helpfully. 'It's a drug that's usually associated with women going through menopause.' 'And why would it be prescribed to a man?' asked Jamieson.

'Well, its main attribute is that it suppresses testosterone. So in a man, it would suppress male urges, usually sexual ones. May I ask was our deceased a sexual deviant?' Briefly, Jamieson considered whether he should release this information but just nodded and said one word 'paedophile'. He didn't even consider using the word 'alleged.' From all he read and been told, there was no doubt in his mind that Lesley Wallace was a fully blown paedophile, and anyway, he'd just remembered it wasn't possible to slander the dead.

It was Doctor Jenner's turn to nod: '*Cyproterone* is the European choice of drug for what is termed chemical castration. As I said, it's a suppressant designed to keep an individual's urges at bay. Unlike surgical castration where the scrotum is slit, and the testicles basically cut out, drugs control chemical castration.' Jamieson winced and involuntarily shifted in his chair, crossing his legs. Once again, the Doctor half smiled.

'So', said Jamieson, 'although the word castration implies the complete removal of the testicles, in the case of chemical castration, this isn't actually the case. Would the patient likely re-offend if he came off his drugs?'

'Possibly. He comes off a drug that has been suppressing his urges, and the urges are likely to come back. Whether or not he acts on those urges, Doctor Jenner spread her hands in front of her and gave a small shrug. Well, that's down to the individual.'

'Can we tell how long he's been using this drug?' asked Jamieson. He was leaning forward. His legs were still crossed.

'There are two clues to this,' said the Doctor holding up two fingers to emphasize her point. 'One is infinitely more reliable than the other. The first is more of a pointer, really. For a man slight in stature, the deceased had considerable signs of gynecomastia.'

Jamieson narrowed his eyes and tilted his head in a questioning manner. Dr Jenner explained: 'breast growth, man boobs. This is a side effect of the drug, indicating that the user had been taking it for a considerable while now.' She paused.

'And second?' prompted Jamieson.

'The dispensing chemist at the pharmacy was an old boyfriend of mine, so I phoned him directly, turned on the old charm. Off the record, this man had been using this drug on and off for at least the past fifteen years.'

'On and off?' asked Jamieson.

'Like any drug, it's advisable to take a break every now and again. Drugs make the body and mind do things they are not doing naturally. Going against their instincts, as it were. Who knows what the end result could be if it goes on too long? So coming off medication and letting the body and mind revert to type occasionally is not always such a bad thing.' Doctor Jenner raised her eyebrows.' That's the theory, anyway. Was this course of medicine enforced under some kind of court order?'

Jamieson slowly shook his head and looked directly at the doctor. 'No,' he said. 'He was never found guilty by any court of law, so he must have undergone treatment of his own volition.'

Doctor Jenner pulled a face. 'Interesting,' she said. 'Acknowledgement that what you are is socially and morally unacceptable and then trying to change to put it right. Not a trait that you'd usually associate with this kind of man.'

'Yes,' said Jamieson, standing up and offering the Doctor his hand, 'but you know what they say about leopards and spots - thanks for your help.'

On the way back through the hospital to receive Jamieson's mobile phone rang. He instinctively answered it. It was the Chief Constable.

'Alex, tell me about this murder case you've got,' he said. Jamieson went through what he considered were the salient points so far, leaving out the last piece of information he had received from the pathologist, which he hadn't yet had time to fully digest himself.

'What's your feeling?' asked the Chief Constable. 'Revenge of some kind?' 'It certainly looks that way,' replied Jamieson. He was suddenly aware of someone tugging at his coat sleeve. He turned to face whoever it was. A purple-faced hospital porter stood there pointing at a sign on the wall telling people that mobile phones were not to be used on hospital premises under any circumstances. Jamieson put his hand up to acknowledge the porter - in his mind, this sign was the universally accepted hand signal for 'I'll only be a few seconds longer' but not according to the porter, who continued tugging at his sleeve and pointing at the sign.

Eventually, Jamieson moved away. Purple Face shouted, 'bloody hooligan' at his back. The Chief Constable asked what all the noise was about. Jamieson said there was a drunk causing a scene. The Chief Constable said, 'Hasn't Stone got some history with the victim?'

The commotion with the porter had blindsided Jamieson. How the hell did the old man know about Stone's previous involvement so soon? He thought on his feet. 'DS Stone worked on the original case, Sir, twenty-five years ago.'

'It had an effect on him if I remember rightly,' continued the Chief Constable. 'Are you sure he's up to it?'

Jamieson subscribed to the belief that when you spoke to a superior on a matter, you weren't fully conversant with, you kept your answers short and to the point. 'Yes, Sir. He's a professional.'

'Mmm...I'll leave it with you. Keep me fully appraised, won't you?' 'Will do, Sir,' said Jamieson before he realised he was speaking to a deadline.

Jamieson thought for a moment. Surely Evason hadn't been onto the old man expressing her concerns about Stone's ability to cope in this case. That didn't sound like the way she worked.

'That's him.' Jamieson looked back down the corridor. Purple Face was approaching with a formidable lady dressed in a trouser suit, clearly some kind of official. The porter was pointing at Jamieson as he walked.

For a split second, Jamieson considered fight or flight, then spun on his heel and briskly walked away towards the hospital exit.

CHAPTER ELEVEN

Jamieson woke early — he checked the alarm clock on the bedside table — just after five o'clock. He closed his eyes again and lay back in the warmth of his bed.

This was normal for Jamieson in the early stages of a case. He found that his brain worked overtime during the day until shut down at around ten or eleven at night. Then sufficiently rested, it started again and, consequently, woke him up. From experience, he knew that six hours' sleep was enough for his brain. His body, however, needed a little longer.

He lay in a state of semi-sleep. His body was sufficiently relaxed to continue resting whilst his brain mulled over the course the case had taken to date. Next to him, Lucy slept soundly, her breathing providing a rhythm to help his thoughts. The case was an awkward one.

Firstly, the victim was a man that no one appeared to care very much about. A rare situation — more people wished him real harm than wished him well —very few people enjoyed that kind of notoriety — The Yorkshire Ripper perhaps, and some of the other serial murderers or child killers that Jamieson could think of.

Also, Wallace's crimes occurred over a quarter of a century ago. Does the passing of time make them any less heinous? In Jamieson's book, it didn't count for anything. Wallace had never been fully brought to account for what he'd done. He hadn't paid his debt to society. Had he ever shown any remorse? It seemed that he never re-offended, and Doctor Jenner's news that Wallace appeared to be on a self-administered rehabilitation came as an interesting, if highly surprising, development. Then there was the motive. It seemed that the motive was revenge. There was no evidence or indication that it was anything but revenge. There appeared to be no other reason for this elderly man, who didn't trouble anyone, to have been brutally murdered.

But could someone harbour such vengeance for over a quarter of a century, and why now? Admittedly, Wallace had taken steps to hide his identity, mainly by legally changing his name, but he hadn't strayed far from his old stamping ground. Without too much effort, anyone consumed with that much vengeance would have been able to locate Wallace's, or Wilkins', whereabouts.

He eventually drifted back to sleep but was woken by the alarm going off at six thirty. He rolled over and kissed Lucy awake. Then got out of bed, showered, dressed and went downstairs for breakfast. Remembering that Johnson was bringing coffee and croissants to the morning meeting, he restricted himself to a cup of tea and one slice of toast. He took a cup of tea up to Lucy, told her he'd see her later, went back downstairs and finished up. He was in the car on the road by ten past seven. The traffic was heavier than usual, and he arrived at the station for the morning meeting twenty-five to nine — five minutes late. The others were waiting for him. 'Sorry, sorry,' he said as he burst through the door. He hung his coat on the rack, put his briefcase down next to his desk and picked up the polystyrene cup of coffee that Johnson must have placed there earlier. He sat on his desk and took a mouthful of the coffee. 'Let's begin,' he said.'Claire, what have you got?'

Evason referred to her notes. 'I had a very beneficial meeting with Mr Hawkesworth of Jeffries Hawkesworth yesterday afternoon. It seems that between the raid and the trial, Lesley Wallace spent his time in police custody not, as we know, under arrest but rather at his own request. There was evidently a real ground swell around this case, and a few vigilante groups had been quickly formed.' She looked to Stone for confirmation. He nodded. 'Yeah, I vaguely remember that. Some of the hard nuts on the estate wanted to take things into their own hands. So a mob of about twenty turned up at the station late one Friday after a few beers. They wanted us to serve Wallace and the others up to them on a plate. The others were on remand somewhere in Central London, but Wallace was down in the cells. He was in a right state. There were three cast iron doors with deadlocks between him and the mob, but he was absolutely shitting himself. He was convinced that a copper would accidentally, on purpose, leave the doors unlocked, and the mob would get him. That was probably the only time I saw that bastard's usual slimy, self-confident veneer slip.'

There was a brief silence before Evason continued: 'Anyway, the police agreed to give him protection until the end of the trial. After that, he had to make his own arrangements. He called Mr Hawkesworth, who came down to the station to see him. He wanted to know the best way he could protect his anonymity, and Hawkesworth told him — change your name, change your address, change your appearance — so there and then, he gave Hawkesworth a power of attorney over his affairs and told him to put his house on the market and begin the process to change his name to Brian Wilkins. After the trial, Wallace and his Mother disappeared. They became completely untraceable. Hawkesworth hadn't a clue where they had gone to. The house sold, and Hawkesworth opened a high-interest deposit account in the name of Brian Wilkins and placed the sale proceeds there. The change of name went through, and, from that point on, Lesley Wallace ceased to exist. Hawkesworth took his fees from the sale of the property and closed the file.

Two years later, the phone on his desk rang, and it was his secretary telling him that there was a Mr Wilkins asking to see him. Hawkesworth told her to show him in. At first, the man who came through the door was unrecognisable as the man for whom Hawkesworth had acted two years previously. Wallace was an overweight slob of a man with bad teeth and yellow-coloured hair. He had no pride in his appearance and had worn the same clothes on each occasion that Hawkesworth had seen him. On the other hand, Brian Wilkins was a completely different man.

He was slim and wore glasses. His hair was much darker and had some style to it. His teeth were fixed, and he was dressed in a suit and tie.

Hawkesworth looked closely at the man and still wasn't convinced. He told me that it was only when he shook the man's hand and felt a shiver of pure evil go through him that he could be sure that it was the same man. Evason stopped talking, picked up her coffee and took a sip.

Jamieson considered this information and then asked, 'Wallace was close to his Mother, wasn't he?'

Evason picked up again: 'Yes, it was his mother who wanted to return to the area. They had found a new house seven miles or so from the old one. Wallace was confident enough with his new identity and appearance that he wouldn't be recognised, so he went with his Mother's wish to come home. He went to Hawkesworth not only to reintroduce himself but to get him to deal with the purchase of the new house. Wallace found himself a job working from home as a data imputer and initially only left the house once a week to take his mother to the supermarket to get the week's shopping and to go to the chemists to pick up a prescription.' 'And the only person who knew the truth was Mr Hawkesworth of Jeffries Hawkesworth. He still has a power of attorney, although there has been no call to use it.' 'What did Hawkesworth think of Wallace?' asked Jamieson.

Evason considered her reply. 'Well, although he shrouded the whole issue with the usual solicitor/client privileges, he did tell me, off the record, that he found Wallace thoroughly disagreeable...' she paused. 'but the more he met Wilkins, and that was quite often over the next twenty-five years, he found himself more accepting of the man. That was the phrase he used, more accepting. It was like dealing with a different person, is what he said.'

This backed up what Jamieson had learnt from Doctor Jenner about Wallace making every effort to erase what he was in the past and try to turn himself into something more palatable.

'One last thing', said Evason, 'Hawkesworth had a copy of Wallace's will on his desk.' They waited. Johnson realised he was actually holding his breath. 'and?' said Jamieson. 'Cremation, no guests or flowers. Ashes to be scattered at the Crematorium Remembrance Gardens, where his Mother's ashes are. The estate has been split equally between two children's charities.'

Jamieson recalled the bank statements he had seen in the desk at the house; the money in the accounts and the house's value trotted up to around half a million pounds. Was Wallace buying redemption for his sins? Who knew? Throughout Evason's recount, Stone sat impassively at his desk. Now she had finished, he spoke: 'So we're to believe that this evil bastard went away, found God or some kind of equivalent, went on a diet, had his hair cut and came back a changed man.' Evason wasn't rising to the bait. 'I'm just reporting back what I've been told by a highly experienced and, from what I understand, well-regarded solicitor. I'm putting no personal perspective on this particular situation, not yet anyway.' Stone didn't comment, merely sat stone-faced.

Jamieson spoke: 'Any more to add, Claire?' Evason indicated that she had finished for now. Jamieson took the floor and told them about his visit to the pathologist and her summation that it was as they'd presumed — death was caused by an injury or injuries to the head and face caused by a blunt instrument — probably wielded by a left-handed assailant. He paused and then told them about the self-administered treatment that Wallace was undergoing. Whilst he did this, he observed Stone. The tightening of Stone's jaw and the thin line between his lips had become betrayed by the anger building up inside him. Finally, he burst. With real ire and heavy sarcasm in his voice, he said, 'so we are officially dealing with the death of an angel here, then. I'm surprised that we haven't halted all other police activity in the region just to try to find the person that, if truth be told, has done what someone should have done a long time ago.' As soon as he'd said it, Stone knew it was the wrong thing to say. He looked down at the desk in front of him.

The words hung in the air. Johnson, unused to police work at this intensity, looked slightly embarrassed. Evason looked annoyed. She knew how unprofessional that little tirade had sounded, particularly in front of a junior officer. She had many opinions about Stone and his abilities and methods, but one thing she had never questioned was his professionalism. She caught Jamieson's eye with a look that said, 'I told you so' Jamieson retained his composure: 'Rog, could you get me another coffee from Georgio's, please.' Johnson jumped up, thankful for the opportunity he had been given to escape the situation. When Johnson had disappeared through the door, Jamieson turned to Evason. She was more senior and didn't need to be given a reason to be asked to leave them. 'Claire', said Jamieson. 'Can you give us ten minutes, please' Evason gathered her jacket from the back of her chair and left. Stone continued to sit, like a penitent schoolboy, staring straight ahead. Jamieson went over to the door and made sure that Evason had closed it properly behind her, then he rounded on Stone: 'What the bloody hell was all that about?' he demanded. 'You and I sat in here the other night, and you assured me that your head was in the right place. That you were professional and that past events surrounding Lesley Wallace would not colour the way that you approached this case, and I believed you. I've stuck my neck out for you, despite what other people said to me.'

'Who's been saying things?' said Stone over aggressively and once more immediately regretted his decision to speak.

'It doesn't matter who,' continued Jamieson, raising his voice. 'What does matter is that they were obviously right to raise these concerns because you're acting like a spoiled brat. You're making yourself look foolish, and what's more, because I've supported you, you're making me look foolish as well.' This time it was Jamieson's words that hung in the air.

There was a knock, followed by the door opening immediately after the duty Sergeant stuck his head around. He looked at Jamieson. 'Everything alright, Sir? Only we heard raised voices.'

'Without taking his eyes off Stone, Jamieson replied: 'Thank you, Sergeant, everything is fine. Would you apologise to your team if we have disturbed them at all?'

The Sergeant said 'Sir' and disappeared back behind the door, closing it after him. The silence lasted another full minute before Stone broke it. 'I'm sorry. I thought I could handle it. I *know* I can handle it. It's just being aware of what this man has done and got away with and now being told that he has changed, and that makes everything alright.'

'No one has said that' cut in Jamieson. 'We all probably agree with your sentiments at some level, but our job is to uphold the law. It's not up to us to decide who does and who doesn't deserve justice. Lesley Wallace has been killed, almost definitely murdered, and it is up to us to find out who did it to the best of our abilities. You said as much yourself not two days ago.' He paused. 'Now you're either involved in this investigation on the same terms and conditions as the rest of us, or you decide that you cannot cope with it, in which case? I'll arrange for you to undertake other duties outside of the investigation. Still, one thing is for sure, if you do decide to stay on the case, one more outburst like the one just now and you'll be transferred straight off the team into the first available Sergeant's role, and I couldn't give a flying fig if its traffic control in the Outer Hebrides, you'll be out of here. Is that understood?' Stone sat up. 'Understood, Sir. I'd like to remain in the team. I think I have a lot to offer.' 'I'm sure you do, Sandy. Now get your head together and prove it to me'. The others came back into the room, and the meeting reconvened.

Jamieson decided not to mention his investigation work into the police officers that may or may not be involved and passed the floor over to Stone. Stone had tracked down David Sargeant and Andrew Soper, two of the three men imprisoned on Lesley Wallace's testimony.

'Soper is a career paedophile,' explained Stone. 'His initial sentence was a fifteen-year stretch. He got out after just over ten for good behaviour. He was out for two years before he was arrested again and went back inside. He's been in and out of prison regularly since then. Spent nine of the last twelve years behind bars. He's currently in the middle of a seven-year sentence down in Wormwood Scrubs. It's unlikely he's got anything to do with it, but I'll go down there and interview him anyway, even if it's just to scrub his name from the list.'

'Okay', said Jamieson. 'And Sargeant?' 'That's an interesting one.' said Stone. 'He was only in his very early twenties at the time of the original offence, so he's only mid-forties now. He went down for twelve years originally. He got a lighter sentence than the others because of his age. His brief argued that he was influenced by the older men and, as such, wasn't as accountable, and the Judge and jury agreed. Additionally, he was given time off for good behaviour and got out in seven years. So he was still only twenty-seven then. He had to agree to parole conditions, one of which was to keep his parole officer fully appraised of his address, which he did, and chance would have it looks as though he still lives at the last address he gave the parole board before they signed him off. It's only up near Leicester, so that's another visit that I can do.'

'Good,' said Jamieson. 'Take Rog with you for both interviews. It'll be a good experience.' Stone nodded.

Finally, Johnson gave a brief appraisal of his previous afternoon.

'I carried on with the house-to-house enquiries in the immediate and surrounding areas where the body was found. Not much luck, though; it seems that nobody saw or heard anything. I've got some more calls to make, but I'm now quite a distance away from where it all happened, up nearer the pub, so it's even more unlikely that I'll turn anything up.'

Jamieson outlined the day ahead as he saw it. Johnson would go back to the house-to-house calls for the remainder of the morning whilst Stone teed up a meeting for the afternoon with Soper at Belmarsh prison. Directly after that, they could both go up to Leicester to interview Sargeant. That would hopefully clear two names from the list of potential suspects. Then, after Stone had arranged the prison visit, he could concentrate his efforts on locating Malcolm Lewis and the Manageress of the foster home. In the meantime, he and Evason would focus their efforts on finding what they could about the Marshall and Hughes families, or rather Evason would. But, first, Jamieson wanted to contact DI Scott and DS Mitchell to set up off-the-record meetings to hopefully eliminate them from the picture.

Johnson left not long after. Stone told him he'd call on the mobile phone and would like to be heading towards the prison in West London by one thirty- at the latest.

Evason and Stone sat at their desks tapping at their computers, and Jamieson made his way back into the glassed-off area at the back of the room. He found the numbers for Scott and Mitchell amongst his notes and stabbed the number for Scott's mobile into his own phone. The phone was answered within three rings: 'DI Scott' 'DI Scott' said Jamieson. 'My name is DI Alex Jamieson. I think we may have met previously on a course.' The line went quiet while Jamieson presumed, Scott thought. Then Scott spoke: 'I remember an alcohol-fuelled evening on the last night of a Community Policing course about six or seven years ago. There was a Jamieson there, played a mean tune on the guitar, I remember.' 'I still do. How are you? Still up in Merseyside?'

They spent the next five minutes catching up and bemoaning the lack of police resources before Scott finally said: 'anyway, as nice as it is to catch up, you must have called for a reason. What is it I can do for you?'

'There's been a development on one of your Father's old cases, and I'd like to meet up with you to get your views. You know, what your Father would have made of it, that sort of thing.' Jamieson had rehearsed this speech beforehand. It was a difficult situation, talking to another copper to judge whether he could possibly have cause to commit a crime.

'Which case is that then, or do I need to ask?' asked Scott.

'Lesley Wallace.' 'That makes sense, I suppose,' said Scott. 'That was the only case he was involved with that could possibly still have ramifications a quarter of a century later! So what developments have there been? Is Wallace up to his nasty tricks again?'

'No,' said Jamieson, as deadpan as he could, 'he's been murdered'

'Ah' was Scott's response.

They talked some more before Scott said, 'look, you're in luck. I'm due down in Birmingham for a one-day seminar on Monday. We could meet up afterwards in the hotel bar, say six; we can talk it through them if you like.'

Jamieson took down the details of the hotel and agreed that he'd see Scott at six on Monday evening. When he hung up, he thought about the conversation that he'd just had. What was Scott's reaction to being told that Wallace had been murdered? Was he surprised? Did he sound pleased? Jamieson scolded himself. Perhaps he should have held back the fact of Wallace's death until he had an opportunity to meet Scott face to face. It was that much easier to judge reactions when you could see someone's face rather than just hear their voice at the end of a telephone line. No matter, too late now.

He made a note of the meeting in his diary. He then phoned the number he had taken from the system for William Mitchell. It was a landline. He dialled, and the person answering told him that Mitchell had worked four consecutive late nights and wasn't due in until tomorrow. Jamieson told them who he was, and he was given a mobile phone number for Mitchell. He checked his watch. It was nearly ten o'clock. He'd give Mitchell another hour in bed before calling.

He went back outside into the main office. Evason and Stone sat at their desks. There was no sign of Johnson. Jamieson assumed that he had gone back to the door-to-door duties.

'How's it going?' Jamieson asked Evason. 'Found the Hughes family. That was easy. They're still at the same address they were at twenty-five years ago. I haven't made contact yet, but there is a phone number. Do you want me to ring?' Jamieson thought: 'No,

I think we'll call round on the off chance. Presumably, they're local?'

Evason checked her notes 'Upton Road. Five minutes in the car.' 'Okay, we'll go in a minute. What about the other family? The one with the two boys.' 'The Marshalls.' said Evason. 'I've put in a call to Birmingham County Council Social Services to see if they can give us any ideas. After what happened, the family was placed on the at-risk register. It's unlikely that they'll still be on it — the two boys will be in their early thirties by now — but the council might be able to point us in the right direction. I should know more later today.' 'Right,' said Jamieson.' let's go and see the Hughes family.'

CHAPTER TWELVE

Upton Road was an untidy part of town. The houses were terraced and cramped, and the roads were lined with cars, many of which, Jamieson was sure, would not have passed current Ministry of Transport regulations. Evason parked up in the first vacant space she found — it turned out to be a good five hundred yards from the house they were looking for.

As they walked down the road, Jamieson looked at the number of houses with satellite television dishes fixed to their roofs. Jamieson found it amazing that even at a time of increasing unemployment and economic downturn, people still found enough money each month to cater for their dose of sport or films. There weren't many, he supposed, who had satellite television solely for the purpose of the History Channel. 'That's it', said Evason, pointing to a house on the other side of the street, 'Number thirty-one.' The house was in a poor state of repair. It looked as though it hadn't seen a coat of paint for many years. One of the upstairs windows was cracked, and it was evident that someone from the inside had done a patch-up job using some sticky tape. The doorbell didn't work, so Jamieson rapped the door with his knuckles. They waited for a minute or so.

'Blast', said Jamieson. 'We should have phoned ahead after all. I thought the Mother might be in, though.'

As they turned to go, they both heard movement from behind the front door, then a man's voice. 'Who is it, please?' Evason stepped forward and bent down to the letter box. 'Mr Hughes? Mr Hughes, it's Detective Inspector Jamieson and Detective Sergeant Evason from the local police station. Could we come in please, Sir? We have a few questions we'd like to ask you.' There was a brief silence and then a reply. 'Hold on a minute, please.'

The sound of various bolts being opened could be heard before the door finally opened. A security chain meant that it could not be opened more than five inches.

A man looked out. Evason held her warrant card up to the space for him to see. The door closed again, followed by the sound of the chain being slid back.

From reading through the past case files, Claire Evason knew that David Hughes was in his late twenties when the original case broke, which would now have made him certainly no older than mid-fifties. However, when the door opened and David Hughes stood before them, she automatically assumed that this wasn't the David Hughes they were looking for. The man standing in front of them was bent double and had a walking stick in each hand. His hair was thin and grey. If pressed, you would have said that this man was in his eighties. His clothes were old, and a stale odour from inside the house washed out past him and hit their noses, almost causing Evason to gag. She regained her composure. 'Mr Hughes, Mr David Hughes?' she asked. 'Father of Darren.'

The man almost imperceptibly nodded his head. 'That's right,' he said.

Jamieson took over. 'Can we come in please, Mr Hughes?'

With a considerable effort, the man backed away from the door into the hallway. Every step was a monumental task. Without the walking sticks supporting him, it was evident that he would be totally immobile. 'Follow me,' he said and turned. Almost immediately, he edged through a doorway to his left. Jamieson and Evason followed. Jamieson pulled the front door shut behind him. Hughes positioned himself in front of an armchair before falling back into it. He groaned, winced with pain, settled, and then indicated a sofa to his left. 'Please sit down,' he said. The room was small and felt claustrophobic. The furniture was far too large for the restricted space, and the curtains were not fully drawn back, heightening the cramped feeling. The light was switched on, but the shadeless bulb which hung above their heads was of such a low wattage that the light thrown only barely cut through the gloom whilst Evason remained standing in the doorway. She had her notebook and pencil ready.

'I'd offer you a drink, but I'm afraid it's beyond me', said Hughes 'Unless you'd like to do the honours' he looked towards Evason 'Sargeant, wasn't it?' Both Jamieson and Evason declined the offer of a drink, but Evason offered to make one for Hughes. 'That would be very kind of you. Tea, please - thank you. Darren usually makes one for me before he goes off to work in the morning and then when he gets back at night. During the day, Social Services turn up just after one with lunch and another hot drink then.'

Evason went through to the kitchen. Jamieson could hear as she filled the kettle and flicked the switch to on. Then the sound of the fridge opening while he assumed she looked for milk. Within sixty seconds, she was back in the room.

'Is it just you and Darren living here, Mr Hughes?' asked Jamieson. 'What about your wife?'

'My Janey?' said Hughes. 'My Janey's been dead over twenty years now', he sighed.

'I'm sorry to hear that.' said Jamieson. 'What happened?'

'A handful of pills when I'd got my back turned. She'd had a tough life.' He paused for thought. 'It was probably always going to end that way.'

The kettle clicked off, and Evason returned to the kitchen to make Hughes' drink. Again. she was back within a matter of seconds. She pulled a table over and placed the drink down. 'Thank you very much', said Hughes. 'I shall enjoy that', Jamieson watched whilst he picked up the cup and blew across the top of the hot brown liquid before taking a sip. With great deliberation, he put the cup back on the table.

'Mr Hughes, does the name Brian Wilkins mean anything to you?' Hughes thought for a moment. Then, finally, he said, 'No.' Jamieson paused, then pressed ahead. 'Does the name Lesley

Wallace mean anything to you?' Hughes' eyes hardened. 'I think that you know that it does.'

'Do you know where Lesley Wallace lives?' Jamieson picked his questions carefully. Hughes looked him directly in the eye. 'The less I know about that evil bastard, the better it is for everyone concerned. So no, I don't know where he lives.' By way of explanation, Jamieson said, 'Lesley Wallace changed his name to Brian Wilkins some years back. He was murdered a couple of evenings ago.' Hughes' face showed no sign of emotion. 'and you're looking for a murderer.' He spread his arms. 'Well, as you can see, whilst I may have had a motive, I didn't have the opportunity. See this, see me. Old before my time, my body wrecked. MS. Multiple Sclerosis. I haven't left the house unaided for the last fifteen years.' Jamieson nodded in acknowledgment.'Is there anyone else who may have had a means and motive you know of? What about Darren, for example?' An ironic smile crossed Hughes' lips. 'Do you know', he said, 'after everything that Wallace had done to him if Darren had found out where he lived and gone there to rid this family of twenty-five years of constant pain, I'd have said to him, 'Good on you, son" he stopped talking and considered his next sentence ', but he didn't. He's not like that. What happened to him all those years ago has conditioned him into accepting that things are as they are. I don't think that he gives scum like Lesley Wallace a second thought. Would killing Wallace bring his Mother back? No. Would killing Wallace change anything about the way Darren is? No. Would killing Wallace mean that my disability would go away? No. Would killing Wallace change anything material in Darren's life? No. So why would he dirty his hands? He wouldn't be the answer. He's way above that.'

Hughes picked up his cup and took another sip. Jamieson waited patiently.

'Besides', said Hughes, bringing the cup down from his mouth. 'He's been away all week. I've had a carer for the last five or six nights.' He laughed a humourless laugh. 'That's probably my alibi for you.'

Jamieson caught Evason's eye. The news about Darren being away was interesting. 'Do you know where Darren is, Mr Hughes?' he asked. 'Not exactly. He said something about a convention somewhere in America. He's big on computer games. That's what he spends his time doing, up in his room. He has very few, if any, friends.' Hughes thought some more than continued, 'That's all he does really — gets up, goes to work, gets home, sits at his computer and goes to bed. I was surprised when he said he was going away for a while. Pleased though, he's my registered carer, and the council offers respite services, so he took them up on it. First time he's done that in fifteen years.' Still standing in the doorway, Evason looked up from the notes she was taking. 'When is Darren due back, Mr Hughes?'

'Well, he's due back in work on Monday, 'said Hughes 'So Sunday at the very latest.' Evason wrote in the notebook. 'We'll need to see him as soon as possible, you know, to eliminate him from our enquiries,' she said without looking up this time. 'Can we call round Monday evening?' Hughes thought about the request. 'It'd be nice for him to have some time back first, you know, jet lag and all that. Can you make it Tuesday?'

Jamieson remembered the meeting he had arranged with Jim Scott in Birmingham for Monday and cut in. 'Yes, Tuesday is fine, Mr Hughes. What time does Darren get in from work?'

'Six'

'We'll be round at six-thirty if that's okay?' Hughes nodded. The effort of this seemingly small movement caused him to wince with pain. He drew air in through his front teeth, which caused a coughing fit. Jamieson watched with concern on his face. Evason, more dynamic in situations, stepped forward from the doorway and leant down, her head level with Hughes' own head. She patted him on the back. Eventually, the coughing subsided. Hughes breathed deeply. Evason went into the kitchen to get some water. Jamieson could hear her opening and closing cupboards, presumably looking for a glass. Finally, fully recovered, Hughes said, 'I'm sorry about that.' Jamieson held his hand up. 'Not at all, Mr Hughes. Is there anything we can do for you before we go?'

Evason came back into the room and handed Hughes a glass of water. His hand shook as he lifted it to his lips and sipped. Hughes looked into Jamieson's eyes and spoke. 'I'm not Darren's biological Father. His real Father had used Janey, got her pregnant and then just upped and left without a by your leave; he's never made any effort to contact Darren since. When I first met her, Janey was still only just turned eighteen, and Darren was two. I fell in love with her there and then. I was in my mid-twenties. I had a decent job, a good wage. Janey was damaged goods; I could see that long before Darren's dad had had his way. Her problems went way back before then. But love does strange things to a man.

Back then, I thought I could sweep them up in my arms and stop any more harm from coming to them. I thought I could make it all better, give her the protection she'd never had. I adopted Darren. Gave him a name, an identity'. He stopped talking. Jamieson and Evason waited. 'I was wrong. My Janey's problems went far deeper than I ever imagined. I found myself trying to hold down a job to provide for my family, but Janey's needs became greater and greater, took more and more of my time, Darren was getting left out, something had to give. I reached a decision; Janey said she agreed, but I'm not sure that she understood the consequences. When he was six, we put Darren in a foster home where I felt he would be better cared and provided for. It was only meant to be a short-term solution. Without Darren, I could hold down my job and give Janey the time and care that she needed to make her better. When she was better, we'd bring Darren back into the fold, and we'd be the perfect family unit — that was the plan, anyway.'

Hughes sipped his water again. 'But Janey didn't get better. If anything, she got worse, and Darren stayed in the home. The stress I was under became almost unbearable. I was close to cracking up myself. This went on for three years without respite until finally, what was happening to Darren at the foster home came to light. Although we visited him three times a week, we hadn't picked up on any of it — he gave off no signs — he was always a quiet kid, very close to his Mother. It seemed that even at his tender age, he knew his Mother was very ill and that, if it meant her getting better, then he would put up with everything that life could throw at him.'

'At first, I wasn't sure what to tell Janey, if anything at all. Her state of mind was so fragile, but finally, her Mother, who had never shown much interest in her previously, insisted that it was her right to be told the truth and went ahead and did so without giving any real consideration to the recourse of doing so. At first, Janey clammed up, refused to believe any of it had happened, then she got very angry, even angrier when she realised that the police had given the man who had defiled her son immunity from prosecution. She couldn't understand how this animal could have done such a thing and wouldn't be punished — where was the justice in that? The Government instigated an enquiry. Janey found out the name of the man put in place to head the enquiry up. She hounded him and phoned his offices eight, nine times a day. Other times, she would turn up and demand to speak to him. When the results of the enquiry were made public, it was the start of the end for Janey. The enquiry was very thorough, and we became aware of what Darren had been through for the first time. Darren had never uttered a word about it himself, but the odious Wallace, safe from prosecution, made sure that the world was aware of exactly what happened — it seemed that he revelled in his moment of notoriety.'

'Finally, Janey was consumed with guilt. Despite what I said to her, she believed it was her fault that Darren was in the home in the first place. If she'd been a better person, then Darren's Father would never have gone off, and they would be living in a nice little house in perfect harmony, and none of this would have happened. I told her that was not how it was, but she wouldn't listen.'

'Around this time, I started getting muscle spasms and feelings of lightheadedness and nausea — I was smoking heavily — I had been for some years — I didn't go to the doctors at first partly through fear — I had the feeling that something was going badly wrong with me. Then one day, I was at work, and I had a huge attack. I ended up in Luton General diagnosed with MS.; Whilst the doctors couldn't say for certain what had brought the illness on; they did say that stress and smoking were big factors — I suppose that's one thing I can't blame Wallace for, the smoking, I mean. I was told that the likelihood was that I'd get progressively worse, but I discharged myself anyway. I carried on working, but the attacks got more and more frequent. Eventually, the company had to let me go. I didn't feel bitter. I understood completely. They were a business, not a charity. They actually made me redundant, which they didn't have to, and made a payment of ten thousand pounds. I was grateful. By now, Darren had started senior school and was living at home. He was more grown up now and, by necessity, had become more independent. Although he was still comparatively very young, he effectively took to caring for both his Mother and me.' 'My bad days were very bad, as were Janey's. Then one day, just as it seemed we were coping, Janey took an overdose of sleeping pills. I was downstairs, couldn't move, shouting upstairs to her. There was no answer. It took me two hours to move four yards across the floor to where the telephone was. When I got there, I dialled 999 and asked for an ambulance. It got there within ten minutes, but it was all over by then. My Janey was dead. She was twenty-six. On her twenty-fifth birthday, she had told me that she'd been alive for over nine thousand days, and of those, she could only really honestly say that she could remember ten, maybe twelve, being what she would call really great days.'

'The day of her funeral, I had a bad attack and ended up back in hospital. I couldn't even say a proper goodbye to her.' Hughes looked down at his hands, pursing his lips, trying to hold his emotions in check. His eyes were watering. With a degree of composure retained, he continued. 'The doctors were right. I have gotten progressively worse, although my rate of decline has slowed down over the years. Darren has done well, considering what he has been through. He's held down the same job for the past fifteen years or so. The pay isn't so good, but as far as his self-worth goes, it's a massive step. He's only ever mentioned Lesley Wallace once to me. That was on his twenty-first birthday. We'd bought a bottle of champagne, and although the doctors advised against drinking with my condition, I wasn't going to let my son celebrate his birthday alone. So we cracked the bottle open and toasted each other. We talked about Janey — not in a maudlin way, but how life may have been different if she'd been around — Darren looked at me and said, 'I think Mum's death came at about the right time. She wasn't looking for happiness, and happiness was never going to find her, so the outcome was probably for the best.' I thought about what he'd said and found myself agreeing with him. Bearing in mind, he was only eleven or twelve when his Mother died; it was really very perceptive of him.'

'Then he said something else, he said 'Lesley Wallace didn't only rape me, in a way he raped our whole family. I took the actual physical rape, but Mum was raped mentally, and you were raped in a different way with your illness. It's all connected, and it's all down to him. I wonder where Lesley Wallace is, and I wonder whether he sleeps soundly at night.'

'That was the only time he ever spoke that name in my presence.' He paused. 'Let me tell you something else about Darren. He is incredibly well adjusted for a human being who has been through as much as that boy. He took an early interest in computers. When he left school, an old friend of mine gave him a job in his office down in North London, nothing fancy, not massively paid, but enough. Took him to the local bank, opened an account for him, lent him three hundred pounds to take lessons, and then helped him buy a small motorbike to get him to and from work when he'd passed his test. I owe that old friend so much. Darren still works there, still got that bank account, still rides a motorcycle, only much bigger and more powerful now. He still doesn't earn much, but what he has got is dignity and self-worth. He's got more dignity than anyone else I've ever known. I am so very proud of how he has turned out.'

Shortly after, Jamieson and Evason took their leave. On the way back to the car, Jamieson asked, 'What do you think?'

Evason considered her answer. 'That's a very damaged family', she said.'I think it's highly unlikely that the Father had anything to do with it, even in terms of getting someone else to do it for him. I just don't think he's physically able.' Jamieson agreed. 'What about the son?' he said.

Evason used her remote to open the car door as they approached.

'Not sure,' she said, opening the car door.' We'll have to meet him and find out where he's been.'

Before he opened the door, Jamieson looked at Evason across the car's roof and said, 'Do you think Lesley Wallace got what he deserved?'

Evason looked him directly in the eye; she thought before she spoke: 'Yes. Yes, I do, but our job doesn't give us the right to make that judgement.'

CHAPTER THIRTEEN

Johnson turned from the door and walked back down the garden path. Another 'no reply' and another visit he'd have to follow up at a later date. He'd been doing house to house for the best part of the last two days, and it hadn't proved very successful. Probably as many as fifty per cent of the doors he knocked at had remained unanswered, which meant follow-up visits. He checked the clipboard he was holding and, with a pen, noted the address and, next to that, entered a cross, indicating no reply.

He looked at his watch. It was ten to two. Stone had called fifteen minutes ago, saying he was on his way. He had arranged to see Soper down in Wormwood Scrubs. No appointment was necessary. After all, Soper wasn't going anywhere. Johnson looked back down the road to see if there was any sign of Stone. He reckoned he was by now equidistant between the pub and where Wallace's body had been found. So far, his enquiries had turned up absolutely nothing. Even those people who were in and had answered their door had nothing to add, had heard nothing, had seen nothing. They had mostly been asleep or dozing in front of the television. It seemed that there were no late-night dog walkers amongst them. Johnson opened the gate to the next property and walked up the garden path. As he pressed the doorbell, Stone pulled up outside and tooted the horn twice. Johnson looked back and held up his index finger to indicate either one minute or that this one was the last house — either way, Stone understood his drift.

The door opened as he turned back. There stood an elderly gentleman with an impatient expression on his face.'Good morning, Sir,' began Johnson. 'I'm Constable Johnson from Bedfordshire Police...'

'Well,' said the elderly man, with more than a hint of sarcasm in his voice, 'that's a first.' Johnson was confused. 'I mean,' continued the man, oblivious to Johnson's baffled look, 'I've called the police on numerous occasions and left various messages, but this is the first time they've actually taken any notice of what I've told them.' The man disappeared back into his house and reappeared seconds later. He was holding a small notebook. 'Here,' he said, tearing the top page out and pushing it towards Johnson.

Johnson took it. 'What's this, Sir?' he asked, still very confused.

'That,' said the elderly man, 'is the details of the car I called the police station about on Tuesday. It was parked there.' he pointed to the entrance to his driveway. 'The rear of it was a good three feet across my driveway. There was no way anyone could have got in or out of the drive with it parked there.'

Johnson looked at his own feet, then up at the elderly man. 'I see, Sir. Actually, I'm not here...'

The elderly man deftly ignored Johnson's attempts to assert some control over the conversation, cleared his throat and announced, 'Traffic Management Act 2004, Part six, Section 86 'Prohibition of parking at dropped footways etc.' Subsection (1)(a) paragraph (iii) In a special enforcement area a vehicle must not be parked on the carriageway adjacent to a footway, cycle track or verge where the footway, cycle track or verge has been lowered to meet the level of the carriageway for the purpose of assisting vehicles entering or leaving the carriageway across the footway, cycle track or verge" Once again the elderly man pointed towards his driveway. 'As you can see, the footway, or in this case the pavement, has clearly been lowered to enable access to my driveway. Therefore, this car was illegally parked.'

Stone, becoming impatient, sounded the horn again.

Johnson spoke, 'Yes, sir, thank you for bringing it to our attention. We'll look into it and get back to you as soon as possible'. He turned and headed towards Stone in the car.

The elderly man called after him. 'You'll need all the details of when the offence took place. I've written them all down along with my name and address.' He held up another piece of paper. Johnson went back up the garden path and took the paper. 'Thank you, Mr.....'

'Allsop. Bernard Allsop, 'said the man., 'and thank you for acting so swiftly.' He smiled. 'My telephone number is noted on the paper if you need to speak to me.' Johnson smiled back and nodded.

Stone asked what it was all about when he got into the car. 'You really do not want to know,' replied Johnson, adding a tick to his clipboard against Mr Allsop's address and shoving the pieces of paper into his jacket pocket.

The journey down the A1 into North London took just over an hour. Stone pulled into the prison visitors' car park at three o'clock. He wasn't sure what to expect from this meeting. He remembered Soper from the original case. The man was a nasty piece of work with absolutely no redeeming features whatsoever. So the fact that he had re-offended came as no surprise to Stone. Of the original four arrested and convicted, Soper was the one most akin to Wallace, although when it became known that Wallace had sold the others down the river to save his own skin, Soper's response was firstly one of betrayal and disbelief quickly followed by anger. Stone wondered what Soper's attitude towards his own personal Judas would be a quarter of a century later.

They entered the prison and went through the formalities that anyone else who was visiting one of the inmates would. Soper was classified as a category A inmate, a testimony that his past demeanours still made the authorities consider him a maximum risk and a danger to the public at large. As such, he could only be interviewed with a prison guard in attendance in the actual interview room.

They were led down a maze of corridors and through secure doors that had to be opened by warders with huge bunches of keys on the end of chains secured to their belt lines. Finally, they were shown into the interview room, which was empty except for a table in the middle and three wooden chairs, one-on-one side of the table and two on the other. There was one barred window providing some natural light. Stone flopped down in one of the two chairs, leaving the other available to Johnson if he should choose to sit down.

Johnson felt nervous. When he had received the call telling him that he had been seconded onto the team looking into the Wallace murder. His initial reaction had been one of great joy; however, since that time, his excitement had somewhat dimmed. He was beginning to feel like a glorified gofer specializing in coffee runs and pointless house-to-house enquiries. But now, standing in a maximum security prison interview room waiting to interview a dangerous man and key witness, his excitement levels began to rise again, and the adrenaline was pumping around his body. Finally, stone spoke: 'You alright?'

Johnson nodded. His mouth was a little dry. 'Fine,' he replied.

'You take notes', said Stone. 'Although I'm not expecting anything useful to come out of this, more a case of eliminating Soper than anything else.'

The door opened, and Andrew Soper was ushered in. He sat in the chair opposite Stone. The warder accompanying him closed the door and stood in front of it, guarding it, in case Soper made a bid for freedom through the door and the other four locked doors they had been shown through.

Stone looked at him closely. Older, less hair, more lines on his face, but definitely the man Stone recalled that Soper was slightly older than himself when he was arrested, which would make him in his early fifties now.

They all sat in silence for a minute or so. Stone could have waited all day, but finally, Soper spoke: 'What's this about then?' He asked, irritated, one up to Stone. Still, Stone didn't speak. This was his interview, and he'd conduct it to the sound of his own tune, not some scumbags like Soper.

Finally, he broke his silence: 'Do you know of a Brian Wilkins?' He asked. Soper thought: 'No, should I?' Stone stalled again before saying: 'Lesley Wallace is dead. Murdered.' He watched for Soper's initial reaction.

A split second whilst Soper registered what Stone had told him, another split second registering surprise. Finally, his face broke into a wide grin. 'Someone finally got the fucker. Who was it?'

At that point, Stone's experience told him that he could have concluded the interview. Soper's initial reaction told Stone that he knew nothing about what had happened to Wallace. His joy was so spontaneous that it could not have been contrived. This was news to him and seemingly very good news. Soper chuckled, 'Best news I've heard in ages.'

'Nothing to do with you then?' Stone asked, instantly wishing he hadn't.

Soper stopped laughing, surprised: 'No, but I wish it was me, I tell you.'

Slowly, something dawned on Soper. 'Hold on a minute. Let me get this straight. You thought that I'd masterminded some kind of hit on Lesley Wallace from my prison cell. Oh, that's flicking rich, that is, you've been watching too much television, you have. What did you think that I put the word out and that the criminal classes of Britain swung into action? You wankers' and he started laughing again. Humiliation burnt into Stone's cheeks as Soper's laughter reached hysterical proportions.

CHAPTER FOURTEEN

The drive up to Leicester was made in comparative silence. Soper's taunting had put Stone in a foul mood, and Johnson wasn't sure how to react. So he just kept quiet. He figured that if Stone wanted to talk about the events back at the prison, then he would. He didn't. They had been driving for almost two hours and were on the outskirts of Leicester before Stone spoke. 'Are you hungry'?' he asked. Johnson was. He hadn't managed to have any lunch and had only a croissant in the office as breakfast. 'Yes' was his simple answer.

Stone checked the clock on the dashboard of the car — five forty-five.

Earlier, he had phoned ahead on the telephone number he had obtained from BT for David Sargeant and was surprised to find himself speaking to Sargeant's wife. He always had a problem associating the type of person he believed Sargeant to be with, having a wife and possibly a family — even though he knew that statistics showed that more than fifty per cent of convicted paedophiles were married men with children.

Sargeant's wife's voice registered immediate concern when Stone told her who he was and that he wanted to speak to her husband. Quite naturally, she wanted to know why. Stone told her that it was connected with standard police enquiries and that there was nothing to be concerned about. She told him that her husband got in from work at around six. Stone told her that they'd be there by six thirty. Stone wondered whether Mrs Sargeant knew about her husband's past. Stone swung the car into a drive-through burger outlet. They ordered and parked up in the cramped car park to eat. Johnson realised he was, in fact, very hungry and ate and drank very quickly. Almost immediately, he regretted doing so as the burger and fries repeated on him, causing a burning sensation at the top of his chest.

Stone ate in a more relaxed manner. Usually, he wouldn't consider eating fast food, but he recognised there were occasions in the job that he did where he had no other option. He left half of his own burger and sipped at the bitter coffee he suspected had been brewing in the pot since lunchtime.

Finally, Stone spoke about the events at the prison: 'What did you make of Soper?' he asked Johnson. Johnson sat back in his seat and made a face: 'He's a piece of work, that's for sure. Is he in solitary?' Not solitary, but he is kept in a secure wing with the rest of the nonces and rapists.' said Stone. 'That must be a hell of a place to work. Imagine Soper then multiply him by a hundred.'

Stone took another sip of his sour coffee and continued, 'Do you think he had anything to do with what happened to Wallace?'

Johnson answered quickly: 'No, he was too surprised when he first heard. It was first-hand news to him, and he reacted accordingly. You can't feign that kind of reaction. Plus, I think he'd like to have had something to do with what happened, and if he had have done, he'd have told us first.'

Stone nodded. 'I didn't handle the situation very well. We may have gotten some information out of him that would have given us more suspects to work with, but I blew it. Let him get the better of me.'

Johnson thought about what Stone had said. 'He goaded you, and you reacted, that's all. It's understandable. I think he would have some ideas as to who may have been involved, but I don't think he would've shared them with us, anyway. Clearly, he hated Wallace with a vengeance and would see whoever did it as doing him a favour, so he wouldn't want to make our job any easier. I think the Guv, Evason and yourself have put together a decent list of suspects, and I think the name we're looking for will come from that list.' Stone drained his coffee and crumpled the paper cup in his right hand. He nodded to himself. 'Let's hope you're right,' he said.

The satellite navigation system took them right to Sargeant's door. They parked up outside and made their way up the front garden path. It was nearly ten to seven, twenty minutes later than they said they'd arrive, and Stone could picture Sargeant sitting inside the house beside himself with worry as to what the visit from Bedfordshire police could be about.

It was a modern house, detached, good-sized garden in a decent neighbourhood. Stone wondered what Sargeant did for a living to be able to afford such a nice home. Before he rang the doorbell, Stone turned to Johnson: 'I'll talk; you take notes. Keep an eye on the way he reacts. It could tell us something.'

Sargeant himself answered the door. He was an overweight, short man with glasses and mid-length curly hair. Stone recalled him as being in his early twenties at the time of the original case, which would make him in his mid-forties now. Sargeant stood back to allow them in and directed them into the living room to the right off of the hall. They went through to a comfortable room housing a leather three-piece suite and a widescreen television, amongst other things. Sargeant invited them to sit down. It was evident from his manner that he was not pleased to see them, let alone have them in his house.

Stone sat down and looked around him. On the table next to him was a picture frame with a photo of Sargeant, a woman who Stone assumed was his wife, and two children, a boy and a girl, who Stone took to be his children. He picked the frame up for a closer look. 'This is your family?' he asked, not unpleasantly.

'Put that down, please. They have nothing to do with you,' sargeant responded. 'I may have little option other than to speak to the likes of you, but I don't need to involve my family in this.'

Stone did as he was asked and replaced the picture frame.

He looked at Sargeant, 'and what exactly do you not want to get your family involved in?' He asked.

'The same bloody thing you people always want to talk about. Something that happened a quarter of a century ago. Something that happened when I was very young and very naïve. I thought that the justice system in this country was built upon conviction and rehabilitation. I was involved in something horrible a long time ago. I was led astray by some terrible men, and I was tried and convicted in a court of law. I was put in prison, and I served my sentence. I deserved what happened to me, and I took it on the chin, kept my nose clean and was released. I have never, ever re-offended, never even contemplated it and yet you people will not leave me alone. Whenever there's a sniff of any kind of sexual offence within fifty miles of here, I get an unofficial visit, always unofficial, so there's no paperwork. Whatever happened to wiping the slate clean? I'm sick of the whole thing.' There were tears close to the surface.

Stone decided to let the outburst pass without comment. Sargeant pulled himself together: 'I'm sorry,' he said, 'I can't seem to get away from my past.' Stone nodded his acceptance of Sargeant's apology: 'We're here about your past; I can't deny that.' Sargeant rubbed his hand across his mouth and looked at Stone expectantly.

Stone continued: 'Lesley Wallace is dead. He was murdered on Tuesday evening. We are here to find out what, if anything, you know about it and, hopefully, to eliminate you from our enquiries.'

Sargeant nodded slowly. He had calmed down considerably and was now able to conduct a reasonable exchange. 'I see', he said. 'Why do you assume that I have got anything to do with it? Wallace was an evil individual. I was an associate of twenty-five years ago.'

Stone explained, 'At this moment in time, we can't find any other motive than the events of twenty-five years ago. There may be some, but we can't find them at present. It seems that Wallace, like you, has kept his nose clean since it all happened, so the only motive we have is what happened all those years ago and who hated Wallace enough to seek revenge all this time later. There are plenty of people who had a motive — you yourself spent the best part of ten years in prison based on Wallace's testimony against you. Some people would consider that that was more than enough grounds to commit murder.'

Sargeant didn't respond immediately. He seemed to be trying to understand the reasoning behind Stone and Johnson's visit. Finally, he said, 'I accept why you're here', 'but I forgot about Lesley Wallace many years ago. Just then, when you said his name, it was the first time I'd given him any thought in over twenty years. I think I'd subconsciously closed him off.'

'No thoughts of any retribution, then?' asked Stone. Sargeant half smiled and shook his head. 'In prison, I was what they term a 'model prisoner'. That meant I accepted what I had done and, more importantly, I accepted responsibility for what I'd done. I didn't blame anyone else. I had the choice to walk away and, at age twenty, I chose not to.' He narrowed his eyes as he spoke, concentrating on the picture in the frame that Stone had picked up earlier. 'I also stumbled across religion — nothing too deep — I just started reading and talking to the Prison Chaplain — it passed the time as much as anything. But it gave me an insight into how other people lived. What was right, what was wrong, values, that sort of thing. By the time I was paroled, I think I was viewed by the prison authorities as completely rehabilitated — a success story.'

'Are you still religious?' enquired Stone. 'Christmas, Easter maybe, but nothing heavy. I like the values, though, but they shouldn't necessarily be restricted to any particular religion. They're just a decent set of rules on how to live your life. They should be transferable to anyone's beliefs.' Stone nodded, not as much in agreement but more to express that he understood Sargeant's point. He paused a moment, then said: 'Back to Wallace. Can I ask what you were doing on Tuesday evening?'

Sargeant thought for a second, then answered, 'Same as every Tuesday evening. Got in from work at around half-past six, had dinner, sat with the kids until their bedtime, then watched television with my wife until after the local news and went to bed at around quarter to eleven.'

'Was your wife with you the whole time?' Sargeant nodded. 'Yes, she was' ... 'and she can corroborate your whole story?'

Sargeant paused briefly before answering. 'She can, but does she really need to be involved?'

Stone picked up on the slight hesitation. 'Does your wife know about your past?' he asked.

Sargeant paused again before answering. 'She knows I spent time in prison, but not what for. After we first met, it became pretty evident that it was going to be a serious relationship, so I told her early on that I'd spent time inside. She didn't want to know anything about it, just that I wasn't the same man then as I was when it first happened. I knew that I wasn't, so it wasn't a problem for me to tell her that I wasn't. We've never talked about it since.'

'What about the visits from the police in the past?' asked Stone.

'She would always take the kids out when the police arrived, and they never wanted her to corroborate anything before, so she never had to get involved any further.'

Stone thought for a moment. 'Okay,' he said. 'There's no need for her to know anything. All she will need to do is sign a statement to the effect that she was with you the whole of Tuesday evening.' 'Thank you,' said Sargeant. 'I appreciate your help with that.'

'Is she back this evening?' Stone asked. 'I could take a statement from her tonight.'

'No,' said Sargeant, 'She's at her mother's with the kids. We thought it would be for the best.'

Stone checked his watch. 'Okay,' he said.'I'll brief some of the local lads in the morning and get them to come and see your wife to get it all sorted out. It's not a big deal — should only take half an hour, tops. I'll leave any explanations to you.' Sargeant thanked Stone once again. In turn, Stone thanked him for his assistance. Back in the car heading south, Stone asked Johnson what he thought of Sargeant.

'Completely different from Soper,' was Johnson's considered reply. 'Seems as though he's made a real effort to put his past behind him.'

Stone agreed. During the interview, he had actually found himself warming to David Sargeant. If he didn't know of his past and met him in a social situation, he may even have spent an hour in his company debating the rights and wrongs of the world.

But thought Stone, as he turned the car onto the Ml towards Luton, that was precisely where his problem lay. Both Sargeant and Wallace had taken steps to change their ways and had seemingly succeeded in doing so — Wallace had reinvented himself completely, and, to a lesser extent, Sargeant had done the same thing. So why was it that Stone felt compassion, even a degree of sympathy, towards Sargeant while still retaining an almost raw hatred of Wallace? It was a question he pondered over but never satisfactorily answered for the entire length of the journey home.

CHAPTER FIFTEEN

Usually, on a new murder case, the team would work weekends to expedite matters but Jamieson took the view that there just wasn't the urgency attached here. There were no grieving family members to contend with, and, although there had been one or two cursory enquiries from members of the local press, none of them had made the connection between Lesley Wallace and Brian Wilkins. That one factor would have made for a more interesting news story, but even then, how much interest would people have in events that took place twenty-five years ago? Jamieson hadn't yet called a press conference to announce the link purely because he was waiting for positive identification of the body.

Jamieson took the unusual step of telling his officers that they weren't required in the office until Monday morning. That they were to give the case occasional thought over the weekend and come back with any new angles on Monday. Jamieson was a great believer that constant thought about a single topic eventually caused the mind to switch off and close down new avenues of thinking. Much better for his officers to spend the weekend relaxing, for the most part emptying their minds of Lesley Wallace. It was in this state of mind he often found his subconscious asking him wider-ranging questions, questions that he hadn't thought of previously.

Jamieson phoned Evason on Friday evening and told her about his plans. She had worked with him now for nearly six months and knew that he tried different approaches from the conventional way of policing. She had things to do this weekend anyway, so she was more than happy to go along with his idea. Jamieson also asked her to consider how they should approach the interviews with Darren Hughes on Tuesday evening and the Marshall family, whom Evason had managed to contact through Birmingham Social Services and with whom she had made an appointment to see Jamieson on Monday afternoon at four o'clock. This dovetailed quite nicely with Jamieson's meeting with Scott, also in Birmingham on Monday at six, although he had yet to decide whether or not Evason would be party to that particular meeting.

Next, Jamieson phoned Stone, who was returning from Leicester with Johnson. They talked about the day's events. Stone dismissed Soper and Sargeant as viable suspects, although he didn't go into great depth regarding either of the two meetings. Next, Jamieson told him about the disintegration of the Hughes family, and Stone went quiet. Finally, he said, 'there was too much pressure going on with no outlet valve. Something was always going to give.'

Jamieson told Stone of his plan for the weekend and asked him to pass the work onto Johnson. Stone was a more dyed-in-the-wool policeman, and whilst he didn't openly say so, Jamieson felt that Stone thought they should all be in the office working the case as hard as possible. Despite being told otherwise, he also suspected that Stone would still go into the office and continue the investigation for at least part of the weekend. Stone remained non-committal with his response to Jamieson's plans, but he did close the conversation with a cryptic comment: 'Its funny,' he said, 'but this feels like a murder that no one really cares very much about.'

Jamieson knew precisely what he meant but wished he hadn't said it aloud.

CHAPTER SIXTEEN

As soon as Claire Evason had pushed the red button on her mobile phone to terminate the call from Jamieson, she began to plan her weekend.

She took an already open bottle of white wine from the fridge, poured herself a good-sized glassful, and returned to the sofa where she had been reading her notes on the current case and listening to music. She picked her notebook up, flipped it closed and put it away in her bag. She wouldn't need to revisit that until some time on Sunday afternoon. She swung her long legs onto the sofa and stretched out, two comfortable cushions propping her head up.

Sunday, she decided she would spend with her parents down in Kent. Her Mother made a superb Sunday roast after which, if the weather held, they'd take a long walk with the dogs. If it didn't, they could sit in watching whatever fayre was served up on Sunday afternoon television these days, and the dogs could run around in the garden. Saturday morning, she would treat herself to breakfast and some treatments down at the local spa. Jamieson did say that they should all rid their minds of Lesley Wallace as much as possible, and what better way to do that than to spend twenty minutes drifting aimlessly around a floatation tank with everything but your face submerged in a thick, warm liquid or having Maeo, the Thai Masseuse, have her skilled hands bully the tension out of your shoulders.

She reached for her mobile to call the spa and book her appointments. As she scrolled down her list of contacts to find the number, she paused for thought. She scrolled back until she found an entry just shown as 'P' on the list of numbers. She pursed her lips and subconsciously gently tapped the mobile phone against them whilst she gazed off into the distance at nothing in particular. She looked at the mobile telephone screen and, using her thumb, pressed the call button. Immediately, her heart rate quickened, and her mind started racing.

The call was answered within three rings.

'Hello'

'Hi, it's me. Can you talk?'

'Yes, there's no problem. Where are you?'

'I'm at home. You?'

'In the car, just finished a meeting. I'm on my way home.'

'I wondered, what are you doing tomorrow? I mean, are you free at all?'

'I've got a civic reception to attend.' Her heart lurched. 'but I'm promised it'll be finished by three at the very latest. I'm around after that.'

Her voice faltered slightly. 'Your wife?'

'At her sister's for the whole weekend.'

'Aren't you expected to be there after your reception?'

'Paperwork that needs to be done. Marion knows the score. It all goes with the job, the salary, the lifestyle' Marion. She hated that name, but not as much as she hated herself at that moment. 'What were you thinking of?'

'Um, dinner would be nice,' she said.

'Great. Where? I mean, somewhere discreet, obviously.'

Obviously, she thought to herself. Can't be seen out in public with me. 'There's a little place I know just off of the A12 near Chelmsford'

'Sounds great.'

'They, um, there's a room, you know, in case you wanted to have a drink.' God, she was so bad at this. She sounded like a tart.

'Good idea. Text me the details of the place, and I'll sort it all out. Any problems, I'll call you back; otherwise, I'll see you there as close to four as possible. Okay?'

'Great. Thanks. Thanks for doing that.'

'No problem. It'll be in the name of ...Erm... Fields. The room will, I mean.'

'Excellent. See you tomorrow.'

'Bye.'

She pressed the 'end call' button on the phone. A strange feeling of anticipation and immense elation filled her, and for that reason, she hated herself even more.

Johnson spent the weekend working overtime. He had no significant other half to worry about, so his time was his own. As soon as Stone had passed Jamieson's message on to him, Johnson was on the phone with the Duty Sergeant at the Station to find out what extra working hours were available over the next two days. There was a shift on Saturday morning, starting at six and finishing at two. That worked nicely. Johnson played rugby on Saturday afternoons, and this week's kick-off was at three o'clock. If he left the station at two sharp as soon as his shift ended, he could easily be at the ground for two thirty, giving him half an hour to prepare for the match.

Then on Sunday, the same shift was available. Johnson said yes to both. It was easy, patrolling a local beat; it was all about the new police initiative of being more visible than anything else. So he and another officer would cover a pre-planned route on foot three times during the shift unless anything more serious kicked off, which it rarely did during the early shift. Johnson hoped it was either Tom Rogers or Fiona Lee, who he was teamed up with. Tom, because he had similar tastes to Johnson, and they could talk rugby or whatever else for eight hours, or Fiona, because she was easygoing and had a great sense of humour.

Working both shifts would put an extra hundred and fifty pounds *net* in his monthly wage packet. However, Johnson considered that this was time well spent.

Stone dropped him off on Dunstable High Street at just before nine. He stopped off for a takeaway at the local Indian restaurant and was home eating it on a tray on his lap in front of the television by nine-thirty. He was twenty-four; he was single, and at this moment in time, he wouldn't swap any of that for the world.

Stone bade Johnson a good night, swung the car round, and headed home. He wasn't hungry, although he assumed something would be waiting for him in the oven at home. Margaret wouldn't be at home, though. She was out with friends, something that was happening more and more recently. Stone thought about the last time they went out as a couple for dinner, to the pictures, to see a show, anything. He came up with a blank.

The truth was that things hadn't been going so well between them lately. Stone had heard of cops being married to the job but had never considered that he had been one of them. He told himself that he wasn't career minded. He did his job to the best of his ability and went home with no baggage.

And initially, that was what Margaret liked about him. He had no pretensions. He worked hard and got results. Every year when it was time for his annual appraisal, he would be asked about his career progression, and he would always make it clear that he was comfortable where he was, doing what he did.

He held that thought for a moment. It had been seven years since he had been asked where he saw his career going. Seven years! 'That fact momentarily stung him. He had spent the last twenty-five years of his career telling anyone who asked that he was happy as a Detective Sergeant, and yet now people had stopped asking him. He felt affronted — completely irrational, he knew, nevertheless — people had assumed that he had no interest in promotion anymore, and they had no right in making that assumption.

Margaret had also grown tired of his attitude. Twenty-five years ago, when Stone was a DS, the wage was a good one. They lived in a nice house; they drove a nice car. But now, Stone had reached the top of his wage band and had no real salary rise in the last fifteen years. Sure, there was the annual rise in line with inflation that all police workers received, but Margaret watched as younger, less able men than her husband joined the force, caught him on the ladder and quickly passed him, many leaving him a long way behind. Alex Jamieson was a point in case, and he wasn't what you'd call a high-flyer and yet here he was four years younger than Stone and earning probably as much as twenty-five thousand pounds a year more. Claire Evason was twenty years younger than Stone and was probably not far short of what he was currently earning now.

He and Margaret still lived in a nice house, but they couldn't afford anything bigger or in a better area. Stone's income just wasn't high enough. This had never previously mattered to Margaret, but just lately, it had taken on greater importance. Stone didn't know why and didn't know what had changed, but something had, and he didn't know what to do about it.

Now he had another problem to cope with. This whole Lesley Wallace business had jolted him back in time to a period when, by his own admission, he hadn't been at his best and nowhere was the spectre of that same name rearing up at him, opening all kinds of old wounds. He knew Jamieson's idea of taking the weekend out was primarily aimed at him.

Jamieson was a shrewd operator and could see that the whole situation was taking its toll on Stone. Having a weekend away from it might give Stone some greater perspective on the matter. A man had been murdered, and it was their job to find out who had been responsible. It was as straightforward as that. Full stop.

But as much as he knew that Jamieson had his best interests at heart, he also knew that he would be in the office tomorrow morning working the case and, probably, Sunday morning as well because that's what he did. Besides, at the moment, he had little better to do with his time.

CHAPTER SEVENTEEN

Jamieson probably hadn't made the best use of his free weekend and now driving to work on Monday morning, he had that strange feeling of a mixture of guilt and regret that one gets when the most of an opportunity hasn't been made.

His weekend hadn't really amounted to achieving very much of tangible worth at all, really. However, following last week's band rehearsal, he had taken time out to practice some of the new songs just in case he found himself available to play in a proper show at any time in the near future.

He had pottered around the garden — God; he hadn't that phrase; it made him sound (and feel) at least seventy — and eventually found himself in front of the television on Sunday afternoon watching some nondescript football match.

Saturday night was the highlight of the weekend. He and Lucy met with friends at a local gastro-pub and enjoyed an excellent meal and some good wine. Lesley Wallace was never far from his mind as hard as he tried to remove all thoughts of the man, but he still hadn't come up with any new angles. This troubled him somewhat. Usually, when he started work on a new case, he had plenty of ideas and energy to work them through, but with this one, he was starting to wonder if Stone was right. Perhaps this was the murder that no one really cared very much about. Jamieson was early today and was pushing the office door open at seven fifty-five precisely. Stone was already there poring over the old files, trying to squeeze some new life into the case. Jamieson wondered whether Stone had been in over the weekend but decided not to pursue the matter. If Stone wanted to come in and work, then that was his business. Jamieson wasn't about to make an experienced officer work in a manner they were uncomfortable with. Jamieson had made the offer of a free week-end. Stone probably hadn't taken it up. Life goes on.

Jamieson and Stone were discussing their respective weekends when Evason arrived. She looked relaxed and ready to pick up from where she'd left off at the end of last week. At least someone had made the most of the opportunity, thought Jamieson.

'Good weekend?' he enquired as Evason settled herself at her desk.

She smiled. 'Lovely, thanks', she replied in a manner that suggested that she appreciated being asked but wasn't about to elaborate any further on her answer. Johnson arrived not long after armed with the usual breakfast order and commenced handing out coffees and croissants.

They sorted themselves out, and the morning meeting began. Jamieson was disappointed but not surprised when it transpired that no one had any new angles on the case. Johnson suggested that it may have been a 'killing for kicks' — a new phenomenon seen mainly in the Mid West of America where someone or some group of people decide to murder for no other reason than just to see what it feels like. It was incredibly difficult to police out there. The sheer vastness of the place meant that they would be murderers could drive unnoticed into a sleepy hick town in the middle of nowhere, commit murder and drive out again with no one being any the wiser until the body was discovered. The idea was based on how many American serial killers operated, the most famous being Henry Lee Lucas, who just drifted from town to town for years in the mid-seventies to eighties, committing murder after murder for no other reason than he could.

Jamieson liked the idea that Johnson had given the case some thought and had found a new way of looking at it, although he did add that he found it to be unlikely without dismissing the idea entirely.

They then caught up on Friday's developments. Jamieson and Evason told the other two about their meeting with David Hughes and heard about the others' meetings with Soper and

Sargeant. The details of the Soper meeting were kept to a minimum. Given Soper's incarceration, Jamieson was happy to move him right down the list of likely perpetrators without removing him altogether. Sargeant, they would keep higher on the list until, at least, the witness statement was received from his wife. Stone made a note to call the local officers to visit to get the statement taken.

Stone confirmed that over the weekend, when he found himself at a loose end, he had visited the nursing home where the foster home manager had been living for the last fifteen years. She was now eighty-six, although she had all of her faculties working. Stone had told her why he was there and asked whether she had any ideas about who may have had cause. At first, she answered his questions as best as her memory would allow, but the longer the interview continued, the more unpleasant the memories she unearthed. Finally, she became very agitated, and Stone was asked to leave in no uncertain terms by the Matron.

There were times when Jamieson disliked this job. Of course, they were dealing with a murder case here, and it was vital that they followed up every single lead they came up with. He also knew that Stone would have handled the situation sensitively; Jamieson had seen him in similar situations, finding empathy for his subject whilst obtaining answers to essential questions. However, at the same time, they weren't there to harass elderly ladies and leave them upset and crying. He wondered whether a formal complaint might find its way from the nursing home to the Chief Constable's Office. He sincerely hoped not as dating the Chief Constable had given him his head on this case, but the team had not yet produced anything significant that might move them nearer to resolution. Ad hoc complaints from angry nursing home managers might change all that.

Jamieson felt frustrated that they appeared to be making very little headway. 'Someone must have seen something,' he said.'It must be impossible for someone to smash someone's skull in without it raising anyone's attention — even at eleven thirty in the evening.' He thought some more. 'Sandy, you and Rog go back to the house, see if there's anything obvious we've overlooked that might help us. Then get hold of the personal stuff we collected from the house, bank statements, cheque books, things like that, see if there's anything there. Rog, how far have you got with the house-to-house enquiries?'

Johnson screwed up his nose: 'Up the hill to the pub, probably another hundred or so houses. Then there's all the callbacks — probably another hundred or so there.' 'Okay, we need to get them finished. Crap job, I know, but it's all part of being a detective. See, if they've got anyone downstairs, they can let us have to help you out. Also, get down to the pub tomorrow evening; that'll be a week on from when it happened; see if there's anything of interest there.' Jamieson turned to Stone and almost apologetically said: 'Sandy, you'll have to help Rog out with the house to house, I'm afraid. We're now over five days in, and we're not getting any warmer. Any news about Malcolm Lewis?' Stone shook his head. The fourth member of the gang, who had been locked away on the evidence of Lesley Wallace, was proving elusive to find.

'Right,' said Jamieson, 'Claire, you do some work of finding him this morning before we set off for Birmingham. Talk to Sandy before he goes off, see how far he's got.'

"Sir' said Evason, an almost indiscernible smile of satisfaction forming on her lips.

Stone looked annoyed that he was being given menial tasks when he was the more senior of the Detective Sergeants. However, he managed to hold his thoughts to himself. 'Okay,' said Jamieson, 'let's get going. Any tangible progress, phone it in on the mobile.

Otherwise, we'll meet again here tomorrow at the usual time. It'd be nice to have made significant progress by then, just in case I get a call from Big Pete.' Johnson looked confused, 'The Chief Constable' explained Jamieson.

Stone told Johnson to get all the paperwork together from the house-to-house enquiries to date, then sat down at his computer. He found the number for the station most local to David Sargeant and dialled. He asked to be put onto a Detective Sergeant when he was put through. The call was connected.

Stone explained that he needed a favour. He needed a witness statement to corroborate an alibi. The DS at the other end of the phone said that wouldn't be a problem. They had an excess of staff at the moment, so it would be good to get out of the office for a while. Stone gave him the details of David Sargeant's wife and the gist of what Sargeant had said about the evening in question and the timings — in from work at six-thirty, dinner, kids to bed and watching television until ten forty-five — just get Mrs Sargeant to confirm that, and that was all.

'That's all we need,' said Stone. 'Do me a favour, will you? Get someone with a bit of nous to take care of it. We don't want to upset any apple carts. We just need the statement for elimination purposes — plain and simple.'

Stone replaced the phone in the cradle and looked at Johnson. 'Come on, then,' he said, 'the sooner we get started, the sooner we finish.'

CHAPTER EIGHTEEN

Jamieson and Evason set off for Birmingham at just after two o'clock. They took Jamieson's car and used his portable satellite navigation system. The machine calculated that the journey was seventy-four miles long and would take eighty-six minutes to complete.

Evason had phoned ahead and ensured that all the Marshall family would be available. Jamieson had decided that Mr and Mrs Marshall would be interviewed together and the two sons, now in their early thirties, individually. Jamieson would interview Mr, and Mrs Marshall and Evason would take the sons.

'How do we approach this?' he asked Evason as they pulled onto the M1. Evason drew in a deep breath.

'Well,' she started ', Mrs Marshall was very defensive when I spoke to her. She said the family had put the whole thing to bed long ago and didn't want it to be disturbed again.'

'I can understand that,' said Jamieson.

'Me, too.' '

What do we know about the boys now?' asked Jamieson.

Evason consulted her notes. 'Seem to be reasonably well adjusted. Privately educated — the older one went to university and is now teaching, and the younger one runs his own business. They're both married with kids.' 'Privately educated?' mused Jamieson. 'Yes, that's what Birmingham County Council said. Why?' 'From the file, I understood that the Marshalls were very much working class. So I just wondered how they could afford private education - even back in the day — and before you say anything, I'm not being judgemental, just a Policeman.'

They drove on in silence for a while. Then, finally, the voice on the satellite navigation system announced that they were ten miles from their destination. Jamieson checked his watch. They were an hour early. He pulled into the next services for a coffee and to kill twenty minutes or so.

Evason went to buy the coffees. Jamieson pulled his mobile phone from his jacket pocket. Last week he had tried to call William Mitchell, the young Detective Sergeant who had required counselling after working on the original case and was now a Hostage Negotiator with the Met. Mitchell hadn't answered, so Jamieson had left a message. He hadn't returned the call, so Jamieson had called again just after this morning's meeting had finished. Again, there had been no answer, and Jamieson had left a more urgent message. That was now seven hours ago, and still no contact from Mitchell.

Jamieson entered the number he had for Mitchell and pressed the dial button. Once again, the phone went to the answering service. This time Jamieson didn't leave a message. The phone number he was ringing was definitely Mitchell's because the message on the answering service started with the greeting 'Hello, you've reached the answering service for Keith Mitchell of the London Metropolitan Hostage negotiation Service...' but for whatever reason, Keith Mitchell either wasn't accessing his messages or was but had made a decision not to return Jamieson's calls.

Jamieson tapped the mobile phone against his front teeth while contemplating the situation. He was still deep in thought when Evason returned with the coffees. When he saw her, he slipped the phone back into his pocket.

Evason handed him one of the two cups she was carrying and took a sip from the other. She grimaced: 'That's been stewing a while', she said. 'I suppose at least it's wet and warm.'

They found a bench on the forecourt of the service station and sat down, enjoying the sunshine.

Jamieson took a sip of his coffee. Evason was right; all in all, it was pretty horrible. He looked at her: 'If this was your case, would you be doing anything differently?' he asked. She narrowed her eyes: 'Nothing drastically different, no', she answered. 'Which, by implication, means you would do some things differently', reasoned Jamieson.

'Some,' said Evason. Jamieson waited for her to elaborate, but she didn't.

'Like what?' he pressed.

'Stone,' she said. 'If it were my case, I wouldn't have him working it. He's got too much history with it. I don't think he can be considered impartial. If, for some reason, we are unable to solve the case and someone comes out of the woodwork and screams that the police haven't done their job properly, could you honestly put your hand on your heart and say that we had the most appropriate officers available on the case?'

Jamieson felt the sting of criticism but allowed it to wash up and over him before he responded. 'Sandy's a good cop. He's got an excellent track record. Besides, firstly I don't think we will find anyone screaming about this case in particular. Secondly, if we did, I'm confident that we could prove beyond doubt that we had the best available officers working it, including Sandy.'

Evason nodded, but Jamieson could see she was far from convinced by his answer. They would have to beg to differ on this particular point.

'Any other comments?' he asked slightly more aggressively than he meant to.

She shook her head; 'No,' she said, 'just the one'. She checked her watch. 'We should be going.'

She stood up without waiting for his reply and moved off towards the car, dropping her empty cardboard coffee cup into a waste bin on the way. Jamieson sniffed and said to himself, 'well handled — nice to see your management skills are still to the fore' before getting up and walking towards the car, dropping his empty coffee cup into the same waste bin.

Fifteen minutes later, the satellite navigation system had directed them to a well-maintained council estate on the southeast boundary of Birmingham City Centre. They were still fifteen minutes early, but Jamieson was tired of waiting and insisted on going on ahead. They found the house they were looking for and parked up outside. Jamieson ensured the car was locked before joining Evason at the front door. The door was opened by Mrs Marshall, a small woman in her mid-fifties, with glasses and a nervous smile on her face. After initial introductions, they were shown inside the living room, where Mr Marshall sat waiting in an old armchair. He had been watching television but clicked the remote control button to off when his wife ushered the police officers through the door. Mr Marshall stood and shook hands with both Jamieson and Evason. He was a big man with grey hair pushed back behind his ears. He was wearing a uniform which Jamieson worked out from the badge on the breast pocket was for the local bus company, and he recalled that Evason mentioned that Mr Marshall had been a bus driver for the last thirty years. Mrs Marshall said that one of her sons, Steven, was in the kitchen, but the other, Duncan, had yet to arrive.

She asked whether they would like a hot drink, which they both declined, although Evason did ask if she could have a glass of water. Mrs Marshall went to the kitchen, and Mr Marshall offered them a seat on the sofa. They sat down, and Jamieson took the opportunity to thank Mr Marshall for his family's time, particularly as it concerned an episode from long ago that he was sure they would have preferred to forget all about. Mr Marshall nodded.

Jamieson explained that to save time, he would speak to Mr and Mrs Marshall whilst Detective Sergeant Evason would speak individually to their two sons. Once again, Mr Marshall nodded. Mrs Marshall returned with a glass of water for Evason. Evason took the glass and thanked her. She stood up, offered her seat to Mrs Marshall, and went back to the kitchen to speak to Steven Marshall. Mrs Marshall sat on the sofa next to Jamieson.

Evason had already filled Mrs Marshall in with the background to the visit. Jamieson began by going through all the details again for the benefit of Mr Marshall. Once again, Mr Marshall nodded that he understood what had happened and why the police were there.

As he spoke, Jamieson frequently looked from Mr Marshall to Mrs Marshall and back again. On each glance, he noted that Mr Marshall wore the same neutral expression, but Mrs Marshall held her hands in her lap and constantly played with her wedding ring. Jamieson concluded his opening speech: 'I'm sure you understand the importance that we find who did this. It was a particularly savage attack on an elderly, defenceless man.'

For the third time, Mr Marshall nodded, and for the first time, he spoke. 'Of course, Inspector.' Jamieson waited for more. The big man shifted in his chair and looked at his wife. 'I think I can speak for my wife and myself in this matter.' This time it was Mrs Marshall who nodded. She also gave her husband a nervous smile of encouragement. He continued, 'we won't pretend it wasn't an extremely stressful time for our family. The twelve hours that the boys were missing were unbearable. The relief when we received the news from the police that they had been found safe and sound was huge. The ramifications of the event continued for many years after that day. My wife had a nervous breakdown, and the boys were seldom out of our sight for a very long time after.

However, we are devout Christians, Inspector; our faith teaches us to forgive and forget. I will freely admit that at that time, my beliefs were sorely tested, and if the police hadn't stopped events when they did, then we may well be having an entirely different conversation today.' He paused and spread his hands in the air in front of him. 'But they did, and my faith remained intact. It still does to this day. I had no thoughts of revenge on any of those men. I prayed for them that they might see the error of their ways, but most of all, I thanked the Lord for delivering my sons back to me before too much damage had been done.'

Jamieson nodded. 'How were the boys?' Mr Marshall responded: 'They were very young at the time, five and seven, and they were, as you'd imagine, very frightened by the whole episode. But the community pulled together, the church was magnificent, and the boys got through relatively unscathed.' 'Were they able to go straight back to school?' asked Jamieson. 'For the next eighteen months or so, they were schooled at home by my wife. The council were also very good in providing a home tutor for them for three afternoons each week.'

Jamieson turned his attention to Mrs Marshall: 'You must be very proud — I understand that one is a teacher and the other runs his own business.' Mrs Marshall looked down at her hands but said nothing. Jamieson felt that there was something that wasn't being said. He continued; 'I understand that they then attended a private school.' He smiled. 'I don't know what the fees were like then, but they are certainly very expensive these days.' Mrs Marshall said nothing. Mr Marshall replied coolly: 'We managed'. Jamieson, still smiling, said, 'I'm sure you did.'

An uncomfortable silence settled across the room. Then, finally, Jamieson broke it: his next question was directed at Mr Marshall. 'You'll appreciate that I'll need to eliminate you from our enquiries, just to tie up loose ends more than anything else. Can you confirm where you were last Tuesday evening between ten-thirty and twelve-thirty?' Mr Marshall reached into his inside jacket pocket and pulled out a folded piece of paper. He pulled it apart and studied it closely. 'I was on the City Centre to Solihull route. Started at six and knocked off at just before one.'

Jamieson reached his hand out. 'May I see?' he asked. Mr Marshall handed him the piece of paper. He gave it a cursory glance and handed it back. 'Can that be corroborated?' He asked.

Marshall nodded: 'Yes, by my line manager.'

Jamieson was intrigued. He never considered the Marshalls real suspects, but there was still the need to eliminate them from the enquiry. He was still of the same opinion; however, now being around the nervous Mrs Marshall and the holier-than-thou Mr Marshall, he felt something was missing but couldn't quite put his finger on it.

He finished by taking down the details of Mr Marshall's line manager, thanked the Marshalls, and moved into the kitchen. The second son, Duncan, had turned up and was talking to Evason. He was explaining how last Tuesday had been parents' evening at the school and having finished speaking to parents by nine forty-five, he and several other teachers had retired to the local pub. They hadn't left until gone eleven. Evason thanked him for his time.

They left shortly after that. It was just before five o'clock, and the afternoon was still pleasant. Children from the neighbourhood played in the communal green area. Jamieson and Evason walked back to the car and climbed in. Jamieson hadn't yet told her about his meeting with Scott. He wound the window down to let some air in. The sound of the children playing carried into the car through the opened window.

'What did you make of that?' He asked Evason.

'Not a lot,' she replied. 'They are both well-adjusted young men, married with kids and mortgages. They barely remembered what had happened. It seems that their Mother and Father did a good job of keeping all the facts from them. I suppose you found out that the family is devout Christians. No thoughts of revenge. Plus, 'she opened her notebook and scanned down the last page, 'they've both got pretty good alibis. Duncan's, you heard, and Steven was at a meeting in Manchester. What about Mum and Dad?' 'Same thing, really, although something didn't feel quite right. He provided all the answers while she sat wringing her hands in her lap.' Jamieson watched a group of young boys outside kicking a football around 'I don't know!"

Their conversation was interrupted by a loud bellow, 'Janice, no!' They both looked up and saw Mrs Marshall running towards them. Mr Marshall stood in the doorway, his face a shade of bright red. He shouted again, 'They don't need to know about it.' Mrs Marshall stopped running and turned to face her husband. He looked at her imploringly. 'They don't need to know about it, love.'

She smiled at him and said: 'I'm sorry Frank, I really am, but it may be important'. She continued towards them, although not running this time. As she came level with the car, Evason lowered her window. Janice Marshall leant down — hands on her knees. She was breathing heavily, and it took a while to regain her breath. Eventually, she pushed her hand through the open window. She was holding a piece of paper between her fingers, which she offered to Jamieson. 'I think you need to know about these,' she said between deep breaths.

CHAPTER NINETEEN

They took up precisely the same positions when they got back to the Marshall's living room — Mr Marshall in the big armchair, Mrs Marshall and Jamieson to his left on the sofa and Evason standing in the doorway — only this time, the whole dynamic had changed entirely.

Janice Marshall was energised. Gone was the nervous woman who had sat in the same seat not ten minutes previously, seemingly weighed down by an unknown force on the one hand and her husband's sheer weight of existence on the other. Conversely, Frank Marshall sat, fixed jaw-line and tight-lipped, hands gripped on the arms of the chair, looking straight ahead.

The couples' sons had left shortly after Jamieson and Evason but had turned left at the end of the garden path, whereas Jamieson and Evason had gone right. Jamieson noted that there had been no effort made to contact them to get them to return. He wondered whether their absence was by design — perhaps Mrs Marshall didn't want them to know what she was about to say.

For the first time, Jamieson looked at the piece of paper he was holding with a degree of detail. He recognised it as being a banker's cheque. It was written out to 'Mr and Mrs F Marshall' dated a week ago and was for the sum of one thousand pounds. The issuing office of the bank was in North London. Jamieson turned it over and looked at the back. It was blank. The most obvious omission was the name of the sender. He looked at Mrs Marshall; 'Tell me,' he said gently. She paused and resisted the strong temptation to look at her husband. 'The first one came about two months after the court case. It was for five hundred pounds. The only other difference was that a branch of the same bank issued it, but up in Yorkshire somewhere, I can't remember exactly. We thought it was a well-wisher. Somebody who had found out about what had happened and was making a donation. The neighbours may be, you know, a collection they wanted to make for us, but to save us from embarrassment, they kept it anonymous.' This time, she did look at her husband. He didn't return the gesture. She continued, 'So we paid it into the bank account, bought the boys some nice things and booked a holiday. Five hundred pounds was a lot of money twenty-five years ago. Frank and I were thankful, but we never told the boys. They still don't know to this day.'

Jamieson nodded. 'What happened next?' he asked. Mrs Marshall raised her eyebrows slightly as if she was having trouble believing her own story. 'Another one arrived the following month, exactly the same.' she stopped talking.

Jamieson prompted, 'What did you do this time?'

Mrs Marshall appeared to stare at a spot on the carpet just in front of the television: 'We talked about it. We talked about it for a long time. We asked close friends from our church group, the local Vicar, and we prayed for guidance' 'and' said Jamieson. 'We kept it. No one we spoke to came out and said it like that, you know, 'keep it'.

'Everyone said it was our decision, and whatever decision we made would be the right one for us.' She smiled more to herself than for anyone else's benefit.' But, gosh, that sounds so woolly, doesn't it? A bit of a cop-out, really.'

'Each time when the next one turned up in the first week of the month, it was an easier and easier decision to make. It helped. The boys were reasonably unaffected by their ordeal, but I was a mess. I couldn't let them out of my sight. The money meant I could give up my job and school at home and still afford some professional teaching a couple of times a week. Then after eighteen months or so, the amount increased to a thousand pounds a month, and once it had remained at that level for a few months, we decided to put the boys into private education. After that, I was much better, more relaxed about things, so I could go back to work and fit my hours in around dropping the boys off at school and picking them up in the evenings. I still couldn't let them, board, though. That was a step too far.'

Unseen by any of the others, Evason allowed herself a small smile and admitted to herself that Jamieson was good. He had homed straight in on the fact that this was a working-class family who had put their children through private schooling. She, herself, had missed the relevance.

Janice Marshall carried on talking. The money had become a regular income. Almost like a Government benefit but with the worrying uncertainty about how long it would last. She stressed that the money was only ever spent on the boys — putting them through private school and university, helping them put together a deposit for when they were ready to buy their own home — and now that her sons were financially dependent, the money was set aside to ensure that their grandchildren could benefit in the same way. In his head, Jamieson roughly calculated that more than two hundred and fifty thousand pounds had been sent over the last twenty-five years. He sat forward in his seat, picking his words carefully. He asked: 'Did you ever think about where the money was coming from?'

Janice Marshall sat frozen. Her eyes were wet. She was unable to speak.

Finally, after sitting in silence for what had seemed like an eternity, Frank Marshall Spoke, his voice was calm and controlled: 'You don't have to say anything, Janice love, we haven't done anything wrong' 'Legally, no' said Jamieson 'You haven't done anything wrong.'

Suddenly Marshall was animated. 'What the bloody hell is that supposed to mean? You do not sit in judgement of us. You do not question our morals. You do not even know us.'

Jamieson debated whether to discuss the morals of accepting money from a man who, if he hadn't been stopped, would have undoubtedly participated in the rape and possible torture and murder of Frank Marshall's sons but decided against it. He briefly wondered what he would have done in the same situation as these simple people. They had given their children the best possible opportunities by accepting blood money. Marshall was right about one thing — Jamieson didn't know them, and it wasn't for him to judge them by his standards. That wasn't why he was here. Instead, for the second time that day, he thanked the Marshalls for their time and apologised, but he would have to take the banker's cheque with him as evidence in the case. It would be returned in due course when it was no longer needed. He offered his outstretched hand to Frank Marshall, who pointedly refused it and then onto Janice Marshall, who took it and looked him in the eye. 'We're not bad people, 'she said quietly. Jamieson nodded, unable to bring himself to speak. Evason finished by adding that they may need to get in touch at some point in the future, and before Jamieson could gather his thoughts entirely, they were back in the car.

Jamieson checked his watch.

It was five-thirty. The hotel was a twenty-minute drive away, so he started the car. He and Evason could talk while he drove.

CHAPTER TWENTY

When they had negotiated the residential streets and finally found their way back to the main road leading to the hotel where Jamieson was due to meet Scott. Jamieson finally had an opportunity to tell Evason about the planned meeting. He apologised for not telling her earlier; however, the events back at the Marshall's house had prevented him. Evason was okay about it. She hadn't got anything planned for this evening and would retire to a corner of the bar to write up the notes she had taken during the meetings from this afternoon. However, she would need something to eat, so Jamieson cleared the purchase of a bar meal on expenses. It was the least he could do in the circumstances. 'Is there any way that money couldn't have been from Wallace?' she asked. Jamieson thought it through and then simply answered, 'no'.

Evason agreed and knew that one of her allocated tasks for the next day would be a fine-tooth comb exercise through Wallace's bank statements to reconcile withdrawals from the bank accounts to the dates the Marshalls received from the banker's cheques.

Evason spoke. 'Well,' she said, 'at least we can cross the Marshalls from our list of suspects. It seems very unlikely to me that Mr Marshall would have done anything that would have stopped that particular gravy train.'

Jamieson went quiet for the next few minutes, evidently deep in thought. 'What's on your mind?' Evason finally asked him.

'Thinking about the meeting with Darren Hughes tomorrow evening,' he replied, 'Wonder whether he's been receiving any cheques in the post?'

'If it *is* Wallace, where has he got his money from?' Asked Evason.

Jamieson puffed his cheeks out:'He was especially close to his Mother; there could have been money there, or he was a computer bod at a time when computers were relatively new, so he probably commanded a good income; his own outgoings weren't exactly high. But, on the other hand, three pints three times a week and dinner for one isn't going to set you back a fortune. Either way, you want to look at it, it was him. I'm absolutely certain.'

Evason looked out the window for a while, thinking things over.'What do you make of the Marshalls?' she asked. 'Did they know where it was coming from?'

'If they couldn't be one hundred per cent sure, then they certainly suspected it', said Jamieson. 'It's the hypocrisy I find hard to deal with. I mean, you either accept where the money is coming from and take it no matter because it helps your family, or you stick to your principles and refuse to take it and look at it like some kind of manna from heaven sticks in my craw. Simply put, it is money from a man who, given the opportunity, would have caused great harm to their children and appears to be seeking some kind of redemption. That's it, live with it!' He winced at his reply. He had a cynical, judgemental streak and, at times, found it difficult to conceal. Sitting next to him, looking out the window, Evason said nothing. Ten minutes later, Jamieson was approaching the bar of a typical hotel chain establishment. The carpet under his feet was the same pattern in countless other hotels up and down the country. Ditto for the design of the bar and the stools that stood before it, as well as the tables, chairs and pot plants, set out for the pleasure of the patrons. Evason had headed off into the foyer for a coffee and sandwich. Jamieson promised her that he would be no more than an hour tops.

He checked his watch: six twenty. He hoped that Scott would still be here and was disappointed that he couldn't see anyone at the bar as he drew closer. He cursed himself for not ringing to confirm during the day. He had delayed his decision whether to include Evason in the meeting for too long when he knew it would be inappropriate for her to be there all along. Then the Marshall thing blew up, and he missed his chance to speak to Scott. Now it looked as though Scott had forgotten or had turned up and waited and then thought that Jamieson must have forgotten and gone. He muttered 'Bollocks' under his breath — a missed opportunity now he'd have to rearrange or speak to Scott over the telephone.

He was annoyed because he wanted to meet with Scott, not just to talk about the case at hand but also to talk about things in the Force generally, about career prospects if, and it was still a big 'if', Jamieson moved further north. He and Lucy had discussed a move before in a bid to revitalise his career. But, in reality, now it was probably the wrong time. Lucy had found a job that she really enjoyed, and Justin was on the verge of the most critical years of his education, so suddenly, his own needs had been relegated down the pecking order. But still, it would be nice to know what was out there for him. To see how highly his stock was considered within the Police Force.

He turned to go and find Evason before she placed an order for an overpriced sandwich and almost knocked Scott over.

'You're in a bloody hurry', said Scott smiling and extending his right hand. 'Sorry I'm late — the course overran — some swot from The Met kept asking irrelevant questions.' he pointed towards the bar. 'What are you drinking?' Jamieson had a pint of the weakest lager on offer, and Scott had the same. Both had longish drives home and, out of necessity to their livelihoods, needed to stay on the right side of the line. So they retired to a table and chairs away from the bar for some privacy. Not that it looked likely to get very busy tonight.

DI Scott cut an imposing figure and was, Jamieson imagined, very popular with the ladies and probably equally popular with the men. Jamieson remembered that he could be both charming and coarse, at the same time endearing himself to all-comers. He stood about six feet two and had a muscular build and stylish dark hair. He wore designer glasses and positively oozed confidence. Unfortunately, Jamieson couldn't remember whether or not Scott was married.

Jamieson asked about the course. 'Same old, same old, really,' replied Scott.' everything is so PC these days. You can't even sneeze without offending someone.' He took a pull on his pint.' How's Bedford?' he asked.

Jamieson's face said everything. Scott laughed. 'That bad, eh?' Jamieson forced a smile. 'Remember that course? That was nearly twenty years ago now. We were all young guns. We were going to change policing in Britain. We were going to put the bad guys away and let the good ones feel safe' 'and all the while, we'd be drinking and playing the guitar,' finished Scott, grinning. 'That was a good course. Happy days,' he said, raising his glass in a toast to days gone by. Jamieson nodded, offered his glass up and took a sip.

Scott continued, 'Do you remember MacDonald? Tall chap wore a kilt on the last evening and did a Highland Fling on the snooker table.' Jamieson smiled at the recollection. 'Well, he's Assistant Chief Constable somewhere north of the border.' They discussed their various careers over the past twenty years or so. There was a kind of reverse symmetry. It seemed that Jamieson had initially moved up through the ranks quickly only to have slowed down to almost a halt in recent years, whilst Scott had stayed as a Detective Sergeant for far longer, but once he started up, the ladder had progressed well. Although they were both Detective Inspectors, Scott was a slightly higher grade and was well placed for his next promotion. When this fact became evident, Jamieson felt a pang of irrational jealousy shoot through him.

'What's it like working in Liverpool' asked Jamieson. 'It's really good,' replied Scott.' they let you get on with it, you know, they're not on your back every other minute asking what you're doing and why you're doing it. As long as the results are there, they're happy. The Chief is a younger guy. Go ahead, big on the police working with the community; it's worked well up to now. Crime rates are down in some of the most violent areas in Merseyside. Happy community, happy police — it's all good!'

He took another mouthful of beer and looked Jamieson directly in the eye. 'Plus,' he said, 'it's a great place to work for career progression. If you do well, you'll get the recognition and the promotion that follows. That has been made very clear to everyone, and so far, he's been as good as his word.' Jamieson broke eye contact and looked down at his glass. 'You thinking about a change of scenery, then?' Scott asked. Jamieson raised his eyebrows in a gesture representing a facial shrug. 'I feel a bit stagnant where I am, is all.' 'Can't have that', said Scott.'Shall I put some feelers out? There are a couple of vacancies on the horizon. It can't hurt, can it?'

Jamieson bought a second drink for each of them. He had mineral water, and Scott had a smaller beer.

'So someone finally got Lesley Wallace, did they?' asked Scott.

'Looks that way," said Jamieson. As he outlined the case to date, he found himself getting depressed about the lack of progress that the team had made so far. 'What did your old man make of it all in the end?' he asked Scott. Scott took his glasses off and used a serviette from a holder on the table to give them a clean. 'Scott Senior was incredibly disappointed in the whole thing, but mainly in himself. You know that he did a deal with Wallace to snare the others? Well, he always maintained that he went in too early — poor lack of judgement on his part — and he hated himself for it. The powers that be knew he'd screwed up as well. They let him finish up the case; then, they retired him. That really hurt him. From the public's point of view, the case was a huge success, the police had managed to get four highly dangerous men off the street, but the fact of the matter was that the most dangerous one had walked away scot-free to resurface and potentially re-offend God knows how many times more.' He held his glasses up to the light and, satisfied that they were clean enough, put them back on and looked at Jamieson.

'Did he pursue the matter in his retirement?' asked Jamieson.

'At first, yes. When Wallace went to ground straight after the case had ended, the old man was determined to track him down and let the local police know all about him. But he soon realised that it was an impossible task without the weight of the force behind him anymore. All of his colleagues closed ranks on him, probably on orders from above, then after two years of getting nowhere, he just gave up. I wouldn't say he was a broken man. He was always much too strong to let that happen, but he was never the same again.' Scott took a mouthful of his drink.

'What about you?' asked Jamieson. 'Any thoughts of revenge for your dad?'

'Ah, revenge by proxy. I see where you're coming from. Sorry to disappoint, but no. I was what, twenty-two, at the time. I was more intent on my own career. I was glad that Scott Senior had been pensioned off in many respects. It certainly made my Mother happier and cleared the pitch for me. You know, it stopped people suggesting that my progress was down, not so much to what I knew, but more by who my Father was.' Scott made a face. 'No,' he said, 'The day Lesley Wallace walked out of that police station in Bedfordshire was the last time anyone from the Scott family saw him.' he leant forward almost conspiratorially and smiled at Jamieson just for the record I was at Old Trafford last Tuesday evening watching United stuff Spurs. I had three friends with me. Just in case you were wondering.' He winked at Jamieson, who smiled back. 'I'll cross you off the list of suspects, then.'

Jamieson checked his watch: it was ten past seven. Then, he remembered his promise to Evason. 'I've got to go. I've got a DS waiting for me in the other bar.'

Both men stood to leave. They shook hands. Scott gripped harder and longer than usually acceptable, making Jamieson feel slightly uncomfortable: 'I'll ask around about jobs that might come up. I'll let you know,' said Scott. 'Keep in touch anyway. It's always good to talk to one of the old hands.'

Jamieson nodded. He knew that Scott probably wouldn't ask about the jobs and also that they wouldn't stay in touch. There was no animosity between the two men. It was just the way it was. 'Thanks for your time,' he said and turned towards the exit to find Evason. As he walked away, he remembered something that he wanted to ask. So he turned back: 'Jim, did your Dad ever mention a William Mitchell? He was a young DS who worked on the original case. He had to have counselling afterwards for a while.' Scott thought: 'There were a couple like that. One of them kept in touch with Dad. Even visited him when he went to the old peoples' home. Stone, his name was. But Mitchell' he shook his head "that doesn't ring any bells...sorry.'

'No problem,' said Jamieson, 'just a thought. Drive safely.'

CHAPTER TWENTY-ONE

Stone thanked the elderly lady and turned and walked away up the garden path. He heard the door close behind him. He took his mobile phone from his pocket, scrolled down, and found Johnson's number. He stabbed the call button with his index finger. Johnson answered within two rings.

'Where are you?' asked Stone. 'I'm just finishing up with the pub landlord,' answered Johnson. 'Has he anything to add to his story from the first time round?' 'No. Nothing at all.'

There was a silence for a good five seconds before Stone spoke again. 'Okay. I'm on my way up. Get them in — I'll be about five minutes.'

He disconnected the call and pushed his mobile phone back into his trouser pocket. His watch showed six fifty-six. They had started at just after ten this morning. 'Shit, that's been a long day,' said Stone to himself and started walking up the hill towards the Happy Farmer and a long overdue pint of best bitter. Johnson was waiting in one of the booths when he arrived at the pub. On the table in front of him were two pints. Stone came over and squeezed into the seat opposite him. He picked up his drink and looked around the empty pub before he took the top three inches from his pint. He smacked his lips. 'I needed that,' he said. He surveyed the empty pub once more and checked his watch. 'Bloody hell, it's empty even for this early in the evening. No wonder the pub trade is on its knees.' Johnson agreed: 'I've been talking to the owner. He's losing money hand over fist at the moment. Says he can't carry on for much longer.'

They sat in respectful silence for the next minute or so. Then, finally, Stone spoke: 'Well, I guess we've done what needed to be done today, although nothing has come of it. No real surprises;

most people are home in bed at eleven on a Tuesday evening. Still, we've conducted as thorough a house-to-house enquiry as we can be expected to, given that there were just the two of us.'

" Someone must have heard or seen something, " said Johnson 'surely', " Not necessarily, " said Stone. 'It's like a leaf falling from a tree in a forest — no one saw it, no one heard it, but it still happened, ask Lesley Wallace. You'll get plenty of days like this when you're a detective, you know. It's not all Starsky and bloody Hutch.' Stone thought that Johnson would ask who Starsky and Hutch were for a moment, but he didn't. Settling instead for an equally cutting 'I've heard of them. My Grand-Dad told me about them.'

Johnson picked up the clipboard on the seat next to him. He flicked

through the pages: 'Just two or three callbacks left,' he said. 'I can knock them on the head over the course of the next couple of Oh Bollocks!'

'What?' said Stone.

Johnson turned the clipboard, so Stone could see the page he was looking at. 'That old boy I spoke to last week. Do you remember? The one that made all the fuss about the car parked across his driveway. I forgot to pass his complaint on to the Desk Sergeant back at the station.'

'Don't worry about' said Stone. 'He's probably complained three more times since we saw him; I know the type. Pass it over tomorrow. It'll keep.'

Johnson started to read through the notes that Allsop had made.

'I don't blame the old boy, really,' said Stone.'I bet he lived there for years before everybody had a car. I expect when he first moved in, only about three people living in the street could actually afford the luxury of a car. But, I don't know; things change very quickly, don't they?'

Johnson didn't answer - staring intently at the sheet of paper as if seeing it for the first time. He suddenly realised that, much to his embarrassment. However, it had been in his possession for over ninety-six hours; it was, in fact, the first time he had given it any real attention - he reread the whole thing giving particular emphasis to the date and times that Allsop had written down.

'How far do you think it is from where this Allsop bloke lives to where Wallace was found?' Johnson asked Stone. Stone shrugged. 'Don't know. Perhaps a couple of hundred yards. Why?' Johnson passed the clipboard to him. 'Look at that,' he said. Stone took the clipboard and read through the sheet of notes. 'What am I looking at in particular?' He asked. 'The date and the timings,' answered Johnson.

Stone held the clipboard at arm's length, allowing his eyes to focus. 'Tuesday 6th,' he said, 'last Tuesday.' Then, finally, the realisation started to dawn on him. 'Between ten thirty pm and eleven twenty pm. That's interesting.'

'It fits very nicely,' said Johnson.' estimated time of death based on the doctor's post-mortem and our own knowledge of Wallace's movements is eleven fifteen pm or thereabouts. How accurate do you think Allsop's timings are?'

'Knowing that sort of man,' said Stone, picking up his drink, 'spot on. But let's go and ask him anyway.' He tipped the remaining half pint of his beer down his throat and was on his feet, moving towards the door before Johnson could react. Feeling like a rank amateur compared to the drinking feats of his colleague, Johnson struggled to drink the next two mouthfuls of his drink before giving up, putting the glass on the table, picking up his clipboard and following Stone out of the door.

On the five-minute walk back down to Allsop's house, Stone belched on three occasions as a result of having rushed his beer. Each time he apologised with a perfunctory 'beg pardon'.

Stone leaned forward and pressed the doorbell when they finally reached the front door. The overly loud 'ding dong inside could be clearly heard from the outside. Allsop answered the door promptly. When he saw Johnson, he smiled: 'Ah, Detective Sergeant Johnson, how nice to see you again. I'm glad the police are taking my complaint more seriously this time.' He turned to Stone. 'You must be DS Johnson's superior officer. Although these days with policemen getting ever younger, you never can tell.'

'Good Evening Mr Allsop' said Stone. 'My name is DS Stone' He held out his warrant card for Allsop to see.

'Ah,' said Allsop smiling ', Equal in rank but no doubt senior in experience. Won't you come in?' He stepped back from the door and held his arm out to indicate the way. Stone made a snap decision. 'Er, no, thank you, sir. We only have a few questions and don't wish to intrude upon your evening.' Nice work, thought Johnson to himself. If Allsop had gotten us in there, we wouldn't have been out this side of midnight.

'We've been reviewing your paperwork about the car parked across your driveway, Mr Allsop, and we just wanted to confirm the times with you.' Stone continued quickly before Allsop could speak. 'Now you say the car arrived last Tuesday at ten thirty pm and was gone by eleven twenty. How can you be so sure of the times?' Allsop looked at Stone as if he had asked him how he knew that two plus two made four. 'Why *Newsnight,* of course,' he answered.

Stone looked at Johnson, who looked back at Stone. Allsop could see there was some confusion. '*Newsnight'*, he repeated 'every weeknight on BBC 2. Starts at ten thirty, unless there's blessed snooker on, and finishes at eleven twenty. Covers all the news stories of the day. I never miss it.'

'I see', said Stone nodding '*Newsnight*.'

'Yes,' said Mr Allsop, 'I distinctly remember hearing the offending car parking up just as the music for *Newsnight* began last Tuesday at ten thirty. By the time I made it round to the front door, the driver had disappeared, so I took down the make and registration number of the car to report it to the police. Then I settled down to watch my programme. Then to my amazement, as the closing music started, I heard the car start up again; it was as though the driver had popped into a house nearby just to watch *Newsnight*.' He chuckled at his own joke.' Anyway, by the time I got out to the front to give the driver a piece of my mind, he'd gone again.'

'You didn't see the driver at all, did you, Mr Allsop?' asked Stone. 'No,' came the reply.

'Did you notice anything unusual about the car at all? Anything in the back seat, for example?'

'Only that the back bumper was parked two feet across my driveway.' Stone could tell that the old man was working up a head of steam and decided that he had extracted all the relevant information. It was time to beat a hasty retreat. 'It must be incredibly frustrating for you not being able to park your car in your own driveway, Mr Allsop,' empathised Stone as he made to turn back down the garden path. 'Where did you have to leave it, a couple of hundred yards down the road?' Allsop looked at him blankly. 'I haven't got a car', he said. 'I can't drive' Stone looked stunned, and Johnson suppressed a snigger. 'Thank you for your help, Sir, 'said Stone.' we'll get back to you.'

CHAPTER TWENTY-TWO

Finally, Jamieson felt some progress had been made. He wasn't sure if anything that had come out of yesterday's meetings was significant, but importantly, it opened doors and avenues of enquiry. On the drive back down south, he had spoken to Stone, who recounted the meeting with Mr Allsop. Magnanimously, Jamieson thought, Stone passed all the credit to Johnson. 'Think there's anything in it?' he asked Stone.

'The times work; there's no doubt about that. If it's not our man, then he may have seen something, so it's certainly worth our time,' replied Stone.

'Good — let's follow it up tomorrow. See if we can get a handle on who owns the car.' Jamieson told Stone about the meeting with the Marshalls.

'So good old Lesley became a Sugar Daddy, did he?' Stone skirting on irony. 'Looks like it,' said Jamieson, 'buying penitence, perhaps.'

Jamieson dropped Evason back at the station and made his way home. He called Lucy on the way. There was no answer on either the home phone or her mobile. She was probably down at the gym. He left a message saying he'd be home in about forty-five minutes. Almost immediately after hanging up, his own phone rang. He reached forward and pushed the answer button without reading the caller identification. He assumed that it must be Lucy returning his missed call. 'I'd imagined you being all sweaty at the gym,' he said. "It was the Chief Constable who let it pass without comment: 'Alex, Peter here, any worthwhile updates on the case?'

Jamieson gave him a full update and stressed that he saw these developments as positive.

'Have we spoken to the press about it yet?' asked the Chief Constable. 'We're waiting for a positive id, Sir.' answered Jamieson.

'I think we should press ahead with it tomorrow. If we can't get the positive identification by then, use words like 'suspect' and 'believe'. We already get enough grief from the media about non-cooperation, so we ought to give them something to feed off. Do you think there will be much interest?' 'Local, perhaps, don't really know about national. It was twenty-five years ago,' stressed Jamieson.

'Maybe you're right. Let's hope so. I wouldn't want a backlash from locals who find out that they've had a pervert living in their midst for the last twenty years. So get a press conference arranged as quickly as possible, will you? Get it out in the open. Show them that we've got nothing to hide. Thanks, Alex; keep me posted, please; good night.' And as quickly as the call came, it was terminated.

This morning Jamieson drove to work with the same optimistic feeling as he had the evening before. A breakthrough was the bankers' cheques sent to the Marshalls. Jamieson would ask Evason to go through Wallace's bank statements to cement the consensus of opinion that he was indeed the Marshalls' benefactor. This could be done by reconciling withdrawals from the account to fall approximately in line with when the Marshalls had received the payments. They would follow this up with a visit to the issuing branch of the bank to see if any of the clerks could give a description that would place Wallace (or Wilkins, as he would be known to the bank) in the bank purchasing the bankers' cheques. It would also confirm if, as Jamieson suspected, Wallace was issuing any payments to his other victim, Darren Hughes. He was due to speak to Hughes that evening but suspected that it would be a difficult interview.

If he could go forearmed with some information, it would make things just a little bit easier.

As eloquently described by Stone during their conversation, the business with the car unearthed by Johnson and Stone was 'either shit or shovel'. By that, Jamieson assumed he meant that it either turned out to be someone who was there purely by coincidence who saw and heard nothing, the 'shit' in Stone's allegory, or it was someone who, when they tracked him or her down, admitted their guilt almost immediately, the 'shovel'. Either way, it was a good lead to progress, which would be Stone and Johnson's main thrust today.

There was another loose end that Jamieson couldn't nail down. His inability to contact William Mitchell was puzzling him. There may be a plausible reason that Mitchell wasn't returning his calls, but it still didn't sit right with Jamieson. He would try again this morning and, if necessary, find out who Mitchell's superior was and go down that route.

When he got to the office, he was the last to arrive. The place seemed to have an altogether different air about it. As if the information uncovered the previous day really meant something. It seemed to have revitalised his team. Evason was at her desk with Wallace's bank statements in front of her. She was making notes on a pad of paper by her side. Johnson and Stone had broad smiles on their faces — a good sign. Johnson had already got the coffees in.

'I'll run yours down to the microwave and give it a reheat, Sir. It's been sitting there for over an hour now.' Jamieson didn't know whether that was a genuine offer to be useful or a dig that the others had been in the office for a good while before their commanding officer deigned to turn up. He took it as the former. 'Thanks', he said. 'Then we'll start. There's a lot to get done today'. Johnson was back in a minute. Jamieson thanked him and took a sip of the piping hot coffee.

He sat at his desk and addressed the others. Evason remained seated. Stone casually leant against the doorjamb whilst Johnson emulated his senior officer and sat on the edge of his desk.

Jamieson began by going over yesterday's events and how he saw the current status of the investigation. Then, he asked Johnson for an update on what was now being badged as 'the Allsop situation.'

Johnson quickly went through how yesterday had panned out for him and Stone. 'After we left Mr Allsop, we asked traffic to run the car's details through their computer. It turns out that it belongs to a car hire company operating out of West London, close to Heathrow Airport. It's a privately owned company, not a national like a Hertz or Avis, so it's not a preferred choice of the airport.' Explained Johnson 'So I called last night and spoke to a ...' He checked his notes '...Mr Mohammed Razza, the owner. He was very helpful and looked up his hirings register. Turns out that between Wednesday 9th and the following Wednesday 16th, the car in question was rented out to one Mr Jason Mannix. Mr Mannix flew in from Pennsylvania on the first Wednesday and out again on the second Wednesday.' Jamieson nodded. Johnson impressed him, and under the guidance of Stone, he had every opportunity of developing into a good detective.

'Anything interesting about the return of the car?' asked Jamieson.

'Not so much the car', said Johnson. 'But when Mannix brought it back, Mr Razza gave it the once over, and something was missing.' Jamieson looked at Johnson, urging him to continue. 'You know the old-fashioned hydraulic jacks that you slide under the car and then fit the handle into a hole and pump, and the car lifts up.' As he spoke, Johnson mimed what he was describing '...you know, effectively the jack itself and the handle are separate.' Jamieson and Evason both nodded.

'Well,' continued Johnson. 'When Mr Razza checked, the handle was missing. Mannix claimed he didn't know anything about it, but Razza made him pay an extra £25 for a replacement, anyway. He couldn't argue, really, because Razza took his passport as a security deposit for the car.'

'I bet he didn't keep a copy', said Evason.

'He did, actually,' said Johnson. 'He's a very thorough man, is our Mr Razza.' 'How much do those handles weigh?' mused Jamieson.

'They're solid iron, so two, maybe three kilos,' said Stone. 'Certainly enough to make a mess of someone's head if in the right hands.' Jamieson nodded thoughtfully.

'How old is Mannix?' Jamieson directed this question at Johnson. 'Passport says he's thirty-three. Razza describes him as just under six feet with a muscular build' came the reply.

A silence fell across the room. Then, finally, Jamieson spoke, addressing Stone and Jamieson.

'Okay, you two, what next?'

Stone spoke.'The owner says the car hasn't been rented since Mannix returned it last Wednesday. So we're going down there to see what we can find. It's possible that we might have to impound the vehicle. Get a local forensics team to give it the once over.'

Jamieson turned to Evason. 'Claire, what have you got?'

Evason spoke 'There's definitely a pattern that matches up. There are withdrawals on what seems to be the first Monday of each month. Fifteen hundred pounds each time.' Jamieson nodded. It appeared to be as he suspected. 'A thousand for the Marshalls and five hundred for Darren Hughes?'

Evason shrugged: 'Very probable', she said.

'Okay,' said Jamieson, 'Ring the Branch Manager. We need to bottom this out as quickly as we can.'

'Already done', said Evason 'We're due there at ten o'clock.'

Jamieson looked at his watch. 'We'd better get going then.'

As the two teams gathered their belongings in preparation for the day ahead, Jamieson addressed them one more time: 'Question of the day.' he said, 'For what possible reason would someone fly halfway round the world to murder a man in his seventies? Answers on a postcard, please!'

CHAPTER TWENTY-THREE

On the way across to the bank, Jamieson phoned the Chief Constable's office while Evason drove. He asked to be put through to the Public Relations Department and found himself talking to a lady called Miriam. He explained that he needed a press conference arranged as quickly as possible. Miriam proved to be very efficient. She enquired where it was to be held and who would be attending.

He told her somewhere convenient in the Dunstable/Luton area and the usual attendees: so local and national newspapers, television channels and radio stations. She asked for details that she could turn into a press release, and he gave her the bones of the story to date. She asked for a contact number, and he gave her his mobile. She said it would most likely be tomorrow morning in the conference suite at one of the hotels the police usually used for this type of thing.

She said she would call back later with the press release for his final agreement before it was issued. Jamieson assumed that in these days of electronic communication, getting press releases out into the media was a far simpler task than it was, say, ten years ago when fax machines were considered cutting edge.

As they got nearer to the bank in North London, Jamieson's mobile rang. It was Doctor Jenner, the pathologist. Having referred to both medical and dental records, she was as certain as she could be, without positive identification, that the body lying in her morgue was, indeed, Brian Whittle, aka Lesley Whittle. Jamieson thanked her for her efforts. That was good news. At least he could stand up at the press conference whenever it was arranged for and be able to identify the victim positively. He tried William Mitchell's mobile phone one more time but disconnected the call when he was redirected to the answering service.

Finally, they arrived at the bank in Enfield. It was a large Victorian building and, Jamieson suspected was regarded as a far more important centre of business back in the day before banks started centralising their operations. His suspicions were confirmed when they walked into the grand banking hall. There were ten till spaces, of which three were open for business and two customers being served. He and Evason made their way to the reception desk towards the end of the hall. Evason introduced herself, and the girl staffing the desk confirmed that the branch manager was expecting them. She showed them into an office and asked if they would like some refreshments. Jamieson asked for a coffee, and Evason went for some water. The office had a desk facing two and four chairs, two in front and two behind. There was a filing cabinet in the corner and some non-descript posters on the wall advertising the bank's services and telling the reader why this bank was better than the others.

Jamieson hoped that this would be a painless experience. Officially, banks did not have to release any information to the police without a court order which, in Jamieson's opinion, meant more paperwork and an unnecessary loss of time in his investigation. Some stick-in-the-mud bank officials were good at digging their heels in and insisting on the court order before even discussing issues with the police, let alone releasing any information.

He spoke to Evason: 'You run the interview, and I'll chime in with any questions I have.' She nodded and took her notebook and pen from her bag. Jamieson knew that would please her, and he also knew she was more than up to the task. The likelihood of him intervening to cover a point Evason may have overlooked was almost non-existent.

Evason sat in the chair immediately behind the desk. Jamieson sat to her right and slightly behind. Without the desk to hide behind, he felt a little open. He crossed his legs, right ankle to left knee, and folded his arms. He quickly unfolded his arms, deciding that it would look too defensive, and finally decided to let his hands sit in his lap.

The door opened, and a round-faced man in his early forties came in. He introduced himself as Derek Forage, Branch Manager. He was clearly nervous talking to the police. Some people were like that when they spoke to authority. They hadn't done anything wrong and therefore had nothing to worry about, yet they acted almost furtively. Derek Forage spoke far too quickly and said too much. Jamieson was pleased. He felt that Forage would help as much as possible without creating unnecessary barriers.

Evason introduced herself and Jamieson. Forage shook their hands. His own hand was unpleasantly sweaty. His handshake was somewhat limp.

There had been some preliminary discussions in the calls that Evason had made to the bank in setting up the meeting, but she decided to go right back to the start. 'Can you explain why somebody would want a banker's cheque, please, Mr Forage?' she asked.

Forage gave the question due thought before answering: 'Well, I suppose the main reason is that it's a guaranteed payment. Because it's issued on one of the bank's own accounts, it's considered as good as cash. The day a bank's own cheques start bouncing, we'll all be in trouble,' he added by way of a joke. 'How can you guarantee payment?' asked Evason.

'Well,' said Forage. 'When the customer comes in to buy one. We take the cash from their bank account and put it into one of the internal bank accounts. So, before we hand the bankers' cheque to the customer, we've already had the equivalent in cash from them.'

Evason nodded.'I see,' she said, 'Can the sender of a banker's cheque remain anonymous?'

Forage thought, 'I guess so', he said 'the name and address of the sender aren't put on the bankers' cheque itself. So, unless the sender puts his or her details in a covering letter, say, all the receiver will get is the bankers' cheque showing their name as the payee, the amount and the bank details.' He paused in consideration. 'I can't think of a situation why someone would want to send a bankers' cheque anonymously, though.' He looked at Evason as if for some clarification. None was forthcoming. 'Thanks,' she said.' that gives us some idea as to the process involved.' She flicked the pages into her notebook. 'Now, more specifically, we'd like to ask some questions about a customer of yours, a Mr Brian Wilkins.'

Forage nodded his big, round head. He spread his hands out in front of him. 'I want to be as helpful as possible here, I really do, but there are some things that my Head Office won't let me do without a court order.'

'We appreciate that, Mr Forage,' said Jamieson. 'Anything you can tell us will greatly help at this stage.' Evason shot him a glance to remind him that this was her interview. Jamieson held his hands up in front of him in a small gesture of recognition that he had interrupted her.

Forage looked at his watch; 'actually,' he said, 'the person you need to speak to about Mr Wilkins is Sandra Bundy. She's due any minute now.' Then by way of an explanation. 'She's our auxiliary. By that, I mean she comes in to cover the lunch hours so the others can go off and eat their lunch. Sandra fits in where she's needed. She often works on the enquiries counter, where the bankers' cheques are issued. She's worked here for years. I think she knows Mr Wilkins quite well.' He rechecked his watch. Jamieson looked at his own watch. It was eleven thirty. Right on cue, there was a knock on the door. Forage leapt forward from his chair and opened the door.

'Sandra,' he said. 'Hello, come on in. These two people are from the police. They just want to ask you some questions about one of our customers. So there's nothing to be worried about.'

Sandra Bundy walked into the room. She was a tall, thin woman in her mid-fifties.

Like Forage, when he first entered the room, she looked worried. She sat down. Evason introduced herself and Jamieson. She showed her warrant card, which seemed to relax Mrs Bundy, but only very slightly.

The trick of interviewing is asking open questions and getting the person you are interviewing to tell you everything they know rather than relying on your questioning technique to get everything out in the open. Evason used the classic and simplest opening line: 'Tell us everything you know about Brian Wilkins.'

Sandra Bundy looked at Derek Forage, who smiled and nodded encouragingly.

'Well,' she said. 'Mr Wilkins comes in here on the first Monday of every month without fail, and I do mean without fail. A couple of times, I've seen him come in with the worse case of flu that you could imagine, and I've said to him, 'you should be home in bed; there's nothing that can't wait' but he'd just shake his head and say something like 'not while there are things to be done'. He's a funny man; I like him.' Liked - thought Jamieson — you liked him.

Evason nodded. 'Why did he come to the bank?' she asked.

Once more, Sandra Bundy looked towards Derek Forage, who again nodded.

'Well,' she said. 'He would come in at as near to quarter to twelve as you could imagine, and each time he would want the same thing.'

Jamieson found himself instinctively uncrossing his legs and leaning forward as if to hear better.

Sandra Bundy stopped talking as if to make up the suspense. Then, Evason prompted her, 'Which was?' she asked.

'Well, he would order two bankers' cheques', she said, pausing for thought ', one for a thousand pounds made in favour of F Marshall and the other for five hundred pounds in favour of D Hughes...'

'You seem to know those details by heart', said Evason.

Sandra Bundy shrugged. 'He's done the same thing for the past fifteen years. It's got to the stage where I have everything ready for when he gets here. The process, which would normally take around fifteen minutes, now only takes two or three, and he's gone. Barely time to pass the time of day, really.'

'He's that predictable?' asked Jamieson.

Sandra Bundy nodded. 'Like I said, he's been here on the first Monday of every month for, at least, the last fifteen years, if not longer.'

Evason cursed herself for not having a photograph of Wallace to get a positive identification, but she was pretty confident that it was their man. She asked Sandra Bundy for a description of Lesley Wallace and was confident enough that the description matched that of the deceased man back in the hospital morgue.

'There is something else that you should perhaps know,' said Forage. 'It may or may not have any bearing on your investigation.' His face reddened as all eyes turned towards him. 'The bankers' cheque for Hughes never clears through the banking system,'

Jamieson looked at him. 'What does that mean?' he asked.

'Well,' continued Forage, 'when you receive a banker's cheque, you pay it into your bank account the normal way and eventually, it works its way back through the system until it arrives at the originating branch - here. Then we reconcile our internal accounts. So, in effect, the banker's cheque coming back offsets the money put into the account from the customer's account. In this case, Mr Wilkins'.

Jamieson thought about what he'd just been told, working it all out in his mind. He was about to speak when Evason beat him to it. He was pleased because he had, after all, told her that it was her interview. 'So Mr Hughes wasn't cashing the cheques?' Forage shrugged before he replied, 'either that or he wasn't receiving them in the first place.'

'What about the cheques for Marshall?' asked Evason, even though she already knew the answer.

Forage looked at Sandra Bundy. She nodded and said, 'They're usually back through the system within five days of us issuing them, which means that F Marshall, whoever he or she is, must receive the cheque and pay it into his bank account on the same day.'

Evason glanced across at Jamieson, who avoided her gaze. Sandra Bundy continued talking. 'It's a strange situation because each time we issue a bankers' cheque, it costs Mr Wilkins twenty-five pounds. We explain to him that the cheques for Hughes are never cashed and that he is wasting his money, but he insists that we keep sending them.' She gave an almost helpless little shrug. 'He is the customer, and they do say that the customer is always right, but sometimes I wonder.' Evason had a puzzled look on her face: 'If the Hughes cheques are never cashed, what happens to the money?'

Forage responded this time: 'Like all cheques, bankers' cheques have a six-month life. After that, they become invalid and out of date. So we add an extra three months for grace; then, if nothing has happened, we move the money back from our internal account into the account where the money originally came from.' The room went quiet for a brief moment whilst everyone collected their thoughts, and then Sandra Bundy spoke: 'It was almost like a ritual for him, I suppose. The fact that it wasn't achieving anything didn't really seem to be of importance.' Jamieson couldn't help but feel a little disappointed. He had seen this as a potential lead in the case, but as an interesting development as it was, it didn't shed much light on who might be responsible for Wallace's murder. Again, stone's words came back to him. This really did seem like a murder that no one cared about.

His mobile phone buzzed in his pocket. He took it out and read the screen — Chief Constable's Office — he said, 'excuse me, but I have to take this', stood and left the room.

Outside, he pressed the answer button and said, 'Jamieson. It was Miriam from Public Relations. She quickly read through the press statement that she had prepared, and save for a few minor amendments that Jamieson wanted to make, he was happy to release it to the press. The Press Conference was due to be held the following morning in one of the conference rooms at the Bedfordshire Grand Hotel. Miriam would monitor interest and give him an approximate number of attendees by five this evening. She would see him at the hotel at eight-thirty tomorrow morning to go through how she saw the morning unfolding. She finished by saying that the Chief Constable himself wouldn't be attending. At present, it was all very low profile, and they wanted to keep it that way. The presence of a senior ranking officer would only raise interest in the case, which they wanted to avoid if possible.

Jamieson thanked her for her help and told her he looked forward to meeting her in the morning. Then, he pushed the 'end call' button and slipped the phone back into his pocket. When he re-entered the interview room, the atmosphere appeared to be livelier; Evason scribbled purposefully in her notebook.

'And this was on every occasion that Mr Wilkins came into the bank, would you say?' Evason asked Sandra Bundy. The tall thin lady thought about her answer and nodded. 'Yes. Well, certainly the majority of occasions.'

Evason turned to face Jamieson: 'It seems that Mr Wilkins had company when he made his monthly visits to the bank.' Jamieson's interest was re-ignited: 'Do we know who?' he asked, moving his gaze from Evason to Sandra Bundy.

Sandra Bundy shook her head; 'It was a man, but he never came up to the till with Mr Wilkins. He always stood over by the far wall waiting.' Jamieson was a firm believer in a picture painting a thousand words. He stood up again: 'Please show me', he said, raising his right arm in invitation for Sandra Bundy to step outside the office and show him exactly what she meant.

They stood at the far end of the banking hall. Jamieson stood next to Sandra Bundy, and Forage and Evason stood behind them. They were looking back down the length of the hall with the entrance immediately in front of them, about forty metres away. To their right were the till positions.

'Which is your till?' Jamieson asked.

Sandra Bundy indicated the end till nearest to them. A sign above the position said, 'Enquiries' differentiated it from the other tills, which Jamieson presumed were purely for transactional banking business. There were still only a handful of people using the bank, one of whom gave them an uninterested glance before returning to their business of waiting in the queue. 'Can you and Mr Forage go to the far end of the hall and come in as if you are Mr Wilkins and the other person? You be Mr Wilkins, and Mr Forage can be the other person. Show Mr Forage exactly where he needs to stand, and then you continue as if you are going through with the usual transaction. Can you do that for me, please?' Sandra Bundy looked confused but eager to please. She and Derek Forage walked the length of the banking hall and out through the double doors at the end. They re-appeared seconds later. As soon as they were through the doors, Sandra Bundy indicated that Derek Forage should split away from her and stand in the corner.

He did so whilst she continued up the banking hall and to the enquiries till. Forage was thirty-five metres away, and the lights were high up on the ceiling, giving off a dim glow. Jamieson knew it would be tough for anyone to give a good description, let alone a successful identification. Sandra Bundy was looking over at him expectantly. 'How long did you say Mr Wilkins would be at the till?' he asked. 'Five minutes absolute maximum,' came the reply.

'And did you ever have cause to speak to or even look at the other person for any length of time? Would you recognise him if you saw him again?' Sandra Bundy shook her head; 'No,' she said. 'He always stayed down that end of the banking hall. I always thought that it might be Mr Wilkins' son. He looked about the right age.'

Jamieson nodded. He turned to Evason: 'Can you take down a description, anyway? It won't be much use, but we should have something on file.' Evason took Sandra Bundy back into the interview room.

Jamieson remained outside, looking around for inspiration. Something caught his eye. He spun round, looking for the Forage. Suddenly remembering that the fat man was still standing in the far corner of the banking hall playing the part of the mystery man. He strode purposefully down the banking hall towards Forage. Forage saw him coming and walked up to meet him.

When Jamieson reached him, he turned and pointed up towards the opposite corner of the banking hall to where they were standing. Above the enquiries counter was an ancient CCTV camera facing out into the banking hall.

'Tell me,' said Jamieson.'Does that thing work?'

Forage smiled: 'It's pretty old, but it's still in good working order.'

Jamieson moved into the corner where Sandra Bundy said the mystery man stood. He looked up at the camera. It appeared to be positioned to take the whole area, including where Jamieson was standing. Forage confirmed that this indeed was what the intention was.

'That one covers the entrance and the banking hall plus all the tills.' He twisted round and pointed above their heads. 'And that one,' he continued. 'covers the far end of the banking hall and again a different angle of the tills.'

'What's the configuration?' asked Jamieson.

Forage thought for a moment, then replied, he could see where Jamieson was coming from, 'During business hours, that's eight-thirty to six these days, allowing for early starters and cleaners after we close, one static shot every thirty seconds. Outside of that, it uses a motion sensor. So if we're raided, and a cashier hits the panic button, it goes on continuously.'

Jamieson rubbed his chin. 'How often are the films changed?'

Forage replied: 'Close of business on the last working day of every month' and pre-empting Jamieson's next question, 'They get sent to the contracting company. They never get developed unless the contractors are specifically asked to. Films are wiped and reused again after three years. As we've already established, this is pretty old technology here. Everything is done on disc, so much quicker and easier these days.' 'So if we were to ask for the static shots, specifically from that camera.' Jamieson pointed to the one above the enquiries counter '...on the first Monday of each month between, say, eleven forty and eleven fifty for the last three years 'In theory' said Forage 'they should be available.' 'How long?' asked Jamieson.

Forage looked doubtful.

'Between you and me', said Jamieson. 'This is a murder enquiry. Someone bashed Brian Wilkins on the head last week, and we need to find out as much as we can about our mystery man as quickly as possible' He knew he was over dramatic but fancied that Forage, who he had surprisingly grown to quite like, would be impressed by some involvement in a murder case.

He was right.

Forage put on a serious face: 'In that case', he said, 'I'll pull some strings and get it pushed through as urgent.' The thought of the fat man pulling and pushing almost made Jamieson's face crack into a grin, but he held it together. 'Here's my card', he said. 'Let me know as soon as possible' and added rather naughtily. 'Brian Wilkins is depending on you!'

CHAPTER TWENTY-FOUR

Mohammed Razza was in his mid-fifties and initially seemed slightly reticent in opening up to Stone and Johnson. Stone took the initiative. He had dealt with members of the Asian community previously and thought he knew what made them tick. 'Mr Razza,' he began. 'We're very grateful that you've proved so willing to help us with this situation. Now I just want to reiterate that we have no interest in any aspect of your business except for the rental of this car by Jason Maddox between the 9th and 16th just over a week ago. So rest assured we won't be looking at anything over and above that.' He flashed his best-winning smile.

Mr Razza observed him a little apprehensively. Johnson stood a little behind Stone next to a local forensics officer, who Stone had rustled up on the journey down.

The vehicle itself was a nondescript car — white and seven years old — there was no in-car stereo system, just a gap in the dashboard with several wires poking out — the registration and description matched the one that the fastidious Mr Allsop had provided them with — the car smelt of previous renters' cigarettes and sweat.

Mr Razza had already told them that the hydraulic jack handle was missing. Johnson noted the model number and used Mr Razza's ancient computer to locate the nearest stockist. They would need a comparable handle for the pathologist to treat to ascertain whether or not it was the likely murder weapon.

Stone turned to the forensics officer. 'Do what you can with it', he said, pointing to the car.

The officer nodded. 'The best I can do for now is to collect up whatever fibres that might be there, but without anything from the suspect, I can't put him in the car.' Stone nodded. 'I understand that, but just do your best, yeah?' He turned back to Mr Razza. 'Now, Mr Razza, I understand you took a copy of Mr Maddox's passport. Do you think I could have a look, please?'

Mr Razza crossed the yard to the small portable office in the corner. Stone

followed but remained outside of the small office. Johnson was already in there using the computer, and there wasn't room inside for a third person in the cramped area. Mr Razza went over to a filing cabinet in the corner and rooted around. Stone looked at the yard filled with cars of all makes and models, colours and ages. He smiled to himself. There was definitely a market for this. Not everyone could afford the more expensive, newer, better-appointed cars the nationals provided. From what he could see, all the vehicles were taxed and probably had up-to-date MoT certificates. Razza probably let some of these out at thirty quid a day, cash in hand, no questions asked. He made a living, and someone got a car for the day — everyone was happy. Well, except the taxman, that is.

Johnson appeared: 'Right', he said, 'an auto parts supplier round the corner has one in stock, same make and model. I'll go and get it now. It'll only take ten minutes.' Stone nodded. Johnson set off and suddenly turned halfway across the yard. 'How do I pay for it?' he asked.

Stone smiled.' You're a detective now,' he said.' You'll work something out.' Johnson gave him a withering look and left the yard. Minutes later, Stone heard the car fire up and ease away.

Mr Razza appeared in the office doorway with a buff-coloured file in his hand. He held it up. 'It's this,' he said and returned to the office. Stone followed him. The file was on the cluttered desk when he got into the office. He pulled a chair out, sat down, and opened the file. There wasn't much in there.

There was an imprint of a credit card in the name of Jason D Mannix with the amount left blank. There was, what appeared to be, a signed rental agreement cobbled together from other rental contracts that Mr Razza had come across during his lifetime and a catch-all insurance document that Stone suspected didn't offer the renter very much protection.

Finally, there was a copy of Mannix's passport. Stone studied it closely. As he suspected, it was an American passport. The photograph showed a fresh-faced blond boy who looked as American as an apple pie. Full name, Jason David Mannix, date of birth, third September nineteen eighty-one, place of birth, Carroll, Fairford County, Ohio, distinguishing marks, tattoo right biceps.

Stone flicked through the pages of the passport that Razza had copied. It seemed that this was the first time the passport had been used to travel. The only stamp on the visa page was that of immigration at Heathrow Airport. Stone turned to Mr Razza and pointed at the passport photograph. 'Would you recognise him again?' he asked.

Razza nodded. 'I think so,' he replied.

'Okay,' said Stone. 'I need to make copies of these documents. Can I use your copier, please?'

Razza looked at him. Stone was unsure whether he had understood the question, but finally, Razza indicated the machine in the corner of the room. It made the computer look like cutting-edge technology. By the time Stone had made copies of the quality he wanted, Johnson had returned. 'Get it?' Stone asked. Johnson nodded. 'Cost me twenty quid,' he grumbled. Stone grinned.

'That's about all we need here,' said Stone. So let's leave the forensics guy here and head back to the station. See what the others have found out today.'

They left their business cards with both Mr Razza, who looked relieved that they were going, and the local forensics officer, who grumbled something about a 'fishing exercise' and 'being too busy for this'.

In the car on the journey back, Stone opened the box containing the new hydraulic jack that Johnson had just bought. He fished out the jack handle and stripped it of the protective bubble wrap. The handle was a nice fit in the palm of his hand and had sufficient weight behind it to act as a serious weapon. He looked across at Johnson, who was driving. 'I think we've got ourselves a contender for a murder weapon,' he said.

Johnson nodded. It was pleasing for him to start to see the case, making some progress at last. He had initially been disappointed that nothing had really happened, but now he felt there were doors opening, albeit not very wide.

Ile said: 'I've been thinking about what the boss said this morning, you know about why someone would fly across the Atlantic to bash someone's head in and then fly back.' It was Stone's turn to nod this time.

Johnson continued: 'I can't answer that. I mean, I can't imagine any circumstances why someone would do that. From what you say about the passport, it almost looks as though this is the first time this guy has ever left the United States and to do what, come here and kill someone.'

Stone smiled the smile of an experienced policeman. 'If he is our man, which is still a big if, then there will be some connection between him and the victim. We can't see it now, but it will come if we keep doing the right things. We'll get there; I'm sure of that.'

They drove for the next fifteen minutes in silence. Then, finally, Johnson spoke: 'I've had a thought. The landlord of the pub said that there was someone with an accent in a couple of nights before Wallace was murdered. I reckon that was Mannix. What do you think?'

'There you are,' said Stone.'Keep doing the right things, and we'll get there. We'll stop off on the way back and show him the passport photograph. See if he recognises him. If he does, that's another piece of the jigsaw in place. It's like I say, keep doing the right things, and we'll get there.'

CHAPTER TWENTY-FIVE

Jamieson took over the driving duties back to the station, allowing Evason to put her notes in discernible order. However, the fact that he spoke to her non-stop throughout the journey made it almost impossible for her to concentrate and, therefore, unable to complete the task, a detail lost entirely on Jamieson.

Evason noted that he seemed more alive since they had uncovered the presence of a mystery man. It was like his senses had been re-awoken, and he suddenly had an interest in the case again. 'It'll be interesting to find out if this man has any bearing on the case. I mean, it could all just be a red herring.' Evason nodded. 'Perhaps', she said, then added, 'but I don't think so.'

'Go on,' said Jamieson, momentarily taking his eyes off the road to look at Evason.

'Well,' she continued, 'from what the people at the bank say, this individual seemed to take a lot of care not to get himself noticed. You know, hanging back, almost hiding in the corner. It was as if he wanted to make sure that Wallace was doing what he was supposed to be doing but at the same time didn't want to get too involved.' 'It's too late for that,' said Jamieson.' he is now officially involved — even if it's just for us to find out who he is and then eliminate him from the case. What was Sandra Bundy's description like?' Evason flicked her notebook; 'Not good. Medium height, average build, average length hair, smartly dressed.'

Jamieson grinned. 'So we're down to four million suspects then.'

Evason raised her eyebrows and then asked, 'Do you think the static pictures from the CCTV will throw anything up?' 'It's an avenue', replied Jamieson. 'It all depends on the quality. Anyway, we've got the Forage on the case for us. Reckons we'll have them the day after next, so Thursday.'

'What do you make of it all?' asked Evason. 'I mean, first of all, Wallace sending the money, then the Marshalls keeping it and Darren Hughes seemingly ignoring it. It's all a bit crazy, isn't it?'

Jamieson thought before replying, 'I suppose it represents people's values. Wallace thinks that paying people off will go some way towards absolving what he's done, and the Marshalls seem to agree with him by their actions in accepting the money. We're not sure what the position with Hughes is yet, but after talking with his father, I wouldn't be at all surprised that no amount of money could buy his forgiveness.' 'We're there tonight', said Evason 'Six thirty. Important meeting, I think.' In his head, Jamieson agreed with her. It was the most important meeting in this case yet. If anyone had a motive, it was Darren Hughes — according to his Father, his was a family ruined by the actions of one man — and that man had been found dead, murdered, not more than a week ago. Jamieson also wondered who the man in the bank could be and what motives he had for accompanying Wallace to the same bank for the past fifteen years.

And try as he might not to make a snap judgement, he found the name of William Mitchell coming more and more into his thoughts. A man so damaged by the events of the original case that he had to undergo counselling and yet a man who had risen above this setback to reach a senior rank in the Met but also a man who, as of yet, had been unwilling, or unable, to return his telephone calls.

Jamieson's mobile rang. It was sitting in the hands-free cradle attached to the dashboard. He leant forward to push the 'answer' and 'speaker' buttons.

'Jamieson', he said.

'It's me', said Stone 'Rog and I are on our way back' Jamieson checked the clock on the car radio — eleven fifteen.

'You're on the speaker — Claire and I are on our way back, too' Knowing Stone's occasional preference for risque language,

Jamieson felt it was only fair that he let Stone know who was listening. Evason already found it hard to put up with Stone's social lapses.

'I won't swear then,' said Stone. Evason sat stony-faced. Jamieson suppressed a smile. Stone knew what buttons to press when it came to annoying his colleague. 'Tell me about your morning,' said Jamieson.

'Yeah, interesting,' replied Stone. 'If it comes to it, I don't think we'll have too much trouble putting Mannix in the car. And from Allsop's testimony, we know that the car was in the vicinity of where Wallace was found at around the time we think the attack took place. The handle of the jack is missing, probably at the bottom of a lake between Luton and Heathrow, and from what we've found out, yet to be confirmed by the Pathologist mind, there's every chance that the handle of the jack will prove to be a match for the wounds found on Wallace's head,' he paused.

Jamieson picked up the thread. 'The word 'circumstantial' springs to mind.'

'You can almost hear the CPS now', said Stone and then adopted what he believed was a posh voice. 'Yes, inspector, we know what you *think* happened; now, if you'd like to back that up with the faintest shred of hard evidence, we'd be more than happy to have a look.'

'There's also motive to consider,' said Jamieson. 'And we haven't got one yet.'

Jamieson left it to Evason to tell the others what had happened at the bank. Occasionally Stone's disembodied voice would pass comment, but overall the feeling was that the door had opened a little wider, and there was more to work with.

Jamieson toyed with asking Stone what he thought about William Mitchell but held off, making a mental note to have a word with him when it was not so public.

Stone signed off by saying that he and Johnson would stop off at the hospital to leave the jack handle at the Pathologist's office and that they expected to be back in the office by half-past two at the latest. Jamieson asked him what he saw as the next move from his side of the investigation.

'Well,' said Stone. 'We need to find out what we can about Jason Mannix, and I think an international call to his local police station in Carroll, Fairford County, Ohio, USA is as good a starting place as any.

CHAPTER TWENTY-SIX

As they made their way up the garden path, Jamieson noticed what he guessed was Darren.

Hughes' motorcycle up on its stand in the far corner of the front garden. His Father had mentioned that Darren's current bike was much more powerful than his first one, and he wasn't kidding. The machine was huge by any standards and must have taken a skilled and extremely competent rider to control it. From the registration plates, Jamieson could tell that the bike was over ten years old but had been well looked after and cared for by its owner.

Unlike their first visit to Upton Road, the front door was opened almost immediately this time. The woman who stood before them was around sixty and wore a green smock and trousers. Jamieson guessed that it was David Hughes' community nurse. She considered them closely without speaking. Jamieson held out his warrant card so that she could read it.

'We're here to see Darren Hughes,' he said, adding, 'we do have an appointment.'

She stepped back to allow them in. As they passed, she said, 'Upstairs, door facing you at the top' Jamieson noted the minimal usage of vocabulary and wondered whether she knew about the family history and had been briefed about their intended visit. Jamieson went up first; Evason followed. Glancing to her left, she could see David Hughes sitting in his armchair in the living room as she reached the fifth stair. He didn't appear to notice them, or perhaps, she thought, he had chosen not to. The curtains were drawn on the landing window, making it quite dark. As he stood at the top of the stairs, Jamieson noted that the door to his immediate right was the bathroom and the separate toilet next to that. The door straight ahead of him was Darren's room, and he could hear noises from a television coming from behind the closed door. Next to Darren's room was another room with the door shut, and on his left at the end of the landing, yet another closed door. Jamieson presumed that these last two doors were unused bedrooms. It couldn't be possible for David Hughes to get up the stairs, so his bedroom must be on the ground floor. Jamieson wondered where he bathed or went to the toilet.

Jamieson turned to Evason and gave her an enquiring look: 'Ready?' he said quietly. She nodded.

He stepped forward and used his knuckles to knock on the door. There was a slight pause, then the sound of someone moving from behind the closed door. Eventually, the door opened. A young-looking man with delicate features, unkempt black, curly hair down over the collar of the rugby shirt he was wearing and a scruffy but trendy half beard stood before them. Evason noticed that he had the darkest eyes she had ever seen.

He looked at them inquiringly.

Jamieson spoke: 'Mr Hughes, we're from the local CID. We'd like to talk to you about an incident that took place last week.'

The man in the rugby shirt grunted and went back into the room. Jamieson took that as an invitation to enter and did so. Evason followed close behind. By the time they had got into the room, the man was sitting in front of a computer screen in the far corner of a cramped room facing away from them. He was tapping at the keyboard. There was no obvious place to sit in the room, so Jamieson and Evason stood looking distinctly out of place in the small bedroom. Hughes moved his right hand, which settled on the computer mouse. The screen showed an image of a computer graphically produced soldier carrying a huge gun and numerous grenades. Jamieson assumed that Darren Hughes was operating the soldier's movements via the mouse.

Jamieson watched the screen closely. An image of a soldier wearing a Japanese flag tied around his forehead came into view.

The soldier under the control of Hughes' right index finger fired a burst of bullets, which almost cut the Japanese soldier in half. The words 'Die Motherfucker' came up on the screen.

The graphics were stunningly realistic, and Jamieson wondered whether this was what his fourteen-year-old son spent much of his time doing behind his closed bedroom door. He looked around the room — an unmade bed, clothes everywhere, posters on the wall, a collection of girly magazines on the table beside the bed — a typical teenager's bedroom — only Darren Hughes was in his mid-thirties.

Hughes continued with what he was doing, making no attempt to enter into dialogue with the police officers. The only sounds came from the computer, a rough American voice issuing commands and occasional bursts of machine gun fire.

Finally, Jamieson began talking: 'Darren, we wanted to speak to you about the death of a man named Brian Wilkins. He was formerly known as Lesley Wallace.' The man seemed not to hear the question or, more probably, chose to ignore it. Instead, he carried on playing the computer game.

Jamieson felt his face redden slightly with a mixture of annoyance and embarrassment. He was aware that the room was so small Evason was standing much closer than someone normally would. He felt crowded, and the situation put him under pressure. He tried again: 'Darren, I understand your reticence in this matter, but a man has died a violent death, and it's our job to investigate what happened to the best of our abilities.' Jamieson was pleased with his choice of phrase, nothing too controversial or presumptuous in respect of what the man in front of him had been through as a child. Then he blew it; 'I understand that you may have some issues,' he said. As soon as the words had left his lips, he knew that it had been the wrong thing to say. He sounded like an amateur psychiatrist.

Understand — that's right *for me- I understand* — not you — *me!*

You may have— not you have — you may have— I'll be the one to decide — remember me from the first two words of the sentence because *I'm* the one who understands — not you! *Some issues — people* who have some issues are talking about the dustmen waking them up too early on a Monday morning or the price of bloody petrol going up. *Some issues* barely cover systematic child rape over a sustained period.

'Jesus,' Jamieson thought to himself. 'an eight-word sentence, and the only inoffensive word you managed to utter was *'that.'*

Hughes was sitting in a swivel chair. He clicked on the mouse, and the image on the screen froze - presumably paused. He pushed against the desk and slowly set the swivel chair in motion. When he had completed a one hundred and eighty-degree turn and was facing in the direction of the two police officers, he used his foot against the carpeted floor to stop the momentum. He stared directly ahead of him at nothing in particular. He had his arms folded across his chest.

Jamieson and Evason waited.

Finally, Hughes looked up, directly at Jamieson, and spoke. He had a nice voice, and his answer was carefully considered: 'Issues, Inspector? First, may I ask, have you ever been sexually abused?'

Once again, Evason couldn't help but notice how dark his eyes were as they held Jamieson in their grip, demanding an answer from him.

Jamieson maintained eye contact and gave a small shake of his head. 'No,' he said quietly, 'No, I haven't.'

Hughes pursed his lips, nodded as much to himself as Jamieson, and gave the briefest of smiles. 'Sexual abuse is such a sanitised term, don't you think? Covers a multitude of sins, really. A kind of 'catch-all.' He unfolded his arms and made a quotations sign with the index and middle fingers of each hand term for the media who don't want to upset their audience too much. People like to think they know what the likes of Lesley Wallace do to defenceless young boys, but they don't really want the warts and all version, so the media use the term 'sexual abuse' His heavily ironic tone made him appear slightly more animated but only just. He was still very much in control.

He continued, 'do you know what Lesley Wallace did to me, Inspector?'

Jamieson had read the files. He had seen a statement given to the police by a very frightened nine-year-old boy who almost certainly did not understand what he had just been through. In front of him now was a grown man who was fully conversant with life and who, over the years, had had plenty of time to relive the horrors of a two-year period earlier in his life. He wasn't sure what his answer should be.

He merely said, 'I think so.'

Hughes screwed up his nose and made a face: 'It sounds to me as though you've had the sanitised version,' he said.

Jamieson didn't respond. Although he knew Evason was in the room, it felt like it was just him and Darren Hughes.

'Do you know,' said Hughes, 'for years and years, I never understood why Wallace singled me out. I mean, there were over a hundred boys in that home, so why me? Then a few years ago, I found out. The foster home had a colour-coded system. A red sticker meant 'normal', whatever that means, a blue sticker was 'at risk' or something like that anyway, right down to a yellow sticker, which meant 'vulnerable'. And the stickers were put on the front of the boys' individual files, which were not adequately policed. So ideal for a predator like Wallace, not only could he walk right in and access the files without anyone questioning him, but the school had very kindly highlighted the vulnerable boys for him. That's what the paedos like. Vulnerability. It gives them something to prey on, something to get their hooks into.'

He stopped and considered what he had just said as if hearing it for the first time. He continued.

'At first, Wallace was nice to me, took me under his wing, looked in on me during the night, that sort of thing. I suppose that was the grooming you hear so much about these days. Then, three days after my eighth birthday, it all changed. He woke me up in the night, told me to keep quiet and took me from my dorm to the night warder's room at the end of the corridor. I remember his breath smelt strange — I didn't know why.' Then, he paused and broke eye contact with Jamieson for the first time since he started speaking. His eyes appeared to be focussed on an indefinable point towards the corner of the room to his left. Evason knew from her training that he was in a state of recall, reliving memories in his mind's eye. 'He told me that he knew all about my mother. He called her a worthless c**t. I had no idea what that meant — I was eight years old — why should I have known? He said it was my fault that my Mother was the way she was. I hadn't loved her enough, and her heart had been broken, and she had to go away to a hospital for mad people. He said she would probably never come out, which was down to me.'

He stopped talking. He showed little emotion as he recounted these terrible events, and it seemed to Jamieson that he had managed to divorce himself from them over the years. Whilst he spoke in the first person, it was as if he was telling someone else's story. 'I remember I started crying. Wallace held me and calmed me down. He said that he knew the doctor in charge at the hospital and that he could speak to him to see if there was anything that could be done for my Mother. The doctor had told him that there were tablets and medicines that may make her better. He asked me if I'd like him to speak to the doctor, and through my tears, I said yes.'

Another pause whilst he gathered his recollections.

'He said I was a good boy. Then he said he could only speak to the doctor if I was nice to him. He said it was what my Mother would want, and did I think I could be nice to him and do the things he asked me to? I said yes. He said the most important thing was that everything had to be done in secret. If anyone ever found out about anything that was going on, the doctor would get in trouble, which would be the end of my Mother's chances of getting out of the hospital. He said she would die in there, and people in hospital die very quickly and in great pain.'

Jamieson, unperturbed by Hughes' speech, continued.

'You'll understand that we have procedures to follow. After all, a man has been murdered and given your past encounters with this individual, you would have a very good motive' Hughes looked back at Jamieson. 'Encounters is a nice word', he said, his voice flat.

Jamieson ignored him and continued. 'We need to know where you were last Tuesday, 8th of April, and can anyone corroborate your story?'

Hughes just continued to stare. The silence between the two men was palpable — it was as if Evason wasn't there. Finally, Hughes spun the swivel chair back round to face the desk. He leant forward and tugged a drawer open. As he did so, his shirt rode up, revealing a tattoo etched into the small of his back. Jamieson arched his neck for a better view but could not read it. Hughes snatched something from the drawer and spun back around. He held it out to Jamieson.

It was a passport. Jamieson took it without looking at it. His eyes held Hughes's eyes. Hughes spoke. 'If you look, you'll see my entry through immigration at Philadelphia Airport on the 6th of April and my departure some six days later.'

'You were in the States?' said Jamieson.

'That's where Philadelphia was last time I looked,' replied Hughes, without a trace of humour in his voice.

'Did you go with anyone?' asked Jamieson. Hughes shook his head. 'No, just me' 'What did you do there?'

'If you haven't worked it out yet, Inspector, I'm a geek. I'm a loner.' He jerked his thumb back over his left shoulder and indicated the frozen computer screen. 'I was at the World's biggest computer games convention, being wowed with the latest technology along with all the other weirdos and saddos for the best part of four days.' Jamieson nodded and considered his next question. 'Can anyone verify that at all?' Hughes grinned and shook his head. 'Do you know I think the answer to that is probably no? I probably spoke to a couple of hundred in a convention hall with over two thousand people when I was there. Was I able to establish a normal relationship with any of these people other than to talk about the latest fantasy game that had just been launched? No, I wasn't. But, Gee, let me think, now, what on earth could have happened in my past to make it impossible for me to establish normal relationships with people? Do you know I really can't think?' Sarcasm dripped from his voice.

Jamieson held his gaze for a further ten seconds, then flicked open the passport. Passing the pages through his fingers, he quickly established that it was Hughes' passport and that the immigration stamps on the dates Hughes had mentioned were in place. He passed the passport back to Evason, asking her to note all the relevant information. Then, he turned back to Hughes. 'Tell me something, Mr Hughes', he said. 'Have you, since the original case, nearly a quarter of a century ago, either seen, heard of the whereabouts of, been contacted by, or tried to make contact with Lesley Wallace?'

Hughes said nothing and shook his head. 'You're sure?'

Again Hughes said nothing but, this time, very deliberately nodded his head.

'If you had seen him and were absolutely positive that it was him, what would you have done?'

Hughes answered immediately, 'Nothing. I wouldn't have dirtied my fucking hands.'

On the way back downstairs, Jamieson motioned to Evason that he wanted to speak to David Hughes. The nurse was nowhere to be seen, so they made their way to the front room. David Hughes appeared to be dozing. Jamieson tapped gently on the door. The prematurely old man's eyes flickered open. It took him a while, but he eventually focussed on the two police officers. He recognised them instantly. 'Did you finish talking to my Darren?' he asked quietly.

Jamieson nodded. The room was in semidarkness with just a ghostly white glow from the television offering any light. The volume was turned right down. Jamieson positioned himself directly in front of David Hughes, crouching down, so the two men were level. He looked directly at him.

'Have you ever received any money from Lesley Wallace?' he asked gently. David Hughes closed his eyes. A tear slid down his right cheek. Then, with great effort, he lifted his misshapen right hand and pointed towards a small drawer tucked away in the sideboard directly behind Jamieson.

Jamieson looked over his shoulder and, still crouching, moved crab-like towards the drawer that Hughes had indicated. He reached his right hand out and grasped the drawer's handle when he was within touching distance. He looked back at David Hughes, who nodded almost imperceptibly. He tugged the drawer open and instantly recognised the same document that he had seen at the Marshall's yesterday. He dipped his hand in and brought out a handful of similar documents. He flicked through them. All bankers' cheques, all for five hundred pounds, all payable to D Hughes.

He took a deep breath and calculated that the worth of these was well in excess of one hundred thousand pounds.

'Darren doesn't know anything about them,' said David Hughes. Not a thing. I never wanted the bloody things — they just kept coming — blood money, I wanted no part of it.' Jamieson tucked all the bankers' cheques back into the drawer. They weren't evidence. They meant nothing to the investigation. They merely closed a puzzling chapter in the case. He pushed the drawer closed and stood up, indicating to Evason, standing in the doorway, that it was time to leave. As he passed David Hughes, he bent down and looked into his face. He reached out and took his hand. 'Darren doesn't need to know', He whispered, 'and he won't hear anything from us. I promise.'

CHAPTER TWENTY-SEVEN

Jamieson and Evason had gone to Upton Road in separate cars, so there was no usual debrief on the way back to the station. Jamieson considered moving into a local pub but decided against it. He felt somewhat battered by the meeting with Darren and felt the need to collect his thoughts, process them, and put them into some kind of logical order. He thought that perhaps Evason felt the same way.

Jamieson explained his thinking as they left the house and walked towards the cars.

Evason was non-committal either way. She understood Jamieson's reasons for not wanting a debrief until the morning but, at the same time, was a great believer in striking whilst the iron was hot, and perhaps the way to deal with the interview they'd just had was to meet it head-on. Jamieson stuck to his guns and made his position very clear. They would meet tomorrow morning before the others had arrived at the office and talk through the major points of the interview, having had a night to get things straight in their minds. After that, he had a press conference to deal with.

As he reached his car, Jamieson checked his watch — eight o'clock, another hour before he got home, and he was putting it crudely, knackered. He wished Evason a good night and waited until she had reached her car, parked some thirty yards further along the street, and had got herself settled before he got in his own car.

He belted up and selected some 'thinking music' from the limited collection of CDs he kept in the car's glove compartment, slipped the disc in, and adjusted the volume. Loud enough to bring him back to reality. And the reality was that people like

Lesley Wallace were few and far between; what he had just heard was uncommon, it was not an everyday occurrence, and an essential part of his job was to isolate these individual cases as precisely that, out of the ordinary events that happened. It was down to him to bring them to a conclusion, to find the people who were responsible and to the best of his ability to ensure they could not do these things again in the future.

He drove home, half listening to the music and half thinking about what direction the case would move in from here.

Moving in the opposite direction, Claire Evason was listening to her car radio. It was a current affairs programme, with Members of Parliament making cases for tightening the knife laws and opponents putting forward their own ideas. It was entertaining and interesting, and Evason easily lost herself in the debate. So much so that it took some moments before she realised that her mobile phone was ringing. She fumbled for the earpiece that came as standard with that particular make of phone and finally got the connector into the socket on the phone and one earpiece into her left ear, all whilst driving along a busy street — very impressively handled but highly illegal — before hearing the connection and almost shouting 'Hello.' 'It's me,' came the voice from the other end of the line. 'Is everything okay?' 'Yep, hold on a minute, though', said Evason. She turned the car radio off, pushed the free earpiece into her right ear, and regathered her composure. 'That's better,' she said.

'Good,' came the reply.'Busy day?'

Evason thought about the interviews in the bank this morning, which now seemed like an age ago, and the one they'd just had at the Hughes' house in Upton Road. 'Yeah,' she said flatly, 'busy day.'

'How's the case going?'

'Definitely in the right direction,' said Evason.' There's been some, urn, interesting developments, shall we say?'

'Oh, tell me more.'

Evason didn't like this and said so. No, when we started all...' she searched for the right word and settled on 'this, I made it very clear that I wouldn't act as your mole in any case, and I won't. If you want to know how the case is positioned, you need to speak to the officer in charge, just as you would in any other case.'

'Ah, DI Jamieson, how's he doing?'

Evason ignored the question and only half-jokingly threatened to cut the caller off. After that, the conversation adopted a more cordial tone, and Evason's general nature lifted. The rest of the call, about nothing in particular, continued for most of the remainder of her journey home and ended with a planned meeting at the weekend. A good end to a tough day.

Across town, Sandy Stone sat at the bar of his local pub. He picked up the glass in front of him and drained the remainder of the fiery brown liquid into his mouth. It burned on the way down and not in a pleasant manner. Stone winced and signalled to the barman that he should refill the glass.

He did so, and Stone sorted through a collection of coins in front of him on top of the bar, pushing the right combination towards the barman to cover the cost of the drink. He, too, had had a long day, but not nearly as satisfying as Evason's.

This morning's meeting with Razza went well but only confirmed the few things they already knew. The forensics officer had called him in the late afternoon, saying that he had collected and bagged up what he could, but without any trace evidence from the suspect, there wasn't much more he could do. Stone thanked him and said he'd be in touch.

On the way back to the station, he and Johnson had dropped in at the hospital and had been fortunate enough to find Doctor Jenner on a break. She looked at the jack handle, referred to her original autopsy, and confirmed her initial thoughts were that this was probably the same make and model as the murder weapon. Stone liked her directness. Many pathologists would have to run countless tests before giving such an opinion. To find one willing to offer up an opinion made a refreshing change. She said she would confirm in the next day or so. Stone thanked her for her help. Johnson had smiled at her aria sne naa smifea pack.

The next stop was at the Happy Farmer Pub. As soon as the barman with the photographic memory saw the copy of Mannix's passport picture, he confirmed that it was the same man that had been in the pub a few nights before Brian Wilkins had been murdered. They stayed at the pub and had a drink and a sandwich before returning to the station. It was very much as Stone had described to Jamieson — they could put Mannix in the car and, now, at the pub, and they could put the car as near to the crime scene as damn it, and they could put the handle of the car jack as the murder weapon — but they couldn't link Mannix to the deceased. That was the key.

Finally, when they got back to the office, they had gone online to discover what they could about Carroll, Fairfield County, Ohio, Jason Mannix's hometown, and more specifically, who they needed to speak to in the police department there. They found out that, according to a census conducted in 2000, the town of Carroll had 488, mainly white, residents. The average age was thirty-four, and the average household income was Forty thousand, two hundred and twenty-one dollars. The most famous resident of Carroll was James Jackson Jeffries, aka *the Boilermaker,* a heavyweight boxer who held the title of World Champion from June 1899 to May 1905, when he retired undefeated.

Johnson then showed Stone how Google Earth worked, and they managed to locate and zoom in on Mannix's home address. It was a building set apart from the other buildings in the village, probably some quarter of a mile or so down the road. Stone was amazed to be able to see what appeared to be a dog in the back garden of the property. Next, they concentrated on finding out what they could about the local police department. Johnson found a contact number. By now, it was four o'clock in England, which meant it was around eleven in the morning in Ohio.

Stone dialled the number. After four rings, the call was answered. Stone asked if he could speak to one of the detectives. The woman at the other end of the line sounded amused. She explained that there was one full-time policeman and two part-time officers at the station. Apart from that, there was only herself as general dogsbody who answered the phones and saw anyone who walked into the station off the street, kept the station clean and, most importantly, the coffee pot full and fresh. Stone explained who he was, but not what he wanted. He asked the name of the senior officer.

'Oh, that's Officer Harry Fenton,' said the voice. Stone asked if he could speak to Officer Fenton.

'He's not here right now. I don't expect to see much of him today. He'll be in tomorrow morning from nine o'clock,' Stone asked if Fenton could keep himself free at nine-fifteen, and Stone would call again then. 'I'm sure that would be fine.' Stone thanked her for her time and said he would call again tomorrow.

He picked up the glass of scotch. It was his third plus the pint he had had at lunch with Johnson. If he was stopped and breathalysed on the way home, he would be over the limit and in a whole heap of trouble. He considered the situation, opened his mouth and tipped the contents of the glass in and swallowed. It was only five minutes from home, and if he was stopped, he would flash his warrant card - that always worked.

Jamieson finally arrived home just after nine, feeling drained from the day's activities. As he entered the front door, he called out. 'It's me' and got an immediate response from Lucy upstairs. 'I'm in the bath. There's a salad in the fridge for your dinner.'

Jamieson dropped his briefcase on the floor in the hall and slipped on his shoes and jacket off. Then, as he walked into the kitchen, he loosened his tie, filled the kettle, and flicked the switch to 'on.'

He went to the fridge and opened the door. He found the salad on a plate covered with cling film to keep it fresh and lifted it out. As he did, he saw an already opened bottle of white wine.

He thought for a brief moment and took that out of the fridge, too. He flicked the switch on the kettle to 'off'. On this occasion, a glass of wine wins over a mug of hot tea.

He grabbed a knife, fork, and wineglass on his way through the kitchen to the dining room. When he got there, he put everything on the table and started by pouring himself a healthy glass of wine. He plucked the cling film from the plate of salad and picked up the cutlery in readiness. Before he started, he looked around and found an old magazine which he put next to his plate. He read about ordinary everyday people as he ate and drank. He became so engrossed in the exploits of these people he didn't notice that Lucy had come into the room. Then, she spoke, and it made him jump.

'Oh, I fancy a glass of wine,' she said, moving across to him and kissing him on the forehead. 'How was your day?' He knew that she didn't expect an answer. In fact, she had started reading one of the stories in the magazine over his shoulder. She was wearing a big, fluffy white bathrobe and had her hair tied up to stop it from getting wet. When she had finished reading, she tutted 'Incredible', she said and yawned. 'Do you know what? I think I'll take that glass of wine up to bed.' She moved towards the door to the kitchen. She turned to him.'You coming?' she asked.

He glanced up, distracted. 'Urn, do you know I think I'll sit in front of the television for a while, wind down a bit?' He went back to the magazine on the table in front of him.

'You sure?' she asked. He looked up. She'd untied the bathrobe, and it hung open, revealing the swell of her breasts, her flat stomach and a dark flash of pubic hair. She looked at him with big, enquiring eyes. He had an immediate stirring. Christ, they'd been married for nearly twenty years, and all she had to do was flash a bit of flesh at him, and he always came running like a little lapdog. Sad old bastard that he was.

'I'll need a shower first,' he said. 'Don't you dare fall asleep.'

As Stone approached home, he could immediately tell no one was in. There wasn't a light on in the place. He parked the car and let himself in, flicking the light switch on as he passed.

He belched involuntarily, and the reflux burned in the middle of his chest. He lurched slightly. He hadn't drunk that much but hadn't eaten much. He had even left the majority of the sandwich that he had at the Happy Farmer earlier. He found his way into the dining room and opened the drinks cabinet, quickly finding the half-empty bottle of scotch. He moved into the kitchen and looked for and found a glass in one of the cupboards. He set it on the kitchen counter and twisted the top on the bottle of scotch. As he tipped the bottle to pour the drink, he noticed a piece of paper further along the counter. He stopped what he was doing and moved down the counter to read it. His lips moved as he read through the handwritten words. His jawline visibly hardened as he read it for the second time. He stopped and collected his thoughts, appearing outwardly quite calm. Then, suddenly and without any prior warning, he hurled the bottle he was still holding against the far wall of the kitchen. It shattered into a hundred pieces, showering the tiled floor. He spoke with real animosity: 'twenty-five years of my fucking life wasted, you bitch.'

CHAPTER TWENTY-EIGHT

Jamieson was woken by the alarm at five-thirty. He had enjoyed a good night's sleep and felt fully rested and relaxed. He looked at Lucy lying next to him in bed. She had initially stirred when the alarm first sounded, but after he had hit the snooze button, she had resettled. He hadn't realised it when he first got home, but the experience they had shared last night was just what he needed. Perhaps Lucy had known intuitively. She was always good at judging his moods when he was working on cases and maybe felt that he was in need of a release. Or maybe not. Maybe it was her who was in need of a release. Either way, he had bloody enjoyed himself. He got out of bed, reset the alarm for seven thirty, and went off and showered.

He was in the car on the way to work by six and had made good time, arriving in the station car park at twenty to seven. He walked down to the café where Johnson normally got breakfast from and grabbed two coffees and two bacon sandwiches. As nice as last night's salad was, it hadn't really filled him up, and as a result, he was now starving. He didn't know whether Evason would eat a bacon sandwich but couldn't really walk into a preplanned early morning meeting with one for himself and nothing for her. As it was, her eyes lit up when she saw what he had bought with him. 'Wow, a bacon sandwich! What do I owe you?' she asked, reaching for her purse. 'You don't know how good that smells after the last week or so of croissants.' Jamieson smiled and passed her the greasy paper bag containing the sandwich. He had never seen her this animated about anything in the past. Maybe it was bacon sandwiches that did it for her.

He put his hand up. 'Nothing,' he said. 'It's the least I could do getting you up at this ungodly hour in the morning.' He put one of the cups of coffee on her desk and moved around behind his own desk. He sorted himself out and then took his own bacon sandwich from the paper bag. She was right — it did smell glorious!

He took a mouthful and chewed, savouring the taste. Then, before he had swallowed, he said: 'Okay, Darren Hughes. What do we think?' Crumbs flew from his mouth. Evason finished her mouthful before replying. 'Definitely damaged goods,' she said, 'but then that's no surprise really, what with everything he's been through.' 'He's got the most reason to want to kill Lesley Wallace,' said Jamieson. Evason, who had taken another bite of her sandwich, nodded and held up two fingers: 'Two problems with that,' she said, and swallowed, 'One. He didn't know where Wallace was. And two, he's got a cast-iron alibi,' Jamieson thought about her answer. His half-eaten sandwich sat on the desk in front of him. Then, finally, he said, 'Yes, I suppose you're right' then, as an afterthought ', he couldn't have doctored his passport, could he? I mean, made up his own stamp with a Letraset, something like that.'

'Unlikely', said Evason,' it looked genuine enough to me. Anyway, I'll call British Airways this morning and make sure he was checked on and off both flights. Since nine eleven, the records these airlines keep are watertight. So if he was on those planes, they'd have it recorded in at least three places.' Jamieson raised his eyebrows.'How do you know he flew British Airways? I mean, why not one of the other carriers?'

Evason allowed herself a smug smile at the expense of her senior. 'There was a rucksack on his bed with a BA label tied around the handle. I even managed to see the flight number, so it'll be much easier.'

Jamieson allowed himself a smile.'Impressive, Miss Marple,' he said. 'I don't suppose he could have flown back into the UK, bashed Wallace and then flown back out to the States again. You know, a sort of double whammy of an alibi.'

Evason shrugged.' It's possible, I suppose, but it all feels a bit unlikely. Besides, he would have the immigration stamps in his passports for departure and re-entry. And all that activity in seven days would surely have rung some alarm bells on an airport security system somewhere.'

'Okay," said Jamieson. 'let's not completely discount it, but we'll assume for now that Hughes was in the States for the whole seven days. So it couldn't have been he who killed Wallace.

'Could he have got someone to do it for him? What about this American that Sandy keeps talking about? Is it possible that Hughes knew him?'

Jamieson nodded. 'Sandy will be doing some work around that today. See if we can't shed some more light on who the guy is and what he was doing in the UK.' He checked his watch. 'I must go. I'm due at this press conference,' he said. He swept up the remains of his breakfast and threw them into the waste bin. He shrugged his jacket on and picked up his briefcase.

'If Darren Hughes had found out where Lesley Wallace lived, do you think he would have done anything about it? I know he said he wouldn't have dirtied his hands, but I'm not so sure, all the things his family went through as a direct result of one man. Surely the temptation for revenge would have been too great.'

Jamieson moved to the door.

'Talking of revenge', said Evason. 'Did you see that tattoo on Hughes' back when he leant forward to get his passport?'

Jamieson turned back to face her. He pursed his lips. 'Saw it alright, but couldn't see make out it said.'

Evason frowned. 'No, it all happened very quickly. I think it said 'Revenge in everything' or 'Revenge is everywhere', something like that anyway.'

Jamieson thought hard. The phrase rang a bell, but he couldn't think why. He raised his eyebrows.' He's certainly a strange one, is Mr Hughes. I'll be back around lunchtime. Tell Sandy and Rog we'll have the usual meeting then. See you later.' And he turned and left.

Miriam from Public Relations was a beautiful woman, but to Jamieson, that was where the attraction ended. She had no sense of humour. She was efficient, a fantastic organiser and, no doubt, a very hard worker, but she didn't smile once. She told Jamieson what he could and couldn't say. She would be with him at the table, and if he were in any doubt, he should cover the microphone with his hand and refer to her for the appropriate answer. Jamieson just nodded but took little notice. He had dealt with journalists before and knew that any sign of weakness would be picked up on. He had absolutely no intention of asking Miriam from Public Relations how to answer any questions from hardened journalists.

In keeping with the Chief Constable's request, this was to be a low-key affair. The conference room being used was one of the hotel's smaller ones. At the front of the room, there was a table set out with two chairs behind it facing the audience. There was a nameplate on the table in front of one of the chairs which said 'Detective Inspector Alex Jamieson', along with a jug of water and two glasses. Behind the table was the usual Bedfordshire Police backdrop, which depicted a smiling policeman talking to two elderly people on a sunny afternoon with the tagline 'Bedfordshire Police Force — keeping it local'. Jamieson had never really understood that choice of phrase. The fact that he was currently dealing with a murder case where the culprit could conceivably be in the United States of America made it even more surreal. In front of the table were around twenty seats spread out for the visiting journalists. On each chair, there was a copy of the press release that had been circulated yesterday. In the corner, there were tea and coffee making facilities and a selection of pastries — the Chief Constable's Office liked to keep the media on their side as much as possible, and they knew the best way to a journalist's heart was through his stomach. Jamieson went outside to get some fresh air. Although this kind of thing didn't particularly worry him, he was prone to a few butterflies and defied anyone who stood up to speak in public to deny they had similar feelings.

At nine twenty-five, Miriam found him. There were two national papers, The Telegraph and The Mirror, Sky news and BBC Twenty Four and a smattering of local reporters from the press, radio and television — around fifteen people in all. At nine-thirty, he entered the conference room and sat behind the table. He introduced himself and thanked them for attending.

He had a pre-prepared statement in front of him but preferred not to read from it verbatim, choosing instead to put the events into his own words. He referred them to the press release and then began paraphrasing the case to date. 'On the morning of Wednesday 10th April, a local paper boy reported finding a body at around six thirty am on Peverall Road in Dunstable. The local police force reacted swiftly and attended the scene. The victim, a male in his seventies, was already dead. The Pathologist's report suggests that death took place between the hours of ten the previous evening, and two o'clock, that morning. The man had been bludgeoned over the head and face with a blunt implement which we have not yet been able to identify. House-to-house enquiries have been carried out, but as of yet, we have no concrete evidence as to exactly what happened.'

He paused for breath. 'The victim's name was Brian Wilkins. A bachelor who neighbours say very much kept himself to himself. He was known to drink locally at the Happy Farmer public house on three occasions each week. That would be Tuesday, Thursday and Saturday evenings. The day and the time of his death suggest that he was attacked whilst walking home from one of these regular evenings out.'

He picked up the jug of water on the table in front of him and poured a drink. He took a sip and continued. 'We are pursuing various lines of enquiry, but to date, nothing concrete has developed. Brian Wilkins had lived in the area for most of his life and was previously known as Lesley Wallace. We would ask anyone who might have any information in connection with this violent attack, no matter how trivial it may seem, to come forward and speak to the police. All information will be treated with the utmost confidence. Any questions, please?'

A journalist put his hand up. Jamieson pointed in his direction: 'Detective Inspector, is this Lesley Wallace, the infamous paedophile who disappeared from our streets some twenty-five years ago?'

Jamieson paused to buy some time before answering. One of the alterations he had insisted upon in the original press release was to confirm that Brian Wilkins was previously known as Lesley Wallace. He felt this was the right thing to do, to be open and transparent, not to leave the force open to future criticism that they may have held back relevant information from the press. It seemed that this journalist either remembered the name from the original case all those years ago or was a good researcher. Judging from his age, Jamieson felt that the former was probably more likely. He answered the question. 'Lesley Wallace helped the police with their enquiries into a gang involved with child abuse in the mid-eighties. He was never charged with any offences.'

'But he was a paedophile, wasn't he, Inspector?' pressed the journalist.

'He was never charged or convicted of any crime at all, as far as I'm aware,' replied Jamieson, deadpan.

'In your opinion, then. You must have an opinion, surely. And remember, you can't slander the dead, so what harm is there in offering up an opinion?'

'I work by fact of conviction....'

'Mr. Harris, Luton Tribune.' The man flashed a smile. His teeth were yellow and nicotine stained.

'Harris. We're talking about events from twenty-five years ago. I don't think I even have an opinion to share with you.'

But isn't it true, Inspector, that the Commanding Officer at the time, a DI Scott, Jack Scott, entered into a plea bargain with this man without being in full possession of all the facts? In fact, of all the men in the gang, Wallace could be described as the ring-leader and almost certainly the most dangerous, and yet he was the only one who escaped being jailed.'

Jamieson kept his patience, 'as I said, Mr Harris, Lesley Wallace was never convicted of anything.'

'What do the people of Bedfordshire think about having a paedophile living in their community for the last quarter of a century? I mean, they must have known what with the sex offenders' register and all that' Harris continued with the same line of questioning.

Jamieson remained calm. 'I've already covered that point on a couple of occasions, and I'm not going to go over old ground again. The fact of the matter is that Lesley Wallace was never convicted of any crime. Additionally, as you are probably all aware, the sex offenders' register was not introduced until the mid-nineties, so anyone convicted before that time did not have to sign the register by law.' Jamieson looked around the room. 'Now, Gentlemen, if there are no more questions, I have a murder to solve. Thank you for your time.' He started to gather his things up and then noticed as one last hand went up.

It was Harris of the Luton Tribune who had raised his hand. Jamieson acknowledged him with a smile. 'Just time for one last, quick question, Mr Harris?'

Harris stood: 'Is it true, Inspector, that this case has been badged by some of the officers in your police force as the murder that no one cares about? I mean, some old ponce has got what he deserved, right? That's all that has happened.'

There was a round of laughter in the room. Jamieson felt himself redden as he stood up to leave. It was ironic, really, because that was exactly what the case was, a murder that no one really cared about. What was so bloody annoying was the fact that someone had been careless enough to call it that in earshot of a journalist.

He left the conference room through the back door. Miriam was close behind him. Jamieson turned to her.'How the hell did he know that thing about this being the murder that no one cared about?' he demanded. Miriam looked affronted. 'Probably through someone at your station. It's not uncommon for reporters to hang around pubs frequented by police officers, many of whom are hardly discreet when they've had enough to drink.'

Jamieson calmed himself sufficiently to apologise.' You're right. I'm sorry.'

Miriam lifted her hand, palm out as if to say it's already been forgotten. Jamieson buried his face in his hands, slowly lifting his head, his face emerged between his fingers. 'When is the Luton Tribune published?' he asked, dreading the answer. 'Tomorrow', replied Miriam.

'I don't suppose there's any chance that Harris won't have written his piece in time?' asked Jamieson hopefully.

Miriam shook her head.'I'd say there's about a million to one chance he won't have done.'

'Let's hope for small miracles then,' said Jamieson.

CHAPTER TWENTY-NINE

Stone didn't get to work until gone ten. His arrival was greeted with a subtly raised eyebrow from Evason and a brief 'hi' from Johnson, who immediately re-buried his head in what he was doing, feeling slightly out of his depth with the fact that one of his superior officers had rolled up nearly two hours late stinking of last night's excesses. Stone had barely slept. After the bottle incident, he picked up the note and sat down in the living room. He read and reread Margaret's words repeatedly, trying to read something into them that just wasn't there.

There were plenty of well-chosen phrases. Margaret was an excellent letter writer, after all, and lots of truths about how they had been growing apart for the last ten years, which he had to acknowledge. But he'd always assumed that they'd get over it, that they'd move on, that they'd be together for the rest of their lives and now this. Although it felt completely out of the blue deep down, Stone knew it wasn't.

She'd met someone she believed could offer her things that Stone couldn't. Not tangible things, but things that she felt had got lost in their own relationship — love, respect — all the things that men take for granted are there but always seem to struggle to show. She'd moved in with a friend *and* would be in touch in the very near future. She appreciated that they had a lot to talk about but didn't feel ready at the moment. She asked him to respect her privacy, and she promised that she would be in touch very soon — she loved and respected him too much not to sit down with him face to face and talk things over.

His initial reaction was to call her mobile phone and demand to know what the hell she was doing and to get herself back home. It took all his willpower not to do that. Instead, he took his mobile out to the car and locked it in the boot. Out of sight, being out of mind. He came back into the living room via the kitchen, where he picked up a second bottle of scotch, which he sat swigging until the early hours. He finally drifted off to sleep at around four-thirty.

When he woke, it was gone eight. The empty bottle lay in his lap. His head thumped, and there was the sour taste of scotch in his mouth. He stood up gingerly and found his balance. Suddenly there was a surge in his stomach, and he was half running, half stumbling to the downstairs toilet. He made it just and emptied his stomach of the scotch that had been sitting in it for more than five hours. He needed to shower and eat to get some kind of normality back into his day.

First, he went upstairs, stripped off, and stood under a hot shower for the best part of twenty minutes. Gradually feeling started coming back to him and the news from the previous evening slipped back into his mind. He threw up again in the shower, watching the brown liquid slosh around his feet and down the plughole. He retched some more, but nothing came up. It hurt his chest. Convinced that he had now completely rid himself of alcohol, he stepped from the shower and dried himself off. His clothes from yesterday were creased from a night spent sleeping in an armchair, so he took a clean shirt, tie and suit from the wardrobe and got dressed. Before going downstairs, he cleaned his teeth for ten minutes and used mouthwash to rid himself of the taste of last evening. He was only partially successful.

He felt nauseous if he looked down, so he didn't. Instead, he kept his head upright. He closed the front door behind him and got into his car. It was nine o'clock in the morning. He knew he would be over the limit if he was stopped, but his plan was to go to the local cafe five minutes drive away and fill himself with a sizable cooked breakfast and at least two cups of coffee.

He drove there, ordered, and found a seat. For ten minutes, he sat looking at the mound of food in front of him, knowing that ultimately eating it would make him feel better but not being quite able to force the first mouthful down. Eventually, when he had worked his way through three-quarters of the food on the plate and had drunk two cups of coffee, he gave in and pushed the plate away. Finally, he felt more alive and ready to tackle the office.

He arrived at just after ten. Evason wasn't impressed. Perhaps she could still smell the alcohol on his breath, but at this point in time, the opinions of Claire Evason were one of the furthest things from his mind. So Johnson just kept his head down. Finally, at ten thirty, Johnson announced he was going on a coffee run down to Georgios Coffee Bar. Stone indicated that he would like another coffee and delved into his wallet, pulling out a ten-pound note and thrusting it towards Johnson. At first, Johnson ignored the offer, saying that he would buy them from the fund, but Stone insisted, and Johnson thought it better to take the money than to get into an argument.

Shortly after Johnson had left, Stone's mobile phone rang. He fished it out of his pocket. 'Stone', he said.

'Is that Detective Sergeant Stone?' asked the voice at the other end of the phone. 'Speaking,' said Stone.

'This is David Sargeant here; thanks a fucking bunch.' Stone's brain reeled as he tried to recall the name. He knew he had heard it recently but couldn't put it into context.

'Hello?' said Sargeant.

Stone put his hand to his forehead. 'Hello, yes, I'm still here.' He said into the phone. Think, Sandy, think. 'You came to see me up in Leicester last week. Do you remember?' Suddenly, an image of Sargeant's face filled Stone's mind. Yes, it was the visit that he and Johnson made last week. David Sargeant. He was one of the original gang who was put away on Wallace's testimony. They went to see him to eliminate him from the enquiry, and Stone had asked the local lads to go in to take a statement from Sargeant's wife to corroborate his story.

'Yes, Mr Sargeant, I remember. What can I do for you?' asked Stone.

Sargeant was animated. 'So much for your soft, soft approach in dealing with my wife. Your local goon squad went in like a bull in a china shop. Told her everything, said it was their 'duty'. Bollocks was it; their 'duty' was to take a simple statement from her as to what I did last Tuesday evening, not deliberately fuck up my marriage.' Even in his current state, Stone resisted the urge to tell the man to calm down. Better to let him vent his anger, and he would calm down automatically.

'She's left, taken the kids, says she doesn't think she can trust me around them. It's funny at five o'clock yesterday afternoon. She would have said I was the best Father in the world, then after your lot had been in, spreading their poison, she doesn't feel that I can be trusted. How does that work? This is for something that happened twenty-five years ago, and I'm still paying now. I've done my time, and according to the judicial system, I've paid my penalty, but it just doesn't work like that, does it?' Stone said nothing immediately. He did feel for Sargeant. When he first met him and assured him that the police wouldn't make his wife aware of his past, he had genuinely meant it. It did seem to Stone that Sargeant had shown regret for his actions, and what he said was true. Didn't our judicial system provide for people who had made mistakes to pay their debt to society and then return with the slate wiped clean? Stone finally responded, but even as the words left his mouth, he knew they sounded lame. His head pounded, and his mouth felt dry.

'Mr Sargeant, I promise you it was never my intention to cause a rift in your family. But, unfortunately, it seems that the officers sent to interview your wife have acted outside of their remit, and for that, I apologise.'

Sargeant's reply dripped with sarcasm and anger. 'Well, that's okay then, as long as you're sorry. I'll explain to my son why Mummy doesn't think it's a good idea for his dad to spend any time alone with him anymore. Fuck you, Stone; I hope you die of cancer.'

The line went dead.

Stone closed his eyes and pushed the knuckle of his thumb into the area between his eyebrows, alleviating some of the pressure he felt building up. The savagery of Sargeant's last words had taken him by surprise. He wondered how he would feel in the same situation. How he would act. After a while, he opened his eyes and exhaled long and slowly through his nose.

'Problems?' asked Evason.

He looked across at her. For a moment, he considered sharing everything that had happened over the last twelve hours with her but instead opted for a brief shake of his head and what he hoped was a wry smile. 'No more than the usual,' he replied. An hour later, Jamieson arrived back from the press conference. They could tell from his face that it hadn't gone well.

'Okay', said Jamieson, taking his jacket off and hanging it on the back of the nearest chair. 'Let's catch up on where we are. Claire, what have you got for us?'

Evason referred to her notebook. 'Well,' she said. 'I've confirmed with BA that Darren Hughes was on the outward and inward flights he claims to have been on. Additionally, they have no record of him being on any other flight with them, so if he did sneak back across the Atlantic to kill Wallace and then go back again, he didn't travel with Virgin. I've also put a call in with the Immigration department to see if he came back in with any other airline. They'll get back to me on that. I've also contacted the hotel where the convention took place, and they've confirmed that a Darren Hughes had a room booked for six consecutive nights covering the dates that Hughes told us about.'

Stone and Johnson looked confused. Jamieson realised they didn't know about the meeting with Darren Hughes yesterday evening. He recounted the episode, including the conversation with David Hughes.

Stone spoke, 'So, on the one hand, we've got Hughes who has a motive but says he didn't know where Wallace lived and has a cast-iron alibi, and on the other, we have an American kid, who we don't know from Adam, who has no motive but has the means, and we can put him in the immediate area around the time of the murder.' This time Johnson chipped in. 'Can we link Hughes and Mannix in any way?'

'Not at the moment,' said Jamieson.

'I've got a call into his Local Police Department,' said Stone, 'but because of the timing differences, I won't get to speak to them until around four this afternoon.' 'Okay', said Jamieson, then to Evason 'Any news from the bank about those stills?' Evason nodded. 'Yep. Definitely tomorrow, the company is copying all the images to disc, so it'll make it easier for us to view.'

Jamieson told them how the press conference had gone. He asked Johnson to pick up a copy of the Luton Tribune on his way into the office in the morning. He added, 'As usual, in these cases, any calls that we get in following whatever is published, get referred immediately to the PR team at the Chief Constable's Office.' Jamieson finished up. 'Okay, yesterday was a better day, and I, for one, feel we are nearer to a result with this one. So let's keep the good work going and see if we can't bottom this out before too long.' They all agreed and began to get back to what they were doing.

Jamieson turned to Stone. 'Sandy, a quick word in the back, please'. Stone followed Jamieson to the small office space at the rear of the main office. Jamieson moved around behind the desk and sat down. 'Close the door and have a seat,' he said.

Stone did as he was asked.

Jamieson spoke. 'When this thing first broke, and I asked you what you were doing the night Wallace got murdered, do you remember what you said?' Stone made a pretence of recalling the situation. 'We had friends round until the early hours', He said finally.

Jamieson looked him squarely in the face. 'I spoke to Margaret, Sandy. It's not how she tells it.'

A surge of anger passed through Stone. 'You phoned Margaret?' he was almost shouting.

Jamieson paused before answering, allowing Stone to calm down. 'You really didn't think that I would just accept what you told me without getting it verified, did you?' He said

'Come on, Sandy, I'm a cop, and cops have to do everything by the book these days, you know that. There's no such thing as a favour anymore.'

This time, Stone stayed silent.

Jamieson continued, 'she says that she was out with friends and stayed the night at one of their houses. She says she left your house at around seven and didn't see you again until the following evening.' Stone sat forward in his chair, head bowed, elbows resting on his knees, fingers locked in the space between. 'What's going on, Sandy?'

Stone rubbed his hand over his face. 'She's telling the truth,' he said.'I spent the evening alone. Well, with a bottle of scotch, to be precise.'

'Why did you lie?' asked Jamieson.

Stone closed his eyes and raised his head to the ceiling. 'I wanted to work the case,' he said.' I thought that if I couldn't give a sound enough alibi, you might consider my presence a conflict of interest and leave me off the case. That's all. I recognise I was being stupid, but I really thought I could add something to this particular case, what with all that went on before.'

Jamieson considered the reply. 'What do you think I should do now?' he asked. Stone shrugged. 'It's your call,' he answered.

'Damn right, it's my call,' said Jamieson.'You could have compromised the whole case by your thoughtlessness. The press is starting to rake up enough police shit on this thing already as it is. What would happen if they got hold of some more muck like this that they could print? 'Copper in phoney alibi headlines.'

A silence fell across the room. Then, finally, Jamieson spoke.' You're bloody lucky that the investigation has moved in the direction it has, Sandy. It's beginning to look a bit more cut and dried now, but if it hadn't had been and I'd found out you'd been giving out dodgy alibis, there would have been hell to pay because, believe me, Sandy, I would have had no option than to go to the Chief Constable to tell him what has happened. There is no room for sentiment in the force these days. Do the right thing, Sandy. Remember that for the future.' Stone raised his head and looked Jamieson in the eye. 'You're right, and I'm sorry. It won't happen again.'

Jamieson considered Stone long and hard before speaking again. 'See, it doesn't. Now go and get on with something that is going to get this case solved, for Christ's sake.' Stone didn't stand up immediately. 'What's wrong?' asked Jamieson.

Stone cleared his throat. 'Margaret has left me, Alex. I found out last night. I thought you should know.' It was the first time he had spoken these words, the first time he had heard them spoken aloud.

Jamieson nodded.'I'm sorry to hear that, Sandy,' he said.' Is there anything I can do?'

'No,' said Stone, 'Urn, just keep it under your hat at the moment, will you? No one else needs to know just yet. Perhaps in a couple of days' time, we could go and have a pint, and you can listen to my woes.'

Jamieson nodded. 'Of course,' he said. 'Do you need any time out?'

Stone shook his head. 'No, I want to keep busy for the time being, keep my mind off it.'

'Fine,' said Jamieson. 'you know where to find me.' Stone stood up and walked across to the door. He had opened it to leave when Jamieson remembered something. 'Sandy,' he said. 'Shut the door for a moment; there is one more thing.' Stone pushed the door shut.

Jamieson spoke. 'Does the name William Mitchell mean anything to you?'

Stone didn't need to think about his answer. 'Yes, he was one of the investigating officers on the original case. Same rank as I was, about the same age as well. It was his first major case, and he took it badly like I did. He also had counselling; from what I can remember, it went on for far longer than mine. Why are you asking?' Jamieson thought about his answer. 'As Senior Investigating Officer, I've been looking into the officers who worked the original case. As you're now aware, that included you amongst others. I'm confident I've managed to eliminate them all except William Mitchell.'

'Why Bill?' asked Stone. 'He's relatively senior now. He's a hostage negotiator with the Met.'

'It's not that I haven't been able to eliminate him,' replied Jamieson. 'I just haven't been able to speak to him to eliminate him. I've left various messages on his mobile and a couple on his landline since this case started and he's just not gotten back to me.

Admittedly, I've pushed it to the back burner a bit given the way the case is going, but it worries me that he's not returning my calls. I've made it clear that it is a murder investigation, so he should be in no doubt about the seriousness of the situation and yet, nothing.'

Stone nodded. 'You want me to do some digging?' He asked.

Jamieson nodded.'My instinct tells me that he's not got anything to do with the murder, but I have pencilled him in for the mystery man who has been going to the bank with Wallace. Don't ask me why. Perhaps it's because we've got a gap there, and there's no one obvious to fill it.'

Stone resisted his natural urge to tell Jamieson that he thought he was barking up the wrong tree. Instead, he just nodded and said, 'I'll see what I can find out' before turning and leaving the room.

As the door shut behind Stone, Jamieson watched him walk back out into the main body of the office. Unsurprisingly, the usual spring in his step was missing, but Jamieson had complete confidence in his man. Stone was a policeman first and everything else second.

CHAPTER THIRTY

Jamieson woke up but didn't immediately open his eyes. Thoughts rushed around inside his head, and finally, the thing that had been nagging away at him fell into place. Only then did he open his eyes, now fully awake. It was still dark outside, and he checked the time on the bedside alarm clock. It was four forty-two.

He pushed the bedcovers back off of himself and swung his legs out of bed at the same time as he sat up. He waited the recommended five seconds to allow the blood flow to get going. His feet found his slippers on the floor at the side of his bed. Finally, he stood up and grabbed his dressing gown, which had been hanging on a hook behind the bedroom door. He pulled it on and fastened the cord around his middle. Lucy remained fast asleep in the bed he had just vacated.

He made his way downstairs, through the hallway, into the kitchen and beyond into the utility room. He flicked the light switch as he entered. He pulled open a cabinet drawer and shuffled through inside until he found what he was looking for. It was a small keyring torch. He turned the light switch off and tested the torch. A small beam of light hit the ceiling. He turned it off again, pushed the drawer shut, went back through the kitchen and hallway, and started back up the stairs again. When he got to Justin's room, he stood with his ear to the door, which was slightly ajar. He could just make out his son's gentle breathing. He pushed the door open and entered. He walked across the floor, taking care not to trip over anything that might be left lying around until he reached the approximate place where he needed to be. He switched on the torch and pointed it at a spot on the wall. His positional instinct was good. The beam immediately picked out the eyes of the girl on the poster that he had first noticed when he was in Justin's room last week. He moved it slowly downwards, past the breasts that were impossibly large when compared proportionally with the far too slender waist, past the gun being offered out of the poster itself, apparently to the observer, down to the very foot where the ever-weakening beam picked out the legend 'Revenge is Everything.'

Not 'Revenge in Everything' or 'Revenge is Everywhere'. Evason was so nearly right about what she saw tattooed in ink on the small of Darren Hughes' back as his shirt rode up when he leant forward to reach his passport. Nearly right, but not quite.

Evason's phrases had sat in Jamieson's mind for the last forty-eight hours, pushing their way to the fore every so often, challenging him to think when and where those words or words like those had crossed his mind before. Then suddenly, lying half awake and half asleep, it had come to him at four-thirty in the morning. On the wall in a room of his very own home.

Justin stirred, and before Jamieson had time to dim the torch, the boy was awake and talking the slurry, nonsensical language of the recently woken.

Jamieson shushed him. 'Jus, it's okay, it's me, Dad'

Justin took a few seconds longer to come fully back to his senses. He sat up and reached over to turn the bedside lamp on. He shielded his eyes against the light with his hand and squinted in Jamieson's direction. 'Dad, what are you doing in my room?' Suddenly it struck Jamieson just how strange this would sound, but he had found it impossible to wait until morning. 'Jus, that poster', he pointed to the girl on the wall 'what is that all about?'

Justin resisted the obvious response about it being the middle of the night and simply gave his dad a straight answer. 'Erm... that's Revenge Trade. It's an online gaming site.'

'Explain,' said Jamieson.

'Well,' said Justin. 'it's a computer game where you play opponents over the Internet.' He thought for a moment. 'In the old days, if you were playing *Monopoly*, say, then all the players would need to be sitting around a table for the game to work. It's not like that now. Because of the Internet, I could be playing a real-time game with someone on the other side of the world.'

'So I could be playing *Monopoly* against someone in, say, Australia?' asked Jamieson. Justin nodded. 'As long as you both have access to the Internet. If there were four of you playing, one could be in Australia, one in Japan, one in Brazil and you, sitting here in the UK — all in real-time — all as if you were sitting around a table in your living room throwing dice and moving counters like the old days.'

Jamieson took this all in. He pursed his lips and looked at Justin '...and this...*Revenge Trade?*' he asked.

Justin rubbed his hand across his face. 'Just one of many millions of games people play,' he said, stifling a yawn.

'But why this one?' asked Jamieson. 'I mean, why do you have the poster on your wall, for example?'

Justin shrugged. 'I like the imagery, I suppose, is all.'

'How do you play it?'

'What *Revenge Trade?*' said Justin. He pulled a face. 'I've only looked at the website itself a couple of times. I think the idea is that you've got a problem that you can't solve, and someone else has a problem that they can't solve but put the two problems together, and there may just be a way of solving both.'

'...and this actually works?' asked Jamieson.

'Dad,' said Justin, 'You're blurring reality with gameplay here. On the whole, it's a made-up world for bored kids sitting at their computers to get involved in. Okay, there may be some really, really geeky kids who swap homework assignments, you know, Jimmy in New York can't do algebra but is very good at biology looking for someone who is good at algebra but hopeless at biology, and he'll 'trade' by doing their biology assignment for his algebra assignment. Quid pro quo, that kind of thing.' Jamieson nodded that he understood, and Justin continued. '...but mainly, it's make-believe. You know, kids and even adults will create their own kind of cyber-world and invent personas and situations they find themselves faced with. If they put themselves in danger, they can ask the other online players for help or suggestions on how they can get out of the problem. Then the player chooses one of the options that they've been given, and the game decides the outcome and everyone moves on to the next stage. There's no real beginning or ending to the game — it just goes on and on until the player opts out.'

'So it's just a game?' said Jamieson. 'Nothing more sinister. What's the point?'

Justin shrugged again. 'What's the point of *Monopoly?* It passes the time enjoyably, I guess.'

Jamieson nodded thoughtfully. 'Dad?' said Justin. Jamieson stirred from his thoughts. 'Yes, Jus' 'Can I go back to sleep now? I'm tired.'

Jamieson leaned over and kissed the boy on his forehead. 'Yes, sorry, son,' he whispered, turned the bedside light out and left the room, pulling the door closed gently behind him.

CHAPTER THIRTY-ONE

After that, sleep was out of the question for Jamieson. Instead, he went downstairs, where he boiled the kettle to make himself a cup of hot tea. He was animated. He couldn't sit, but equally, he couldn't stand either. He felt that *the Revenge Trade* would provide the link they had been looking for between Hughes and Mannix. He was confident that this would tie the two men together. What was it that Stone had said? '*On one hand, we've got Hughes, who has a motive but says he didn't know where Wallace lived and has a cast-iron alibi, and on the other, we have an American kid, who we don't know from Adam, who has no motive but has the means, and we can put him in the immediate area around the time of the murder.*' Now Jamieson hoped they were on the verge of proving a link and were one step closer to finding out exactly what happened.

At five fifteen, Jamieson could stand it no longer. He found his mobile phone, which he had left on charge in the living room. He scrolled down the menu to 'text' and, in his clumsy, technophobic manner, typed in 'Possible big development in case — I'll be in the office from seven onwards' then found the numbers for Stone, Evason and Johnson and sent the text message to each of them before going off to shower in the downstairs bathroom so as not to wake anyone in the house.

By the time he returned to his phone some fifteen minutes later, showered and dressed for a day's work, three messages were waiting on his phone. The first was from Evason and simply said 'See you then', the second from Johnson which said 'Seven it is' and the last and most intriguing from Stone which said 'ditto — see you there' Jamieson scribbled a note for Lucy and Justin — 'Couldn't sleep, gone to work — see you later — Jus, sorry for waking you up'- grabbed his briefcase and was out of the house and in his car. It was five forty-five.

Within fifty minutes, he had parked up and was pushing open the office door. Johnson and Evason had beaten him to it and were already there. Johnson had provided the obligatory coffees, and he and Evason were huddled around her desk reading a newspaper.

They both looked round when Jamieson entered, tense looks on their faces. Jamieson saw that the newspaper was the Luton Tribune, and his heart sank. Amidst all the recent events, he had forgotten about yesterday's press conference.

'Christ,' he said. 'I'd forgotten about that. How bad is it?'

Johnson started to speak, but Evason cut across him. 'Have a read for yourself,' she said and stepped back from the desk, allowing Jamieson to move closer to get a better look. But unfortunately, the headline didn't give him much hope that it would be a sympathetic piece. 'Child abuser found dead' read the big headline. 'Pervert lived unchallenged in a neighbourhood for twenty years', read the smaller by-line. Jamieson winced and read on:

A child abuser who lived in a neighbourhood, including families with young children for over twenty years, was found murdered in the early hours of last Wednesday morning. The gruesome discovery was made by a paperboy during his delivery round at approximately six thirty in the morning.

The victim was quickly identified as Brian Wilkins, 74, who lived alone on Penrose Avenue. Initially, neighbours were quoted as saying that Mr Wilkins 'was a harmless, old man', and those interviewed expressed shock that such a thing could have happened in their 'sleepy suburban neighbourhood'.

However, things took a more sinister turn as the day's events unfolded. Police have now openly admitted that Mr Wilkins was formally known as Lesley Wallace and had been involved with a police investigation dating back twenty-five years involving the procurement of young boys for sexual purposes.

Four men were convicted at the time and have served sentences for their crimes, but due to a botched police investigation, Wallace, who was rumoured to be the ringleader of the sick group, went unpunished and walked free to do as he pleased.

When this new information came to light, neighbours' attitudes quickly changed. Mandy Watkins, who lived three doors down from the deceased and has three children aged six and under, had earlier said, 'I can't believe that someone would want to hurt a man who kept himself to himself.' However, she soon changed her tune when she found out about the double life that Mr Wilkins was living. She said, 'It's disgusting. How can the police let a man like this live and move around unchallenged? It makes me feel sick to my stomach.'

The police investigation is being led by Detective Inspector Alex Jamieson, who has responded to the events by telling the press that 'he had no opinion that he wanted to share' with waiting Journalists....'

When he reached this point, Jamieson snorted and explained to anyone who was listening, 'That quote has been taken so bloody far out of context.'

«...Wilkins, or Wallace as he was formally known, died from a series of blows to the back of his head, delivered sometime in the late hours of last Tuesday or the early hours of Wednesday. As of yet, no witnesses have come forward."

Jamieson's eye was drawn to a feature running alongside the main story, which ran with the headline *'The murder that no one cares about'*. He scanned the first few lines:

'Police insiders have dubbed the slaying of Brian Wilkins as the murder that no one cares about. Wilkins, who was considered by many as a defenceless old man, was savagely battered to death yards from his own front door last Tuesday. One neighbour said last night, 'It doesn't matter what a man is supposed to have or haven't done; he should expect a degree of protection from the society around him. For the police to give this investigation, such a

degrading nickname speaks volumes for why this country's legal system is in the state that it currently is....»

Jamieson gave up reading.

In short, it was a complete hatchet job by an experienced old hack like Harris of the Luton Tribune. Harris had trampled over any lines of respect and implicit agreement between the police and the press; worse, his editor had apparently allowed him to do so. A complaint would be issued by the Chief Constable's Office to the appropriate commission, and given the general misleading nature of the report, it would be upheld. Harris and the Luton Tribune would have their wrists slapped and be forced to issue an apology, which they would hide away on page fifteen, some considerable time after running the original story, at a time when people would have either forgotten or no longer cared. Gutter press journalism at its finest.

The damage had been done with this first report. Jamieson's decision now was whether to call the Chief Constable's Office first or wait for them to call him. He made a mental note to get his call in first to Miriam at around eight-thirty. He only hoped that was early enough. He felt deflated after the promising start to the morning. He pushed all negative thoughts from his mind and called Evason and Johnson over to Evason's desk. There was no sign of Stone yet. Jamieson said, 'Claire, fire up your computer. There's something I want to show you both.'

Evason sat behind her desk and logged herself into the system. The desktop page appeared.

'Okay,' said Jamieson. 'Type the words 'revenge trade' into the search engine. Evason tapped away at the keyboard and pressed 'enter'. Within seconds, the various sites were listed. The very top one was the one that Jamieson was looking for. He held his breath. He hadn't yet visited the website and wasn't sure what they would find. He nodded. 'The top one,' he said to Evason.

She moved the arrow across the screen and clicked on the first site listed. The screen went black at first, followed by a clock-type graphic showing how much of the download had happened.

They waited whilst the percentage of completion ticked off. Finally, at one hundred per cent, the site's front page unfurled from the top of the screen downwards. It was the picture Justin had on the wall in his room, the image of the girl offering the gun. Jamieson glanced at Evason. Her facial expression gave nothing away until the page had fully unfurled, revealing the legend at the bottom. She narrowed her eyes. Her memory banks were working overtime. She spoke the words as if somehow that would help her to remember, 'Revenge is everything.' It was almost painful to watch. She closed her eyes to concentrate.

Finally, she spoke 'The tattoo on Darren Hughes' back. I thought it said 'Revenge is everywhere or something like that, but it didn't. It said 'Revenge is Everything'. It said that'. She pointed at the words on the bottom of the screen.

Jamieson nodded. Johnson looked confused, so Jamieson quickly filled him in.

Evason moved the mouse across the 'entry site' banner. 'Have you looked at this yet?' she asked Jamieson.

'No,' he said.'I thought it would be better if we looked together.'

Evason clicked the mouse. The image rushed towards them, and as they watched, it felt like they were falling onto the screen. Jamieson subconsciously pulled away as if to stop it from happening.

Suddenly, the rushing ended. Finally, they had arrived at the welcome page. It was, to be honest, slightly disappointing.

The graphics didn't live up to the poster girl picture. The artwork was nowhere near as technically good. The picture showed a group of teenagers (Jamieson presupposed) dressed in hooded sweatshirts, their faces indistinguishable in hidden shadows. They were all wearing jeans fashionably low on their waists, showing the brand name of their underwear and branded pumps. Some had their arms folded across their chests in a kind of gesture of solidarity. They were on what appeared to be a desolate street — maybe post-apocalyptic — and again, the legend

'Revenge is Everything' was prominently shown on the screen behind the figures.

The tags across the top of the screen read 'The Game,' 'The Characters,' 'The Situations,' and 'The Outcomes.' Evason moved the icon across to the tab that read 'The Game' and looked at Jamieson. He gave a small nod, and she pressed the mouse. There was a small 'click.'

The new page filtered down from the top, replacing the home page. But, again, it was disappointing, not what Jamieson was expecting at all.

The opening text read:

revenge

NOUN 1 Revenge involves hurting someone who has hurt you. >
VERB 2 If you revenge yourself on someone who has hurt you, you hurt them in return.

(sense 1) retaliation, vengeance

(sense 2) avenge, retaliate

trade

NOUN 1 Trade is the activity of buying, selling, or exchanging goods or services between people or countries. 2 Someone's trade is the kind of work they do, especially when it requires special training in practical skills, *E.G.* a joiner. >VERB 3 When people, firms or countries trade, they buy, sell or exchange services. 4 If you trade things, you exchange them, *E.G. Their Mother had to trade her rings for a few potatoes.*

(sense 1) business, commerce

(sense 2) deal, do business, traffic

Evason widened her eyes and looked at Jamieson. 'I'm no expert', she said, 'but those definitions don't read as though they've come from the Oxford English Dictionary' 'No', agreed Jamieson, 'it sounds like it's been self-written, or more likely, an entry from a schools' dictionary. Strange example to give — *The Mother had to trade her rings for a few potatoes'* — sounds like Communist Russia.'

They read on…

Join our World

Join our Reality

Trade your Revenge

Feel the satisfaction of vengeance

The following text talked of the cyber world of *the Revenge Trade* and how your problem would be considered by millions of online visitors around the world. How their suggestions and answers would be collated by the system, and the optimum solution would be provided to provide your cyber vengeance. Johnson, who hadn't said anything up to now, finally spoke. He reaffirmed what Justin had said in his sleepy state the night before.

'It's not real,' he said, shaking his head. 'It's make-believe. I think it feels real to us because we *want* it to fit with what we're looking at because it does fit quite snugly; you know, Darren Hughes finds a website and types in all the details of his hurt and pain, and the cause of that hurt and pain is found battered to death with the main suspect out of the country. He's spoken to the all-powerful Internet, and the Internet has acted with speed and precision. It's just not real.'

Jamieson nodded. 'It sounds farfetched, I agree, but it's as good as we've got at the moment. I don't think that the website is involved, but it is possible that the *idea* has come from Hughes visiting the website. There is the tattoo which means that, unless there's a huge co-incidence, he has a connection with this website. Rog, make this your priority this morning. Go online with them, make up something you want revenge for, and send it off into cyberspace. See what comes back. Try to find out more about the site itself — where it's based? Who hosts it? Who is it registered to? That kind of thing. Try to build up a picture, see where it takes us.'

Johnson smiled — some proper detective work at last — Evason chipped in, 'You might find the technical department in Central London are useful if you come up with anything that you don't understand' She turned to Jamieson 'What about Hughes' computers at home and work, should we be taking them so that the forensics boys can have a look at the hard drives, see who he has been communication with?'

Jamieson pulled a face 'Decent call, but I still don't think we've got enough to go in heavy-handed. We need more evidence first.'

Jamieson checked his watch — eight twenty-five — time for him to put his call into the Chief Constable's Office. As he moved to the office area, the main door opened. Stone, red-faced and out of breath, carrying his briefcase in one hand and a padded envelope in the other.

'Sorry,' he said. 'the bloody car decided to play up this morning. I've had the AA round since about six this morning. It took them nearly two hours to put it right.' He tossed the envelope to Evason. It spun in the air, landed on her desk, skidded across the surface, narrowly missing a collection of half-filled coffee cups, and dropped off the edge. Evason shot him a glance of sheer annoyance before stooping to retrieve the envelope. Stone irritatingly grinned at her. 'That's just been handed in at the front desk,' he said.' it's got your name on it.' Stone put his briefcase down and shucked his jacket off. 'Anyway, what is the big development?'

Jamieson told him about the tattoo and the Revenge Trade website. Stone listened without interruption, a serious look on his face. Jamieson heard himself talking. The longer he spoke, the more farfetched the theory sounded. He finished up with a rather pathetic 'so that's how it looks. Perhaps it wasn't the big development it felt like at four thirty this morning. Maybe I was getting ahead of myself.

Stone nodded and said, 'that's not so unbelievable. There's some sound theory in which there.' 'Maybe', agreed Jamieson and turned to go. He looked back. 'Anyway, Sandy, work with Rog this morning, but try to find time for that other thing we talked about yesterday. Let me know how you get on.'

'Hold on,' said Stone. 'You'll want to hear this.' Jamieson turned to face him. Stone continued talking. 'I got a call from the States late last night. It was an Officer Harry Fenton from the Carroll Police Department in Fairfield County, Ohio. I was due to speak to him at one o'clock yesterday afternoon, which is around nine o'clock their time, but I couldn't get hold of him. I kept trying him for most of the day, but it felt a bit like I was being spun a line about him not being available. Anyway, in the end, I phoned him from home at half past ten, told them I'd hold until he was available if necessary. Finally, he came to the phone and talked to me. I told him what we were looking at and asked him a bit about Jason Manni....»

'What did he say?' asked Jamieson.

'Not much really,' replied Stone. 'He said it didn't sound like the Jason Mannix he knew. Sounded very defensive of the lad. Couldn't believe that he'd be mixed up in anything like what I'd described. Then he turned very defensive himself, wouldn't say much more, except to say that our case appeared to be very high on circumstantial evidence but very low on anything concrete...'

'He has got a point,' said Jamieson.

'There was one more thing he said, though,' continued Stone, pausing a while for effect. 'While he was in the UK, Jason Mannix's Father was murdered back home in Ohio!'

CHAPTER THIRTY-TWO

Before Jamieson could fully comprehend the implications of what Stone had just told them, his mobile phone rang. It was the Chief Constable's Office. He moved to the back of the office, away from the hubbub that Stone's announcement had caused.

He answered, 'Jamieson.'

It was Miriam. 'Have you seen the Luton Tribune?' She asked. He said he had.

'Scandalous', she said. She told him they had had previous run-ins with the publication and, in particular, Mr Harris, who, she explained, appeared to have no interest in maintaining relations between the local police force and the newspaper he represented. Jamieson could tell that she was as close to seething as her professionalism would allow her. But, suddenly, he liked her a lot more. She was human, after all.

'I've already lodged a complaint with the Press Commission,' she said. 'And I've spoken to a couple of friendly journos who were at the press conference. They're as outraged as we are, and they'll happily give evidence to support you at any hearing the commission decides to hold.' Jamieson looked at his watch. Miriam didn't hang around. She had done all this, and it was still only eight forty. He was impressed.

She went on to explain that neither of the nationals had taken up on the story. A scandal with an MP broke yesterday, consuming all the headlines, so their murder case had slipped through without anyone showing great interest. That wasn't to say that it wouldn't be filed away and may resurface at some point in the near future. That was how the media worked. On quiet days the editor would get some junior staff member to trawl through recent press releases to see what could be resurrected and turned into a scoop. Sometimes press releases from three weeks ago would find themselves front page news, much to the surprise — and chagrin — of the Public Relations Department.

'For what it's worth, Alex,' said Miriam, 'I thought you conducted yourself with great professionalism under intense provocation from that little weasel Harris. So we'll back you all the way. Don't worry about anything.'

'I wasn't until I spoke to you,' thought Jamieson, but merely answered, 'thanks.'

'One more thing,' said Miriam, 'the Chief wants to see you in his office at two thirty. He wants to know how your case is progressing.'

'Thanks', replied Jamieson. 'I'll be there,' he pressed the 'end call' button and walked back to where the remaining team members were waiting for him.

Evason held up the padded envelope. 'It's from the processing company who services the bank's CCTV cameras,' she said. 'There are around two thousand images to look through. They're all on disc, though, so I can get going on them straight away — see what we can find.'

Jamieson nodded. 'Good,' he said. 'It seems as though our Mr Forage has come up trumps. We should phone him and thank him for his efforts.'

'On my to-do list,' replied the ever-efficient Evason.

Jamieson turned to Stone. 'Okay, Sandy, tell me more about your call from the States,' he said.

'Not a great deal more to add,' said Stone 'as I said, Officer Fenton was quite evasive. Apparently, Mr Mannix Senior was attacked the night after our own victim on the way home from his local bar after leaving just after twelve. He, like Wallace, was beaten about the head with some force evidently — fractured skull, left cheekbone and eye socket, right arm broken, presumably a defensive wound — and was found dead early the following morning.'

'Any obvious suspects?' asked Jamieson.

'That's just it,' said Stone. 'The Police Department has closed the case already. They've put it down to either some itinerants carrying out a so-called 'killing for kicks.' You mentioned them earlier in the investigation, where they just steam into a small town, murder someone and move out again.'

' *They've closed the case after just seven days of investigation?'* repeated Jamieson incredulously. 'Can you believe that?'

Stone shook his head. 'They reckon they've got two witnesses who say that they saw a couple of bums acting suspiciously not a mile from where the body was found earlier that evening and another witness who says he saw two men board the bus out of Carroll early the day after — paid cash for their tickets, got out at the big terminus in Philadelphia which services cities all around the States. The police reckon that these two men could have got onto any bus to over one hundred and twenty destinations that day alone. So they are untraceable, and on that basis, the police believe it is impossible to make any arrest and rather than have the case sitting dormant on the books, they would rather close it as unsolved.'

'What do we know about Mr Mannix Senior? Raich, was it?' asked Jamieson.

Stone shook his head. 'Fenton wouldn't say anything, said it was wrong to speak ill of the dead.'

'How far is Philadelphia from Carroll?' asked Jamieson.

Behind them, Johnson was tapping away at a computer. 'Hold on just a minute,' he said Bright lad, thought Jamieson, one step ahead.

Johnson spoke again. 'Around four hundred miles. That's nothing in the States. That would take around ten hours on a Greyhound Bus.'

'Forget about Greyhound Buses,' said Jamieson.' that's bullshit. There were never two men acting suspiciously. That's a smoke screen. How long would it take to drive four hundred miles on a powerful motorbike?'

Johnson thought, 'Well, I guess you could push it a hundred miles an hour on some of the quieter roads. Then allowing for slower roads and stops for breaks...I'd say you could do it in what? Six or seven hours?'

'So there and back in fourteen hours', said Jamieson, 'leaving Philadelphia at five in the evening and getting back at seven the next day, give or take an hour either way.' 'It's a tall ask', said Johnson, 'and you'd really need to be compelled to do it '..and you'd need to be comfortable on a fast bike', chipped in Stone, 'but it is possible', concluded Johnson.

Jamieson nodded. 'What does Darren Hughes drive to work?' He spun round to face Evason.

'A motorbike', replied Evason.

Now, said Jamieson. 'What possible compulsion could Darren Hughes have for taking an eight hundred mile round trip in fourteen hours to a non-descript destination like Carroll?'

CHAPTER THIRTY-THREE

'You must admit, Alex, that it's all a little bit flimsy. To base a trip to America on the evidence, or should I say, lack of evidence, that you've accumulated to date is a big ask, especially when budgets are as tight as they've ever been' The Chief Constable sat with his elbows on the desk in front of him and the fingers of each hand touching, forming a peak. He reminded Alex of the Headmaster from his schooldays.

To a point, I agree,' replied Alex. 'but I don't see any way forward in this matter. As far as I can see, we've got their murder, and they've got ours. For some reason, they've buried theirs, and the only way I can hope to bottom our case out is to get an understanding of theirs and hopefully come face to face with who we believe to be or murderer.'

Peter Jarman was a career policeman. He had made Chief Constable at age forty-six and had somewhat stagnated there. He was now fifty-two. He earned a good wage and had a healthy pension pot waiting for him whenever he should decide to retire. He had a wife and a mistress whom he enjoyed seeing in all too infrequent clandestine meetings in faraway restaurants where no one would ever know who they were and why they were there. A wholly satisfactory arrangement for him, but he couldn't for the life of him see what it gave his co-conspirator. She was young, intelligent and going places in the force. She wasn't what you'd call classically beautiful, but to him, it was her charm and vivacity mixed with a touch of vulnerability that he found so attractive. Jarman acknowledged that he'd never been a detective, unlike Alex Jamieson sitting before him and with whom he had a lot of time. No, he was more like a politician, listening, nodding, smiling and saying the right things.

'You think these two men arranged for each other to carry out the other's murder as personal acts of revenge, thereby removing motive and because whilst they were carrying out each other's murder, they were providing themselves with an alibi.' Jamieson nodded. Put like that; it did sound borderline ridiculous.

'What would you do in my shoes, Alex?' asked the Chief Constable.

Jamieson thought out his response, 'Today's Thursday; I could fly tomorrow, hire a car from the airport and be in Carroll by late tomorrow evening. I can spend two days there carrying out my enquiries and be back on the plane on Sunday evening and back in the office for Monday. I'll fly second class and hire the cheapest car I can get from the airport. I'll stay in cut-price accommodation. The cost of actual pounds to the force would be around nine thousand pounds. It's got to be worth that even if all it does is confirm that the whole thing is a huge coincidence.'

Jarman rubbed his chin with his hand, apparently deep in thought. 'Alex, against my judgement, I'll trust your judgement on this one. I'd feel happier if you could put a more definitive link in place that ties Hughes in with Wallace sometime during the last two or three years, but I'll acknowledge there is something not right going on here. Go to the States, but be back by Monday. Phone ahead and tell the American Police that you're on your way and that you'd appreciate their time in assisting you with some loose ends in a murder enquiry that you are conducting. Don't presume to tell them that you are right and they are wrong. If you do that, then you will lose my backing. If you approach the matter in the manner that I know you are capable of, then I am confident you will get answers to your questions.'

On the way out of the office, Jamieson's mobile phone buzzed — he had an incoming text from Evason — 'Get back here as soon as you can' — he stopped and doubled back. His Mother had always taught him to be polite, so he sought out Miriam and thanked her for her efforts from the previous day. She smiled at him and said working with him had been a pleasure.

He arrived back at the station at quarter to four. He ran up the stairs taking two at a time, and hurried along the corridor to the office that served as their operations room. He burst through the door. All faces turned to him. There were smiles. 'Okay', said Evason. 'Who's first?'

'Yours is the best, Claire, so you go first,' said Stone, sounding more accommodating than he ever had before.

'Fine,' said Evason. She spun the computer screen in front of her round so that Jamieson could see it properly. 'Look at that and tell me what you see.'

Jamieson looked closely. It was an image from the bank camera facing out into the banking hall behind the reception desk. The date and time were shown at the top of the image: Monday 4th October 2007 11.37.30am.

The picture was remarkably clear for a still image from a CCTV camera. In the foreground, at the first, till Jamieson could easily make out the person they now knew was Lesley Wallace. He was smiling. In his hand, he held something, a piece of paper. What it was actually irrelevant. Jamieson moved his eyeline up to the top of the image, which showed the entrance to the banking hall, then off to his left, to the corner where the bank employees said that the person who came into the bank with Wallace stood. There stood a tall figure which could only be a man, and immediately Jamieson knew who it was.

'Bastard,' he said.

Stone came up to him, smiling. 'You've not seen it,' he said.'You think you've seen it, but you haven't. Look again.'

Jamieson pointed to the man in the photo. 'But that's....'

Stone interrupted, 'I know who that is, and so do you, but it's not the most important thing in that picture. Look again,' he repeated.

Jamieson looked at the screen again. His eyes scanned everything. Wallace's smile, the back of the cashier's head, the one person in the queue, an old lady in her seventies, the cashier next in line, the customer at the next counter...staring straight at Wallace like he had seen the devil embodied. Eyes wide with apparent disbelief, seemingly unable to tear his stare away.

Darren Hughes. It was undoubtedly Darren Hughes. 'Spotted him?' said Stone

'Spotted him', replied Jamieson, stunned; 'we've made the link.'

'More by luck than judgement,' said Stone. 'and of course, the eagle eyes of Detective Sergeant Evason.'

Evason took over. 'I've phoned Derek Forage at the bank, and he's confirmed that Darren Hughes holds a bank account at that branch and that he paid in a salary cheque at till number two on the date shown in the picture.'

'Look at the images before and after.' She used the mouse to scroll back first. 'Here,' she said. 'This is the first one.'

The first shot showed Wallace already at the till. Hughes had entered through the front doors and was halfway down the banking hall. He is carrying a crash helmet. There was no queue, so he would have been able to walk straight up to the first available till. Jamieson remembered for their visit to the bank that outside of peak periods, only till numbers one and two were open.

'Then this,' said Evason, clicking the mouse to reveal a new image.

This time Hughes had reached the till and was pushing a piece of paper towards the cashier, presumably his wage cheque. He was looking straight ahead and hadn't noticed Wallace yet. Wallace was still engaged in banter with the cashier at till one. 'Then the picture you've already seen.' Evason scrolled the image forward.

'We think that between the last one,' she scrolled back to the previous picture '...and this one,' she scrolled forward again to the current picture of Hughes staring straight at Wallace, 'something must have happened. Remember, Wallace had changed his appearance beyond recognition, so it's more likely to have been his voice that Hughes recognised. Perhaps Wallace said something that acted as a trigger in Hughes' brain, or Hughes may have even heard Wallace mention his name; you know, when asking for a banker's cheque payable to D Hughes. Of course, we now know that would have been David Hughes, but possibly Darren heard the words 'D Hughes, 'and that was what initially caught his attention.'

Evason drew a breath slowly. 'Either way', she said, 'recognition was apparent' She scrolled the following three images, which represented a minute and a half in time. They all showed Darren Hughes staring at Wallace with the same intensity as the first image. Conversely, Wallace was completely unaware of the interest shown in him by the young man.

The next image shows that Hughes has finished at the till and, as there is now someone in the queue, he is unable to linger, so the next images show him moving off and arriving at a brochure dispenser where he pretends to be reading some of the bank literature, but the whole time he is staring at the back of Wallace's head. Then Wallace has finished and starts moving away from till one. Hughes is holding back, standing by the dispenser. In the last image, Jamieson could just make out Wallace and the mystery individual disappearing through the doors at the end of the banking hall. Darren Hughes has started walking back up the banking hall.

'There's a small car park round the back of the bank,' said Evason. 'It's likely that Wallace, his friend, and Darren Hughes were all parked there. Hughes probably took his time in getting his helmet on and getting settled on his bike. Then when the car carrying Wallace pulled out, presumably taking him home, Hughes just pulled out behind them, followed them home at a safe distance and lo-and-behold. Suddenly, Darren Hughes has reunited with the man of his nightmares, but he also knows where he lives.'

Stone picked up. 'The rest is pure conjecture, but Hughes probably staked Wallace out, got to know his routine, when and where he would be and then worked out his next move. The date on the pictures is October 2007; we're now in June 2009, so it's taken him nearly two years, but it very much looks like he's taken his vengeance.' Jamieson sat down. Sometimes you got results from great police work; other times, you got lucky. Jamieson was happy enough to know that his team had worked hard and deserved any luck that came their way.

'Well done everybody, great work,' he said. 'Let's get Hughes in and see if we can't get a sympathetic judge to issue a search warrant for home and work so we can get his computers and look at them. What else was there?'

'Well,' said Stone. 'Somewhat irrelevant now, but I've managed to make contact with David Mitchell. You already know that he wasn't the mystery man, anyway. He hadn't returned your call because he had been in New York for the past ten days. He was called out on short notice to help them with an emergency situation. They needed a top hostage negotiator, and he got the gig. He took the opportunity to fly his wife out for a brief break for the last few days. He apologises for not getting back to you, but in a rush, he had left his usual mobile at home and had been issued a different one by the NYPD while he was out there. So your calls hadn't been getting through.'

Jamieson nodded. Things were moving quickly. He gathered the team around and issued orders.

'Tomorrow I go to the States...' Surprised, looks at everyone. '.....if we're right and Hughes and Mannix have crossed the Atlantic to commit murders, it's important that we understand as much as about what happened out there. Also, we need to get the Americans on our wavelength. At the moment, it seems as though they are content to sweep this under the carpet because their murder was committed by a person or persons who are untraceable. That's okay for them. The murder rate out there is so high anyway that one more unsolved case won't greatly affect their figures. But for us, it's a matter of personal pride.'

He looked at Evason 'Claire, could you get in touch with admin at Head Office Operations and get me booked on a flight for as early tomorrow morning as possible?' We know that BA flies to Philadelphia, but if we can find another cheaper carrier, then that will work just as well, and I'll need a car at the other end. I've got an eight hundred-mile round trip, so it needs to be something that I can drive in a bit of comfort. I'll need to be back on the return flight sometime Sunday evening.'

Evason nodded. She didn't like being treated as secretarial staff, but Jamieson knew she was good at detail, so he had no reservations about asking her to take it on. He turned to Stone 'Sandy, can you look into getting that warrant sorted out and getting a team together to pick Hughes up when he gets in from work tonight at just before seven. Then could you get in touch with your American colleagues and set up a meeting for me with them as early on the Saturday morning as possible? It sounds as though this Fenton guy is the man I should be talking to, but also, I'd like an opportunity to talk to Jason Mannix at some point over the weekend. Just a chat, nothing more. Remember Sandy; softly, softly, we want their cooperation with this. Also, find out whether Mannix has a tattoo. You know exactly what I mean by that.'

'Rog, how are you getting on with the website?'

Johnson referred to his notebook.' It's hosted out of Utah. Registered owners are Keith Anderson and Raoul de Villiers. Both live in Utah. From their ages, I'd say they were probably students. The site gets on average 1,000,000 hits per day, so it's not a YouTube by any means, but it still sees a considerable amount of traffic. Unfortunately, there doesn't appear to be a facility on the site for a player to be able to contact another player. The best you'll get is a first name and where the player is from..' He spread his hands '...so, for example, I'm Roger from England. So I can contact and correspond with other players in the confines of the game itself, but I can't communicate with them outside of the game.'

'Did you give them a situation to deal with?' asked Jamieson.

Johnson smiled. 'I did,' he said.'I told them I suspected my wife was cheating on me with a work colleague.'

'What came back?' asked Jamieson.

'Well, all the responses are collated and categorised and then you get the most popular three suggestions routed back to you. This happens after one hour, twelve hours, and then twenty-four hours. The situation stays 'live' for twenty-four hours and only then disappears from the game.'

'So what do we have?'

Johnson pulled a face and referred to his notes.'After the first hour, we had 'confronted her and talk it through' with six thousand, three hundred and forty-one votes. Then we had 'have an affair of your own with eleven thousand, nine hundred and sixteen votes...' Johnson cleared his throat '...and finally, with twenty-two thousand seven hundred and seventy-nine votes, we had 'murder the bitch'. 'Jesus', said Stone, 'so in the first hour, over forty thousand of these players have responded, and the advice of over half of them is for you to kill your wife.' Johnson smiled. 'Remember though, Sandy, it's not real.'

'Good job so far, Rog," said Jamieson, but I think it's time we got the real professionals involved. See if you can make an appointment tomorrow with that department in the city that Claim spoke about. Show them what we've got, see what advice they can give us?"

The team disbanded and made their way back to their desks. Spirits had been lifted. The recent developments made a clearer picture of a muddled situation. It was becoming clearer what the team thought had happened, whether they could prove it was an altogether different matter.

Jamieson picked up his mobile and headed towards the door.'I've got a call to make,' he said, 'I may be some time.'

CHAPTER THIRTY-FOUR

The phone rang three times before it was answered. 'Jim Scott,' said the voice.

'What the fuck are you playing at?' said Jamieson. He rarely swore, so when he did, it carried real venom. A pause at the other end of the line. 'Ah, Alex, 'said Scott.

'Don't 'Alex' me; just answer the question, Scott. You sit in front of me and tell me that you haven't had any dealings with Lesley Wallace since God knows when and then this afternoon, someone shows me a photograph of you and Wallace together in a bank in North London. Not only that, but a very thorough bank clerk assures me that this arrangement has been going on for at least the last fifteen years, if not longer. Now what gives?'

Another pause, Jamieson had visions of the man at the other end of the phone taking off his glasses and massaging the bridge of his nose between his index finger and thumb — a man under pressure looking for an answer to give that would make everything alright. He couldn't find one.

When he eventually answered, his voice was resigned, almost weary. 'Twenty-two years actually, Alex, ever since Dad went into that home.'

Jamieson felt his initial anger subside. He didn't want it to. He wanted to stay angry. He wanted to demand an answer from this fellow police officer who hadn't shown him the profession, courtesy of a simple answer to a simple question.

However, the irony of the situation was not lost on Jamieson. If Scott had been honest in the first place, there would have been no need to get the pictures from the bank's CCTV camera and without the pictures, they would never have put Wallace and Hughes together.

219

'You've very nearly derailed my investigation,' he said with slightly less venom than he could have used. 'Now, you'd better give me some answers.'

Scott sighed. 'Of course,' he said. 'Dad knew exactly where Wallace went after the case. Wallace had already got the better of him once, and he wasn't prepared to let that happen again. Wallace headed north with his Mother to Leeds to keep his head down for a couple of years until everything had blown over. He doted on his Mother, and she had always made it clear that she wanted to return to Bedfordshire one day in the not too distant future. So Dad called in the old boys' network. The police in Yorkshire tagged Wallace as soon as he stepped off the train. They watched him check in at the local hotel and followed him whilst he registered with a letting agent the next day.

Pretty soon, Wallace had found himself and his Mother a small furnished cottage in the Yorkshire moors. They took a two-year let and moved in within three days. In the meantime, Dad had visited Wallace's solicitor, Mr Hawkesworth, a happily married man with two children and a secret penchant for the local prostitutes; not as secret as he thought apparently, anyway, he happily traded Wallace's new identification for some police discretion. So within a week of Wallace leaving to set up a new life and a new persona, Dad knew exactly where he was and what he was calling himself. He left it a further couple of weeks for Wallace to get settled, then paid him a visit.'

A pause. Jamieson could hear what he thought was the click of a lighter, and then Scott blowing out what must have been smoke from his first drag of his cigarette. Scott sniffed.

'Dad told me that the look on Wallace's face when he answered the door to him that first time was priceless. 'How the fuck did you find me?' he said. The old man just smiled and said something like scum always rises to the surface somewhere. Dad went in and sat down and told Wallace exactly what he wanted him to do — initially five hundred pounds a month to the Marshalls and two hundred and fifty a month to the Hughes family — Dad knew that Wallace could easily afford that; he'd been left a fair amount when his Father had died, and he was a shrewd investor — and, Dad added, he wanted Wallace to undergo treatment to stop him being what he was — a danger to small children. Wallace said what if he disagreed? Dad thought about it and said he hadn't decided, but he would either reveal Wallace's whereabouts and what he'd done to some members of the local mining community and let them dispense their own justice, or he would arrange to plant so much evidence on Wallace that he'd be lucky to see the light of day ever again.'

'It won't surprise you to hear that, Wallace agreed.'

'After that, they made arrangements that on the first Monday of every month, Dad would collect Wallace and take him to the local bank where they would do the transactions and get the money sent. Dad usually drove up on the Sunday and stayed at a local bed-and-breakfast. It was almost as though he'd make a short break of it.'

'Did his relationship with Wallace ever change?' asked Jamieson.

'Never mentioned it,' replied Scott. 'Then Wallace and his Mother moved back south, and the routine continued. This time, though, there was no need for Dad to stay overnight. He would pick Wallace up and drive him to a bank far enough away so that no one would ever conceivably recognise him.'

Not far enough, thought Jamieson humourlessly.

Scott continued, 'then one Sunday, Mum fell ill, and Dad couldn't make the usual Monday routine....'

'What happened?' asked Jamieson.

'Wallace called for a cab to take him to the bank. He was conditioned to do it. He saw that it was the right thing to be doing. It couldn't put right what he had done, but it went part way to doing so. Mum died, and dad went downhill very quickly. He was put into a home and began to lose his memory. Before it had gone completely, he asked me to do one thing for him: to continue with what he called Wallace's recuperation. See, Dad only saw the money being paid to the families as part of what this was about. The other part, perhaps the main part, was the rehabilitation of the monster, Lesley Wallace, and who's to say it hadn't worked? So I took over the routine. At first, it was very difficult to accept that the man in my car had been a serial child abuser, but as time passed, I became more accepting. Can people change? Can they rehabilitate? As policemen, we have to hope so because that's what our judicial system is based upon, isn't it? Serve your sentence, repay your debt to society and come out as a changed individual. I'd never say I liked Lesley Wallace, but I appreciated what he'd come from and what he moved onto.'

Scott took a deep audible breath before he continued.

'Eventually, Dad forgot all about Wallace. Dementia kicked in, and his memory banks just erased him. Wallace went to the home to see him. Dad didn't have a clue. They sat and talked about the weather, cricket, politics, you name it. Two men brought together under the strangest of circumstances, passing the time of day like old friends. I only took Wallace the one time. I felt like I was betraying Dad. It felt wrong.'

'And you've been doing the same thing for the last twenty-odd years?' asked Jamieson. 'Why didn't you stop and rely on Wallace to keep going without you being there?' 'Two reasons.' Said Scott, 'Firstly, I'd promised Dad that I'd do it, and secondly, I thought that if I stopped, there might be a chance that Wallace would fall back into his old ways, and I didn't want that to happen.'

'Do you think he would have? I mean gone back to his old ways,' said Jamieson. Jamieson imagined that Scott was shrugging. 'Who knows?' was all he said.

'Has anything else changed in the last twenty years?' asked Jamieson.

'The only real thing of note was that not long after I started with the routine, I was driving Wallace to the bank, and he told me that his investments were doing well and wanted to double the payments to the two families. He also wanted to draw up a will, leaving everything to children's charities.'

'What did you say?' said Jamieson.

'Outwardly, I said I thought it was a very good idea,' said Scott. 'Privately, I looked up to the Old Man and gave him a smile.'

'Anything else I need to know?' asked Jamieson.

'Alex,' said Scott. 'You have to believe that I meant no harm to your investigation. I was just carrying on with a promise to my dad.'

'Yeah, I'm sure,' said Jamieson somewhat unkindly. 'Let me ask you one final question — do you think Lesley Wallace got what he deserved?'

Scott paused before answering. 'If it had happened twenty-five years ago, then yes. But now, I'm not so sure.'

Jamieson hung up.

That was the problem with this case: everyone had a different opinion.

CHAPTER THIRTY-FIVE

They set out for the Hughes' house at just before seven. Jamieson, Evason and Stone in Jamieson's car and Johnson in the squad car following. The squad car would bring Hughes back with them providing. That was, he agreed to come.

Up to now, Stone had been unsuccessful in obtaining a warrant to search the home and work premises. The Judge, who had always previously been sympathetic to the needs of the police, called it a 'fishing exercise' based on not much more than some rather flimsy co-incidence of circumstances. This caused a problem. Jamieson knew that Hughes worked with computers but was unsure how adept he was. After this evening's interview, Hughes would be on notice that the police had made various connections, and it could be that forearmed with this knowledge, Hughes may have the wherewithal to wipe any traces of activity from either of the computers to which he had access to the *Revenge Trade* website or to anyone else for that matter including Jason Mannix. That was a chance Jamieson was prepared to take. He had no arrest warrant, and tonight was an invitation to Darren Hughes to come to the police station to answer some questions. If he declined, then they would come back with a warrant. Jamieson always found it easier to obtain a warrant from a Judge if the individual refused to attend informal discussions at the station based on 'what has he got to hide.'

He had phoned Lucy earlier and told her he'd be home late tonight and that he was up and out early in the morning for a short trip to America. She sounded surprised but not put out. She knew what being married to a policeman was all about. She said she'd pack a small suitcase for him.

They were able to park closer to the house this time. Jamieson asked Stone to wait at the end of the garden path whilst he and Evason went to knock at the front door. The squad car had pulled into a space further back down the road.

Darren Hughes answered the door himself. Initially, his face registered confusion as he struggled to recognise their faces from two nights ago. Then it came back to him, and he assumed a more self-assured and confident attitude.

'Am I under arrest?' He asked.

Jamieson shook his head. 'No, it's just an informal chat. There have been some developments since we last spoke. We'd like to clear up one or two things.'

'Do I have to come?'

'No, Sir, but we could come back with a warrant for your arrest. Then you would be obliged to attend. It would make it more formal. Taped interviews, solicitors present, that sort of thing.'

'Okay', said Hughes. 'I'll come, but I can't leave my father on his own. His condition worsened a couple of nights ago, and he needs someone to be here with him in case he has a relapse.'

Jamieson thought, 'We'll be no longer than an hour, and I can leave an officer with your Father for that time. How does that sound?'

Hughes considered the proposal and nodded. 'I'll just tell him,' he said and went back into the house. He reappeared not more than thirty seconds later. The driver of the second car stayed with David Hughes. Darren Hughes rode with Johnson, who took over as driver. By the time they had returned to the police station, ten minutes of the promised hour had elapsed. They got Hughes into one of the interview rooms. Jamieson and Evason sat opposite him. Coffee and biscuits were ordered. As promised, the interview wasn't taped. However, Jamieson asked that the video camera be allowed to run without audio recording to keep in line with protocol. This protected the officers in the room from accusations of police violence. Hughes didn't object.

They settled down—Jamieson and Evason on one side of the table and Hughes on the other. Stone and Johnson stayed outside.

Jamieson began by talking first.

'Mr Hughes, you will remember our conversation from Tuesday evening regarding the murder of Brian Wilkins aka Lesley Wallace?'

Hughes nodded.

'As I said, there have been some developments, and we'd like to talk more about events.'

Again Hughes nodded.

'Mr Hughes. Have you ever visited a website called Revenge Trade?'

Hughes made a play of thinking hard about the question before answering, 'I don't think so; why do you ask?'

Jamieson gave a wry smile — so this was how it was going to be — 'You have a tattoo in the small of your back which says 'Revenge is Everything' — that happens to be the same wording found on the website that I just mentioned. It just seemed a co-incidence is all.'

Hughes nodded. 'What a coincidence,' he said.

Jamieson continued, 'do you know of someone called Jason Mannix?' he asked. Again Hughes thought 'No' came the reply.

'When you were recently in the USA, am I right in saying that you remained in Philadelphia for the whole time you were out there?'

Hughes nodded. 'Yes,' he said.

'You didn't hire a motorcycle and travel anywhere?' Jamieson pressed. Hughes thought hard. 'I don't think so,' he replied.

'Mr Hughes, said Jamieson patiently. 'You were only there last week. Surely you can remember whether you hired a motorbike or not.'

Hughes was considering his options. If the police had found out that he had hired a bike, was there any point in denying it?

'I was going to,' he said. 'But then I changed my mind.'

'Have you ever been to a town called Carroll in Ohio, USA?' Asked Jamieson.

'No,' said Hughes. He shifted in his seat.

Jamieson made a moue with his lips while he thought about his next move.

'When we spoke on Tuesday evening, you said that you had had no contact with Lesley Wallace, aka Brian Wilkins, in the last twenty or so years, is that correct?' Hughes nodded

'That is correct,' he confirmed.

Jamieson turned to Evason. She took out a 10" by 7" black-and-white photograph from a large brown envelope and passed it to Jamieson. Jamieson looked at it and then placed it on the table in front of him, simultaneously using his fingertips to spin it round, so it faced Hughes. He pushed it forward so that Hughes had a better view. It was the first picture that Evason had shown Jamieson, the one with Wallace in the foreground laughing and Hughes at the next till eyes transfixed on Wallace.

'Have a look at that picture, please,' said Jamieson. Hughes looked. 'Is there anyone that you recognise?' He asked.

Hughes pushed back his seat; it shifted a good six inches. He leant back into the chair and stretched his legs out under the table. He crossed his arms in front of him. All defensive measures. A typical posture of a man about to go into denial. He sat like that for a while in a state of contemplation. His jawline had hardened. Any semblance of the earlier humour he had shown had disappeared.

Suddenly, he sat forward. He appeared to have reached a decision. 'That's obviously me,' he said, jabbing a finger at the photograph.

'Anyone else you recognise?' asked Jamieson.

Hughes hesitated, then pointed at the figure in the foreground. 'That's Lesley Wallace'. It was Jamieson's turn to hesitate, using the silence to great effect. Then, finally, he spoke, 'You told us that you hadn't seen Lesley Wallace for years, but this is dated October 2007.'

Hughes shrugged. 'I lied, so shoot me. It still doesn't mean I had anything to do with him being murdered,' Jamieson agreed, 'but it does put a different complexion on things, I'd say. Tell me, something about Lesley Wallace has changed a great deal over the last twenty-five years; how did you know it was him?'

Hughes sat back in his chair again. His eyes focussed on the corner of the room. 'When I was eight years old, that man made me put his penis in my mouth. He told me that I had to look into his eyes when I did it and tell him that I loved him. That is one voice and one pair of eyes that I will never, ever forget for as long as I live.'

The room fell into an uncomfortable silence, broken only by a knock at the door. Evason stood up and opened it. It was the coffee and a plateful of biscuits. It was seemingly inappropriate after the last passage of the interview, but nevertheless, it broke the unease that had fallen across the three people in the room.

Evason took the tray and placed it on the table. She put a mug of coffee in front of Hughes and two more in front of Jamieson and herself. She put the plate of biscuits and a sugar bowl in the centre of the table. Hughes immediately reached for the sugar bowl and shovelled three heaped spoonfuls into his mug.

Jamieson checked his watch — nearly seven forty-five — he had promised Hughes that he would only be an hour. That gave him another fifteen minutes at most. He decided on a more direct approach.

'Mr Hughes, can I tell you what I think happened?' without waiting for an answer, he continued. 'I think that you blame Lesley Wallace for everything that has gone wrong in your life, your own situation, your Mother's suicide and your father's illness — and I'm not here to say that you are right or wrong in your belief.' Jamieson looked at Hughes, who simply looked back. 'I think that you have had thoughts of taking some kind of revenge for a long time, but you have never known where to find Wallace. He disappeared directly after the trial and reappeared with a different identity two years later. I don't know whether you have ever tried to find him during the last twenty years. It may be that you haven't because that way, you could keep control of yourself. If you didn't know where to find him, then you couldn't do anything you'd regret.'

Jamieson paused.

'Then, on the 4th October 2007, you pay a visit to your bank, and there he is, the subject of all the hatred and bitterness that you have been harbouring for the last quarter of a century, standing not more than five feet away from you, laughing and joking with the cashier, and suddenly the whole dynamic changes. Now you do know where he is. He's standing five feet away. You've found him in spite of yourself.'

Right on queue, Evason showed Hughes the next six photographs in succession.

'I think you decided there and then to find out where Wallace lived. You moved away from the till and pretended to read some brochures. You followed when Wallace had finished what he was doing and left the bank. These photographs confirm all of that. Then I think you followed Wallace to the car park at the back of the bank. He got into a car, and you didn't recognise the driver, but that didn't matter. You waited for the car to leave the car park and followed on your motorbike — you had your crash helmet with you in the bank, so it's evident that you had your motorbike with you — you tailed the car at a safe distance and were lucky enough to find that it led you straight to Wallace's house. In the space of thirty minutes, you had not only found Wallace himself, but you also now knew where he lived.'

Hughes sat with a blank expression on his face. Jamieson continued.

'Over the next few weeks, you probably staked Wallace out to get a feel for any routines he may have had, and you got lucky. He was a creature of habit. Every Tuesday, Thursday and Saturday, he spent three hours at the local pub a half-mile walk away. He came home just after eleven; the streets were quiet, an ideal time to strike.' 'The problem you had was that you would be a major suspect if Wallace was found dead, and you couldn't afford to be imprisoned because no one would be around to look after your Father.'

Jamieson paused to gather his thought process, then continued. 'You're a big computer game fan. So you've probably come across a website called *Revenge Trade*. Here I get a bit woolly because computers aren't my specialist subject but either through this website or using the ideology of the website; you decide that it would work if you got someone else to murder Lesley Wallace for you. In return, you'd murder someone for them. Hence the trade of revenge...' Jamieson opened his hands to demonstrate the simplicity of it all. 'Somehow, you get in touch with a like-minded individual in the States who needs someone to commit murder for him and is willing to murder in return. The beauty being that when the murders are committed, the main suspects will be ten thousand miles away. A pretty strong alibi by any standards.' 'I think that you flew to the States for the convention; three days in, you hired a motorbike and drove four hundred miles to Carroll where you murdered Raich Mannix, Jason Mannix's Father, then you drove four hundred miles back to Philadelphia in time for breakfast. Around the same time, Jason Mannix did for Lesley Wallace in a similar manner. Then each of you finished their time abroad as if nothing had happened and flew home with the trade having taken place. It was a good plan. What you didn't reckon with was a nosey neighbour who hated cars that parked across his driveway, a tattoo in the small of your back and a poster on my son's wall at home.'

The last part confused Hughes.

Finally, he sat back and gave a sardonic round of applause. 'Bravo Inspector,' he said. 'That really stretches the imagination. I suppose you've got hard evidence that all this happened exactly the way you say.'

'No, not at the moment,' said Jamieson, 'but it all fits very nicely, you have to admit.' He smiled at Hughes. 'Hopefully, I'll find out more when I fly out to the States in the morning.'

Momentarily, Hughes lost his composure. His mouth opened slightly as if he were about to speak, but nothing came out. Finally, he managed to talk: 'you're going to the States?' He asked, a little too hurriedly.

Jamieson nodded. 'We like to be thorough,' he said.

Hughes regained his composure and gave a brief smile. 'Well, good luck with that.' he said. 'Now, as I am here voluntarily, I think I'd like to go home and make sure my father is alright.'

Jamieson spoke cordially. 'No problem. Thank you very much for your time. DS Evason here will arrange for you to be taken home.'

Hughes left the room with Evason. Stone appeared moments later. 'How did it go?' he asked.

Jamieson made a slight movement with his hands. 'Fine, I think. You?'

'Yep,' said Stone. 'Got the warrant here.' He held up a piece of paper. 'As soon as Hughes admitted to having known that it was Wallace in the bank. The Judge was happy that a link between the two had been established. He signed right away. His secretary has just faxed it across.'

'Okay', said Jamieson 'If I'm right, Hughes will try to make contact with Mannix in the States to warn him that I'm coming and to get his story straight, and he'll do this using either email or his mobile phone. He'll want to move quickly, so give him a couple of hours, then get across there and get hold of his computer, mobile phone, and anything else that might give us a bit more leverage in linking the two of them.' 'Will do,' said Stone 'have a good trip.'

CHAPTER THIRTY-SIX

Jamieson was very hot and tired.

The satellite navigation system in the rental car was telling him he was still some forty miles from Carroll. He'd been up since four thirty — Greenwich Meantime—and it was now eight o'clock Eastern Daylight Time. Allowing for the five hours lost across the time zones meant that Jamieson had been awake for the past twenty-one hours. He hadn't managed to sleep on the flight, having found himself sitting next to an initially interesting if somewhat over garrulous American lady who said she was in her mid-sixties, but Jamieson thought it was more likely that she was in her mid-seventies. She wore lots of makeup, and her eyebrows had been drawn on with an eyebrow pencil. First, she told him about her trip to England and about everything she had done. Then, she asked him about his trip to the USA. Jamieson, wanting to avoid discussing the case, told her he was going to a computer games convention in Philadelphia — how ironic, he thought.

The lady looked confused: 'Strange', she said. 'I thought that was a couple of weeks ago.' Feeling somewhat chastened, Jamieson noted never to underestimate old ladies again. He passed her concerns off with a feeble. 'Oh, that was another one. They're always having these conventions.'

They talked solidly for over an hour, at which point the old lady started repeating herself. Over the remaining six hours of the flight, she told Jamieson about her pet dog on seven separate occasions. Jamieson was trapped. He was aware that he should try to get some rest for the journey ahead, but his common decency prevented him from asking the old lady to keep quiet, so he just put up with it. The airline provided breakfast shortly after takeoff and lunch just before landing. A headwind had shortened the journey by about twenty minutes, so they touched down at just after ten thirty in the morning. Jamieson had brought hand luggage with him, and his car had been pre-booked from the UK. Clearance through immigration was reasonably speedy. As he queued, Jamieson looked around and tried to imagine Hughes going through a similar process just over two weeks ago.

Finally, at ten minutes to twelve, Jamieson took temporary ownership of his upgraded rental car. The upgrade wasn't at the expense of the Bedfordshire Constabulary; moreover, the usual car rental office scheme offered an upgrade. When Jamieson refused this, they admitted that they have no smaller cars anyway, so the upgrade was made without incurring any extra cost.

The Satellite Navigation System soon put him on the right major road, and Jamieson spent two hours driving, getting used to the car and touching the speed limit most of the time. When he checked the milometer, he saw that he had travelled just over a hundred miles in the first two hours. Not too bad, given that the first twenty minutes were spent getting out of the vast airport complex.

Once he reached the main highway, it was a relatively straight road, with roadside diners liberally dotted along the way. After the first three hours of driving, he pulled into one to use the toilet facilities and grab something to eat. He ended up with a bowl of chilli and a (twice) refilled mug of coffee. He paid up and left, forgetting to leave the mandatory tip for the waitress. He hurried back in and pressed a five-dollar bill into her hand, apologising for his forgetfulness.

Out of the car, he was suddenly aware of how hot it was. The vehicle and diner were equipped with air conditioning, but Jamieson realised that a short walk across the car park and into the restaurant had left him with a damp back and rivulets of sweat running down his forehead. Back in the car and on the Interstate, he quickly got the car up to the speed limit of one hundred and five kilometres per hour before flicking the cruise control button.

He drove on and on past miles and miles of what he assumed was farmed land, past towns positioned in small pockets away from the general noise of the main road and passed out-of-town shopping centres with parking for what seemed like thousands upon thousands of vehicles. He watched the sun move across the cloudless sky and listened to various classic radio stations as he passed in and out of the range of their transmitters. He smiled when he heard the Chuck Berry version of Johnny B. Goode. At seven o'clock, he pulled into roadside services for petrol. He had one hundred miles to go. He grabbed a coffee to drink on the move and, within ten minutes, was back on the road. Fairfield County started to appear on the roadside signs with around sixty miles to go. It was, by now, cooler, although he kept the air conditioning on full blast and aimed at his face to prevent the tiredness from washing entirely over him. Finally, just before nine o'clock, he crossed the Fairfield County Line and five miles later, he was in downtown Carroll. Downtown was represented by a small supermarket (Jamieson suspected that there would be a Wal-Mart somewhere in reasonably close proximity), a small old-fashioned petrol station, and a farm feed shop. There was a bar called Dusty's opposite the police station; a one-storey wooden building painted white with a sign announcing it was 'The Carroll Police Department'. There were no lights on at the police station as Jamieson passed by. He half expected a handwritten sign reading 'Please come back tomorrow.'

Further through the small town, Jamieson found what he was looking for. It was the town diner. Jamieson pulled up outside. The diner had big windows, and as Jamieson looked inside, he could see the bar in front of which there was a row of around ten stools. The rest of the place was filled with booths. There were a handful of people sitting around. A waitress, carrying an order pad with her pen thrust into her hair, moved around between the customers carrying a pot of coffee. A sign was hanging in the diner's window that said 'rooms available.'

Jamieson stepped out of the car and stretched. It had been a long journey. Finally, the day's heat had disappeared, and a cool breeze blew. He retrieved his jacket from the rear seat of the car and his overnight case from the boot, pressed the remote to lock the doors, and walked up to the diner's glass door. With his jacket in one hand and his bag in the other, he had to shoulder open the door. As he entered the diner, the waitress came out from behind the counter with every ready coffeepot in her hand. She smiled pleasantly. 'Take a seat, hon; I'll be right back' she said over her shoulder as she set off to replenish coffee cups to the customers sitting in the booths.

Jamieson put his case on the floor and hauled himself up into one of the stools at the counter. He looked around the diner. Unlike films where a stranger shows up in a small Midwest town, and all the locals look up from what they are doing to see what the new guy in town looks like, no one paid him a blind bit of notice. Instead, the diners continued with what they were doing — eating, drinking, talking, laughing.

The waitress reappeared. She put a mug down on the counter in front of him and prepared to pour some coffee. Jamieson held his hand up. Right now, he was really tired and needed to get some sleep. Caffeine coursing through his veins would only delay that process. He only had one full day here and wanted to feel as alive as possible. A good night's sleep now was paramount. 'Thanks, but no coffee,' he said to the waitress. Her badge said 'Lena'. Lena pulled a suit yourself face and lowered the coffee pot. 'Well, what can I do for you?' she asked. Jamieson half-expected her to add the word 'Stranger' to the end of the sentence, but she didn't.

'My name is Alex Jamieson,' he explained. 'I've booked one of your rooms for a couple of nights. Well, I mean, a room has been booked for me.'

'Okay, Alex Jamieson,' she said. 'Let's look in the bookings register.' Lena went round behind Jamieson and appeared on the other side of the counter. She reached behind the till and pulled out an A4 diary. She opened the journal, licked the end of her finger and flicked through the pages until she reached the point where today's date should have been. But instead, it appeared to have been torn out. 'Wow, that's odd,' she said. 'The page is missing. No problem, though, we've nobody staying for the next couple of nights, so I can easily put you up....»

'Lena, no...' A man had appeared from the kitchen doorway behind her.

Jamieson estimated that he was about forty-five ten and weighed a hundred and eighty pounds. He stared intensely at the waitress. 'There are no rooms available for the next two nights. Not for strangers, anyway.'

The diners within earshot had stopped what they were doing and watched as events unfolded.

Lena acted swiftly and with conviction. 'Now Conrad, don't you be so rude? It looks as though Mr Jamieson here had travelled a long way and could do with a good night's rest. You go back to doing what you were doing.' She turned to Jamieson.'I'm so sorry about that, Mr Jamieson. I don't know what he was thinking.' She looked back at the man called Conrad, who still stood in the doorway staring over at where they stood. Lena turned her attention back to Jamieson. 'There's a room made up ready upstairs for whenever you want it. The key is right here..' she handed him a door key with a red tag and the number '5' on it...it's round the back and up the stairs, fifth door along.' The diners went back to what they were doing.

'Thanks,' said Jamieson, taking the key. 'Do you want to eat now?' asked Lena.

"No, thanks," said Jamieson. "I just need to get my head down and get some sleep. What time is breakfast served?'

'Oh, any old time', replied Lena, 'we're open from six in the morning until eleven at night every single day except Christmas Day and New Year's Day — we close at six then!'

Jamieson laughed. 'Thanks for your help just then', he said. 'I don't know what his problem was.'

Lena smiled. Jamieson decided that she was pretty, in a tired sort of way. She was probably in her mid-thirties with her blonde hair tied up. Although her eyes looked weary (no surprise, thought Jamieson, if she worked all year round), they had a sparkle to them. Her nose was small and slightly turned up. Her lips filled out when she smiled. She spoke. 'Oh, don't pay any attention to Conrad. He doesn't mean anything by it — it's just his way.'

Jamieson wished her a good night and made his way back out of the diner. He turned left round the back of the building and found the staircase Lena had mentioned. Five steps up, he heard a noise in the darkness behind him. He instinctively turned round.

It was the solid figure of Conrad. He stood at the bottom of the flight of stairs, some five feet lower than Jamieson. Jamieson could just make out the outline of his facial features. 'You made me jump,' said Jamieson, 'sneaking around like that.'

Conrad spoke: 'We don't like strangers poking their nose around here, 'You'd be best going back to where you came from.'

Before Jamieson could reply, Conrad disappeared into the shadows as quickly as he had appeared. Jamieson strained his eyes to see where he'd gone. His heart still raced.

When he realised that Conrad had gone, he turned and continued up the stairs until he reached the landing and went off to find room five.

CHAPTER THIRTY-SEVEN

The sun peaking through the blind eventually woke Jamieson. He lay with his eyes shut for a few minutes, weighing up the situation. He had slept well, but as was often the case, he still felt desperately tired. Last night he had driven for the last hour or so purely on a mixture of adrenaline and caffeine, and this morning his body was letting him know in no uncertain terms that that behaviour like that was not to be tolerated. Finally, he opened his eyes and reached for his watch, which he had left on the bedside table. He turned the watch over in his hands and looked at it. His initial reaction was panic until he remembered that he hadn't made the necessary adjustment to his watch to reflect American time. His panic subsided. On the other side of the bed was another bedside table with a clock on top of it. The time showed it was seven-fifteen. He had slept for around ten hours.

He got up and went into the small bathroom. He ran hot water into the sink, foamed up his face and started shaving. When he had almost finished, he heard a knock on the door. His mind flashed back to his encounter with Conrad yesterday evening. He grabbed a towel and warily crossed the room to the door.

'Who is it?' he asked.

'Its Lena', came the reply. 'I heard you running the water, so I guessed you were up. I've brought you some fresh coffee to help you get going.'

'Hang on,' said Jamieson. Then, before opening the door, he wrapped the towel around his waist and pulled yesterday's shirt on.

Lena stood there holding a tray with a coffee pot, milk, sugar, mugs, and spoons. She smiled at him.'How d'you sleep?' she asked. He stepped back to let her enter. She put the tray on the old chest of drawers in the corner.

'Good, thanks,' he replied, 'out like a light as soon as my head touched the pillow.'

They made some more small talk while he poured himself a coffee — Lena couldn't join him in a mug as she was expected back downstairs for the morning rush — he asked her what time she went to bed. She told him that after the last customers left, there was still tidying up to be done to get the place ready for the morning, so it wasn't much before midnight until she had a chance to get to bed. She was up again at five-thirty to get the diner opened again.

Jamieson said that was a full day every day. Lena said that she didn't mind and that she and Conrad had been doing this for nearly twenty years now, and on the whole, she quite enjoyed it.

'Conrad is your husband?' asked Jamieson.

Lena laughed. 'Good Lord, no,' she said.' he's my big brother. We've worked the diner since our folks died.'

Jamieson apologised, but Lena just laughed again. 'No problem,' she said. 'I thought it was funny.' Jamieson didn't tell her about his encounter with Conrad last night. Lena said she had to get back downstairs. Jamieson said he'd be down in a while for some breakfast. He realised that he hadn't eaten since yesterday's bowl of chilli, and he was famished.

Lena said he would need a full stomach for his meeting with Harry Fenton. Jamieson looked a bit taken aback and asked how she knew about his meeting. Lena smiled. 'Oh, everybody in the town knows,' she said, opening the door and stepping out onto the landing. 'The detective from England coming to little old Carroll,' she smiled again. 'See you downstairs,' she said and pulled the door closed behind her. Jamieson showered and dressed in a clean shirt. He wore the suit he had travelled in but didn't wear a tie. The suit was slightly crumpled from the journey, but it would have to pass muster — he was travelling light and had brought no alternatives. As he left the room, a blast of heat hit him. 'Christ,' he thought. 'It's not even eight o'clock yet.'

He breakfasted well and had another cup of coffee. A full stomach gave him some more energy. He settled up and said goodbye to Lena. He jumped in the car and drove the half mile or so back down to where he'd seen the police department yesterday. He parked up and entered the building via the glass doors.

The building looked deserted. He checked his watch. It was only eight forty-five, but still, Jamieson reckoned, somebody should be about. He stood waiting at the counter for around five minutes. There was no bell to ring for attention, so he coughed a couple of times politely. Still no sign of life.

He sat in the waiting area. At ten past nine, the glass doors swung in, followed by a solid-looking man in his early fifties. He wore the khaki-coloured uniform that Jamieson recognised from television programmes, with a dark brown wide-brimmed hat. Around his waist, he had a belt with a holster. Jamieson could see the handle of the police-issue revolver peeking out of the holster. He was what Jamieson would call a sheriff rather than a policeman. He had brown hair edged with grey and a moustache. On first impression, Jamieson felt that his demeanour was not a happy one. Jamieson wondered whether this was Officer Fenton.

The officer looked at Jamieson sitting in the waiting area. He appeared to scour his memory for some clue as to why this man should be waiting. Then, finally, he got there. 'Detective Jamieson?' He asked.

Jamieson nodded and stood up.

'My name's Fenton. I'm the Chief round here.' He held out his hand. Jamieson shook it. 'Good to have you in Carroll, sir.' His manner betrayed his words. Fenton clearly wasn't happy that Jamieson was there.

'Officer Fenton,' said Jamieson. 'Glad to be here.' Fenton's facial expression didn't change. He just nodded.

'Sorry no one was here to meet you,' he said. 'Alice, who usually holds the fort, was called away last night and hasn't made it back into town yet, so we're a little light-handed right now.'

Jamieson smiled. 'No problem,' he said. 'I appreciate you seeing me.'

Fenton's face hardened, but he remained noncommittal. 'If you'll give me five minutes more', he said, 'I just need to complete a few early morning procedures, including putting a pot of coffee on to brew.' He turned and passed through a door to the back office. Jamieson sat down and waited. He thought about his initial meeting with Fenton. Jamieson's presence clearly put the man out, and Jamieson didn't think that he was in for a particularly accommodating meeting. Finally, after fifteen minutes, Fenton reappeared. 'Sorry, it all took a bit longer than I first appreciated. Com'on through to my office at the back.'

He followed Fenton through to a small, cluttered office. The walls were covered with framed citations and photographs, mainly of Fenton shaking hands with various dignitaries, the sort of photo opportunity that Jamieson would run a mile from. Fenton offered Jamieson a chair and walked round to the far side of the desk. Jamieson listened for the telltale hiss of the coffee machine but heard nothing. Fenton made no offer of coffee - no matter, Jamieson had already had more than his fill for the morning. Fenton sat back in his chair and hoisted his legs up onto the corner of the desk, crossing them at the ankles. He picked up a pen and tapped the edge of the desk. He was sending out a clear message that he didn't appreciate Jamieson's presence in his town, let alone his office.

Fenton smiled a humourless, insincere smile. 'So what can I do for you, Detective Jamieson?' he asked.

Jamieson leant forward in his seat. 'My team and I are working on a murder case back in England. I understand that you have been working on your own murder case here in Carroll. I think there are some distinct similarities that connect the two cases. I wanted to discuss them with you as the senior officer in charge of the case to see whether we could work together towards a conclusion.'

Fenton drew a deep breath. 'The only murder we have had here in the past two decades was the killing of Raich Mannix, so I guess that's the one you're referring to.' He paused for substantiation, but Jamieson neither denied nor confirmed. Fenton continued regardless. 'Truth is, Detective Jamieson, we've closed that murder investigation. Under guidance from the Ohio State Judiciary appointed representative, Judge Linus Reinholt, the case has been designated as unsolved or indeed unsolvable — the verdict being unlawful killing by people or persons unknown.' Jamieson nodded. 'That's pretty swift action', he said. 'I understand that the murder took place only a matter of ten days or so ago.'

Fenton bristled slightly. 'Well,' he said. 'when the evidence is as clear as it was, there seemed no point in dragging our heels. That's how we do things in America.'

'May I ask?' said Jamieson. 'What the evidence was?'

Fenton took his feet off the desk. It was his turn to lean forward. He was struggling to keep the exasperation from his tone of voice. 'We had three reliable witnesses who provided sworn statements that placed two male itinerants, firstly very close to the place that the body was found, and secondly, boarding a bus to Philadelphia the next morning. Just about everyone else in the town has an alibi....'

'.....including his son Jason, who was in England at the time,' cut in Jamieson.

'.....including his son, Jason. There appeared to be no motive for the killing, but that is the case with many murders of this type in Mid-West America. There are a lot of sickos around who take great pleasure out of whacking someone for no reason and leaving them for dead. In England, you guys call someone who kills two innocent people a serial killer, and it's front page news for weeks and weeks. In America, there are so many of the sick fucks murdering who knows how many that sometimes all we can do is tidy up after them and thank the Lord that they've moved on through our town without causing too much damage.'

'What can you tell me about the victim?' asked Jamieson.

Fenton shook his head 'white, male, sixty-six years old, unemployed living off the state, some minor criminal activity in his younger days but no convictions in the last twenty years at least, spent his evenings in Dusty's and his days sleeping off his hangover. Five kids, wife died some ten years back....' He spread his hands in front of him as if to say that was all.

'That's all on record', said Jamieson 'what about off the record?'

'We work with fact, Detective, not hearsay.'

Jamieson pressed, 'did my Sargeant explain our theories regarding the two cases?'

'Yes, he did,' confirmed Fenton.

'and?' asked Jamieson.

Fenton shrugged. 'And that's all they are, theories. There's no hard evidence to support them. No witnesses; it's all circumstance. Yes, at a push, it could all fit, but equally, you could put forward a case that two spaceships landed and little green men jumped out and killed both victims, then flew off again and without evidence; who's to say it did or didn't happen?'

Jamieson thought about the situation. He'd come a long way to be knocked back five minutes into a conversation. 'I'd like to talk to Jason Mannix,' he said. 'Can you arrange that for me?'

It was Fenton's turn to pause for thought. 'I will ask Jason Mannix if he wants to speak to you in an off-the-record interview. If he doesn't want to do that, then there's nothing either you or I can do. You have no jurisdiction out here, and I have no case to solve, so officially, I'm not obliged to do anything. Unofficially, well, that's down to Jason Mannix.'

Jamieson nodded.'Thank you for that. Do you think it would be possible for me to see the Mannix case file?'

Fenton thought about the request. 'We've nothing to hide. It doesn't run too much more than an autopsy report, three witness statements, a request to the State that we can close the case and their confirmation that we can do so.' He reached forward and flicked through some files on his desk. He finally pulled one out of the pile and passed it across to Jamieson. 'There's an empty office next door; feel free to use it.'

Fenton was right, the file was skinny, and Jamieson assumed it wouldn't tell him a great deal more than Fenton had just told him. Jamieson looked around the office that he was sitting in. He suspected that police stations and offices were pretty much the same all over the world. He opened the file and pulled the papers out.

The autopsy showed that, like Lesley Wallace, Raich Mannix took a severe beating with an unnamed blunt instrument. The attack was described as frenzied. The first blow was probably the fatal one. A powerful strike from behind caught the base of Mannix's skull with such venom that the skull itself split, causing massive and immediate swelling of the brain. Death was instantaneous. The majority of injuries were post-mortem. The assault continued after Mannix had died.

The witness statements didn't say very much, just as Fenton had alluded. The first talked of two mysterious men seen in the town centre just after ten in the evening. The second was timed at around forty minutes from the first and placed the men on the road heading out towards the Mannix place. The third was timed at seven the following morning, placing the men boarding the early morning bus to Philadelphia.

Any statements taken at face value on their own may have held water, but the three together gave Jamieson severe doubts about their validity. In all three statements, the descriptions of the men and their clothing were exactly the same, down to the exact wording on the back of one of the men's sweatshirts. In Jamieson's experience, three separately taken statements rarely, if ever, threw up such precise descriptions as these three. It left him feeling deeply unsatisfied.

The name of the witness on the third statement, the one that placed the men boarding the bus the morning after the murder, was Conrad White. Jamieson wondered whether that was the same Conrad who he had already met.

The last two pieces of paper were an application to the State outlining the events leading up to the murder and requesting confirmation that the case may be filed away as unsolved and an acknowledgement from the State Court that the application had been received and was being considered. So Fenton had lied. The case wasn't officially closed, merely pending.

Jamieson gathered up all the papers and put them back in the file. He went to find Fenton. He was in his office drinking coffee. 'Thanks for this', he said, holding up the file before placing it back on top of the pile on the desk. 'Interesting reading'. Fenton just nodded.

'Just two questions before I go, if I may', he said.

Fenton formed a forced smile. 'Go ahead', he said.

'Whereabouts was the body found?' asked Jamieson.

Fenton took a sip of coffee. 'About a half mile out of town on the road heading east, about five hundred yards further on is where the Mannix place is. If you're going out there, there's probably still some crime scene tape around the area. We haven't had time to clear it away yet. Perhaps you could help us out by doing it for us'. he smiled again; this time, it was genuine. It was Jamieson's turn to force a smile. 'Maybe I just will', he said. He turned to go as he reached the door. He turned back. 'I'm staying in the accommodation above the diner', he said, 'for when you've made arrangements with Jason Mannix'. Jamieson opened the door to go

'Wait', called Fenton after him 'you said there were two questions' Jamieson turned back, a thoughtful look on his face. 'Yes', he said, 'thanks for reminding me. The Conrad White who witnessed the suspects boarding the bus, is that the owner of the diner?'

Fenton's face darkened. 'Yes, it is', he replied. 'Have you met him?'

Jamieson pulled his most enigmatic face and nodded. 'Oh yes,' he said. 'I've certainly met him.'

Fenton watched Jamieson disappear along the corridor. He then turned his head to look out of his office window. He picked Jamieson up as he reappeared at the door to the police station. As he watched him walk back down the road towards his car, Fenton picked up the phone on his desk and dialled a number.

'Con?' he said. 'Is that you? What have you been up to, your dumb son of a bitch? I told you to leave the Englishman to me.'

CHAPTER THIRTY-EIGHT

Jamieson got back into the rental car, cranked up the air conditioning and drove the half a mile or so out of town until he reached a spot at the side of the road where the remnants of the police tape still hung limp.

He pulled in just beyond the taped-off area. He checked his watch, which he had by now synchronised with local time. It was twelve-fifteen - the hottest time of the day. He killed the engine and stepped out of the car. The oppressive heat hit him instantly. It felt particularly close after the ice-cold air in the car. Jamieson walked back along the road to the taped-off area. In truth, there was very little for the lay detective to see. Forensics may have had a field day in an area no bigger than four square metres, but looking at the space now, some ten days after the event, nothing sprang out to catch Jamieson's eye. Jamieson assumed that Fenton had involved a forensics team immediately following the finding of Raich Mannix's body, although nothing about the handling of the case would surprise him. It was evident that the theory involving the two mystery men was the one to which Fenton was sticking, and Jamieson felt that would still be the case despite any evidence he could produce.

After half an hour at the scene, Jamieson set off on foot back into the town. Twenty minutes later, he had reached Dusty's bar. His shirt was soaked with sweat, and he needed something to drink. He pushed the door and entered.

He took a stool at the bar and asked the bartender for an iced tea. While he waited, he looked around the rest of the bar. Apart from two men sitting in one of the booths at the window, the place was empty. It wasn't a big place to service a town of four hundred people, of which probably one hundred were male drinkers between the ages of twenty and sixty with apparently little else to do with their time.

The bartender came back with the iced tea. Jamieson thanked him, took a long sip, and let it slide down his parched throat.

Jamieson called the bartender across. He introduced himself and asked whether the man was working on the night that Raich Mannix died. The man smiled, which encouraged Jamieson, and replied that he worked every night and most days, so, yes, he was working the night that Raich died.

Jamieson asked how much Mannix had had to drink. 'No more or less than usual,' said the man. 'I'd say he was drunk but not roaring.'

Jamieson asked how often Mannix was in the bar. 'Every night,' came the reply ', and you'd better believe that takings have gone down since he died.' He smiled again.

'I thought that he didn't work," said Jamieson. 'Where did he get the money to get drunk every night?'

The man looked as though he was about to answer when someone entered the door behind Jamieson. The bartender just smiled and said, 'enjoy your drink' before moving away to the far end of the bar. Jamieson looked round to see who had come in. It was Conrad White. At first, White just stared at Jamieson; then, it seemed he remembered his manners and nodded to him, walked to the other end of the bar and ordered a drink. Jamieson downed his iced tea and left a five-dollar bill on the bar. Then, he walked back out into the heat.

Jamieson checked his watch and started off at a pace he thought a mildly drunk man might adopt. Before long, he had sweated through his shirt again. He took out his handkerchief and mopped his brow. There was no pavement (or sidewalk, Jamieson guessed), so he had to walk towards the oncoming traffic. There wasn't much to bother him, though, and Jamieson assumed that there would have been even less last Wednesday after midnight.

It took him seventeen minutes to reach the car, not that this was significant in any respect. He continued walking, remembering what Fenton had said about the Mannix property being a further five hundred yards further on.

He soon found it. An overgrown property with the name Mannix painted on the mailbox. A dirt path led up to the front porch. In the front garden, there were two pickups, neither of which looked to be in any kind of working order. It looked deserted, although Jamieson thought he saw the curtains twitch; then again, maybe not. He set off back to the car. It was all very similar to what had happened to Lesley Wallace. A man going through a routine attacked in the optimum place on his way home late at night when witnesses were unlikely to be around. It felt pre-planned; it didn't have the feel of an impulse attack. He wondered whether Jason Mannix would speak to him and, even if he did, what good it would do. Fenton had already clarified his position and added that Jamieson carried no jurisdiction over here. Perhaps it had been a flight of fancy. Maybe he should have accepted it for what it was and treated it as murder or even murders that no one cared about.

He got back in the car. It was now two fifteen, and he realised he was hungry. So he set off back to the diner for a sandwich and some more coffee.

When he got there, it was almost empty aside from two elderly ladies sipping coffee in one of the booths towards the rear of the floor. Lena was there and smiled when she saw him. 'You must be hungry,' she said. 'What can I get for you?'

Jamieson slid into one of the vacant booths. 'Coffee please,' he said. 'and a club sandwich of your choice, I don't mind which.'

'Tuna melt?' she said.

'Sounds great,' said Jamieson. But, even with all the coffee, he had been drinking, he was still beginning to wilt in the heat.

'Coming right up,' said Lena. Jamieson wondered how she kept up her cheery exterior when she appeared to spend eighteen hours a day on her feet.

While waiting for his order, Jamieson shut his eyes and probably drifted off to sleep.

He was woken by Lena shaking him gently. His coffee and club sandwich were on the table before him. 'You should probably eat this and then go upstairs and take a nap,' she said. Jamieson nodded. 'You're probably right,' he said.

He ate half the sandwich and sipped the coffee. Both were very good. Lena saw to the only other two diners, then poured herself a coffee and slid into the booth opposite him. She smiled.'How was Harry Fenton?' she asked.

Jamieson pulled a face. 'Not very forthcoming' was his reply. He carried on eating, and she watched him for a while. Finally, he put his sandwich down and looked at her. 'Tell me about Raich Mannix,' he said.

'Well, he's dead, for one thing,' replied Lena.

Jamieson gave her what he hoped was an old-fashioned look.'That much I know,' he said. Lena screwed up her eyes. 'Why, Mr Detective?' she said. 'I do believe that you are pumping me for information.'

'And I believe you are the only person in this town who I think will tell me anything near the truth,' said Jamieson.

Lena took pity on him. 'Well,' she said. 'I will say that the very second Raich Mannix died, the world became a nicer place. He was a mean man, the meanest I've ever met.' Jamieson's heart jumped, but outwardly he checked his emotions like all good detectives. At last, someone who was willing to share some information with him. 'Tell me about him,' he said flatly.

She considered his request. 'Oh, here goes,' she said, 'but if you say it was me that told you, I'll deny it, and they'll run you out of town. I'm not joking.'

'You have my word,' promised Jamieson.

'The Mannix family has lived in Carroll for as long as anyone can remember,' she said. 'The family used to own a big cotton mill over on the far side of town. Everyone in Carroll either worked for them or knew someone who did. That would be Raich's grandfather's time around the turn of the century. On the back of that Cotton Mill, Carroll thrived and prospered, and everyone was happy. In the thirties, Raich's Father took over the running of the mill, and nobody noticed any change — things were exactly the same.

Raich was born around the end of the war. In the early seventies, the mill hit problems. Another mill had opened up nearer Phili and was able to undercut Mannix significantly. Business dried up. Raich would have been in his late twenties by then, and he begged his Daddy to let him take control of the mill, take it forward, and take on the competition; I hear he had a good business brain, and many people think he would have made a decent fist of things, but the old man said no, said he didn't think that Raich was the right man for the job. So he carried on running it himself, well into his eighties. But it sank. The fortune the family had amassed was put back into the business to keep it afloat. When the old man finally died, and the business became Raich's, all that was left was the old mill itself, no order book, no customers, no staff. The mill was mortgaged to the bank, and they foreclosed almost immediately. Raich pleaded with them to give him a chance, but the bank had a buyer lined up and sold the business from under Raich's feet.'

She paused and sighed. 'The battle took a huge toll on Raich. He became unbelievably bitter and twisted. It's not difficult to understand why. He had married a girl from a nearby town, and she had given birth to a boy, Jason. With the business gone, all Raich could afford was the shack just out of town. The more he drank, the meaner he got. His wife Lorraine would appear at the store with bruises and blackened eyes. She'd say that she was just clumsy and that she walked into a door, but that didn't sound right. She'd stand by her man, though, and she had another three kiddies, another boy and two girls. Young Jason had to grow up quicker than most. He had his fair share of bruises and broken bones, but Lorraine would joke that her boy was just as clumsy as she was.'

'I had a friend working at the hospital, and the doctors there pleaded with her to report to her husband, but she never would. She always said she married him for better or worse, and that was that. Jason and the other children grew up to be pretty well adjusted, but they had a fear in their eyes that was plain to see.'

'Then, around ten years ago, Lorraine was admitted to hospital with a ruptured something or other. As usual, she said she'd fallen, but the doctors could see fist-shaped bruises all over her body. They knew what was going on, but without Lorraine to press charges, there was nothing they could do. They kept her in the hospital for the night, and at around two o'clock, she took a turn for the worse and died. Even on her deathbed, she stuck to her story. The hospital sent word to Raich Mannix at home that he should come in, but he was so blind drunk that he couldn't manage it. Poor Lorraine, she died alone without anyone she loved around her.'

Lena's eyes brimmed with tears. She wiped them away, annoyed with herself for letting her emotions get the better of her. Just then, Conrad appeared in the doorway to the kitchen. He glared at Lena.

'Oh, Conrad, 'said Lena. 'Just you go and get on with whatever you should be doing, and don't worry yourself about me.' The big man continued staring for a further ten seconds before turning back into the kitchen.

'What happened then?' asked Jamieson gently.

Lena sniffed. 'Well, for a short while, things got better. There were no trips to the hospital. No 'accidents'. The kids settled well at school, especially Jason. He was very nervous around people, but he was good at computers and all that sort of thing. Not that the local school could provide him with a computer to learn on — he used to go to Philadelphia for weekends to stay with friends, still do occasionally — they had a computer there that he could use. He hated going away, leaving the younger ones with Raich, but he had no choice. Otherwise, he would be stuck in Carroll for his whole life with the rest of us, and he had a bit more to offer the world than that. Anyway, Raich started drinking again, bruises started appearing again, and trips to the hospital. That sort of thing, he was getting out of control. Finally, one of his daughters, Josie, was admitted to hospital with bleeding, you know, in her woman's areas. Seems she'd had a miscarriage. She was thirteen. She wouldn't say who the father was, but we all knew that Old Raich had been sticking it to his own daughters.' Lena dabbed at her nose with her handkerchief.

'They've got a three-year-old lives in the shack with them. Louise, the sixteen-year-old, is the Mother. Although there's no proof, it's more than likely that the kiddie is Raich's. He is a violent, vicious man, but because the kids wouldn't testify, there was nothing that could be done.'

Jamieson resisted the urge to say that there was. Someone had taken revenge on their own hands. A revenge that didn't need scared and scarred people to stand up in court fearing for their and their loved one's safety.

'Did anyone from the family ever fight back?' asked Jamieson.

Lena thought, 'Couple of years back, one of the kids was kept in hospital with a fractured skull. Jason had been at the hospital all afternoon, got back to town at around eleven in the evening, and went straight to Dusty's. Hell, he was mad. He found Raich propping up the bar, well on the way to his usual state. Jason grabbed his shoulder and spun him round, told him that enough was enough, that it had to stop. Raich just looked at him, then burst out laughing, said who was going to stop him? A skinny ass bastard like Jason? He told him to go home before he regretted it. Jason stood his ground. He just said, 'one day, old man, one day,' she paused. 'And I guess he was right!'

The telephone behind the counter started ringing. Lena looked around. There was no sign of Conrad to answer it. 'Excuse me,' she said, standing up and walking behind the counter. She picked the phone up and had a brief conversation with the person on the other end. She put the phone down and came back to where Jamieson was sitting. 'That was Harry Fenton,' she said. 'Jason

Mannix will be at the station at five o'clock for exactly half an hour, but no more.'

CHAPTER THIRTY-NINE

Sitting across the desk from Jamieson, Jason Mannix looked both younger and smaller than the description given in his passport, the copy of which Jamieson was currently scanning. The passport put Mannix at thirty-three and a touch over six feet tall. In reality, he looked to be barely out of his teens and with his shoulders hunched as they were, he struggled to pass for five feet eight. Probably, Jamieson decided, a result of years of physical and mental abuse.

They were in Fenton's office. This time, Jamieson was on the business side of the desk, and Mannix was sitting opposite. Standing almost furtively by the door, behind and to the left of Mannix, stood Fenton, his hands on his hips, jacket open, revealing his holstered weapon perhaps as a deliberate reminder to Jamieson that things were different this side of the Atlantic.

After receiving the call at the diner, Jamieson decided to get some rest before meeting Mannix. He asked Lena to call him after an hour before going up to his room. He lay on the bed and fell asleep almost immediately. When Lena knocked on his door to wake him with a seemingly obligatory mug of coffee, it felt as though no time had passed.

He showered, put on his last clean shirt and suit, now looking very crumpled, and drove down to the police station for the meeting. It was just coming up to four thirty in the afternoon.

As Jamieson entered the station, he could see that the front desk was unmanned, so, without breaking his stride, he lifted the counter and made his way straight to Fenton's office. He was bored with the pleasantries and couldn't have cared whether Fenton objected or not.

As it happened, he didn't. He looked up from what he was doing as Jamieson entered his office and gave a brief nod towards the chair. Jamieson sat down. 'Coffee?' asked Fenton.

'No thanks,' said Jamieson.' Two days in the States, and I've probably drunk more coffee than I would in two weeks back home. I'm feeling pretty wired.'

Fenton nodded. 'You don't mind if I do?' Jamieson spread his hands. 'Be my guest', he said.

Fenton stood and walked across to the coffeemaker. He had his back to Jamieson as he prepared himself a drink. 'I understand that you've been talking to Lena at the diner', he said. Then, without waiting for Jamieson to respond, he continued, 'nice girl, but you wouldn't want to share your deepest secrets with her. The whole town would know everything within hours.'

Fenton turned back to face Jamieson. He had a mug in his left hand and a spoon in his right to stir the contents. 'I guess you've heard all about the Mannix family?' Jamieson nodded. 'Pretty much', he confirmed.

Fenton stirred the coffee, then removed the spoon and gave the side rim of the mug three solid taps. 'Then you'll know that Raich Mannix was the meanest son of a bitch that ever lived', said Fenton.

Jamieson nodded. 'Sounds that way', he said before adding, 'It still doesn't mean that you boys taking things into your own hands was the right thing to do.' He stared defiantly at Fenton.

Fenton smiled, tipped his hat forward and scratched the back of his head. 'Now, don't be thinking y'all can come out here and be tricking us simple country folk with your big city ways', he said in a mock accent.

Jamieson remained tight-lipped. 'I know exactly what happened and what's more. I think you and some of your fellow townsfolk have provided false statements to shift the emphasis on the murder. The two itinerants never existed, yet alone did they kill Raich Mannix. That was a man called Darren Hughes. He did so around the same time that Jason Mannix was in

England carrying out a murder on behalf of Darren Hughes. In effect, they swapped murders.'

Fenton walked back to his chair behind the desk and sat down. 'That's some fancy theory you've got there. I'm sure you've got the evidence to back it up.' He made a clicking noise out of the corners of his mouth and pulled a face that feigned concern. 'Even then, you've got to get Jason Mannix and whoever else you suspect back into England to prosecute them, and from what Jason's been saying about your country, he sure ain't in no hurry to go back of his own accord. I guess that'd be the same for any of them.'

'There's always extradition,' said Jamieson, immediately wishing he hadn't. He was on the ground unfamiliar to him and had a feeling that he was playing into Fenton's hands. Fenton took a slug of coffee.

'Well now, extradition, you say. Let me ask you something. Have you ever dealt with the United States judicial system?'

Jamieson shook his head.

'Well, let's just say it don't move too quickly. We've had vicious murdering Mothers, just sitting on death row for thirty years before now while the lawyers talk about this and talk about that, appealing this and appealing that.'

Fenton looked thoughtful.

'You've heard of Polanski, right?' Jamieson nodded.

'We've been after that guy for over thirty-five years. Some folk are saying that because it's been so long, we should give up and forget it ever happened.' Fenton shook his head in bewilderment. 'I don't believe that. I believe he should return and face up to whatever he's done. If he's telling the truth, then what has he got to worry about?'

'The point is that extradition doesn't seem to have worked there none too good, and we're supposed to have good relations with the Swiss about these things. It just seems like a good idea to the politicians. You know you scratch my back, and I'll scratch yours until it comes to a point when a country actually wants to extradite somebody, then it becomes a political hot potato. Nobody wants to hold it long enough to drop it!' Fenton let out a sigh.

'The US legal system is not always designed to help the good guys and punish the bad ones. We had one son of a gun wipe out an entire family — Mama, Papa and four kiddies — cut 'em up with a knife for fun one night, and just because the officer who made the arrest screwed the words up, the case fell apart — it breached his rights — what about the rights of the family? Guy walked out of that courthouse just like that, free as a bird.' He paused, then spoke again.' Not for long, though. I heard that some 'itinerants' caught up with him, too. Who knows, they may have been the same ones as our guys.' He gave Jamieson a rueful smile. 'Point is, people who break the law don't always get what's rightly coming to them. Other people feel cheated, feel it's not right.'

Jamieson spoke.' I think that Jason Mannix and Darren Hughes broke the law. Will they get what's rightly coming to them?'

Before Fenton could answer, the bell on the front desk sounded. Fenton craned his neck to see who it was. 'Speak of the devil, and he will appear,' he said and inclined his head towards the front desk. Jamieson craned his neck to look over his shoulder. He recognised Jason Mannix from the passport photograph. He was wearing a short-sleeved shirt and a pair of jeans. He looked nervously about him as if a police station were a foreign place for him to find himself.

Fenton stood. 'I'll get Jason settled into one of the spare rooms, and then I'll be back. But, first, we need to put some ground rules down.'

Fenton was gone for no more than two minutes. When he returned to the room, he pulled the door shut behind him. Then, he sat in the chair behind his desk.

'Just to reiterate,' he began. 'You have no jurisdiction here. Jason Mannix has presented himself here at my request. He has come of his own accord; he is not under arrest or any kind of caution, so anything he says is inadmissible in a court of law. Furthermore, he has no legal representation present. He is here to answer your questions as best he can. If he feels unable to answer any, I have advised him to remain silent..."

'Plead the fifth amendment, if I remember rightly,' interjected Jamieson.

Fenton was unmoved '...and Inspector, if I feel that you come anywhere close to overstepping the boundary, I will conclude the interview and send Mr Mannix on his way.' Fenton stared defiantly at Jamieson, who held his gaze for a full five seconds before nodding his head imperceptibly to confirm he had understood.

Fenton stood. 'Let's go,' he said.

Jamieson looked at Jason Mannix. He explained who he was and why he was there. Mannix didn't say anything, just viewed Jamieson with dead eyes. 'You recently visited the UK, Jason, is that correct?' asked Jamieson. Mannix nodded. 'While you were there, did you go to a place called Luton?' Mannix paused for a few seconds and then nodded for a second time. 'Why did you go there?'

'Friends,' murmured Mannix.

Jamieson nodded slowly. 'Do you have their names and addresses? It could be important.'

Mannix shook his head. 'No,' he said softly.

Jamieson rubbed his forehead.' How did you get there?' he asked. 'To Luton, I mean.'

'Car,' said Mannix, his voice cracking. He cleared his throat and spoke again, this time louder and clearer 'Car. I hired a car.'

'Can you remember what the make of the car was?' pressed Jamieson.

Mannix shook his head. 'Small, white one, that's all I remember.' he said.

'Did you need to use the jack at all?' asked Jamieson.

Mannix looked confused. Jamieson elaborated, 'for jacking the car up, I mean.'

Mannix understood the question and thought about the answer. His eyes inadvertently flicked towards Fenton, who had moved further into the room. He answered flatly, 'no,' Jamieson leant back in his chair. He wanted to increase the pressure on Mannix but knew that if he went too far, too soon, Fenton would bring an end to the interview.

'Jason,' he said. 'Do the names Darren Hughes or Lesley Wallace mean anything to you?'

Again, Mannix's eyes flicked towards Fenton. He closed them, annoyed with himself for giving away a signal. 'No,' he said finally.

Time for a change of approach thought Jamieson.

'Jason,' he said. 'How did you feel about your father's death?'

Fenton stepped in, hands raised. 'Now that's going…..' He started to say before Mannix cut across him. Then, for the first time, the young man was animated.

'Nothing,' he said it so loudly that it stopped Fenton in his tracks. The room fell silent for what seemed like an eternity before Mannix continued speaking. This time, he had more control over his voice. 'I felt nothing for him. Perhaps relief for my sisters and closure for my Mother but nothing else.'

'When did you find out about your Father's death?' asked Jamieson, apparently ignoring Mannix's emotional outburst and Fenton's warnings.

Mannix was distracted. 'Um, I can't say. I don't really remember.'

'Is that because you already knew it was going to happen while you were in England? It was part of the deal, wasn't it?' Fenton was moving forward again.

'That's it, Buddy, you've stepped over the line.' He stepped protectively between Jamieson and Mannix. Jamieson ignored him and continued talking, peering around Fenton and watching for Mannix's reactions.

'How did you get in touch with Darren Hughes, Jason? Was it through the Revenge Trade website? Did they somehow put you in touch?'

Mannix instinctively raised his arms across his chest to protect himself. He visibly whitened under the barrage of questions from Jamieson. Fenton picked the young man up under the armpits and lifted him to his feet. He started forcibly moving him towards the door. Mannix shuffled, unable to get into any kind of stride.

Jamieson continued with his verbal battering.' Why did you hit Lesley Wallace so hard, Jason? The first blow almost certainly killed him. You must have known that. So the other four weren't necessary. The old man must have been on the floor already when you continued to bash his head in with a jack handle. Did it feel like you were hitting your Father, Jason? Causing him pain for all the hurt he had caused you. Your Mum. Your sisters.'

Fenton turned to face Jamieson. 'That's enough now. Stop it. The interview is over.' He turned back to Mannix and half guided; half pushed him through the interview room door and out into the corridor. Mannix seemed to be in a stupor and just allowed himself to be manoeuvred by Fenton.

Jamieson shouted after them, 'This was never an interview. It's a cover-up.'

Fenton slammed the door closed behind him. The sound of wood hitting wood reverberated around the bare interview room.

Jamieson slumped down into his seat. He felt angry and ashamed. He was angry because he knew that the law had been broken, and it was his job to uphold it. Furthermore, he felt that Fenton was instrumental in encouraging such laws to be broken. Fenton, a sworn upholder of the law, was a senior United States Police Department officer involved in murder and cover-ups.

However, the overriding feeling was shame. He had conducted himself badly in front of both Mannix and Fenton, despite his promise to Jarman that he would remain calm and, above all, professional. That clearly hadn't happened, and he wondered what the repercussions would be should Fenton decide to lodge a formal complaint. He knew despite his suspicions, despite all the blocks fitting snugly into place, that he had no hard evidence, and without that, he had no case. He knew the interview had been going nowhere. Fenton had primed Mannix too well, and even if Mannix had let anything slip, Fenton was well placed to step in to stop proceedings before too much damage could be done. That still didn't excuse Jamieson's actions. He tried to browbeat the suspect into confessing in the presence of a badged US policeman. That was poor judgement; furthermore, it hadn't come close to working.

He felt drained and annoyed with himself. Tactics like those belong in the past. He gathered his papers to return to his motel to prepare for tomorrow's journey home. The door opened, and Fenton came back in. He sat down in the chair Mannix had been sitting in less than sixty seconds ago. He had a calm, almost re-signed, look on his face.

He spoke. 'Well, Inspector, I wouldn't say that was your finest hour, would you?'

Jamieson stopped packing papers into his case and looked directly at Fenton. 'No,' he replied. 'No, I wouldn't.'

Fenton pursed his lips. 'Sit down for a minute, will you, please?' Jamieson did as he was asked.

Fenton took his hat off and threw it gently onto the table. He leant forward and rested his forearms on his knees, hands clasped in front of him.

'When I heard you were coming over here, I did some checks on you. I've got some friends who work in the British Police Force. I called in some favours. It's amazing the speed that the networks move at. I made a call on Friday, and by Saturday morning, I had a pretty good picture of what you were like as a man and a police officer...' He paused. When Jamieson didn't respond, he continued. 'I know that you're a good man and a thorough cop. I know you believe in doing the right thing. I know you trust the law to do the right thing every time.' Again Fenton paused. 'Me? I'm a bit more cynical. I've seen too many bad people walk away. But, hey. Mebbe, that's just the good old USA for you.' He raised a half smile. 'Take Raich Mannix, for example. Okay, circumstances made him what he was. I'm told that before he lost everything, he was a good, hardworking man. He wanted to keep that mill open because he knew what it meant for the town of Carroll — it gave people jobs, and if the towns- folk have jobs, they have money in their pockets to spend in the town's shops and bars and restaurants, Carroll used to be a thriv- ing town until the mill closed down —when the bank foreclosed, Raich went to some dark places. But, make no mistake, Raich beat his family, he beat his wife, ended up killing her, he beat his kids, started when they were real young, raped his kids, in- cluding young Jason, who you just met, he fathered the youngest daughter's baby.'

He paused for a third time to allow his words to sink in. 'Trou- ble was that no one would ever report him to the police. Every- one was scared of the repercussions. So it just went on and on.'

'Then, about eighteen months ago, young Jason came to see me. Despite everything, the kid had made something of himself. He was very good with computers. He'd come up with a plan that he'd worked out with someone through the Internet. Seems like they'd got their own Raich, who they needed taking care of. Any- way, Jason and the kid in England had worked everything out between them, and Jason asked me what I thought.' Fenton gave a slight shrug and widened his eyes. 'I thought it looked pretty clever for two youngsters to come up with for all the reasons that you're finding it almost impossible to get anywhere now. There's no connection between the victims and the killers. Plus, one is in the USA, and the other is in the UK. I heard it was only because Jason parked in the wrong place that any connection was made. The kid parks in the right place, and you're probably not here talking with me now, am I right?'

Jamieson knew he was right. Despite all their hard work and effort, they only had a couple of breaks that enabled them to get anywhere close to closing this case. He nodded and merely said, 'yeah!'

Fenton nodded back. 'The two kids worked it all out themselves. My only involvement was getting the whole thing to bed as soon as possible. The English kid biked across from Philadelphia and was there waiting for Raich when he stumbled by, pissed, just past midnight. The kid was back on his bike on his way back to Phili within five minutes. We made sure that all possible suspects had alibis, and the main one, Jason, well, he was thousands of miles away. We left Raich where he was until well after nine the next morning when one of my deputies' found' him by the roadside. Some of the other townsfolk had previously agreed to put forward statements to say they'd seen two itinerants around town earlier in the day who were almost certainly responsible, and we managed to convince the State to close the case off as soon as possible.'

'Raich Mannix was a bastard who deserved everything he got. I have no doubts about that.'

Jamieson spoke. 'What do you know about the man that Jason Mannix killed?'

'That he was a child abuser.'

'He was never convicted of anything like that.'

'My point exactly. Just because he was never convicted doesn't mean he didn't do it.' Jamieson thought about Fenton's answer.

'We can't work outside the law like a bunch of vigilantes. It's not how it works.'

'Ninety-nine point nine, nine per cent of the time. I'd agree with you. We just happen to have come up with the point zero one time that I don't,' said Fenton.

'Twice', Jamieson pointed out.

'Yep', agreed Fenton, 'Twice.'

Jamieson stood up to go. He picked up his case and stuck out his hand to Fenton. 'Thanks for your time and your honesty.'

Fenton took the outstretched hand and shook it. 'Look,' he said. 'There's nothing personal here. In another time and place, we'd meet and have a beer. But if you try to use the conversation of the last five minutes to further your case, I'll deny that it ever took place. I just wanted you to know that you are right about what happened and how it happened. I just happen to think that the world is a better place now than it was two weeks ago. Why and how we got there, I don't know, mebbe I don't care.' Jamieson smiled and released Fenton's hand. He passed through the door and out into the reception area of the police station. As he put his hand on the glass exit door, Fenton called from behind him.

'Inspector' Jamieson turned back. Fenton continued. 'This is a God-fearing country that you're in. So tonight, when you're back in your hotel room, take the Bible out of the bedside cabinet. Go to Matthew 7.2, read the words. Perhaps it will all make more sense to you then.'

CHAPTER FORTY

Jamieson checked his watch and saw that it was three forty local times. His flight left Philadelphia International Airport at nine oh two, and he had around one hundred miles to go to reach the airport. He worked out that he should have returned the rental car and would be checked onto the flight by six thirty at the latest. That would give him time to grab a coffee — he was worried that he had become addicted over the last two days — and a sandwich in the departure lounge. He had thought about buying a book but decided that the in-flight entertainment plus some much-needed sleep would be a more productive way of spending the seven-hour flight.

He had set out at six-thirty this morning. Lena was up and made sure that he had had a good breakfast and more coffee to keep him going throughout the day, and he had stopped off on a couple of occasions throughout the journey to take rest breaks. After yesterday's meeting, he returned to the motel and showered again. Then, standing with only a wet towel wrapped around him, he recalled what Fenton had said to him and reached across the bed to the bedside cabinet. He pulled the drawer open and found a Gideon's Bible inside.

He flicked through the pages until he found what he was look-ing for: Matthew Chapter 7.2. He read the words and tried to understand how they fitted in with the case. 'Give, and it shall be given unto you. For whatever measure you deal out to others, it will be dealt to you in return.'

So revenge is behind it all, he supposed, was the point that Fenton was making. Although the more he read the words, the more he thought it was about being rewarded for charitable acts instead of punished for less than charitable acts. Still, he'd never been that big on religion and decided that the whole point of the Bible was that it was open to all different kinds of translation. If Fenton felt that the translation of these words was to do with acts of revenge, then who was he to disagree?

He put the bible back, dried himself off and got dressed in jeans and a T-shirt he had bought from the local store on the way back from the Police Station. He sat on the bed, and before long, tiredness had overtaken him, and he had drifted off to sleep again. He was woken by a knock on the door. He checked the time. It had just gone seven-thirty, and he went across to open the door. It was Lena. For once, she was not wearing her dinner uniform. She asked whether he would like to have dinner with her somewhere away from Carroll. There was a nearby town with a reasonable bar cum restaurant not more than ten miles away. It would probably be ribs or steak and fries, but she thought it would do him good to get out of Carroll for an evening. At first, he was concerned that she was looking for something he couldn't provide, but then he changed his mind. She was a good person looking to do a stranger in town a good deed. Moreover, she was probably a little lonely herself and would like nothing better than to exchange stories with someone from another walk of life. He told her he needed to freshen up and would meet her downstairs in ten minutes. As it turned out, they were both right. He about her — she was great fun, and they talked all evening about different things but not what he was doing in Carroll. She had no hidden agenda, and he felt that she would have been affronted if he had suggested anything untoward — and she was right about the food.

Jamieson went for ribs and was genuinely astonished by the amount of food on the plate set in front of him. He made a great effort at clearing the plate but eventually had to give up, a beaten man with almost half a rack of ribs still uneaten.

They drank nothing stronger than Coca-Cola and got back at just after eleven. Jamieson thanked her and gave her a goodnight peck on the cheek. He told her he'd see her before he left in the morning. She said that breakfast would be available at six.

As it happened, the evening away from Carroll, from the case, was exactly what

Jamieson had needed. For the first time in days, he felt relaxed. For more than three hours, he gave no thought to the case and felt all the better for it.

After breakfast and as he drove out of Carroll, he passed Fenton standing with Conrad White passing the time of day. He assumed; he raised his hand in a farewell gesture which Fenton returned with a smile and a nod. White did not move a muscle.

Once again, he found a radio station playing his type of music and settled in for the long drive to the airport.

As he drove, he thought about the case. The plain truth was that no matter how correct he believed his appraisal of events to be, there was not a shred of hard evidence to support his theories. Fenton had admitted exactly what had happened on this side of the Atlantic but had made it clear that he would deny everything if pressed. Hughes and Mannix had remained silent, and if they continued in that vein, there would never be sufficient evidence to even charge them with murder, let alone convict them.

He thought about Jim Scott's role in all this. If he had come forward from the very beginning, then there would have been no need to get the still photos from the Bank's CCTV camera, which put the connection in place between Hughes and Wallace. And the Marshalls up in Birmingham, taking the money every month without considering where it was coming from or, indeed, if they did know where it was coming from, putting the events leading up to it to the back of their minds. At eleven thirty, he pulled into a roadside diner and had coffee and a sandwich. As he left, he pulled out his mobile phone and switched it on. There were a few missed calls showing on the screen, which he ignored. He scrolled down until he found Sandy's home number, briefly considered the time in the UK — it would be about 6.30 or thereabouts — and pressed the call button, anyway.

The phone rang seven times before it was answered.

'Hello', said Sandy's voice thick with sleep. 'It's me,' said Jamieson.

A brief silence before 'Oh, Alex. Sorry, it's a bit early.'

'No, I'm the one who should be apologising,' lied Jamieson. 'I didn't realise how early it was there.'

'What's new?' asked Stone, stifling a yawn.

Jamieson briefly recounted the events of the last two days. Stone said, 'So the Yanks aren't interested in taking this one forward.'

Jamieson said, 'It seems that Raich Mannix is their Lesley Wallace.'

'What', said Stone, 'the murder that no one really cares about?'

Jamieson flinched when he heard the phrase, even five thousand miles away, but nevertheless agreed.

'What's happening to your end?' he asked Stone.

'Well,' began Stone. 'Forensics has got Hughes' home and work computers but can't get anything out of them. It seems he may have deliberately released a virus into them once he knew we had made the connections between him and Wallace and him and the Revenge Trade. Perhaps we got a bit closer than he ever envisaged. Johnson took his concerns about the Revenge Trade website to the Technology boys in London, but he says that their attitude was 'So what! Put it at the back of the queue behind the other three thousand dodgy websites that were being investigated."

'Okay,' said Jamieson. 'It looks like dead ends all round, really.'

'Looks that way,' said Stone.

'Sandy, do me a favour,' said Jamieson.' My flight is due in at five tomorrow morning. Could you pick me up from Heathrow? I think we'll drop in on the Hughes family before Darren gets off to work for one last try to see if anything gives. The Americans might not be interested, but let's see if we can get Darren Hughes on some kind of conspiracy to murder charge for the Wallace killing. He might just crack, and we can lose this 'nobody cares' tag. That is the thing that bothers me the most. The fact that the press and everyone else thinks that we really don't give a damn about getting this case solved.'

'Okay,' replied Stone. 'Landing at five. Bloody hell, I'll have to be up by four to get there.'

'Get to bed early then', said Jamieson' See you tomorrow, bright and early.'

CHAPTER FORTY-ONE

As it was, Stone need not have worried about being up at four. Jamieson made it to the airport without any problems and onto the plane. But there was a delay, a mechanical issue which took over an hour to put right. This meant the flight lost its original slot and had to go on standby until the next available flight became available.

By the time the plane was in the air, it was running almost an hour and three quarters late. As Jamieson wasn't allowed to use his mobile phone on board, he could not get a message through to Stone about the delay. Stone would be at the airport early and know from one of the overhead monitors that there was a delay. He may or may not be in a bad mood. More to the point, Jamieson's idea of getting to the Hughes' house before Darren had left for work was now unlikely to happen. The originally scheduled landing was five. Even allowing for a headwind, the new scheduled landing was going to be no earlier than six thirty, then getting through immigration and out to where Stone had parked would add another half an hour or so. Leaving Heathrow at seven in the morning to get to Luton, around forty miles away, before eight, through rush hour traffic, wasn't going to happen, even for a driver who tended to ignore speed limits such as Stone.

Jamieson slept for most of the flight back, even missing the meal termed 'supper,' which was served at two in the morning local time. He changed his watch to UK time early in the flight. When he awoke, the first thing he did was to check the time — five-thirty — a friendly air hostess passing noticed that he had woken and asked if he would like the breakfast, which had only just been served. Considerately, they had let him sleep on, but there was still some available if he wanted. He was hungry and said 'Yes, please'. The hostess returned with a tray. Jamieson lifted the plastic lid to reveal a croissant, a pot of jam, two sausages, some dried scrambled egg, and some fruit juice. Jamieson ate the lot and settled down for the final part of the journey into Heathrow Airport.

By the time the plane had landed, and he had passed through immigration, it was just before seven. He spotted Stone as soon as he came through arrivals. For someone who had been up since four o'clock and waiting for a plane to land since five, Stone looked remarkably calm and unruffled. This was in direct comparison to Jamieson, who was still dressed in the jeans and t-shirt he had worn out on Saturday evening along with his, by now, a rather forlorn suit jacket and his work brogues.

As Jamieson made his way across the concourse towards him, Stone spotted him. He smiled, which was good news as far as Jamieson was concerned. It meant he was in a reasonable mood. 'I didn't know whether I should have held up a sign with your name on it,' he said, reaching down to take the holdall from Jamieson's grasp. 'Good trip?' Jamieson let him take the bag, and they started walking towards the exit. 'Interesting,' he said. 'Not sure that it justified the money spent, though. 'Can't see that we're any nearer to resolving anything.'

Stone fed coins into the parking machine and collected the ticket that appeared out of the slot near the bottom of the machine. They walked and talked until they reached the car. Stone put Jamieson's case on the back seat, and they both settled into the car. Just outside the airport car park, they hit the first traffic of the day and queued as they battled with the taxis and other vehicles, making the early morning run to collect family, friends, business colleagues and associates and anyone else who had flown in on the early flights.

The remainder of the journey was a stop-start affair. Now and then, they would have a clear run and would travel uninterrupted for ten, even fifteen, minute spells. Then suddenly, without warning, they would grind to a halt.

Stone remained remarkably calm. Jamieson, by comparison, felt edgy and frustrated by the delays. In his mind, he had drawn up a plan involving catching Darren Hughes early and seeing if his previously impenetrable guard had dropped. The more delays they encountered, the less chance there was of getting to Hughes before he left for work.

Jamieson told Stone all about the trip. Stone was philosophical about what Jamieson had told him. Jamieson had assumed that Stone would rattle on about the 'damn Yanks not playing ball', but instead, he merely said, 'Raich Mannix sounded like a right piece of work.' Jamieson felt that perhaps Stone was starting to think, regardless of police involvement, that this whole situation, on both sides of the Atlantic, had reached the right conclusion. He mentioned it to Stone.

Stone sighed. 'Alex', he began, 'I've been a copper for a long, long time, and I've always believed in the process, you know, bad people do bad things, and we catch them, they get a fair trial, and the system deals with them. But this one...' he puffed out his cheeks and slowly released air through his pursed lips. 'Well, it didn't happen like that. The process fell down for one reason or another, and the bad person who did the bad things, very bad things, never saw justice. So maybe, just maybe, in this case, things that have happened outside of the process have corrected the position.'

Stone sniffed and shrugged. 'Don't get me wrong, I'm not condoning all our vigilantism, but...well, you know what I'm saying, I guess.'

The traffic queue they'd been sitting in started moving again for no overt reason. Finally, half a mile down the road, they passed the cause of the holdup - two cars that had been pushed to the side of the road — one with a bashed in front end and the other with a bashed in rear end — Stone gave a rueful smile 'What a way to start the week' he said.

Jamieson checked his watch. It was just past eight, and they had around ten miles still to travel. He considered the options. 'What about Wallace?' he asked Stone. 'Do you not give him any credit for trying to change what he was?'

Again Stone sighed before he spoke: 'I've thought long and hard about Lesley Wallace since we found him lying on the pavement, and whilst I'll acknowledge that he has taken steps to become more acceptable to the rest of us, I still believe that he sidestepped justice in the terms that we all relate to. He didn't face a jury of his peers and let them decide what course of action should be taken. I knew the Lesley Wallace from twenty-five years ago. I know what that man was capable of, so the fact that he's dead, well, I'm not going to lose any sleep.'

'I suppose that's the whole point,' said Jamieson. 'Twenty-five years is a long time. Was it a different person?'

A silence steeled over the car for the next five minutes, during which they made good progress. Then, a mile or so from both the Hughes' household in one direction and the police station in the other, Stone asked Jamieson where he should be heading. Jamieson looked down at his creased jeans and T-shirt, not exactly the attire of a Detective Inspector and thought momentarily. Then, finally, he spoke: 'The Hughes place,' he said. 'I expect Darren is on his way to work, but at least we can speak with his Father.' Stone flicked the indicator stick down and turned left at the next junction towards Upton Road.

When they arrived some two or three minutes later, the bright sunshine of the early morning had given way to fine misty rain. As they drove past the Hughes' home, searching for a parking space, Jamieson glanced toward the house. Darren Hughes' motorbike was parked in its usual place in the front garden.

'We could be in luck," he said to Stone, indicating the bike. 'It doesn't look as though Darren has left yet.'

Stone pulled into a vacant space and parked a hundred yards down the road. They climbed out of the car and stretched their legs before setting off in the direction they had just come from.

'You worked out what you're going to say'?' asked Stone.

'No,' replied Jamieson.' I'll play it by ear.'

They arrived at the front gate and made their way down the path. Stone arrived first, pressed the doorbell, and then, for good measure, rapped his knuckle on the front door itself.

After two days in the sweltering heat of Ohio, Jamieson could feel the cold damp of an English morning. An involuntary shiver ran through his body.

Stone pressed the doorbell again. This time he spoke loudly or shouted softly, whichever way you looked at it: 'Mr Hughes. This is Detective Sergeant Stone. Can you hear me, sir?'

Another thirty seconds passed by, and still no response. Jamieson moved forward to look in the front room window — the one where David Hughes, Darren's Father, spent most of his time — he used his hands as a shield across the top of his eyes to prevent too much light from coming in. The windows were grimy, and Jamieson could not make out much more than a few shapes from previous visits he knew were the sofas and David Hughes' armchair.

He moved around, across the front of the house, to the side gate which led to the back garden. He tried the latch and found that the gate was open. He turned to Stone and spoke, 'Wait here, Sandy, just in case someone answers.' Stone nodded, and Jamieson moved down the alleyway to the side of the house.

When he had travelled the length of the house, he reached the back garden. The garden hadn't been tended in a long time. The lawn was just a mass of knee-high grass. There was a dilapidated shed in the far corner with every window smashed. The smell of cats' piss was prominent and initially caused Jamieson to gag. He put his hand over his nose and took two steps forward, causing a big old black and white cat to hiss at him before scrambling off, up and over the fence, into next door's garden.

The back door to the house was over to his left, and he made his way across to it, avoiding bottles and other rubbish which sat randomly on the patio floor. He tried the handle, and although the door rattled, it was locked from the inside. Once again, he held his hands up to his forehead and peered in through the glass. As he expected, this was the kitchen. Here, it was brighter and easier to make things out. He could see the sink, cooker and refrigerator, a table and chairs pushed away in the far corner, but no signs of life. He straightened up, made a fist and rapped three times on the pane of glass before bending down again to look in the window for any movement. Nothing.

He made his way back towards the side gate, stopping at another set of windows. He leaned in and pressed his face against the glass. The curtains inside were drawn, so he moved slightly to his right, where the curtains met and had fallen slightly open, leaving a small gap. Jamieson peered in. There was a light on. It was a small bedside lamp with its sheathed beam pointing directly downwards onto a bed with white sheets. Jamieson assumed that this must be where David Hughes slept. It would make perfect sense, given his disability, that he should sleep in a downstairs bedroom.

Jamieson edged to his left to get a wider perspective of the bed. Although the gap was small and the room poorly illuminated, he could make out the body of David Hughes lying in the bed. It looked as if he might be asleep, but instinctively, Jamieson knew he was dead. It wasn't that Jamieson had seen many dead bodies or was indeed any kind of expert in these matters. It was just that laying there on the bed, the twisted and battered shell of a man he knew as David Hughes had a serene look about him. The pain that was etched into everything that Hughes had done in Jamieson's presence was no longer there. The man looked at peace. A noise to his left made him jump. It was Stone. 'Anything?' he asked.

Jamieson stepped back and motioned towards the window. 'Have a look,' he said. Stone stepped up and looked in. Then, after a short while, he stepped back. 'Dead?' He asked. Jamieson nodded. 'I'd say so,' he replied.

'Who is it? The father?' asked Stone.

Jamieson remembered that Stone hadn't met David Hughes. He nodded again. 'We'd better look inside,' he said, remembering Darren Hughes' bike outside. 'You'd better ring through for an ambulance and some backup. Evason and Johnson should be in by now. Get them over here.'

Stone took out his mobile phone and made a call to Evason. Jamieson moved across to the back door. He lined his shoulder up against the wood to the side of the glass, stepped back, and then lunged forward, driving the fleshy part of his upper arm against the wood. He remembered the rugby-playing days of his past. It was like tackling an opposition winger. Under the power of his drive, the lock on the door gave way easily and without causing too much damage.

Stone came up and looked at the door, impressed. 'Claire and Rog are on their way. They'll have an ambulance with them,' he said.

'Okay', said Jamieson. 'You go into the old man's room. Make sure he's dead, but it goes without saying don't touch anything. It may be a crime scene. I'm going to look around the rest of the house.'

They passed through the kitchen, which was surprisingly clean, thought Jamieson, probably the home help that the council provided. The hallway was next. Jamieson indicated to Stone the door to his left as the room they had been looking in from the garden. He continued walking into the hallway, aware that Stone had stepped into the room.

He pushed open the door to his right - the room where David Hughes spent his days.

Everything was as it had been on both previous occasions that Jamieson had been in the room, except for David Hughes himself. The room looked exactly as it did before.

Jamieson turned to the staircase and began climbing the stairs. He wasn't sure what he would find if anything, and this uncertainty caused his heartbeat to increase. As he neared the top of the stairs, he could hear music, not loud, coming from the room, which he knew to be Darren's. He reached the landing and stood in front of the door to the room. He reached up and gave the door a light push. It swung open easily. Through the open door, the music sounded louder. He paused and then stepped into the room. Without realising it, he was holding his breath.

He looked around the room and saw nothing untoward. The music was coming from the computer. It had a melancholy, cloying tone, adding to the unease Jamieson felt growing in the pit of his stomach. The bed didn't appear to be slept in. Jamieson let out his long-held breath and backed out of the room. He closed the door and stood on the landing with his eyes shut. The door directly to his right was the bathroom. Again, he gave a light push on the door. This time it started to move freely inwards but stopped, apparently prevented from moving further by something behind it. Jamieson pushed harder, but the door wouldn't open further than five or six inches. He put his weight behind it and leaned in. It opened slightly further — sufficiently wide enough for him to get his head around and see the object preventing the door from fully opening.

He poked his head in. A towel had fallen from the rack behind the door and was rucked up, preventing a clean door swing. There was nothing else out of place in the bathroom. Jamieson hooked his foot around the door and kicked the towel out of the way. The door opened fully, and Jamieson bent down to pick up the towel and replace it on the rack. Jamieson moved back into the hallway. There was one room left to check. He moved across the landing and stood in front of the last door. Again, tension pulled at his chest, and his heart seemed to batter the inside of his rib cage. He pushed the door open.

Downstairs, Stone had confirmed that David Hughes was, as they suspected, dead. An empty bottle of sleeping pills was on the floor next to the bed. The man didn't appear to have died a violent death. His eyes were closed, and his hair appeared to have been combed. The pillows behind his head were plumped, and he had been tucked into the bed with just his head and neck exposed, much like a mother would tuck her five-year-old up at bedtime. There wasn't anything else that Stone considered looked unusual about the scene. He pulled the door closed behind him and went to look for Jamieson.

CHAPTER FORTY-TWO

Even before he had stepped into the room, Jamieson's instincts told him what he would find.

Nevertheless, the shock still hit him.

The curtains were only half drawn inside the room, and the gloom from outside provided the room with an eerie, iridescent kind of half-light. The door's opening caused a ripple, lifting dust mites and swirling them round. The room clearly wasn't used regularly.

To the right of the doorway stood an enormous old dressing table covered with walnut veneer. It had a big mirror facing the front and two winged side mirrors providing the user with an alternative view. There were lace doilies arranged on the surface to prevent any unnecessary scratching. Jamieson caught a glimpse of at least fifteen framed photographs, mainly black and white.

Darren Hughes sat in an armchair in the far corner of the room. He was wearing a white T-shirt and ripped jeans. His head was tipped back, and his hands were folded across his chest, where they nursed a silver picture frame. From where Jamieson stood, he could only see the back of the frame, but he had a good idea of who the photograph would be of.

Blood covered the white T-shirt from the middle of Darren's chest downwards. It had pooled in his lap and then seeped between his thighs onto the cushion of the armchair. Finally, it had dripped onto the carpet. In the half-light, it looked almost black. Jamieson stared at Darren's wrists. From where he was standing, he could just make out the jagged tears across the radial artery from where Darren Hughes' life had drained away.

Suddenly Jamieson felt light-headed. The events of the past few days had suddenly caught up with him. He staggered forward slightly, reaching out to balance himself against the dressing table. He closed his eyes and pinched the bridge of his nose. He stood like that for a short while, regaining his senses.

Finally, the nausea passed, and Jamieson was able to open his eyes without the sensation of dizziness disorientating him. He pulled a deep breath in through his nose, held it, and then slowly released it through his pursed lips. He glanced down at the picture frames arranged on the dressing table as his eyes traversed the tabletop taking in the photographs. He quickly established the common denominator in each picture. It was a young blonde-haired woman, pretty, perhaps even beautiful in some people's eyes. She was on her own in many photos, posing before some landmark or another. In another, she was caught completely unaware by the photographer, her hand held up across her smiling face, a natural beauty shining through. In other photos, she was with a baby, a toddler and a young boy, all the same person passing through formative years. Finally, the only colour photograph, faded by time, showed the woman, the boy and a man — older than her — probably on a family holiday. Although the sun shone, there had been a sudden gust of wind that had lifted the man's fashionable shoulder-length hair and the woman's skirts. Each of them was laughing as they tried to get the situation back under control. But to Jamieson, the overriding factor of this image was the man with his arm protectively round the shoulder of the young woman, who, in turn, offered her own motherly protection towards the boy.

The man was just about recognisable as David Hughes. By deduction, the boy was Darren and the young woman, Darren's Mother and David's wife, Janey Hughes. And then, thought Jamieson, along came Lesley Wallace.

Stone appeared in the doorway. This time Jamieson had anticipated his arrival, and he had not been surprised, as he was in the garden. Jamieson stepped aside to allow Stone to get into the room.

On seeing Hughes' body, Stone's reaction was short and to the point. 'Bollocks,' he said without anger, 'not this.'

Jamieson left the room and went and sat on the top stair. He could hear Stone moving around the bedroom. After a minute or so, Stone came out. He had moved into police mode, removing any vestige of emotional attachment to the case. He leant on the handrail running along the top of the landing and spoke straight ahead of him. Jamieson was seated down lower to Stone's left.

'There's an empty bottle of some kind of prescription medicine on the floor in there. My guess is that it is a sleeping tablet of some kind. There's also a kitchen knife on the floor by his side. It doesn't look very sharp. It must have hurt the poor bastard like hell.' Jamieson nodded. 'What about downstairs?' he asked.

'Again, I'm making an assumption, but I'd say that son gave Dad a hefty amount of pills and then, when Dad was under, Son pushed a pillow into his face. Whether it was by mutual consent is anyone's guess.'

Jamieson picked up the drift '...and then Son comes upstairs, takes the remaining pills, slits his wrists with a blunt knife and then sits down and waits to die. What a mess.' Downstairs, the doorbell rang. It was either Evason and Johnson or the ambulance. Stone looked at Jamieson and spoke: 'Alex, listen to me. We've got a crime scene to organise. We've got to be professional about it. Put any emotions to one side, you know?'

Jamieson stood. 'You're right,' he said. 'Let's get going.'

It was Evason and Johnson at the door. Jamieson and Stone filled them in on what they would find inside the house. The ambulance turned up and was quickly sent on its way.

A call was put into the Pathologist's Office instead. Within half an hour, the pathologist on call had arrived. It was Doctor Jenner, the pathologist who had attended the death of Lesley Wallace. The irony was not lost on either Jamieson or Evason.

In the same efficient manner she had previously shown, Doctor Jenner confirmed Stone's theory, subject to a formal post-mortem, which would be carried out over the next for-ty-eight hours.

The bodies of David Hughes and his son, Darren, were put in black body bags and carried out of the house where they had lived for the past quarter of a century. They were put into the back of two waiting cars from the Coroner's Office, not the old-style hearses but brand new, shiny cars. They could easily be mis-taken for an everyday family car if it wasn't for their colour and tinted windows.

A small crowd had gathered outside to see what the commo-tion was. They were being held back by police tape and two uni-formed officers—people with nothing better to do. The photo-graph in the frame that Darren Hughes had died clutching to his chest was taken on the same day as the holiday snap. It showed David, Janey, and Darren Hughes sitting on a tartan blanket on a shingle beach. Darren was about five. David Hughes' left arm was extended towards the camera. It was one of those photo-graphs where everybody wanted to be in it, and no one was left to take it.

Consequently, David Hughes did one of those things that all proper Dads did. He tried to take the photograph himself *and* be in it. The result was a skewiff picture with too much sky showing and far too close to the subjects to be considered by a profession-al to be a good photograph.

But it was.

They were all smiling and imagining happier times ahead. Now twenty-five years later, Darren Hughes had died remembering those times and trying to forget everything that had happened in between.

Doctor Jenner came and found Jamieson when she had fin-ished. He was in the kitchen, having made himself a strong coffee — withdrawal symptoms from his brief stay in America.

'That's me done,' she said. 'Do you want to be at the autopsies, or do you want to do the same as last time?' She asked.

'Same as last time, I think,' replied Jamieson. 'Unless you feel I need to be there.'

The doctor shook her head. 'No,' she said. 'I don't think I'll find out more than what it appears. It's all very sad, isn't it?'

'It is,' agreed Jamieson.

'Last thing before I go,' said Jenner. She pulled a plastic evidence bag out of her briefcase and handed it to Jamieson. 'I found that when they moved Darren's body. It had slid down between the cushion and the arm of the chair. I put it straight in the evidence bag. It hasn't been tested for prints yet. In fact, no one else has seen it.' She paused. 'It's addressed to you,' she finished.

Jamieson turned the plastic bag over in his hands. Inside was a sealed envelope with 'Inspector Jamieson' written in block capitals on the front.

'Would you like me to wait while you read it?' asked Jenner.

'No. No, but thanks for the offer,' said Jamieson. 'I'll call your offices in a couple of days to make an appointment with you. Thanks again.'

Doctor Jenner smiled. 'No problem,' she said and turned and walked towards the kitchen door.

When she got there, she turned back.' You've had a bad experience today,' she said. 'If you want to talk it through with anyone, you can always call me. I'm a good listener.'

It was Jamieson's turn to smile. 'Thanks,' he said.

After Jenner had left, Jamieson walked to the kitchen door and closed it. He returned to the table in the corner of the room and put the evidence bag and the envelope on it.

He opened the nearest kitchen drawer, scoured inside it, and quickly shut it. He tried two more drawers before he found what he was looking for. He sat down at the table.

The knife was from the same set as Darren Hughes had used to slit his wrists, only it had a thinner blade. Jamieson carefully took the envelope from the evidence bag and slid the knife's blade down behind the sealed edge. The knife wasn't sharp but, nevertheless, slit the envelope open with ease.

Using his fingertips, Jamieson reached inside and pulled out a single sheet of paper. He carefully unfolded it and laid it on the table before him. His mouth was dry, and the same thumping started again in his chest. He started reading far too quickly and realised he wasn't taking the words in properly. He made himself stop, collected his thoughts, and started reading for a second time. This time pacing himself far better. When he had finished reading, he stared back at the beginning for the third time.

When he reached the end for the second time, he placed the paper on the table and thought about what he'd just read. He wondered when it had been written. Was it before the death of David Hughes (in his mind, he refused to call it the murder of David Hughes), or was it after? Was it the words of a madman or a man in control of his situation?

He studied the words again.

Dear Inspector Jamieson

I hope that you are the first to read these words — my Mother always taught me the importance of respecting one's privacy; I hope that this maxim extends to the Bedfordshire Constabulary; I am, after all, addressing this missive to you, so it is only right and proper that you should be the first to read it.

I trust that you had a successful trip to the United States; not my favourite race of people by any stretch of the imagination, but the only other country I have visited outside of our own fair Island.

Why am I writing to you? Well, in the absence of anyone else, I found I made a connection with you in our, all be they, brief and fractious meetings.

Correct me if I'm wrong, but I felt a struggle within you, a choice, right versus wrong, good versus evil.

Is there ever an acceptable cause to take another human's life? No matter what evils that person may have bestowed upon others. I suspect, rather I know for a fact, your professional self would say not. That part of you would say that there are laws, long-standing laws which make provision for dealing with those kinds of people. But what of your private self? What does one think when one slips the net like Lesley Wallace or, whisper it, Raich Mannix? Is it in order to take matters into one's own hands? I'll leave you to consider that.

Before I sign off, there are two things I want, no, need you to know.

Firstly, I, and I alone, am responsible for both the deaths of Lesley Wallace and Raich Mannix. There was no one else involved, and this is my confession. I'll not insult your professional pride by giving details of how; please just accept my word for it.

Secondly, and I feel most importantly for your own wellbeing, this outcome, that is, the deaths of my father and myself, was always how this whole sorry episode was going to end. From the moment I heard Lesley Wallace's voice in the bank almost eighteen months ago, I knew that this would finish with Wallace, my father and myself dead. Raich Mannix was a bonus, a vile, twisted man. The world is better off without the likes of Mannix. Once Wallace was dead, it was only a matter of time before the rest fell into place. Your investigation and trip to America, as coincidental as it was, had nothing to do with what happened at Upton Road. I need you to know that fact. Please accept it for what it is, and know that there was nothing you could have done to prevent it from happening.

Finally, with a little indulgence on my part, I have a vision of where my family is reunited in a far-off place where the likes of Lesley Wallace do not exist. My Mother is well and looking beautiful, my father is healthy and looks after his family and, as for me, well, I take the greatest pleasure in their happiness as it was before it was so cruelly ripped away from us all those years ago.

I remain.

The letter was signed off Darren Hughes.

CHAPTER FORTY-THREE

It was unseasonably cold and rainy — in Jamieson's experience, these occasions always seemed to be carried out under such conditions. He parked up and checked his watch. He was ten minutes early. He climbed out of the car, turning the collar of his raincoat up against the elements as he did so. He hurried across the empty car park and into the small red brick building. He went through the vestibule into the chapel and sat at a pew on the right, four rows from the front. The place was deserted, and the only sound apart from the patter of rain on the roof was the mournful offerings of appropriately sorrowful organ music. No one was sitting at the organ, so Jamieson assumed the music was a feed being relayed through the internal PA system. He sat solemnly and thought about the case, which had now been wound down and would eventually be officially closed.

Jamieson had submitted Darren Hughes' letter as evidence. The Chief Constable was content to accept it as a confession to both killings — Lesley Wallace's and Raich Mannix's — and even though Jamieson knew it was impossible for Darren Hughes to have committed both murders, he decided not to contest the decision. A copy of the letter was submitted confidentially to Fenton in Carroll — Jamieson wondered whether he would use it to reopen the Mannix case or just stick with the story he already had. Probably the latter, he decided. There was no tangible benefit in reopening the case, only to close it again. Fenton liked things simple, and that was currently how he had it. Why confuse things?

At least the Coroner had released Brian Wilkins' body (Of late, Jamieson had taken to calling the deceased by his legally adopted name. He didn't know why). The case was merely adjourned for now, but Jamieson knew that in time that would become classed as an unlawful killing, probably by people or persons unknown.

Four people were dead, all told. Two unlawful killings and a murder-suicide.

He thought about Lesley Wallace, Raich Mannix, David Hughes, and finally Darren Hughes. He hoped that the Hughes family were now out of their pain. That the death of Lesley Wallace somehow gave Darren Hughes the release he was looking for. He wondered whether it was always going to end the way that it did, with the Father/Son death pact or whether, if the police hadn't got as close as they did, Darren Hughes would have just continued with his denials. He thought probably the former, in a strange way, the way things have turned out, felt about right.

His thoughts were interrupted by the sound of the door opening behind him. He turned. It was Jim Scott.

Scott looked across at Jamieson. He went to speak but was unable to. The undertaker was entering the chapel, followed by four Pallbearers, with the coffin held high on their shoulders. Scott moved out of the aisle and sat opposite where Jamieson was. The whole episode was surreal to Jamieson.

The Pallbearers made their way slowly to the front of the chapel, where they gently placed the coffin onto the conveyor belt. In accordance with Brian Wilkins' wishes, nothing was said. There was a pause of some thirty seconds, time for reflection, supposed Jamieson, before the undertaker reached forward and pressed a button behind the conveyor belt. Curtains opened, and a mechanical sound from within could be heard.

Presumably, thought Jamieson, the sound of some kind of doors opening. The music had stopped, so everything sounded amplified, bouncing around the high ceilings of the empty chapel. The noise of the doors rumbled on for a short while and then stopped. Another pause, and then the conveyor belt whirred into life.

The Pallbearers and the undertaker stood with their heads bowed. Jamieson watched as the coffin started moving through the opened curtains. Then, finally, it could no longer be seen. The curtains closed, and the mechanical sound was heard again.

Then it stopped.

That was it.

The Pallbearers and the Undertaker waited for what Jamieson assumed was considered an acceptable length of time before they filed out of the chapel. As he passed, the undertaker gave Jamieson a nod. Jamieson nodded back. There wasn't a lot to say. Jamieson stepped out from the pew and followed the line of men. He was aware that Scott had done the same and was now close behind him. They all passed through the vestibule and out into the car park. The rain had eased up from earlier. Jamieson watched the five men from the funeral parlour disperse. Three crossed the car park and went to the official hearse which had bought the body. The other two climbed into a red saloon car parked fifty yards away.

He was aware that someone was standing close by and knew that it could only be Scott. So he turned to face him.

Scott said 'Alex', and Jamieson nodded an acknowledgement.

Having reached an uneasy accord, Scott continued, 'shitty day', He said.

Jamieson nodded for a second time. 'Fitting really; the whole thing has been shitty right from the beginning.'

Scott sniffed. 'Why did you come?' He asked.

'I don't really know,' said Jamieson. 'Closure, perhaps? That's a buzzword these days. What about you?'

'Whether I liked it or not, Lesley Wallace had become a big part of my life over the last quarter of a century. I can never say that I grew to like him. Quite the opposite in the very earliest days. In fact, I loathed him. It took all the willpower I had not to beat him senseless back then.' Scott looked away, then back at Jamieson. 'Perhaps I had a sneaking admiration for how he tried to change after that. I mean, you are what you are, whether it's your own fault or not. He recognised that he was despicable, and I think he fought against all his natural instincts and urges to change that. If you judged him on the last twenty-five years of his life, he's probably led a more giving existence than most people,' he shrugged. 'Perhaps even the likes of you and I."

'Darren Hughes didn't think so,' said Jamieson, immediately realising his manner was churlish.

'No,' replied Scott. 'No, he didn't.' They stood facing each other.

'What'll you do now?' asked Jamieson.

'I've resigned from the force,' answered Scott. 'They gave me a choice. Resign now and keep the pension or fight it out and risk losing everything. I've got twenty-six years of service, so that's worth protecting. It's better this way; not so much damage for them to deal with. It wouldn't look good for the force if it came to light that one of their senior officers had been withholding information on a murder case. I think if I'd tried to stand and fight, I'd've lost anyway, and lots of stuff about Dad would've come out, and I didn't want that.'

'It's been a long time,' said Jamieson. 'Would anyone have remembered or even cared anymore?'

Scott nodded. 'Yeah,' he said. 'I would have.'

Scott stuck his hand out. 'Alex, I really didn't want to mess up your investigation, and if I did, I'm truly sorry. I may have been misguided, but all I was trying to do was protect Dad.'

Jamieson momentarily held back and then took the offered hand. But, in truth, if Scott had told him about his involvement from day one, then they would never have got the photos from the bank, which in turn would never have given them Hughes in the same shot as Wallace, so the investigation would have stalled anyway — perhaps never to recover.

Scott released his grip and smiled.' Take care,' he said and turned and walked away. Jamieson watched him go and wondered whether he would have done the same thing in a similar situation.

He hurried across to his car and got in. He fixed the seat belt across his chest and fished into his pocket for the car keys. As he did so, his mobile phone, which he had left in the car's glove compartment for fear of it going off in the chapel, buzzed. He reached forward, flipped open the latch, picked out the phone, and pressed the answer button.

'Hello'

It was Billy Watson.

'We've got a gig lined up on Saturday night. Wondered if you fancied it?'

'Do I get to play Johnny B. Goode?'

'Of course. Highlight of the evening.'

Jamieson smiled for what felt like the first time in a while. 'Count me in', He said.

Printed in Poland
by Amazon Fulfillment
Poland Sp. z o.o., Wrocław

23616152R00165